THE ROMANCE LINE

LAUREN BLAKELY

COPYRIGHT

ABOUT THE BOOK

The first rule of handling PR for a hockey team? Never hook up with a player.

That shouldn't be a problem since the last man on earth I want to give an image makeover to is our goalie. He's infuriatingly hot, famously grumpy and lives to spar with me after every game.

But shining up his rough edges is my path to landing the promotion I desperately need, so I grit my teeth and do my job. No matter how hard he makes it (especially with that sexy smirk and cool blue eyes.) As we travel from pose-with-a-pet photo opps to cuddle-a-kitten fundraisers, we bicker like it's foreplay.

Turns out it is.

. . .

Because as I get to know the man behind the broody iceman exterior, it's me that melts – right into his arms as he devastates me with a kiss that turns into the hottest, most forbidden night of my life.

Only once turns into *every night* as Max shows me how much he wants to take care of me. His possessive touch makes me feel adored for the first time in my life.

But the man is entirely off limits and I can't risk my job for more of those soul-deep kisses.

Because the only thing worse than hooking up with a player is falling head over heels for him.

DID YOU KNOW?

To be the first to find out when all of my upcoming books go live click here!

PRO TIP: Add lauren@laurenblakely.com to your contacts before signing up to make sure the emails go to your inbox!

Did you know this book is also available in audio and paperback on all major retailers? Go to my website for links!

For content warnings for this title, go to my site.

THE ROMANCE LINE

By Lauren Blakely
Love and Hockey #2

1

ZIP IT UP, MAN

Max

Look, I can pull off pretty much anything in the clothing department, but this *might* be outside my wheelhouse. Especially since I definitely didn't pack a purple pair of underwear with little flowers all over the waistband and so little material that nothing is left to the imagination. Even mine, and I have a very active one.

Intrigued, I hold the scrap of purple fabric in front of me in my hotel room. Studying this less-is-definitely-more piece of lingerie, I have to wonder—who even wears this almost thong and also, does it hurt?

I should probably stop pawing around in this bag that's clearly not mine but looks just like it. Must have grabbed it in the lobby by mistake, and I'm guessing this suitcase doesn't belong to one of my teammates either. Not that there's anything wrong with that. To each his own and all. But this cornu-fucking-copia of lace and satin doesn't look like it would fit a pro hockey player.

There are only a handful of women traveling with the team on this road trip to Seattle. The athletic trainer, the team doctor, and the publicist.

My mind catches on that last possibility.

This can't belong to her.

It just can't.

Not straightlaced, rule-following, pantsuit-wearing Everly Rosewood. She's the kind of woman who owns exactly seven sets of cotton bras and panties, in the same matching shade of nude, same matching style, so she can grab and go at the crack of dawn all while devising new ways to torture me with press requests and promo shoot ideas.

No way does Everly own anything that's not navy, black, or beige. Best I return this bag to its rightful owner, pretend I never saw what's in it, and then never think about it again. Searching for the luggage tag, I find one attached to the handle and flip it over.

I freeze. Then, I heat up everywhere. We're talking inferno levels. This bevy of beautiful lingerie belongs to the team's publicist after all. The clever, mouthy woman who hates me. Yep, the one and only Everly Rosewood, who accomplishes more before her workday begins than most people do in a year. But this does not compute—she can't possibly dish out a list of promo duties in that teacherly way of hers while wearing a purple thong.

This is a test. This is clearly some kind of test. No, it's a downright moral dilemma.

Do I slam it shut or hunt around in her things a little more?

I need some distance from temptation. Spinning around, I pace toward the window overlooking the city of Seattle, rainy because of course it's rainy, and the arena where I'll be defending the net early tomorrow against one of the toughest teams in the league.

"All you have to do is zip up that suitcase, return it, and go the fuck to sleep," I mutter.

Great. Just great. Now I'm talking to myself. They say goalies are a little unhinged but this is next level even for me. I grip the windowsill, staring at the Space Needle lit up against the night sky, then I tear myself away, stalk right back over to the bed, ready—I swear I'm ready—to zip that suitcase all the way up and say goodbye to it.

Or, really, I'm almost ready.

I scrub a hand across my beard and gaze a little longer at the treasure trove of lace and satin, like a siren calling to me in the most tantalizing voice.

How do you think the slay-the-world-one-member-of-the-media-at-a-time queen would look in purple lace? Or in soft blue satin?

Does she have a date tonight? My jaw ticks. *Is she meeting a secret boyfriend in the rainy city tomorrow?* It ticks harder. *Does she—oh, hell—wear these every day to work under those pantsuits that drive you crazy?*

And it ticks the hardest.

I haul in a breath, trying to locate my moral compass. But it's hard to find right now. I try again with a pep talk. "All you have to do is reach for the zipper. Pull the teeth closed around one side, then the other. Done."

But I don't move. I stand here stupidly because all those sexy things are scrambling my brain. Taking up all the space in my head now that I know Everly Rosewood wears red lace panties, the color of my dirty dreams.

"Doesn't matter," I mutter. "It really doesn't matter what she wears." Squaring my shoulders, I get ready to perform the most herculean task—zip it up.

As I reach for the bag, my phone buzzes. Saved by the bell. I grab it from my back pocket at Mach speed, grateful for the distraction from a moral dilemma worthy of that vintage board game Scruples.

It's a text from my agent, Garrett.

> Been talking to Thrive about your sponsorship. Need to run some things past you. Let's chat when you return to SF.

That has to be good. Why else would he text me late at night? Dude isn't going to text with bad news like, saying, *you lost your last sponsor less than a week into the season.*

So, clearly this is a good sign. I dictate a reply.

> Works for me. Maybe I'll even let you take me to that new kebab place on Polk Street and give me the good news.

The bubbles dance for a minute. A long minute that should cool me off so I stop obsessing over this bag. Finally, Garrett's reply lands.

> Don't think I didn't notice you finagling a free meal. And sure. Kebabs will do. Just know this—I'm working hard to make this happen. I know you've got plans.

I furrow my brow. Well, no shit. That's his job. He always works hard. Doesn't need to tell me that twice. But I'm not his easiest client lately, so maybe this is just his nice guy way of reminding me he's juggling all the broken plates I've thrown his way.

So I should take this exchange as a win, return this bag, and crash.

Except, what is that scrap of sinful red lace taunting me from the top of the stack of neatly folded blouses in the center of her bag? I shove the phone back in my pocket and then my curious fingers have a mind of their own. One look can't hurt. Fine, one touch. I snatch up the soft strap poking out of the blouses and fish out—what is this? A demi-bustier? A halter half bra?

I lift it to get a better view. It's sheer red lace, the color of a cherry, with the daintiest ruffle along the top. Maybe it's a bra of sorts. I don't even know. Then, with a new kind of reckless abandon, I reach for the next thing, and the next, and the next.

Until...what have I done? I've plundered her bag. Yep, I'm a lingerie pirate.

This is bad, man.

But this is also an opportunity. I smirk as I get to work neatly folding every single silky item.

An opportunity to give her hell.

I pack them all back up, except for this little red thing, and head to the door, like a good boy.

Well, not really. Because tonight, I've been a little bit bad.

2

YOU SEXY LITTLE SNOOP

Everly

It's official. I am a thief. Crouching back on my heels on the plush hotel room carpet, I steal a whiff of the grumpy goalie's cologne.

It's bold and spicy, but strong too, starting with chili pepper and finishing with cedar, and it smells like the kind of guy you can't stop looking at when you go to a club with your girlfriends. That unknowable man with the dark gaze who leans against the sleek, silver bar and surveys the scene with cool blue eyes. The man whose stare is undressing you as you dance for him.

Someone so cocky you hate yourself for wanting him.

I shudder as I close my eyes, catching the final after-notes from this sapphire blue bottle. When I open my eyes, I force myself to cap it.

Blinking off the heady fog, I set the cologne back down in Max's black travel kit as I stare at the evidence in front of me. A wide open suitcase that isn't mine—one I didn't shut when I discovered we'd accidentally grabbed each other's bags when we arrived after our flight to Seattle from San Francisco.

It's damning. I'm not just a scent thief. I'm a veritable snoop.

Why don't you just lick his tube of toothpaste too? Rub your thigh on his shampoo bottle? Mark his things a little more?

Ashamed, I jerk back from the suitcase that's been my downfall for the last five minutes since I noticed the luggage switcheroo when I arrived at my room. I undo and redo my ponytail again and again. What have I done? Did I really look through one of the hockey player's things?

Girl, you sure did. And you relished every single second of it.

Embarrassment crawls up my chest. I can't believe I rooted through his clothes and his travel kit instead of just, oh say, closing the bag and texting him about the mix-up.

LIKE AN ADULT WOULD DO.

But I'm evidently a cat. I now know what cologne Max wears, what color his boxer briefs are, and what flavor lip balm he likes. Also that he uses a coveted face moisturizer that's made from the best grape-seed oil. I wish I could afford this stuff. But I can never let on to Max that I know all these details of his life.

I can definitely never admit I pilfered an inhale of his Midnight Flame—such an annoying cologne that annoying men who like to needle helpful women wear.

Especially since he probably didn't even toss a glance at my things. The man's so uninterested in anything but his own agenda.

Hustling, I hunt for my phone so I can text him. I spot the device, then quickly dictate a note.

Hi, Max! There's been a little mix-up, and I have—

A loud knock on my door startles me, then a deep, masculine voice calls out: "Room service. We have the Veuve Clicquot you ordered and the birthday cake in bed."

What?

I didn't order that. Or anything. Plus, that's way over my per diem. My boss would reprimand me with a cool smile, and I hate reprimands, especially ones I don't deserve.

"Coming," I say, before I can close the suitcase. Once I cross to the door and peer through the hole I gasp, then drop down even though he, obviously, can't see through the peephole.

It's Max Lambert, the wearer of the cocky cologne. The owner of the bag I snooped through. The man who's hated me since before I worked for this team.

Think fast.

Several feet away from me, his suitcase is wide open. He might hear if I head back over there. I slip off my heels as quietly as a mouse. "One sec," I call out in a muffled voice, like I'm far away from the door, then pad back to the bag and zip it up, but the zipper snags.

Fuck a duck. It's stuck on a pair of his boxer briefs.

Kill. Me. Now.

"Coming," I say, hastily.

"No worries, Miss Rosewood," he says in his fake room service voice. "Happy to wait all night with your special cake."

I barely have the time to roll my eyes, but I manage even as I shout brightly, "I know it's you, Max."

"And your champagne. Don't forget I have your champagne," he says as I yank harder and harder.

"I still know it's you," I say, trying to stay cheery as I tug the damn zipper. But I just. Can't. Get it. Squatting in front of the suitcase, I put everything I have into pulling on it, but then I land on my ass.

"You busy rooting through my things?"

I cringe, mortified. Actually, what is worse than mortification? Because that's what I'm feeling right now. Exponential mortification.

But I am a problem solver by nature. I didn't land this plum gig handling press for the NHL team because I can't handle problems. I can so handle them. I wiggle the zipper a little to the left, a little to the right, using a soft touch, and voila.

It's closed.

I take a breath, smooth out my navy blue blouse, run a hand down my ponytail, then head to the door, chin up, smile on, *never let them see you sweat*. Max won't know I was a bad girl. I swing it open and paste on a smile as I meet the face of the man who's made an art form of vexing me. Ice blue eyes, fair complexion, a chiseled jaw covered in a trim beard, and dark brown hair that's a little wild, a little wavy, a little too long. The net effect? All you want to do is run your fingers through it. A scar cuts through his right eyebrow, unfairly making him even sexier, and also a bit scary. He's six-foot-four, and when he's on the ice he looms over the net like some kind of Arctic monster guarding his frozen cave. He's a fearsome goalie, and he's big everywhere—with thick thighs, strong arms, a broad chest, and a hockey butt. This sport does unholy things to players' backsides. Right now though, he's resting one forearm against the doorframe, the other is out of view, and he's smirking.

I'd like to say it's a welcome change from his scowl. But I'm not so sure. Still, I like to fight fire with fire, so I smile wider. "How's it going? Do you need anything? Like a debrief on all the fabulous things we can discuss with the media tomorrow? If memory serves, Seattle is where you started out." I splay out my hands like I'm creating a headline. "The hometown boy makes good."

It's a story the press would eat up, even though he plays for the visiting team. Still, there's little the media likes more than a returning sports hero.

Well, a scandal. They like a scandal more. Which is exactly what I don't want him to ever face again, though the last one was no fault of his own—at least as far as I know. I don't have all the details. Max is notoriously tight-lipped.

But he isn't now, as he scoff-laughs at my request. *Jackass.*

"Let's take a raincheck on that feel-good story," he says, then tips his chin behind me. "By the way, the zipper's a little wonky on that. But you probably already know."

My cheeks flame, but I ignore the splash of heat, holding my chin up high. "Thanks for the heads-up," I say.

Looming in the doorway, he hoists up my suitcase and I try to grab it, but the jerk is too tall, too strong, and too tricky. "And I believe you left this with me. But you probably figured that out when you opened mine."

"I did not leave it with you," I say, momentarily exasperated. Does he think I wanted him to look through my luggage? Oh, crap. Did he give it the same examination I gave his? I really hope not. The last thing I want is Max knowing a single detail about me outside of work.

"Fine, fine. It was just a mix-up. But I have one question."

I groan privately, but smile publicly even though it's just the two of us here in the hallway of the Luxe Hotel late at night. "Yes?" It's asked sweetly, with sunshine, like how I usually try to behave around him. *Around everyone.*

He motions to my room. I sigh but open the door the rest of the way, and he strides inside like he owns the hotel. That's how he walks. Oozing confidence. Radiating sex appeal. Looking like sin. I hate how sexy he is, and he can never know.

As the door shuts with an ominous click, he sets down the luggage on the carpet and raises his other hand. My eyes widen in shock as he asks, "What is this called? Out of curiosity?"

I gasp.

One of my favorite little lacy things is dangling from his finger. And I was dead wrong about him spying. He's as bad as I am. I snatch it from his big hand. "It's a bralette," I say defensively as the sunshine in me starts to fade, clouds rolling in. "Why did you go through my things?"

He shrugs nonchalantly. "How else would I know if the bag was mine?" Max bats his ice blue eyes so innocently. But of course he's not innocent.

Then again, neither am I. "You take one quick look, then shut it when you don't see a thousand and one pairs of gray sweatpants," I explain in my best helpful tone.

But as I say that a voice in my head tsks me. *You didn't take one quick look. You scratched and sniffed.*

"Please, Everly. I travel with a thousand and two."

"Appreciate the correction." I stare him down, not giving an inch. "Though I presume once you saw it wasn't full of your things, you would've just returned it."

Instead of taunting me. But I keep that to myself. I don't need to give him more ammunition.

His gaze drifts pointedly to his suitcase behind him. "Right. I probably should have done that. It would be wrong to go through someone's stuff. To discover their, say, black boxer briefs, raspberry-flavored lip balm, noise-cancelling headphones, secret journal that they keep every night listing all the good things that happened that day or could happen one day, and their expensive moisturizer because God only gave them one face, and it's a fucking great face so they treat it well?"

Is he an evil wizard? Or just the biggest pain in my ass? "I'm sure you don't keep a secret journal," I say brightly.

But I remind myself that the season just started and I can't let difficult people irritate me. My boss told me a few days ago there's a promotion available this year, so I'm going to have to keep my eye on that prize, and not on the prickly problems.

"Are you, Everly?" With one dubious brow arched, he stares at me, like he's a lie detector test. "You sticking to that?"

I cross my arms. "Yes. And you?"

He waves a muscular arm at the suitcase he's returned. "Oh, I already admitted I looked through it. I was damn curious. And I asked what that piece of lace was. A bralette, if you recall. I'm just wondering if you did the same. It's a simple question really."

I swallow and school my expression. "Of course I didn't."

Liar, liar, pants on fire.

"If you say so," he says, smiling, leaning an inch closer. "But I think you're a terrible liar."

I burn, but I'm not a team publicist so I can fight with players. I'm a team publicist so I can fight for them. I swallow down my ire, and say, "It's a good thing you stopped by actually. I've been meaning to connect with you. I'm thinking about putting together a promo event with a local animal rescue once we're back in San Francisco. And I thought, how adorable would it be if we had the big, bad goalie posing with a little kitten?"

Max will hate that for ruining his icy image. He loves it when the other teams think he's an unapproachable dick. Well, guess what? He is.

"Does that work for you?" I ask.

He steps closer. So close I catch another hint of the Midnight Flame. Only this time, it's mixed with his skin. It's muskier, darker, sexier. More virile, and it sends a rush of heat down my belly as he drawls out my last name. "Rosewood." He says it like he's playing with me, ready to pounce. "Good thing I love kittens."

Damn him. I want to stomp my foot, but I'd never give him the satisfaction. "Wonderful. When I think of you I think of kittens. And don't you forget to put it in your secret journal of good things that might happen some day, 'kay?"

"I'll be making an entry tonight, alone in my bed wearing only my black boxer briefs," he says dryly, as he grabs his bag. Then, without a smirk or a scowl, he wheels it to the door. "Enjoy the bralette, Rosewood."

I can't let him get the last word in. "Lambert!"

He turns my way. "Yes?"

I tilt my head. "Where's my cake? It sounded so good."

His eyes narrow as he draws in a sharp breath. Then

his gaze drifts to the bag he returned, and he asks, a little strangled, "Got a hot date here?"

Like I'm going to tell him. I bob a shoulder. "I don't wear my bralette and tell."

He grabs the door handle. "Shame. I was about to send you the birthday cake."

My mouth waters. I want birthday cake. But I want the satisfaction of not revealing that the lingerie is for me and only for me. I wave happily to him. "I guess I'll order it myself for my company and me."

His eyes flash with something almost feral, then he huffs out an annoyed goodnight, and leaves.

Heart beating too fast, I shut the door, catching one last hint of his fading cologne. Max Lambert is the bane of my existence and if I could wish for one thing this season, it'd be to never have to deal with him again.

If only wishes came true.

3

PRETTY AND POWERFUL

Everly

As I pull on the bralette the next morning, I try not to think about its misadventures last night. Like a twelve-year-old might, did Max slingshot it across his room for fun? Toss it up and down in the air for kicks? Inspect it like it was an item in a curio shop? Or just laugh at me for wanting something like this?

Something extravagant. Something pretty.

I believe in splurging on underthings but I have my reasons. Ones he'll never know. Especially since he assumed I must have sexy lingerie for a man. *Please.* My reasons have nothing to do with a hot date.

But as I adjust the bottom of the cherry-red lace bralette, I picture his big hands on the soft lace and I unexpectedly shiver. What an annoying reaction to an unbidden image. I squeeze my eyes shut to get rid of it, but that does nothing to erase the image of Max touching my lingerie, or the chill that rushes through me.

I open my eyes and shake my head in frustration, then pluck at the left strap. Maybe I should just retire this bralette. I don't need the reminder every time I wear it of a man I once stupidly crushed on when I was a reporter. Before I worked for the team. Then, when I stuck a phone recorder in his face post-game, he'd toss me a useful comment or two, offering something fun for my network —*what can I say about all those saves? Sometimes you just get lucky*. He was friendly then. He's an enemy now.

And yet the fucker still makes my skin tingle. Why am I wired to be attracted to men who don't give me the time of day?

Nope. Don't answer that, brain.

But rather than get lost in my thoughts of all the things I need to change about myself, I wiggle the strap around a little bit more, lifting it gingerly over the scar cutting across my left shoulder. As my fingers skim the raised, reddish-pink skin, a familiar image flickers through my mind—a painful one and I wince, feeling the inexorable pull of time. The way it wants to swallow me into that evening three years ago.

But rather than let it, I fight back. Rooting myself to the here and now, I take the opportunity to catalog my surroundings. How does the wall look? Beige. What about the floor? The creme-colored carpet has a diamond pattern on it. How many windows are there? Three, and then beyond the glass is Mount Rainier, rising up, steady, strong, powerful.

With that strength in me, I cross the room to the full-length mirror, hanging by the door. Time for the hardest parts of the getting ready ritual. The last thing I do before I leave every morning for work, whether at home or on the road.

I look.

I'm wearing black slacks and a bralette. My arms are toned. My body is tight. My legs are strong.

I look pretty and powerful, I tell myself. I say it out loud anyway. "You're pretty and powerful." Maybe one day I'll believe it.

I turn sideways and gaze at the jagged row of scars that travel from my shoulder down across my back to my hip, cutting zigzags into my skin. Most are pale, faded over time, but they still mark a map on my body. Some are mean, refusing to go quietly into the night. Together, they are all a story told in one act of what happened one horrible night.

I am pretty and powerful.

I return to the bed and grab the shirt I left on it. Then, with a simple silver gray blouse I cover up the lingerie that makes me feel like I'm more than these scars. When I do the last button, it's hidden. No one would know I'm the kind of woman who doesn't simply like wearing pretty things—but I need to.

Max doesn't know. And he never will.

I leave my hotel room so I can head to the lobby to meet up with one of our centers, Miles Falcon. Miles is from Seattle, and we're going to meet with a local sports talk podcaster, who I pitched doing a feature piece on one of our players from the Pacific Northwest. The podcaster —a persistent and affable guy named Ian Walker—liked my idea, but kept asking for our star goalie too, who grew up here before moving to the Bay Area as a teenager. I kept saying *sorry he's not available.*

There's a coffee shop-slash-recording studio right across from the Seattle team's arena, and the shop hosts several podcasters, including some sports-centric ones that draw live audiences. The guy who runs the whole coffee shop-slash-podcast setup—his name is Joe—has emailed me a couple times to let me know there's a full house this morning. The place holds about seventy-five. "They better not heckle my star center," I said to him in my last email.

As I head to the elevator, I spot Joe's reply on my phone. "Fans'll be fans," he writes, but there's a winky face, so that's good. Plus, Miles is a veteran who's been playing for ten years so he won't be bothered by a rowdy crowd member if one speaks up.

After I push the button for the lobby, another email lands on my phone from Ian. *Last minute, but I had this idea! We do this segment on Five Fun Places to Go in the PNW. Would Max do that? It's not even hockey talk. I promise I won't ask about that game.*

Hope really does spring eternal. And maybe it does in me too. My boss would be thrilled if Max started talking to the media more, especially in a feature-style piece. It's a low-risk way for him to get back out there, and the powers that be have been telling me for months to keep asking him to chat with the press now and then, especially in safe forums like this. I send Max a cheery text. I don't even sass him. I opt only for directness.

> Everly: This would be such a great chance to make a rare appearance in a controlled environment. He's not going to ask about that game—just about your favorite places here. We'll do it at the Pick Me Up coffee shop right across from the arena. You can join in at the end, and you can even talk about your favorite cat café in Seattle. C'mon, you know you have one.

His reply comes quickly.

> Max: I do. I'm there right now. There's a calico rescue cat draped around my neck, and she refuses to budge. Which means I won't be able to make it over to the coffee shop in time. Shame.

I roll my eyes, then drop the upbeat attitude for a few seconds as the elevator chugs down.

> Everly: If I had a dollar for every excuse of yours…

> Max: What would you do with all that dough?

> Everly: I'd have enough for a lifetime supply of blowouts from my stylist Aubrey.

I wish I could say I don't understand his reasons but the thing is—I do. I get that we all have secrets and scars we don't want anyone to see.

* * *

The coffee shop is massive, even by Seattle standards, and this city worships its beans. Pick Me Up started as a college radio station several years ago, then expanded into podcasts recently, and now has a state-of-the-art studio, a dais with comfy chairs for interviews, and, of course, coffee by the IV drip. As Miles grabs an espresso, the fans filter in, some of them wearing gear for the Seattle team, some for the Sea Dogs, and most just in hoodies and jeans. I'm by Miles's side the whole time, and as he downs his drink, Joe emerges from behind the counter. He's in his late thirties, sports a goatee, and has warm brown eyes. He looks like he never sees the sun, which is probably true here in this city.

He smiles a little awkwardly when he sees me. "Good to see you again, Everly. Would love to show you the setup if you have time. We've done some cool stuff with the space."

"Sure. That would be great," I say, since it can't hurt to be nice to the guy who hosts so many sports shows from here.

"Come find me when you're done. I'll be ready."

"I will," I say.

He returns to the counter. As the fans fill the seats in front of the dais, I snag a chair off to the side. Miles and Ian take the seats on the stage in front of two standing mics set on a table. Once the interview begins, I answer emails quietly on my tablet but keep my ears trained on the conversation as Ian chats affably with Miles about playing in his hometown. It's an easy conversation and after twenty minutes, Ian asks him his five fun places to go in the area—the question he also wanted to ask Max. I grit my teeth. Would it be that hard to answer those?

After a thoughtful pause, Miles rattles off a hiking trail he likes, the Hello Robin cookie shop in Capitol Hill, anywhere at all in the entire region but The Gum Wall in Pike Place Market, Snoqualmie Falls, and then, with a happy sigh, he says, "And Dick's."

I sit up straighter, my ears pricked.

Ian nods, a friendly grin coasting across his weathered ebony complexion. "Right on. Love that place. You all do too, don't you?" he asks the audience, and they hoot in agreement, nodding heads, shouting *hell yeah.*

Oh, right. Dick's is the drive-in fast-food chain here that the locals love to drop into casual convo. From the stage, Miles looks to me, sliding a hand through his floppy hair to push it off his forehead. "Everly, you ever had them? Their fries are next level. Back me up here, Ian."

A stocky guy in a ball cap jerks his gaze to me, then shouts at me from the front row. "Falcon is right. You gotta eat a bag of dicks, lady."

Lady. It's such an annoying thing men can say, but I fasten on a brighter smile. "I will take that under advisement."

Miles turns back to Ian, intensity in his eyes. "When they opened one up in Bellevue, the local paper said, *The town welcomes Dick's with open mouths.*"

Another guy, this one with a Seattle jersey, barks out, "Fact: dick jokes never go out of style."

I might beg to differ. But since Ian has the crowd under control, I keep my head down as they wrap up with zero heckles. I seriously don't get why Max can't do this. It was...painless. Miles and Ian chat briefly, then Miles hops off the dais, shakes some hands, signs some autographs, and finds me a few minutes later. He points his thumb toward the door. "Thanks for setting that up. I should hit the weight room for some cardio before morning skate."

"I'll stick around to talk to Ian and Joe, but thank you again for doing this," I say.

"Thank you again for the opportunity," Miles says, then takes off, and I join Ian at the dais as he breaks down his podcast gear, folding up the legs of the mic stands.

"I'll post that interview before the game. We get the best traction then," Ian says as the crowd thins, most of them filtering out.

"Awesome. I appreciate that."

"Nah, I appreciate you making this happen. Shame we couldn't get Max, but maybe next time," he says, as he tucks the mics into a sturdy silver case.

I don't have the heart to say *maybe never* so I reply, "I hope so."

As he rolls up the cables, he stops suddenly mid-roll. "Oh, did you hear?"

The words *did you hear* never lead anywhere positive. I glance around, making sure no one's within earshot. "Did I hear what?" I ask with false bravado, pretending this will be good news when my gut already tells me it's not.

Ian flashes an apologetic smile. "Lyra Raine's in town."

My smile takes a dive straight into the Puget Sound. "She is?" I scratch out.

A sigh of resignation comes from the podcaster. "She's here for a surprise show tonight. Although I guess her concert's not a surprise anymore," he says. "She dropped it on social this morning."

This is bad. This is really bad. The entertainment press will leach onto Max after the game, trying to corner him, to find out if this means he's back together with the pop star who broke his heart more than a year ago. The press loves a second-chance romance, and they won't stop until they get a response or a rise out of him.

I'll have to run some serious interference for the goalie who hates me. "Appreciate the heads-up, Ian," I say, grateful for the tip and ready to track down Max and warn him. "I should get out of here. I'll find Joe and let him know I have to take off."

The tour will have to wait.

"Take care, Everly," Ian says, then snaps his podcast case closed.

"And hey, be sure to eat a bag of dicks," I say as he heads to the door.

With a chuckle, like he can't believe what he's saying, he calls out, "And you...eat a bag of dicks yourself."

Laughing, I shoo him off, then spin around and beeline to the coffee counter. As I walk, I tap out a message to my counterpart on the Seattle team, asking for some help tonight with security. When I reach the counter, I look up again, tucking my phone away. Joe's serving a customer, and once he's done, he flashes me an awkward smile. "Can I show you around?"

"Actually," I say, frowning apologetically, "I've got a pressing thing I need to take care of."

He frowns too. "Shoot. I'm sorry to hear that." In no time, he moves around the counter, leaving a tattooed gal with a pierced nose to handle the rest of the customers, while he comes to me, standing awfully close. I don't need to know what he ate for breakfast—sausage and coffee, I think.

I inch back, and now I'm the awkward one. "Me too. I was looking forward to the tour. Maybe next time."

He steps closer again, not getting the hint. "Definitely. Also, I've been expanding in San Francisco and would love to get your thoughts on that."

Hoisting up my bag higher on my shoulder, like I'm using it as a wedge to shoehorn myself a little bit of personal space, I inch away a second time. "I'm not sure how I can help, but if I can I'll do my best," I say. It's not quite a no, but I'd like it to be one without being rude.

"And maybe," he says, his lips crooking up as footsteps echo behind me, likely coffee shop customers milling about and grabbing their drinks, "I could take you out to dinner there? They might not have a bag of dicks but I'm sure we can find something good."

Well, that escalated quickly.

"I'm not sure," I begin, working on an excuse that'll be diplomatic since we sort of have a business relationship.

He slides closer, cuts in with, "It'll be fun. I promise."

But before I can say another word, a wall of a man is right next to me. Like he came out of nowhere.

He's tall and glowering as he stares at Joe like he wants to rip him apart. "She's busy that night."

Max Lambert is here, turning down the date for me.

What gives him the right to speak for me? I scrunch my brow and turn to him. "How do you know?" The question flies out of my mouth.

Max lifts a coffee cup, then takes a long, leisurely sip. When he's done, he says, "You're booked most nights." There's zero remorse for butting in—only certainty that he's done the right thing.

I narrow my eyes at the big hockey star who's inexplicably here. "You don't know my schedule or when he's coming to town."

Max shrugs, like he's completely unfazed. "I took a guess. Bet I'm right."

I'm so shocked he'd turn down a date for me, even one I was hunting for a way to turn down myself, that I don't even know what to say next to him.

But Joe, evidently, does. He holds up his hands in surrender. Now it's his tone that's awkward as he says, "My bad. I'll let you two sort this out."

"No worries," Max says, in an offhand way. Like the guy just bumped into him on the street. That's all. "She's got a packed sked."

"I don't," I say, because he should not be turning down dates for me. I can say no myself.

But Joe is well past the rejection it seems, since he directs his gaze to Max. "Don't take this the wrong way, but hope you lose tonight."

"We won't," Max says confidently as Joe gets the hell out of my space at last. He disappears behind the counter, then into the back of the shop, out of sight.

I swivel back to Max. He's got another cup of coffee in his other hand, probably for one of the guys. But other than that—he's standard Max. Inscrutable and broody. I flap my hands. "What was that about?"

He gives a careless shrug. "You didn't want to go out with him."

True, but that doesn't even matter. "It's not your job to turn down my dates."

"He's not your type, Everly."

"How would you know what my type is?"

"Not that guy," he says.

He's exasperating. "Okay, I'll take the bait. Why not that guy?"

"He's a little crass. The bag of dicks thing?" he says, dismissively. "C'mon. You can do better."

I stare at him, trying to figure out what is going on with Lambert. "Why are you here?"

4

A NICE INTENTION

Max

That's a really good question. And an easy enough one to answer. I lift my drinks. "Can't a guy get a cup of coffee or two?"

"At the place where the interview you turned down was being held?" she counters, one eyebrow raised. Fuck, she's hot when she's irritated. How is that possible? Witchcraft, I'm guessing.

I look around the massive space as if I'm seeing the exposed brick walls, the dais and the lounge chairs for the very first time. "Hate to break it to you, Everly. But it *is* a coffee shop."

"Max," she says, exasperated. "Why did you..." She waves to where that pushy dude was crowding her but then shakes her head, like she's letting go of the whole thing. "Forget it. Let's go."

Good. The less she asks, the better. I'm not even entirely sure why I pulled that shit other than I had a feeling he was going to ask her out since I walked in, and she doesn't need that kind of hassle in her day. From the second I stepped in here to get in line to grab a cup, his eyes were tracking her as she helped Ian pack up. He was totally unable to focus on making a latte for the customers in front of me since his gaze was lasered in on my publicist.

So yeah. I butted in. Everly barely needs a defender, but she got one anyway. "Look, if I was wrong, I'm happy to go find him and play matchmaker for ya. Maybe you two can have a nice stroll in the park and a cup of tea," I say dryly.

She heaves a sigh as we walk to the door. "No, Max. Obviously I don't need you to set up the date you already turned down for me."

"You don't want to date someone in Seattle anyway, do you?" I ask casually, grabbing the door and opening it. "I mean, aside from last night. You had company, right?"

I'm fishing. I'm totally fucking fishing.

"How would I have had time to see someone last night? With my *packed sked* and all," she says, throwing my words back to me.

"So I was helpful, then, to turn that dude down for you," I say. And I've just learned, too, that she didn't have a hot date last night, which makes me way more pleased than it should. "Bummer that you didn't get that cake from room service though."

"What goes better with working late in your hotel room on upcoming publicity plans than cake?" she asks, then quickly types something on her phone. She puts it away once we're outside the shop-slash-studio and shoots me a serious look. "Why are we having this conversation about dating?"

That's a fair question too. I don't care who she dates. Or where she dates them. She vexes me. She pushes me. She drives me crazy. The feeling's mutual. But it was the principle of it. Some men are just pushy fuckers, and he was looking like he was veering too close to that territory.

And she deserves that answer. It's not the easy answer I gave her at first, but I should probably say it. "Because you shouldn't have to deal with that," I grumble as we head to the arena. "And before you can say it, I know you had it handled."

"I did," she says firmly. "I was going to turn him down. You didn't have to do it for me."

True. I didn't. Guess I wanted him to get the message loud and clear. "Look, I didn't like his dick joke, and he was getting in your space, and it was rude."

She whips her gaze to me, brown eyes flickering with curiosity. "You noticed that?"

"I noticed it, and I didn't like it," I say. "He looked like he was trying to touch your arm. You kept stepping away. He kept stepping closer."

"True, but he was never inappropriate."

"Good. He shouldn't fucking be," I say, breathing fumes. There's a special place in hell for men who don't listen to women. "Look, I saw the crowd of guys he courts. They're all kind of...a little crass. Shouting stupid jokes. I could tell you didn't want to be near any of them, let alone him. I took care of it. So sue me."

She chuckles, rolling her eyes too. "*So sue me*? That's your answer?"

"Well, yeah," I say as we reach the crosswalk.

While we wait, she pins me with her sharp gaze. "See, Max? You do something borderline nice, then you're kind of flippant."

I arch a brow. "Was that nice? Not sure I'd agree."

"It was a nice intention," she says.

I shudder.

"Aww. Don't worry I won't tell anyone about your kind thoughts," she says.

"Good," I say, as the pedestrian light blinks green. We're quiet as we cross, and she seems like she's mulling something over. When we reach the other side, she tilts her head in question, her brow furrowed, like she's adding something up that doesn't quite equate. "You heard the whole thing. You were in line right as he was asking me out?"

I take the alibi she's offering—the idea that it was a coincidence. Like in a movie when the guy overhears the villain monologuing. Mostly it was. I won't let on I'd popped into the shop for a cup of coffee, but when I heard those dick jokes I hung around, keeping an eye out. Good thing. I'd figured it'd be a fan getting fresh with her instead of the owner of the shop and the podcast network. So yeah, maybe I was on patrol. Not like I'm going to tell her. She doesn't need to know I was playing the body-guard. "Yup. Needed a morning boost. Glad I left that calico at the cat café when I did. But she was so darn cute," I say, then since I don't want any of this to seem like a big deal, I nod toward the players' entrance. "I should go join my teammates for practice. I like to give them a target they can't get past."

"Actually," she says, but her expression is soft and so is her voice, "there's something I need to discuss with you."

That sounds serious. "Let me guess. I'm in trouble again."

"Would that even matter?"

"Probably not," I reply before she pulls me aside outside the arena entrance to a quieter area.

She moves closer to me now, so close I'm distracted by the whoosh of her hair in that high ponytail, the way it swishes as she moves into my space. "Lyra's in town. I don't know if you know."

The blood drains from my face. "Seriously?" I croak out.

It's not my ex I don't want to see. I'm so over the woman I was going to propose to.

It's the attention that comes with her. The attention that comes to me. I'd give my left nut if it would erase from existence the breakup song she wrote about me. The one that was a lie. But, then again, I like both nuts a whole helluva lot. Maybe I'd give up my spleen to make "Surprise Me" disappear from every playlist in the world and public memory.

"She's doing a surprise show," Everly adds.

"How nice," I mutter.

"I've got it covered," she says, then holds up a finger. Quickly, she scans her phone, then looks up. "I checked with security for the Seattle team. There's a back exit out of the locker room that'll help you avoid the press. I can let the team bus know what time and to look for you, and you should be able to leave unnoticed after the game."

Wow. I'm seriously grateful for that. And for what's unsaid. She won't even ask me to talk to the media tonight. "Thanks. Appreciate it," I say, then I square my shoulders. "I do."

"And don't worry. This changes nothing." She narrows her eyes and holds up a finger. "You get one night off from my requests. And then it is on again."

"I would expect nothing less."

She's made a one-upmanship-style approach of asking me to talk to the press after every single game even though I've made it crystal clear I don't do media.

This is merely a brief detente—not an end to our battle. Then, because she might have noticed I'm holding two cups, I thrust one her way. "For some reason, they gave me two London fog lattes," I say, then offer one of the Earl Grey concoctions to her. "You like them, right?"

Curiosity flickers across her eyes, and she studies me for a beat, her lips curving up. "I do."

"Cool," I say, waggling the cup. "It's yours then."

She takes it. "Thanks. They're my favorite."

"Even better," I say, as if I didn't know that already.

Once inside, she heads one way and I go the other way to the locker room, then hit the ice, the one place where no one really bothers me.

* * *

That evening, the Seattle winger barrels toward me, swift, determined. But I'm not in the mood to let any goals in.

Nothing to do but deflect the puck.

A minute later, one of their guys is flying around the back of the net, flipping the little black disc to a forward who aims then shoots.

Not on my watch. I drop to my knees, my leg pad blocking the shot.

Better luck next time.

And the next time, the puck flies at me and I knock it down, where it lands harmlessly on the ice.

For another period, they come at me, as they should. But I'm feeling impenetrable tonight.

Imagine that.

By the time the game clock winds down, I swear every player in their lineup has tried and failed to take a shot.

When the buzzer blares, I've nabbed a shutout.

My closest friends on the team, Wesley Bryant and Asher Callahan, skate over to me, clapping me on the back as we head off the ice.

In the tunnel, I rip off my helmet, and as promised, Everly's waiting at the end. She gives a crisp nod, and I nod right back, then move on as she asks some of the other guys to talk to the media. Technically, all players are supposed to be accessible.

Twenty minutes later, I'm dressed in my suit and out of there, earbuds in, an online course playing that I really need to focus on as I head for the team bus that'll take us to the airport.

But when I hop on it, the driver is nodding her head, rocking out to "Surprise Me." It's so loud, I can hear it even as the instructor in my ears rattles on about navigational tools used in the eighteenth century.

"Can you shut that off?" I ask.

"Lyra? No way. She's the best," the driver says, but then her eyes widen, her lips part, and something must click. "Oh. Shit. You're..."

Yeah, I'm the guy who inspired the break-up song that America's sweetheart sent to the top of the charts. Only that's not the way things went down.

"Whatever," I mutter.

Doesn't matter. I head to the back of the bus, slump down and listen to the class so I can take a quiz later this week to see how much I've memorized. I don't miss the way things used to be. Really, I don't.

* * *

The next morning, I'm back home in jeans and a Henley, about to head out to see Garrett at the kebab place. I'll be skipping today's team yoga class for this, but I've got the distinct impression that this meeting with him will be more important than one with the yoga mat. I'm heading downstairs, phone in hand, when a text from him lands.

> Best we have this meeting at the office, Max.

Doesn't take a genius to know bad news is coming my way.

5

THE LIKEABILITY QUOTIENT

Max

What do you wear to an execution? I want to make a good lasting impression and go out with a bang, so I trot back upstairs and grab my best dress shirt from the closet—a light blue one along with a pair of black slacks. I change quickly, trying my best not to obsess on what might happen in my agent's office.

Dun dun dun...

With my best ready-for-the-guillotine attire on, I head downstairs again and stop in the hallway with a groan. A little silver tabby with white paws is hanging from the blinds on the window overlooking Pacific Street but trying to hoist herself higher. She's determined to reach the ceiling for fuck-all-knows-what reason. I hustle over to Athena and do my best to untangle the kitten from the blinds without losing an eye.

Not sure that's likely, since she is stronger than ten men. "How are you four pounds and a hellion already?" I ask, extricating her from the wood slats, then setting her on the floor, where she shoots me a look of utter disdain, then jumps right back up on the blinds, hurling her way up like a ninja warrior.

"Let's do this again," I say, then remove her once more. "Try to be a good girl and not climb to the ceiling for the rest of the day," I tell the kitten I've been fostering for three whole hours.

The rescue volunteer dropped her off bright and early.

As I set her down on the floor, Athena attacks my forearm, wrapping her little ones around me. Carefully, so the she-devil won't scratch me, I unwrap her from my wrist. "Fine, have it your way. Climb the blinds," I tell her because cats are going to be cats.

They're going to do whatever the hell they want and fuck you.

I get it. I really do.

But instead she scurries down the hall, done with the find-the-ceiling plan. With the terror off to terrorize a lampshade or a mug, I head to the garage and hop into my car, where I tune back into the online course. Something I'm taking to keep my brain sharp, but it also keeps my mind off the blade that's coming down on my neck *any minute*.

Fifteen minutes later, I arrive at Garrett's agency just off the Embarcadero, a prime location since it's near both one of the city's baseball parks and a football stadium. I nab a spot in the underground lot easily. That'll probably be the last thing that goes my way today. Maybe I'm a pessimist but I like to think I'm a realist. The world is a dumpster fire, so it's best to meet the world on its own terms. Bonus? With my attitude, I won't get blindsided. Been there, done that. Don't want to get blindsided again.

I go to the parking garage elevator, then I hit the button for my agent's office. When the elevator dings open on the seventh floor, I turn down the hall, making my way to the corner suite. The Garrett Emerson Sports Management Agency is a force. My agent left one of the big agencies a few years ago to branch out on his own, and the dude can pull. His client list is impressive across the major pro sports, as well as the Olympic ones.

I push open the sleek, modern doors. Glass walls reflect the sunlight on this October day in San Francisco, polished wooden floors gleam underfoot, and sports memorabilia is tastefully displayed around the waiting room.

The air is filled with a faint scent of leather and success.

The second the receptionist sees me, he flashes a courteous smile. He doesn't look a day over twenty-one. "So glad you could make it on short notice, Mr. Lambert," he says, ready and eager to help. "I'll let Mr. Emerson know you're here."

"Thanks," I say, but before he can even dial the boss, Garrett's already here in the lobby, a warm smile on his face as he strides over to me and extends a hand in greeting. "I see you dressed like you're meeting with the team owner," he says wryly, knowing me too well.

"I can read subtext," I say.

He claps me on the back. "Let's head to the conference room and talk business."

And he doesn't deny that I'm reading his text tone correctly. I follow Garrett down a corridor lined with framed jerseys and signed tennis rackets and golf clubs. There's even a volleyball in a glass case from one of his gold medalists in that sport.

Are these other clients as difficult as I am? But I dismiss the thought. I brought him a cup a few years back. Doesn't get much better than that. We pass by offices bustling with other agents making deals over the phone. The conference room we enter is just as swank as the rest of the office—a long mahogany table surrounded by comfortable leather chairs.

I stop in the doorway though, tilting my head. We're not alone. A young woman I don't know is here. She shoots me a cheerful smile that lights up her curious green eyes. She's with my financial advisor too—John Saito. He played baseball in Japan, where he's from, for a brief stint. Love the straight shooter and his investment strategies, but I'm not sure what to make of him showing up. Plus, there's a whiteboard in the corner, with a sheet of paper covering it.

What the hell have I just walked into?

Garrett gestures to the woman. "This is Rosario Valdez, who's in our branding division. And you know John."

"Nice to meet you, Rosario," I say warily as I shake her hand. I'm not used to meeting with the whole crew, but then again, it's been a long-ass while since Garrett called me to his office. Come to think of it, has he ever?

A sense of foreboding wraps tighter around me as I take a seat. I'm beginning to wish I hadn't skipped the team yoga class for this meeting, since I bet I'll be needing something to chill the fuck out after this meet-and-greet is over.

"Good to see you, Max," John says, but I'm wondering —*is it?* "Do you want water, coffee, tea?"

He doesn't offer me an energy drink. It feels like a purposeful omission. "I'm good," I say, and the tension in the room is obvious in their smiles and their graciousness.

Not one to mince words, I sit back in the chair and say heavily, "Just get it over with. Thrive dropped me. I've put that together already."

Garrett's smile of acknowledgement is at least kind. "Max," he begins as he sits, his tone more serious than I've ever heard it. "Thrive has decided not to renew their sponsorship with you."

Even though I knew it was coming, my lungs feel crushed, like I'm gasping for air. Thrive had been my biggest sponsor for years, providing not only financial support but also a sense of legitimacy in the sports marketing world. Without them, I'm going to lose more than just a paycheck.

It's weird that you can brace yourself for something, that you can read the writing on the wall, and yet it's still a gut punch when it happens. But I don't want to let on how disappointed I am. When you let down your guard, that's when you get sucker punched again. "Okay," I say, trying to keep my voice steady. "Any reason in particular?"

Well, besides the obvious. I'm one of the most hated men in America. That's what happens when the world thinks you broke up with America's sweetheart.

Garrett exhales, then steeples his hands together. "It comes down to visibility, Max. You're not as active on social media as they would like. You're not seen at events or engaging with fans. You're not in the game highlights on ESPN."

I scoff. "I beg to differ. I *was* the highlight of the game last night."

"Yes, a shutout is impressive. It's even better when you give a comment to the media," he adds, then with a *hate to mention this* smile, he adds, "Also, you are *kind of* supposed to be available to talk to the press after games."

I give him a look. "You know what happened when the press tried to talk to me last year. It was *not* about hockey." It was all about the split with Lyra and about her new guy.

"We know," Garrett says. "And the front office is certainly aware of the media attention that came with your last romance."

"The breakup," I correct, since there's no need to be coy here. "You can say it out loud. I do know we've split."

Garrett moves on with the smoothness of a good agent. "And the front office understood that a lot of things happened—"

"A lot of things happened? That is the fuck-all euphemism of the century. The press showed up at my sister's house."

Garrett nods, still the picture of calm. "Yes, and the front office understood you needed a break. And then, after that, they tried to help by having their PR ask you to do features and soft pieces."

Features—like the thing Everly asked me to do in Seattle. I don't mention that though. He probably already knows I refused. Dude probably knows what I ate for breakfast too. I stay quiet, waiting for him to keep going.

"But it's been over a year," he adds. Translation: the team's patience is running out. "And it'd be good for you to get out there. Give a softball comment now and then after a game."

"Like, *I'm just focused on helping the team*," I say, rolling my eyes.

Rosario clears her throat, beaming as she chimes in. "Actually, that's a great start. Our market research shows that a simple team-centric comment to the press can go a long way to endearing the public to a professional athlete."

"Long enough to make them forget a pop star wrote a song about you that was dead wrong?" I counter. Not to mention *the fight* that came before that too.

Garrett levels me with a serious stare. "Not gonna lie— it'll take some work, but it'd be a start."

"You want me to tell everyone, too, why we split? Does the world need to know the truth of that?"

"No, Max," he says, deadly serious. "It doesn't do you any good to air dirty laundry. But it doesn't do you any good to be so reclusive about yourself and the sport either. As it is, your reluctance is sending you backward."

I sigh heavily. "There's a reason I don't talk to the press," I say. And it has little to do with that song. Little to do with *the fight.* It has everything to do with what happened a week or so later when the press tried to track me down at my sister's house after the fight. I burn with anger as I remember that night more than a year ago.

"We know," John cuts in, his voice even more no-nonsense than Garrett's. "But still."

Then I get pissed. Like I would if I missed a save in a game. "This is bullshit from Thrive. I've promoted their product in every way possible. I did promo shoots and commercials."

Garrett nods solemnly. "I know, Max. But the numbers don't lie. Your marketability has decreased significantly. And they aren't the only ones who have moved on."

I bristle at the reminder. I lost Power Kicks, a sneaker company. I lost the watchmaker Victoire. Hell, I couldn't even get a sponsorship with Seductive, the company that owns the cologne I actually wear every day.

The last year's been a long, slow march away from me.

I'm nuclear to brands. But Thrive felt like a lifeboat, consistently keeping me afloat.

"We have nothing compared to the other season," John adds.

The one *before* I discovered Lyra's lies. The one before the world blamed me for her lies. Lies she spun in her song of heartbreak. "Surprise Me" in-fucking-deed.

"And it's affecting your likeability quotient," Rosario puts in.

Frustration bubbles inside me. "What the hell is a likeability quotient?"

"It's a measure of how appealing you are to audiences, Max," Rosario chimes in gently, popping up from her chair and heading to the whiteboard. She rips off the paper covering it and shows a thermometer drawing, with only a small section at the bottom colored in red. "And right now, yours has gone way down."

I scoff. "That sounds like a BS marketing term they use in ad agencies in TV shows. Or like a sign at a bank that's trying to raise funds for something."

Garrett nods, giving me that much. "Maybe, but the thing is, market research matters. Brands use it. They rely on it. Guys like Carter Hendrix?" he says, naming the star receiver for the San Francisco Renegades. "Very high likability quotient."

I groan. Love the guy. He's a friend. But of course he's beloved. "He took his best friend on dates to farmers' markets and chocolate shops and shot videos for a dating app. Of course everyone loves him."

"So you understand how the likeability quotient works," John says, his tone precise, ready to move on.

Wait. Hold the hell on. "Are you about to suggest I fake

date someone? Because no, no, and more no. That is not going to happen."

After a far too public relationship with a pop star went south, no way am I smiling and kissing for the camera. Besides, I don't want to lie. I'd rather have zero sponsors than spin a fake love story for the world.

Rosario chuckles as she returns to her seat. "No, we're not suggesting that. Studies show in your case that'd be worse for your image."

My head spins with all their market research. "You did studies on the possibility of *me* fake dating?"

"Of course. But we don't phrase it like that. We have subtler ways of asking the audience if it would be good for someone. But we feel that based on the, how shall we say, rather public attention of your last romance, a fake romance to improve your image is just too risky."

Translation: I'm too risky.

"You think I'd fuck it up," I say to Garrett.

He holds his hands out wide, an admission. "We think there are better ways for you to improve your likeability," he says.

I roll my eyes. I'm not sure I can do anything but roll them. "I'm fine. I make enough playing," I bite out because let's be honest—pro athletes are not hurting for dough in most cases.

John lifts a finger. "Sure. But we've talked about your future plans frequently."

I grit my teeth, hating that he's right, but he's right.

"We've talked about this," John continues, "you want to make sure you have enough for your parents."

We had so little growing up. Money was more than tight. My parents were and still are teachers. Hockey's not cheap, so they put anything extra into the sport, including money they didn't have. I was lucky I played at an ice rink where a pro hockey player had donated funds for the program. I want to take care of them now that I can. "Right," I grumble.

"And we know that you could, god forbid, get hurt," Garrett says sympathetically.

"Don't remind me," I say. A sprained wrist sidelined me for a few weeks my rookie season. It was hell. I was sure my career was over. The dark cloud of dread that followed me around those weeks off the ice has never fully cleared.

"That's where sponsorships come into play because they provide that security even when a career ends," Rosario says, cheerful and chipper.

I'm about to argue that smart savings of my salary will help, and they will, but why argue with them? They're on my team. Besides, facts are facts—I *want* to take care of my parents, since they took care of me, and I can do that better if I have more guaranteed income. I draw a big breath, ready to let go of my irritation. It's not going to win me any friends, and fact is, they're right. I do want to save more and do it quickly. You never know what could happen tomorrow. And you never know what could happen later in life, when you're older, when you can't play, when you can't maybe do a lot of things.

Briefly, I picture my grandfather in his final years, and my throat tightens. I breathe deeply, past the pain of those visits, and focus on the present. "So what do you have in mind? A new sponsor? A shoe company? A body spray company? A dating site? I mean, I don't have to use it, do I?"

Garrett pushes his palms toward the table, like he's

saying slow down. "Actually, we think you need to rehab your image before we can get you a new sponsor."

"It's that bad?" I ask with more vulnerability than I'd expected.

Rosario smiles kindly, like she wants to pat my head in kindergarten class. "Your LQ is so low—it's a one," she whispers, nodding surreptitiously to the thermometer drawing on the whiteboard. "But we know how to boost it right back up," she says, pointing to the top of the thermometer with a certain amount of...market research glee.

"Okay," I say, hesitantly. "Why do I feel like I won't like this?"

"That's a good question. But does it really matter?" Garrett asks, sitting forward in the chair and parking his elbows on the table. He takes a beat, then pulls no punches when he says, "Max, I hate to be the bearer of bad news, but the team isn't happy with you. They could fine you for not talking to the media, but they don't want to do that and we don't want that, do we?"

That's bad. That's basically at the level of *you get one more strike and we don't renew*. What's more, everyone in the league would know I was a problem child.

I gulp. "What do I have to do?"

"Well, we've been talking to the team about a great opportunity for you."

I have a feeling my likability quotient for this idea will be below zero.

6

THE END OF THE FUN FACT ERA

Everly

Finishing my London fog latte, I work my way through emails and interview requests back at the office. As I go, I catch up on listening to podcasts and on-air interviews our players have done over the last few days.

Most I already sat in on, but if I can't be there—since, well, I can't be everywhere at once until I can clone myself —I like to listen to them. I don't want to be blindsided with something I've missed. I hate surprises, which is weird since I work in sports, and literally every game is a surprise.

But sports are at least predictable.

What I aim to avoid is someone tipping me off to something I should have known—a problem I should have anticipated. I'm done listening right as I finish answering emails before they can pile up. When I hit send on the last one, my phone rings.

Perfect timing.

It's Erin, the on-air talent at one of our broadcast partners, and I've been eager to hear from her. After researching other sports broadcasts, as well as the ways fans interact on social media, I proposed they add some new segments to their broadcast to increase engagement. Crossing my fingers, I pick up the call, hoping she's keen on my ideas. I chat with Erin for a bit about the game plan the next few nights, then she says, "And we liked your engagement ideas and want to start doing some fun facts about the players. The fans really love that, especially since fun facts are all the rage," she says, almost apologetically.

"Fun fact: I can tell you're wishing for the end of the fun fact era."

She laughs. "Is it that obvious?"

"Yes, but I'll keep your secret. Especially since fans love them, and I can make this happen."

I'm already thinking of the first few players to ask. Our team captain, Christian Winters, our outgoing center and all-around charmer, Chase Weston, our rising star right winger, Wesley Bryant, and our fan favorite left winger, Asher Callahan. Briefly I think of Max Lambert, and I roll my eyes. Fun fact: he'd rather eat nails than supply fun facts.

Erin and I chat some more about the project, then catch up on the latest sports news. We've been work friends since I started in the business—there weren't many of us women covering the team, so we bonded. But I check the time, then say goodbye since I've got a meeting with my boss in twenty minutes, and I'm never late. I made a vow three years ago, after my life shattered one evening, to never run late again.

I grab my tablet and leave my office to meet my boss

on the other side of the arena. It's only a five-minute walk but not only does this allow me to arrive early, it also gives me a chance to catch up with anyone I run into in the hallways, which is always a good thing as the team's PR person. You learn the most about the people you work with from these casual, unexpected moments.

It's part of what I need to be good at my job, and my goal is to be the best publicist possible. Work got me through one of the hardest things I ever had to deal with, and this job in particular helped me to finally emerge from the darkest days of grief.

It's funny in some ways, since being a publicist wasn't ever part of my life plan. When I went to college, I thought I was going to study environmental science, which didn't make a lot of sense because I'm not a science person. I liked the planet though, so it seemed like a good idea at the time—until I met college science classes.

I shudder at the memory of formulas and equations.

Briefly I toyed with English, but it turned out I didn't want to read a lot of outdated books written by dead white men. I didn't want to read modern essays either. But I did like trying to understand the world and how it worked, and I liked helping people. When I was twenty and drinking boba and eating French fries during spring break with my best friend Marie, she plunked down her milk tea and waved a fry airily, saying, "Why don't you study journalism? You like to make sense of how things work. And it's a helper's profession. You're helping the public understand the world too."

I hadn't seen it that way at first, but like with most things, she was right. Journalism was a perfect fit for me, and after I graduated I landed a coveted job with The Sports Network, then worked my way up to become the beat reporter there, covering the San Francisco Sea Dogs hockey team.

At first I loved it, but a few years ago I became disillusioned with the sports reporting world. It's cutthroat and relentless, and it started to feel like a race to the bottom. Trying to devise new ways to say "slapshot" or "shutout" was stressful, and I didn't need that kind of stress in my life then. It was a fight to be more creative than the competition even as readers and listeners increasingly tuned you out.

Mostly, though, I wasn't sure I was helping anyone.

When Zaire Mandavi, the VP of Communications for the Sea Dogs, pulled me aside after a hockey game one night and said, "I like your style. You're not afraid of anything and you hold your own in a male-dominated field. Would you like to interview for a post?" I agreed faster than a puck flying down the ice.

And when they offered me the gig, I leapt. I had a feeling that Marie would have told me to go for it, even though I couldn't ask her anymore. But her mantra was "if you can say yes, say it."

I'm now more than a year into the job, and I've learned I'm damn good at being a publicist. For a lot of reasons, but first and foremost—I like helping people. It's in my DNA, and while the job is stressful, it's also joyful. Sports bring out a lot of emotions in people, and when fans love a team, it's such a thrill to help bring the team and the players even closer to the community. Makes me feel like I'm bringing a little joy into people's lives as well. We could all use a little more joy in our lives—that's definitely good for the planet.

I head down the corridor to debrief my boss on the latest press requests, as well as my plans for an upcoming slate of charitable events, which I'm sure Max will try to wriggle out of.

As I walk toward the executive suites, I cut to the hallway that'll take me past the locker room when I spot our yoga instructor up ahead, her lavender yoga pants like a calling card. "Hey, Briar," I call out.

She stops and turns around, a smile coasting across her face. "Hey, Everly. You ready to join us for class today? No heels though."

I snort-laugh as I glance at my Louboutins. They definitely make me feel pretty and powerful, and the latter helps especially on days when I meet with my boss. "Doing yoga with thirty rowdy hockey players sounds like a whole new level in the world's hardest video game," I say.

"It is. But I keep them in line."

"You sure do," I say, then remember a debate I heard on the flight home. "Also, isn't yoga supposed to be non-competitive? Wesley and Asher were arguing on the team plane about whose half-moon pose was better. What's the deal with that?"

She smiles, shaking her head. "Next thing you know, they'll try to have a contest in class."

"And they'll place bets. But what even is a half-moon pose?"

With zero hesitation, she shifts into a wide-leg stance, turns her torso to the right then drops her right hand to the floor. Once her palm hits the concrete, she lifts her back leg up, flexing her foot and tilting her hip toward the ceiling. It's daunting and gorgeous at the same time. "You look like a beautiful half-windmill," I say, and I also can't decide whether to applaud or check if she has any bones left after contorting herself like that.

"Thanks. It's all about having fun," she continues when she pops out of the pose as seamlessly as she moved into it. "If you ever want a one-on-one session, I'd be happy to teach you. I bet you can do it," she says, and my brain latches onto those positive words—*I bet you can.*

That's what Marie said, too, when I told her I'd never be able to pole dance. Fun fact: I was wrong. Though, the un-fun fact is this—there are things in pole I can't do. Or really, things I don't do.

A memory of the night that changed my life three years ago grips me tight for a few seconds—the sounds, the sirens, the pain—but I do my best to shake it off and stay in the present. I continue down the hall as the guys start streaming out of the locker room, presumably to Briar's afternoon class.

Wesley and Asher are the first to enter the hallway and Wesley tips his chin toward me in greeting. He's involved with our team captain's sister, Josie, who's become a good friend of mine, so Wesley and I are sort of friends now too. "How's it going, Everly? Anyone new you need to keep out of trouble? Besides Asher."

I go on high alert as I shift my focus to our left winger by his side. Asher is one of the golden guys. He never causes problems. "Asher, what could you have possibly done?" I ask with some alarm.

But he simply flashes me one of his trademark nice guy grins, then says, "I was arguing with some fans online today."

Worry slides down my spine, though I try to shove it aside and focus on fixing the problem. It's triage time. "What did you say? Where did you say it? And who was there?"

Once I know that, I can devise a solution.

"Ev," Asher says reassuringly. "You don't need to worry. I do this all the time."

And that does not help whatsoever. The hair on my arms stands on end. "That doesn't make it better, Asher."

"It was from my burner account, and I was only arguing about baseball. No one knows it's me," Asher explains.

Oh thank god. I breathe a sigh of relief, but it doesn't last long. I stare sharply at him, waggling a finger. "But why? Why is that necessary, Asher?"

This guy signs autographs after every game. He rolls down his window when he leaves the players' lot sometimes to snap selfies with fans. Why would he be arguing about baseball, even from a burner account?

Asher's clever green eyes spark, like a flame's been lit in them. "Because the trades some of the teams are making in the off-season are insane. Did you know that the Cougars let go of one of their big bats, and now the New York Comets think they're going to land Julio Martinez, and it's ridiculous. We needed Martinez and his RBIs. I swear I should have been a baseball general manager because I could do this better in my sleep."

"And I ask again," I say, kind but firm, "why are you arguing with fans online?"

"They don't know it's me," he says with a casual shrug.

"Yet, Asher. They don't know it's you *yet*."

Wesley clears his throat. "Asher likes to get in fights online because if he does it in person, Max always points out where Asher might be wrong. But with the Internet trolls, Asher can just fire off scathing insults about the other teams, so it's a more satisfying argument for him."

Asher shoots Wesley a look like his teammate has

wounded his heart, when it's more like Wesley wounded his pride. "Dude. You don't like my arguments?"

"Dude, I tune them out," Wesley says.

"So, you can see why I need to argue online. It's an outlet." Then Asher looks around, spinning in a full circle. "Speaking of Max, where is our resident Eeyore?"

Wesley shrugs as he scans the hallway. "Good question. Max usually tries to make it to yoga class."

It is odd that he's not around, but Max tends to follow the rules less than guys like Wesley and Asher, who show up for every morning skate and every yoga class.

"Goalies. What can you do?" I ask with a shrug as Hugo and Miles emerge from the weight room.

Hugo's our teddy bear of a defender, a burly guy with a happy grin. He must have heard most of the conversation, since he says like an announcer, "And today, playing the role of Max Lambert is Hugo." Then, he clears his throat, narrows his eyes, and adopts a dry tone, sounding uncannily like Max as he grumbles, "Dude, it doesn't matter who the Cougars traded for. They're gonna suck next year anyway."

The guys all crack up, and I fight off a laugh since I can't be seen laughing at a player's expense. I clear away any remaining amusement in my tone, then look again to the winger with the golden-streaked light brown hair. "Why don't you just argue in person with Max then?" I ask Asher.

Miles strides over to Asher and claps him on the shoulder, taking the question. "Because Asher's trying to keep up his points streak in his baseball Reddit group."

Oh for Pete's sake. I've heard enough. I press my palms together, imploring Asher. "Asher, my sweet Asher who makes my life easy, I promise if you keep this up it will bite you in the butt. Please stop. Someone will find out it's you."

Asher sighs, frowning. "Do I have to?"

I can tell this is hard for him. It's a hobby he clearly enjoys, so I try harder. "I'll find you a support group if I have to for former online arguers. I'll help you find some employees here in athletic training or equipment who like to debate baseball trades, but no more burner accounts, okay?"

Another frown. "If you say so," he says with the world's most forlorn sigh.

"I do. And I appreciate you so much. We could even include the fact you're a big baseball fan in the fun facts our broadcast partner will do about our players," I say, then quickly explain what we're doing with that initiative.

Asher's trademark cocky smile returns. "Can mine be —fun fact: he'd be aces at managing a Major League Baseball team?"

Since I know he'll actually stop arguing now that I've asked him to, I nod, giving him that victory. "Yes."

"Mine is: can imitate all his teammates uncannily," Hugo puts in.

"And mine is: beats all his teammates easily in pool," Miles says.

Not to be outdone, Wesley reminds them he bests the boys in poker. I have a feeling they're going to stay on this alpha male competitive merry-go-round until it runs out of steam so I excuse myself and say goodbye.

As I head down the corridor to my boss's office, my phone buzzes with a text from my former physical therapist. Who I went out with once over the summer after I was no longer his patient. Interesting. I didn't know he was back in town. But I don't need a single distraction now, so I set my phone to *do not disturb.*

A few minutes later, I'm knocking on Zaire's office door when heels click against the concrete floor behind me. "Actually, we're meeting in the GM's office today."

I try not to flinch in surprise at the sound of her smooth, rich voice. Or worry. Because that's serious, if we're meeting Clementine Carmichael on her turf. I don't let the GM's sweet name fool me. She's the ice queen. If she says *you're not unpleasant,* that's a compliment.

But she's British so everything sounds lovely coming out of her mouth.

I turn around to face Zaire. Her parents named her after where they're from, and she looks like a woman who can pull off being named after a country. She's statuesque and strong, with elegant box braids. I put on my best roll-with-it face and head to the general manager's office with her. Along the way, she lowers her voice. "I need to warn you—Clementine is going to want a yes."

Yes. There's that word again. But the context feels ominous. "For what?" I ask, trying to mask my worry.

"A project that should be perfect for you."

Why do I feel it won't be?

We enter Clementine's immaculate office. Her black lacquer desk is so shiny, she can touch up her makeup in its reflection, and she is dusting more blush onto her porcelain cheekbones as we enter.

She looks up and sets down the brush. "Good to see you, Everly. How are you doing these days?"

She asks that of everyone, but I've learned it's best to never truly answer with anything but "great." For all the talk about employee mental health these days, the mental health most companies want is theirs—that you're not going to sue them. And I'm not, so it's true enough when I say, "Great."

"And has Zaire informed you about the promotion you're up for?"

I do my best not to smile. Clementine might perceive it as a sign of weakness. "Yes, she has. I am excited about the possibility."

"Good. I'd love to have a healthy competition for the Director of PR job."

Not me. I just want the job, not to fight for it. It'd be a step up from manager, my current post—more pay, better benefits, a chance to grow…"I'm ready for it," I say, since my job is to spin things.

Zaire clears her throat and says, "As I was telling you, Clementine, Everly has increased our social media engagement by fifty-two percent in the last year, which has led to a thirty-nine percent increase in jersey sales coming from our social channels."

Clementine barely cracks a smile as she looks at me. "Which is why we have a wonderful opportunity that will help you show exactly what you can do for the team," she says in her cool British voice.

"I'm up for anything. I'm currently assembling fun facts from all the players," I say as if that proves my mettle.

Clementine shoots me a curious look but it's one that says *don't bother me with the details* when she waves her hand dismissively. "Then this shouldn't be a problem." She leans back in her white faux leather chair. "We have an opportunity for one of our players to be featured in *The Ice Men*."

I sit up straighter. "The Webflix documentary?" I squeak out, then quickly correct to, "The Webflix documentary. I love that show."

"Yes. Team bank accounts do too," she says.

The top-rated sports documentary premiered last year and airs about six episodes a season. Each hour-long episode follows one player around for several weeks with behind-the-scenes access to him. The ratings for the show are off the charts, and the subsequent viewership for teams' broadcasts have shot up when their players are featured. I've pitched Webflix a few times on featuring one of our players, but I've never heard back.

"That's exciting. Is it Christian? Chase? Asher?" I ask. "Those guys would be great choices with their charm and stats."

Clementine laughs, then shakes her head. "Darling. I wish it were that easy. It's Max Lambert. And we need you to whip him into shape before the shoot begins in January."

My face falls. I can't even fashion a cheery publicist face right now. "You do?" I gulp.

"He's like a diamond in the rough, isn't he?" Zaire says with a grin.

"More like a piece of coal," I mutter, and *oh, shit*. Am I getting myself fired for that?

But Clementine is laughing, for the first time ever. "He truly is, darling. And you'll have your work cut out for you to make him likable. But the thing is—we want this. Badly. He has the stats. He certainly has an interesting reputation. Webflix wants the league's best players for *The Ice Men*, and Lambert is indisputably one of the top goalies. I've heard what this kind of exposure has done for other teams. My friends in Calgary, Boston, and Miami have all been bragging about the revenue it brings in," she says, dollar signs flickering in her eyes, and lust in her voice. That's the magic word—revenue. This opportunity will bring attention and money to the team. "We need this to go smoothly. And you, my dear, are a wunderkind."

As much as I want to relish in the compliment, I'm fighting off a grimace. This is an impossible mission. I can't give Max Lambert an image makeover. Especially in less than three months. He hates everything. "I can't wait," I say, as if I mean it.

"Fantastic," Clementine says, then clicks on her computer, and hits the mouse. "There you go. All the details on *The Ice Men* episode should be in your email. I assume you're in."

It looks like I just became a makeup artist and manners coach in one afternoon.

And because I can fake it when I have to, I say brightly, "I'm in."

* * *

A few miserable hours later, I'm packing up to leave, bracing myself to text Max to schedule our first...is it a session? A lesson? A debrief? I don't even know. When I hit pause on the text, my gaze drifts down to the earlier message from Lucas. He worked with me when I was rehabbing after the car accident, then we reconnected over the summer and went on a date. But he was called out of town shortly after to work in a clinic in Los Angeles for a few months. We never hung out again.

Looks like he wants to now.

> Hey, Everly! I'm back in town and would love to take you out again. Let me know if there's a statute of limitations on a second date. I hope not.

We *did* have a nice time. He's kind and caring, like you'd hope someone in his profession would be. I wouldn't mind seeing him again. But my head's too full right now to respond. It's pinging with this new assignment and what it'll require, and thoughts of Max and what a pain in the ass he is. I'm a little frazzled, so rather than write to either guy, I compose a message to my friends instead, texting Josie, Maeve, and Fable. It took me a few years to even want to have friends again, but I love this group of women and need them now more than ever.

I ask if they can get together with me tonight. Then I grab my things and leave, working on a text to Max as I head down the corridor to my car.

But I stop short at the weight room. He's alone in there, on the leg-press machine, pushing an ungodly amount of weights with his thick thighs, bulging with muscles. The scowl of all scowls is etched on his too-handsome face. His blue eyes are ice. His cheekbones could cut glass.

Welcome to a new hell, Everly.

My stomach twists. I rap on the doorjamb, but I'm not sure he'll hear me, since he's wearing earbuds. But he's a goalie, so his peripheral vision is better than a hawk's. He must notice me out of the corner of his eye, and he looks mad as hell. He presses hard down on the weights one more time, then lets go of them. The loud clang they make rattles my heart.

Pushing up to sit, he pops out his earbuds. "Well, well, well, if it isn't my brand-new babysitter."

Fun fact: this is going to suck.

7

GOOD GUY BOOT CAMP

Everly

The thing about jerks is this—you can't kowtow to them. When they're sarcastic, it's best to disarm them. You do it by being honest, kind, and direct. I've read employee handbooks and guidelines about how to handle difficult people, be they reporters, colleagues, or fans. *Defuse* is the watchword.

Right now, I really should respond to the *if it isn't my brand-new babysitter* with something like "I don't plan to be your babysitter, but I do look forward to working more closely. Let's set a time to review strategies."

And yet the words that fly out of my mouth are dripping with pure sass and served with a syrupy smile as I fight fire with sarcastic fire. "Actually, I prefer *professional* babysitter, Lambert."

Grabbing a towel and wiping his hands then the back of his neck, he says dryly, "I prefer none of this."

"And I see we're in the no stage," I say like a preschool

teacher. Wow, does he bring out my worst behavior too? I think he does. But since I'm on a roll, I stroll into the weight room and add, "Alternatively, you could call me your makeup artist," I say then dust my fingertips against my cheekbones like a fabulous YouTube makeup influencer. I even add a pout for effect. "Would that be more amenable?"

After he sets down the towel on the weight bench, he grumbles, "I don't wear makeup."

And I don't back down. I step closer. "Then think of me as your brand-new...*attitude coach*," I say with the most over-the-top smile. Two can play this game after all.

Slowly, he rises from the weight bench, stretches his neck from side to side, then takes his sweet time staring me down. His height is intimidating. That steely gaze is penetrating, unwavering. My pulse stutters from the way he stares, and I hold my breath. No wonder other teams are afraid of him. He arches a dubious brow as he eyes me up and down, then says with a smirk, "Coach? More like drill instructor."

I breathe a small sigh of relief. At least he's no longer saying no. "That's me," I say.

"I can't believe I have a fucking drill instructor," he says, as he drags a hand over his beard, a distracting move because his hand is so big, and his beard is so beardy, and my mind is so traitorous wondering how that scruff would feel against me.

Shake that all the way the fuck off, girl.

I fasten on a smile to counteract my dirty thoughts. "Then I suppose we should discuss when boot camp begins? Bright and early tomorrow at 0600?" I ask even though I know he won't actually show up then, nor do I want him to. I need to devise a battle plan first.

"This is boot camp all right."

"And I trust you'll be a good soldier at Good Guy Boot Camp?" My smile widens, selling this most fabulous boot camp. *Right. Sure.* But a girl can try.

He doesn't answer right away. Just picks up his towel, tosses it on top of his gym bag by the weight bench, then looks back at me, expression stony. I could snap a pic of him and slap the caption: *The Max Lambert Glower* across it right now. "Rosewood, you do know the last thing I want is a makeover, right?"

My smile promptly vanishes, and I heave a frustrated sigh. He makes it so hard to be sunshine sometimes. "Yes, Max, I picked up on that from context clues," I say dryly, even though I know—I absolutely know—that's the wrong approach with him. Like a GPS rerouting in a new direction, I try again, opting for straightforward and honest. "Listen, I get that this image revamp is the last thing you want. I understand it's a personal affront to the —" I stop and wave an arm in front of him, dangerously close to the strong pecs that stretch his T-shirt quite nicely. Too nicely. I focus on finishing the thought. "...the whole fuck-off-world mystique you have going on. But the reality is—"

He comes closer, his mouth amused. "Mystique? You think I have a mystique?" It's asked with avid curiosity.

I should be nice. I should be nice. *I really should be nice.* "It wasn't entirely a compliment," I say.

His grin turns smug. "You sure about that?"

"Umm, yes, why?"

"Mystique does mean a fascinating aura of mystery, awe, and power surrounding someone or something."

Fuck him. "Are you doubling as a dictionary?"

"No. I looked it up the other night when I came across

it in this online class I'm taking. And you did say mystique, ergo, that sounds like a compliment."

There's entirely too much to unpack in that statement —Max takes online classes?—but now's not the time to delve into his hobbies so I bookmark that in my head. "Yes, I know what the word means." *Deep breath. You can do this. Don't let him get to you.* If I'm going to have to give him charm lessons, I might as well lead by being charming myself. "Max, let's give you a whole new mystique then." I wave a hand toward him like a magician sprinkling, I don't know, now-you-see-it-now-you-don't dust. "The mystique of marketability."

He pauses for a second, his eyes hard, but then he sighs as he slumps down to the bench once again. He drags a hand through his wild, messy hair. It's not quite shoulder-length—it's more unkempt-length, and it works for him. It's dark, a little long, a lot messy, like you've just run your fingers through it. "Yeah, I guess we have to. And I thought hell was line drills in full pads after a loss."

I shudder. That does sound awful, and I feel a pang of sympathy for him. This really must be hard for the man. "Does Coach McBride make you do that still?" I ask.

"No way. That was youth hockey. But the memory still stings."

Be charming. Be sweet. Be upbeat. "I promise this will be better than line drills. Just imagine you're the Beast when he has his claws filed and hair styled."

He narrows his eyes and snarls like a beast when he says, "No bows. I will not wear a bow in my hair."

And I'm finding my rhythm since I say playfully, "Someone knows his *Beauty and the Beast*."

"Yes, I do, sunshine."

I pause on that word. He's called me that a few times,

when we've been out with a group of friends, which happens not by choice but by default because of our friends in common. But maybe it's a good sign. It's not the worst nickname. "Good then. You'll know what to expect. Just think of this good-guy boot camp as a movie makeover," I say, then stop and consider that, holding up a finger. "But not one of the sexist ones."

"The sexist ones? Which ones are those?"

I screw up the corner of my lips, thinking. "Actually, most movie makeovers are because they show the woman being transformed from having braces and baggy clothes to a brand-new hairstyle and tight top—no glasses, naturally—so she looks sufficiently hot for the male gaze. To which I say fuck off."

That earns me the very first hint of a smile. "They can fuck off then too," he says, then strokes his beard. "But don't get any ideas about new hairstyles. The beard stays." Then he shakes his messy mane. "Same for the hair."

"Aww, I guess I am a makeup artist."

He crosses his arms and stares me down.

I roll my eyes. "Fine, the hair and beard stay. But the bad attitude? It goes." I hook my thumb toward the door.

He gives a small nod, then looks away. When he glances back at me, there's a hint of some new emotion in those ice blue eyes. A flicker of sadness? Of hurt? I'm not sure. And I honestly don't know what got him here besides a very bad breakup that he handled badly. But be that as it may, no one likes to be told they aren't good enough. I certainly didn't like it when my dad said that to me as a kid, so I try to both give Max the benefit of the doubt and also offer him a ray of hope. "Max, I know you don't want this, but I'm going to do my best to make this work for both of us. I'll devise a plan and then text you about a time to meet. You have my word that I'll give this everything I have." I meet his gaze, hoping he believes my sincerity, especially when I add, "Trust me."

He scoffs. "That's not my style, sunshine."

I bite down a slew of comebacks, pasting on a smile I don't feel as I head to the door.

Then I leave, knowing it'll take more than movie magic to transform this beast.

8

TELL ME YOUR FORTUNE

Everly

"*Pretty Woman*. Hands down the best movie makeover out there."

That's Josie's declaration that night as we dine on the salted caramel flight at Elodie's Chocolates, since what's a get-together with friends without chocolate? I'm here at the artisanal shop in the heart of Hayes Valley with Josie, Maeve, and Fable, who have become—it's still strange to say—my new crew. And we're debating the best movie makeovers of all time post Max run-in.

"And why's that retro flick the best?" Maeve asks as she absently shuffles her deck of tarot cards. She's been learning tarot and wants to practice on us soon, she's said. Which I've learned is very, *very* Maeve.

I jump on her question. "Because the Julia Roberts character isn't doing it to be hotter for the guy but rather to fit into his world. He's already attracted to her, after all. And the best part is she gets revenge in the end when she goes back to the snooty store with the clerk who put her down," I explain, then pop a salted caramel into my mouth.

Maeve seems to give that some thought as she shuffles once again. "I do love a revenge tale. But hey...what about dude movie makeovers? Are there even any?"

Fable flicks a strand of auburn hair off her cheek as she chimes in, "Of course. Hollywood loves its men. But, with the exception of *Can't Buy Me Love*, where he pays her to date him and she gives him a zero-to-hero makeover that comes rudely crashing down on him, those flicks are almost always about the man transforming into a badass superhero, the world's best spy, or the universe's greatest hitman. Or he goes from nerd to a super jock. Or realizes he has some awesome new power, like he can fly. Seriously." She shakes her head, clearly annoyed with Hollywood. "It's never—*oh, I'm suddenly pretty without my glasses*," she adds in a faux feminine voice.

Josie pointedly removes her glasses, setting a hand under her pale chin. "Look at me, friends. Am I not super hot now?" She offers up an over-the-top smile, batting her lashes.

I laugh, and it feels good to laugh with friends again. I missed this so much for the first couple years after Marie died, when I mostly kept to myself. When friendship was simply too painful to try. Like swimming after a boating accident, I couldn't go near the water for a long time. Friendship was its own form of PTSD for a while there. "You are the hottest, Josie," I tell my librarian friend. "You're now a gorgeous duckling."

She blows a kiss my way, but her expression turns serious as she slides her glasses back on. "Why can't we have a movie makeover where the heroine's fairy godmother transforms the heroine into a badass assas-sin?" She points at me. "You're kind of like an image assas-sin, aren't you? You're going to rid the world of his rough edges as you shine him up."

I didn't tell them the details of what I'd be up to with Max Lambert, but since the grumpy goalie and I will likely be doing more public events soon, it won't be a state secret that he's getting a makeover, so I've told them the basic plan—*put him out there more.* "Just call me Everly Rosewood, Bad Image Assassin and Head Drill Instructor at Good Guy Boot Camp." I wince, though, as the words make landfall. "That's a mouthful."

"That's what she said," Maeve mutters under her breath, then looks up from beneath a swoop of light brown hair streaked with blonde. The smile coasting across her fair skin is downright devilish.

Fable stares at Maeve, unblinking. "You couldn't resist that, could you?"

"As if you could either," Maeve retorts.

"Of course I could not," Fable says.

"Then you get me," Maeve says.

"We all get you," Josie puts in, then reaches for the final piece of chocolate on the tray, asking with her eyes if she can take it. We nod *go for it* then she plucks it, her nails painted with decals of the titular character from *Fleabag* on them, and the hot priest she bangs, which is giving me all sorts of forbidden thoughts I should not be having about men in hockey uniforms—not men of the cloth.

After Josie chews, she looks my way pointedly. "So, have you thought about how you're going to handle all the sexual tension between you and Number Thirty-Three?"

Did Josie read my mind? "What?" I ask, like I don't know what she means when I damn well do.

Maeve bursts into peals of laughter, then when she recovers, she says to me, "That was good. Did you practice that?"

"Practice what?" I ask, this time legitimately meaning the question.

Fable smirks, jumping in with, "That whole *oh so shocked* look you had right there."

"I do not have sexual tension with Max Lambert," I say, denying that hard. I have to deny it.

Maeve lifts a doubtful brow. "Louder for those in the back."

I stare her down, like I did Asher earlier today. "I don't."

Or really, I *can't*.

Getting involved with him in any way, shape, or form would be a bad idea. It's frowned upon at work—athletes are our stars, they are our assets, and their talent pays *all* our bills. So it's best not to tango with the talent. It's one of the unwritten rules of working for a pro sports team, and something my boss even warned me about when I first started. Zaire gave me a tour of the facility I already knew well, then introduced me to all the players. When a couple were a bit flirty, she pulled me aside after and said, "With athletes, it's best to keep things strictly professional."

Tonight, with my friends, I repeat those two watchwords. "It's strictly professional with him," I say, and it is, but I also don't like lying to these women I've grown to care for. "And even though it is," I say, relenting, "he's maybe, possibly, admittedly handsome."

Fable lifts her arms in victory. "Ladies and ladies, let

the record reflect that Everly finds the man of the hour *admittedly handsome*."

"Oh, c'mon. I at least admitted you were right. Was *admittedly handsome* not enough for you?" I ask.

Josie taps her chin. "I'll allow *admittedly handsome* because it's so you."

"And how is that so me?"

Josie wastes no time answering with, "Because it's professional and a little detached."

My face falls. My heart sinks. "You think I'm—"

She reaches for my hand, warmth flooding her eyes. "Oh, babe. I didn't mean you're detached."

I swallow past a stone of emotion—an annoying one. "Okay."

"I meant it as a compliment," Josie adds, squeezing my fingers. "Because it's very you to detach from someone you work with when the rest of us are being pigs."

Josie comes over to my side of the table, and gives me a hug, and I feel foolish all over again that I thought she might have meant something else. It's just so hard to learn to, well, love again in this platonic way.

When we break the hug, Maeve waggles a tarot card at me—on it is an illustration of a hand curled around a wooden wand. It's incredibly phallic. "I drew the Ace of Wands for you, Ev. You know what that means?"

With some dread, I ask, "What does it mean?"

"It means someone is going to be getting some good dick," she says, then winks.

Playfully, I snatch her deck away. "I'll tell my own fortune." I straighten my shoulders, clear my throat, and say, "It means someone is going to be getting some good... *news* at work in the form of a promotion, since she will *not* be entering a forbidden romance and sleeping with the player she's helping."

Maeve sighs. "I like my fortune of you better."

Yeah, I did too. But I'm not going to do a thing about it. I have a boot camp battle plan to devise, and a potential date to dissect.

"Speaking of dick." I whip out my phone. "Help a girl out." I show them the text from Lucas, letting me know he's back and asking me out again. "Do I want to go out with him again? He was my rehab therapist after the accident."

"Is he hot?" Maeve asks immediately.

"Is he nice?" Fable inquires.

"Is he funny?" Josie wants to know.

"Did you feel the zing on the first date?" Maeve asks, diving right into a second round of questions.

"Did he ask you questions or was he a conversational hog?" Fable asks.

Josie waggles her brows. "Was he good in bed?"

I can't even catch my breath to laugh, but I try. Oh hell, do I try. Then, one by one I tackle the friendly interrogation. "Yes, yes, I don't really know. A hint of a zing? He was good at sharing the convo. And no! I didn't sleep with him."

Josie shakes her head, tsking me. "Shame. Because then we could really decide if he was worth a second round. Um, I mean date. Of course I mean date."

I roll my eyes. "Sorry to disappoint, but I did not see his dick."

"No worries. That's what second dates are for," Maeve says, but then she leans closer. "Seriously, go out with him again. Whether you have sex with him or not isn't the point. It sounds like he's passed the most basic tests. Now you want to know if you have chemistry."

"Gotta have chemistry," Fable adds.

"It's magic," Josie says, and her eyes are a little fluttery. Pretty sure she and Wesley are magic together in all the ways.

I mull that over for a few seconds. "You're right. It's worth seeing what's out there. And if there's anything more to explore with us," I say, then tap out a yes to Lucas. He's not a bad boy or a troublemaker. Sometimes a girl just needs a good guy, especially if she has a history of being attracted to the wrong ones.

Plus, I don't have to tell Lucas about the scars all over my back, my hip, and my shoulder, like I did with the last guy I dated. A guy who said nothing when he saw them, but his eyes—wide, shocked, taken aback—said everything.

I don't have to explain my body to Lucas. He already knows I have scars.

9

THE BOY WHO PULLS ON PIGTAILS

Max

It's a dilemma all right—do I go for a pineapple and coconut smoothie with honey or the banana one with peanut butter? I've always been a peanut butter lover, but then again, honey is really fucking good. But maybe I should skip a smoothie today. Wouldn't that be the wiser choice for the wallet?

Behind the counter, a college student with sleek black hair and a smiley face apron covering her university sweatshirt patiently waits for me to give her the final order from our group. We've just finished morning skate, and I stare at the chalkboard menu for The Oasis a little longer, like the decision's going to materialize before my eyes.

Wesley's busy on his phone, but Asher's in no mood for my antics since he cuts in, scanning her name tag, then saying, "Yuki, he'll have the banana and peanut butter one, with added honey."

I turn to Asher, annoyed and grateful all at once. "Am I

keeping you from an important appointment with...your hairstylist? Massage therapist? Nail tech?"

Asher scoffs. "Please. I'm naturally beautiful. Also, you're keeping me from something—namely, my bed and a nap."

"There's plenty of time before the clock strikes one, sleeping beauty," I say, but facts are facts. Wesley and Asher ordered right away, and I took my time, hemming and hawing, like I usually do. Some days I still can't believe I'm spending thirteen dollars on a fucking drink. My middle-school self who never went out for a meal and scrounged together every spare dollar for new skates would have freaked.

I turn to the server once more. "What he said. And, um, thanks for your patience."

"No problem." Yuki inputs my order, then she's hesitant, maybe even nervous, for a beat as I take out my phone and open the wallet on it. She chews on her lower lip, then says, "And...I really hope you win tonight. I love the Sea Dogs so much. And I've been meaning to tell you that every time you come here, but I didn't have the guts because everyone said you were unapp—" She stops, shakes her head, before she corrects to, "Because everyone said it's not cool to fangirl, but I had to say it. Hockey is the best."

"Yes, it is," I say, and because I heard what she didn't say—everyone says I'm *unapproachable*. And I hear, too, what Rosario and my agent said yesterday. That I don't interact with fans, so I add, "And we'll do our best to win tonight."

"How long have you been a fan?" Asher asks, setting his elbow on the counter in the we've-been-pals-forever kind of way that he has about him. "And more importantly, how long have you thought I was better than Bryant?"

Looking up from his phone, Wesley thumps Asher on the head. Yuki laughs, then says to Asher, "I don't know... Wesley had a pretty big goal the other night."

Asher's mouth falls open, as if he's aghast. "Blasphemy."

"Yep, and don't you forget my blasphemy, Callahan," Wesley says, then as he tucks his phone into his jeans pocket, he turns to Yuki as she begins making the drinks. "Really appreciate you rooting for our team instead of the Golden State Foxes."

That's the other hockey team in the city and one of our fiercest rivals. Though I hate the Los Angeles Supernovas more. Especially their starting forward, Fletcher Bane, who'd serve Earth better if he were shot in a spaceship to Mars and left to rot there forever.

But I do my best to never think about my biggest enemy except when we're playing those cheating fuckheads.

"Never the Foxes," Yuki says. "Sea Dogs always."

"That's what I like to hear," Wesley says.

"You chose well, Yuki," Asher adds as she works on the drinks.

They chat with her more as I busy myself with finishing the transaction. I double the amount of the smoothies I bought for myself and my friends and set that as the tip. That's not new. I always do that—tip well. Because I can, and because I was that kid behind the counter once upon a time, working at a quick-serve restaurant, taking orders and hoping for decent tips.

Normally, if someone recognizes me, and that happens from time to time, I say something nice and move on, stat. I figure shit can get awkward real fast, so a simple thanks is all that's needed. But Wesley and Asher? These guys brought her into the convo for a while. Had a real chat with her.

Do I need to do more of that to help my likeability quotient? I hate fake conversations. They didn't seem fake though...But I don't know that me being more outgoing with the college student who makes our post-morning-skate smoothies is enough to change my...likeability quotient.

That stupid term makes me want to kick a garbage can. Instead, I grab my drink roughly when it's done, grunting out a thanks as Asher picks up the pineapple drink while Wes grabs his kale shake. The dude loves his greens. As we head to our regular table in the back of the shop, Asher says, "Did you guys catch up on the end of *Twisted Nights*?"

That's the domestic thriller on Webflix we're all addicted to. "That was wild," Wesley says, sliding into the booth. "I can't believe they crossed the border."

"Don't cross the border," Asher booms in a deep warning tone, reciting the tagline for the show. I could jump in, but I'm a little lost in thoughts of what's next, like what exactly it means to turn my reputation around and how painful that'll be, especially with Everly breathing down my neck. But if even the server here knows my rep, it'll be harder than unsticking a container ship from the Suez Canal.

As I take a thirsty sip, Asher tips his drink my way, catching my attention. "What's up with you, Lambert? You usually mock Wesley for his theories on the next season."

"And yet, all my theories came true," Wesley points out.

Didn't even realize they were debating what might happen in the future. Looking up, I blink off the haze of my own thoughts. "Have you ever heard of a likeability quotient?" It's asked with some derision.

Asher's brow furrows. "No, but I can figure it out."

Wesley shakes his head. "Sounds like marketing mumbo jumbo."

I'm not always the most forthcoming guy, but I trust my friends, and hell, they already know my rep—Asher's the guy you bring home to mom, Wesley's the guy who helps anyone out of a jam, and I'm the guy you'd send to the door to scare off strangers on your porch. "Evidently" —I stop to sketch air quotes—"my *likeability quotient* is in the toilet."

I roll my eyes because I can't not.

"Explain," Asher says as he swirls his compostable straw—he picked this spot as our regular stomping grounds since everything's compostable here.

I take a satisfying suck of peanut butter and banana, then lean back in the booth and 'fess the fuck up. "I lost my last sponsor yesterday," I say, and hell, that's more embarrassing to admit than I'd thought it'd be. They know that's been happening to me ever since *the fight* against Los Angeles, but it still makes me feel like a fool to talk about the ramifications out loud. "And my agency's marketing department told me to shape up. Basically, they put me on notice to make some changes, or else."

"Ouch," Asher says with obvious sympathy.

"Shit, man. That sucks," Wesley says.

Trash talk is our first language, but they must sense my situation has reached code-red levels. I seriously appreciate them not giving me a hard time.

"And yes, I know it's my fault because I don't talk to the

press, but man, that convo still kind of made me feel like shit," I admit honestly.

"You gotta do your own thing. Make your own choices, Lambert. That's what I learned last season," Wesley says.

I mull on that for a few seconds. I suppose Wesley's proof, though, that talking openly can be a good thing. Last season, he spoke up in a big way about his life. That kind of honesty and vulnerability made a huge difference to the team and the community and to his personal life— it's the reason his girlfriend is happily back in town, shacked up with him.

"You did, man," I say, offering a fist for knocking. He knocks back. "You showed the fuck up in all the ways." I heave a sigh, and it's not so much one of resignation but maybe...acceptance that I've got to make some changes. "I guess I have to do a better job of that. When my agent called me into his conference room and showed me a fucking whiteboard with the likeability quotient, it was a rude awakening. But then again, it was a pretty rude awakening a year and a half ago when I walked into the home I shared with Lyra and saw Fletcher Bane from the Supernovas balls deep in her, so..."

Asher shoots me a sympathetic frown. "That's enough to make anyone shut down."

But that was only the start of it. That wasn't *why* I stopped talking to the press. It wasn't why I killed my social media either. What happened a week or so later at my sister's house was—after the fight on the ice with Bane. After the media wouldn't leave me alone. After they hassled my sister.

"But apparently my attitude isn't sitting well with team management, and I need to figure out how to be nicer...or else."

"Just let 'em know you treat us to smoothies—that's nice," Asher says.

"You could treat the whole city," Wes puts in, and I smile, appreciating their effort to fix this.

I roll on, building up a head of steam. "But it's not like I'm going to grab a mic or fire up social media I don't have and say, *well, folks here's why I think the world is a shit show,* and *here's why that song isn't about me.* I'm not going to air my dirty laundry. It won't change anything and the media will demolish her," I say, getting fired up. I can't stand my cheating ex, and I despise Bane, but I detest the press even more. They twist everything and they'd contort the truth in ways I couldn't even imagine.

I guess this reputation makeover is the only way through. I rake a hand through my messy hair, resigned to whatever's next, including the details Garrett shared with me, the part where the team has an opportunity for me to participate in *The Ice Men* documentary series. "And all of this means I'll be hanging with our cheery, chipper, smiling publicist more. Yay me," I say dryly.

Asher snort-laughs, not even trying to hide his amusement. "Good luck with that."

"Yeah, the whole thing is going to be hard, but especially because we're like a bottle of tequila and good choices. We don't work well together."

Wesley clears his throat. "I think Asher means *good luck with working closely with the woman you're hot for.*"

"Yeah, I'm sure you're going to hate it," Asher adds.

I narrow my eyes. "I never *said* I was into her."

Said being the operative word. I'm not denying I think about her at night. I'm not pretending she isn't starring in some seriously dirty dreams. I've just never voiced it to these punks.

Besides, there'd be no point in liking her, especially now. I can't mess up this image makeover. It's too important for my goals. For a life beyond hockey. For the future my parents and sister deserve. Everly's the key to making this happen, so it doesn't matter how sexy she is, how much I want to unbutton those staid work blouses she wears and discover the woman underneath—the one with the alluring lingerie. I'm dying to discover the other side of dangerously sexy Everly, with her pouty mouth and big brown eyes and that sleek ponytail that drives me crazy. The fact that she can't stand me inexplicably turns me on more, which says something about me I'm not sure I'm ready to face. She's a challenge, all right, and what's even more messed up about this lust I feel for her? I can't stand her either, yet she still haunts my mind late at night.

My brain is an asshole.

And I'm going to have to ignore its taunts.

Asher stares at me like he's a lawyer busting me in court, pulling my focus back to the conversation and away from filthy thoughts. "You didn't have to say you were into her," Asher says. "It's clear, man. You're the boy who pulls on her pigtails in class."

And yeah, I'd like to tug on that sleek blonde ponytail more than I should want to, so I do what I'm good at—I shut the hell up, effectively ending the talk about Everly. I drink my smoothie, then head home.

As I swing the door open, I call out, "Honey, I'm home."

But I can't find Athena anywhere in my penthouse. Where is that she-devil? I hunt all over, checking the laundry basket, the cupboards, the pantry, the guest room, my bedroom with its sweet view of the Golden Gate Bridge, until finally I look up in the kitchen.

She's curled up asleep on an exposed beam cutting across the kitchen ceiling.

"How the hell did you get up there?" I ask, scanning the room for the cat path. She must have jumped on the stove hood, then the top of the cabinets, then the beam. Cat parkour.

Grabbing a step stool, I position it under the beam, then climb up and snag the little critter. She unleashes a wild yowl as I pick her up.

"I don't like being woken up either, girl," I say softly, then carry her in my arms down the steps till I can set her on the floor, where she immediately administers bathing protocol to wash the touch of human off her perfect catness.

I head to bed for a nap, smacking the pillow a few times to get it just right before I settle in. Normally, I crash right away on game days. But Asher's remarks gnaw at me. Sure, Everly's beautiful. Yes, she's smart. But we don't get along. Hell, she looked like she wanted to hurl liquor bottles from the hotel room mini bar at me the night I returned her bralette and suitcase to her room. Probably wanted to chuck my cologne bottle at my head too. Admittedly, I'd have deserved her hellfire and fury. Still, she drives me up the wall day in and day out, always asking me to do this kind of feature, or that kind of feature, this cute piece, that little piece—devising her clever ways to try to get me to break. One time, she dangled concert tickets for me if I'd share with a streaming service ten songs I listen to when I work out. I told her to ask Bryant instead. She did and he gave them his entire playlist. Another time, she even said if I talked to the media after a late game, she'd hire a limo to take my teammates and me to play pool afterward. I told her I'd require a yacht.

I was a little surprised there wasn't a yacht waiting for me after the game. The woman doesn't back down. She's as relentless as I am stubborn, and I'm sure it pisses her off that I don't play her game. But it bugs me that she thinks she can wear me down and get me to talk to the media about anything. I don't trust them, and I'm not even sure I trust her. Before she worked for the team, she was one of them. No, she didn't show up at my sister's house late that night, demanding answers and harassing her, but she stuck her damn phone in my face after games, asking questions.

Then, she switched sides, and came to work for the team.

But, as much as I hate to admit it, she did help me out of a jam the other night in Seattle when Lyra landed in town. Things might have been so much worse if not for Everly's clever smuggling of me out the back door at the arena.

I smack the pillow again. Flip to my side. Try to crash.

But something else gnaws at me now—the fact that she helped me out in a big way. I should at least say thank you for what she did. Sighing heavily, I grab my phone, and google a bakery near the arena. Then I send her a slice of cake. Chocolate, since that's the most sinful. I ask the bakery to add a card and the words—*I hear cake goes well with working on upcoming publicity plans.*

Like she said to me.

With that done, I close my eyes and drift off in no time.

When I wake up an hour later, Athena's curled around my neck, purring up a storm, and I don't want to get out of bed.

But I do it anyway. I have a game to win.

10

THE SUMMER GARDEN DINNER TRICK

Max

Phoenix is aggressive from the second the puck drops. They're working me hard, taking shot after potent shot on goal. I can't get a break. Our defenders aren't getting their sticks on the rebounds enough, and every time one of our forwards snags the puck, Phoenix strips them of it.

I'm lunging for the bullets flying my way. Slapping most down, but not enough.

By the end of the second period, Phoenix is up by two, and it's been the workout to end all workouts. My muscles are screaming and my eyes are exhausted from watching every nanosecond of the game. As I skate off the ice, I grab my water bottle, down some, then glance at the stands. That's something I rarely do, but tonight my sister, Sophie, is here with Kade and they're sitting center ice. I tip my chin toward them and Kade waves wildly to me, then I disappear.

That kid is pretty much the cutest thing I've ever seen

—well, Athena *is* cuter, but cats aside, my nephew is—and I'd like to win for him.

In the locker room, I do my best to refocus as Coach prowls the room. "They don't get to come into our house and clean up like that. We need to be getting in their faces. Taking shot after shot on their net. I want you to get back out there, be aggressive, take control of the game, and don't let them get all the damn shots. Get creative. Get a power play. And get some points, men." He breaks down the game, then highlights the opportunities we're blowing, talks up the plays we should be taking, then pauses, scanning the room. Noah McBride looks like a CEO in his suit. He's tall, sturdy, a former player, and now, a methodical, coolly strategic coach. His inspo speeches aren't long. They don't need to be, because he commands the room with his mind. "You've got this, team."

When the intermission's up, we hit the ice again with renewed focus. Aggression even. And it works.

Bryant attacks the puck fast and hard, sending it screaming into the net at the start of the third period. Ten minutes later, Falcon goes on a tear, flying down the ice, then flipping the puck to Callahan who sends it screaming past their goalie's legs.

Yes, fucking yes! I'm cheering from the other end of the ice. We're tied now. All we need is another goal, and for me to shut them down.

Trouble is, Phoenix slips one past me, and that's all she wrote.

I'm pissed when I leave the ice, but one look at Kade, and I've got to let it go. He's clapping as I head to the tunnel, barely seeming to care about the final score.

Truth be told, I don't let the day in and day out eat away at me. Hockey is a long season, and I intend to have a long career. I don't beat myself up over the losses. I focus on the next game and doing better.

A little later, after I'm showered and dressed, I track down Sophie and Kade in the corridor, where I told them to wait for me, away from the media scrum. They're hanging out with Josie, Wesley's girlfriend. When he told me she was coming to the game tonight—which she often does—I asked if she could hang with my sister and nephew at the end. She said yes. It's not the first time she's done this.

She's showing Kade some of the trophies. No, wait. She's reading to him the words on the plaques inside the trophy case. Of course. She's a librarian, so everything's a reading opportunity. When she spots me, she waves, and I head over.

"Thanks, Josie."

"Anytime. And next time I'll bring my hockey little reader for you," she says to Kade.

His blue eyes pop. "Yes! Thank you, Jo-Jo-Jo," he says, trying to say her name.

"Jo-Jo-Jo works for me," she says, then takes off.

I scoop up Kade, who's all smiles—the life of an almost five-year-old.

"You *almost* won, Uncle Max," he says. "But I don't care because I got popcorn. They have my favorite popcorn here. Do you know what else they have?"

"What else?" I ask the cutie as I set him down in the corridor.

"Mushroom jerky! I thought it was going to be gross, but it's so good."

I laugh, turning to Sophie. "Mushroom jerky? They're serving mushroom jerky here now?"

My sister sweeps her arm in the direction of the arena. "Have you seen this place? Of course they serve it."

"Yeah, makes sense. If mushroom jerky doesn't say bougie, I don't know what does."

The vendors are chichi, the offerings are organic and expensive, and the ticket prices are outrageous. Also, every game's sold out. Pretty sure my sister would never be able to afford the tickets on her own. She's a nurse raising a kid solo with some help from our parents, so outrageous hockey ticket prices are not in her budget. Fortunately, I get comp seats, so I get to treat her to the best seats in the house.

I turn my attention back to Kade. "What's your favorite flavor of popcorn?"

"Everything bagel," he says, then shakes his head. "But I didn't pick it. Mommy did. I wanted kettle corn, but she got the everything kind, and I didn't think I'd like it. But I did. Just like the jerky."

"You know what that means, Kade?"

"What?" he asks, bouncing on his sneakers.

"You're a savory," I declare.

He scrunches his brow. "That's a weird word."

Sophie runs a hand through his brown curls. He's the spitting image of her, but with a more golden complexion thanks to his dad, who was Puerto Rican. Good guy who adored my sister, but he died when Kade was one. "It means you like salty snacks more than sweets," she says.

"I like sweets too though," he says, then his whole face lights up. "We should get ice cream."

Sophie yawns. "It's late, baby. I need to get to bed. And so do you. I'm a bad mommy for letting you stay up this late."

"Nah, good moms let their kids watch hockey," I say to

Kade, because it's not that late. We had a five-thirty puck drop on a Wednesday night, so it's almost eight forty-five. "Which is why I'll take you out for ice cream tomorrow. How about I pick you up from daycare and we can do it then?"

Kade pumps a fist. "Yes!"

"Max," Sophie chides.

"What? Ice cream is always a good idea. Grandma and Grandpa can come too. And we can taste test the sweet and salty flavors," I say to the little guy. "Then you can meet Athena."

"Who's that?"

"A kitten I'm fostering," I say, then whip out my phone and show him a pic.

Sophie checks it out too, but she's yawning again. I nod toward the end of the corridor. "Let's get out of here," I say. "I'll drop you guys off."

"But we're all the way over the Bay Bridge," she protests.

I roll my eyes. "Like I don't know that."

"It's not drop-off territory. We can take a Lyft," she says.

That's way too pricey. "Nope. I'm driving, and that's that." It's said like there are no two ways about it. I set a hand on her back and head down the hall. I'm almost out of here, when Everly pops out of the media room, calling out to someone in there, "We'll talk tomorrow, Jenna."

"See you then," Jenna calls back. Pretty sure she works in Everly's department.

When Everly spins around, her gaze lands on me. Surprise registers in those brown eyes, but she composes herself quickly as her gaze swings to Sophie then Kade, then me. Damn, she looks good tonight in those trim, dark gray slacks that hit a few inches above her ankle, exposing the skin of her lower leg, making me wonder for some annoying reason how her ankle would taste.

Floral? Tropical? Like a summer garden? An orange blossom? The sea? A hunger rolls through me as I imagine brushing my lips over that ankle, ideally while she's wearing only those impossibly sexy black heels. I bet she'd taste like...a garden bursting with flowers in June.

A rumble works its way up my chest, and I tamp it down before it makes landfall. I tear my eyes away from her legs, dragging my gaze up to her face, like that'll snuff the lust. But goddamn, her eyes are so expressive. They're big and brown, deep pools that flicker with emotions, amusement, or excitement, depending on what's going on inside her. She has zero poker face. She can't hide her feelings because of those eyes.

Right now, there's curiosity in them. "Hi, Max," she says, her lips curving up. "I was looking for you. Thank you for the cake. It was delicious."

I'm picturing her eating it, licking frosting off the fork seductively, her tongue flicking over the tines. This is getting to be a bigger and bigger problem, so I give a casual, "No problem." But I replay my response. Ah, hell. I sound like a jackass who thinks he did her a favor by sending cake. It was a thank-you gift. I need to make that clear. "Thanks for the save. In Seattle."

"Happy to help. It's my job. And it did, in fact, help me work on publicity plans," she says, then shifts her focus to Sophie and Kade. "This must be your sister and nephew?"

And the door slams shut on my desire. My hackles go all the way up. Does she think my family is part of her publicity project? No fucking way. "Don't get any ideas," I warn her.

"Um, I was just going to say hello," she says, a little defensively.

But I don't trust her. Or anyone.

Sophie sets a hand on my forearm through my suit jacket but directs her attention to Everly. "Forgive him. He's part Doberman."

"What's the other part, Mommy?" Kade asks eagerly.

"Honey badger?" my sister suggests.

"Black bear?" Everly asks next.

"Snow leopard?" Sophie offers.

"Ornery kangaroo," Everly suggests, with some finality.

They are having entirely too much fun at my expense when the fact is I have a right to be concerned. But first things first—this convo. "All right, all right," I say, pushing my palms down, the sign for *that's enough*. "I'm not a kangaroo."

"Kangaroos are cool," Kade shouts, then bounces a few times, hands curled, marsupial-style, above his imaginary pouch.

Sophie sticks out her hand toward Everly even though they're obviously besties already. "I'm Sophie Lambert-Morales, Max's sister, and this is my son, Kade."

"So nice to meet you. Everly Rosewood. I do PR for the team."

"Yes, I've heard about you," she says, and her voice is dripping with sisterly amusement.

I snap my gaze to Sophie. What the hell is she talking about? I haven't said a word about Everly to anyone besides the guys.

"It must have been a couple years ago. When you were a reporter," Sophie continues, talking to Everly.

But no way did I say anything about this unchecked

lust. I was with Lyra then, and I didn't start having these irritating thoughts about Everly till she started working for the team and needling me after every goddamn game —thoughts that escalated ever since I saw the lacy lingerie in her luggage. "I don't think I said anything about her," I say to my sister.

"Yes, you did," Sophie says, too pleased. "You said she was smart and tough and easy to talk to."

Everly's mouth parts, and she's now enjoying this too much. "Max Lambert. That's another nice thing you did."

I narrow my eyes, muttering, "I did not do something nice."

Kade grabs my hand. "You're a nice honey badger, Uncle Max."

"I'm not," I grunt.

"You kind of are," Sophie says. "Except you were kind of a j-e-r-k too when you got on Everly about Kade and me."

Get on Everly.

I'd like to get Everly on her back, spread her legs, and fuck her into next year.

And fuck, fuck, *fuck*. I've got to stop thinking about her in this way. My dickhead mind is spending all its time in the triple-X cinema when it comes to her, but I've got to do a better job at keeping it in the PG theater, watching innocent cartoons, not filthy reels that have no place in this situation. Everly's a work colleague, whose expertise I unfortunately desperately need.

"All right, now that you've had your fun at my expense, the answer is no," I say to my *work colleague*.

"You don't even know the question," Everly points out. She has no problem going toe to toe with me on anything.

"I do," I say, firing right back at her. "You want to take a pic of me with my sister and nephew. You said you were working on publicity plans."

It's an accusation, a cold one, but she ought to know my family's off-limits.

She squares her shoulders, holding her ground. "Well, yes. Of course. I would love that. But I know better than to make that request. I do understand that's not happening," she says, and I blink, briefly taken aback. She does? Okay, that's good. "But that's not what I was coming here for. I wanted to see if we could get together soon to discuss our battle plan. That's what I was working on while eating the world's most sinful chocolate cake. And I have some ideas mapped out already."

I was wrong. I was too quick to assume. I should probably admit that, but instead, I say, "Sure. How about Friday?" I've got plans with Kade tomorrow, but it'll be good to get this meeting on the calendar right away. Good to move quickly. The sooner we tackle this, the sooner it'll be over. I'll fix my problems, make the team happy, do the documentary, and move the hell on.

Which'll have the added benefit of me spending *less* time with the object of this inappropriate lust. Goals.

"Do you want to meet here in my office or one of the media rooms?" Everly asks.

I glance around the corridor, weighing if I want to meet here in the thick of it or go someplace with a different vibe. Not sure the convo is going to be my favorite so I'd rather the whole organization not be wandering the halls as we have it, but before I can say a word, Sophie chimes in helpfully, "Or you could do coffee or lunch or even dinner. There's a great new coffee shop in the Marina District called Republic of Coffee, and a cute new café in Russian Hill called Morning Glow. There's also sushi in Japantown. Which is great for dinner. I love Japantown. Don't you?"

Everly reins in a smile. "All of that sounds great. Max?"

"Sushi's good," I say, then Everly tells me she'll text me later with details. Finally, she continues down the corridor, and I side-eye my sister as we leave and head through the lot. "Coffee? A café? Sushi?"

She smirks, "Well, I was right. You picked dinner."

Shit. She's an evil genius. She tricked me, but I try to shrug it off. "It's a work dinner," I insist as we weave past a Mercedes.

"Keep telling yourself that," she says with the smugness only a younger sister can pull off.

"It is," I say.

"Of course it is, Max."

"What else would it be?" I ask, since evidently I'm in the mood to double down.

"Gee. I can't even imagine." She stops walking, forcing me to look back at her as she gives the smuggest of smug smiles. "You sent her cake."

"She helped me out of a jam in Seattle! I was thanking her."

"Ohhhh. So it was a work cake," Sophie says as we reach my car.

"Yes, exactly."

"Do you send cake to everyone you work with who helps you? Like, did you send Hugo a slice for blocking that shot on goal the other night?" She parks her hands on her hips.

I don't back down though. "Thanks for the reminder. I'll get right on that."

She stares at me without blinking. "I can't wait to find out what he thinks of it next time I come to a game."

"Me too."

While she opens the back seat door, I grab the booster from the trunk, then buckle in Kade. He's already yawning as I shut the door.

When I get behind the wheel, I add, "And you are not going to try to set me up with my publicist."

"Of course I would not," she says as she settles into the front seat. "But now that you mention it...have you thought about dating again?"

I stare sternly at her before I pull out. "Do I look like I enjoy torture?"

"You do play hockey for a living. So maybe."

"Touché," I say, and shift topics to her work, then to Mom and Dad and how the school year is going for them as I drive her across the Bay Bridge.

"Mom says this is her best dance class ever," Sophie says of our mom, who teaches dance at a performing arts school.

"And let me guess. Dad says it's the best class of actors ever?"

Sophie laughs. "Of course that's what a drama teacher would say."

"Gotta love their optimism," I say, and we chat more about them as we head over to Oakland, where she lives a few blocks away from them. After I carry a sleeping Kade inside, then make sure the alarm is on and no one's out front, I hop back in my car. Before I head back into the city, I stop at a local Whole Foods and order a breakfast platter for my parents, sending it to the school where they teach for delivery in the morning. Bagels and fruit are the key to their hearts.

I return to my car. Alone at last, I turn on the Bluetooth and toggle over to the app for the class on navigational tools used in the eighteenth century. It's not my favorite topic, but I'm not taking this online course for fun. As the lights of San Francisco guide me home, I recite the facts I'm learning so I'll be ready to take a quiz in a few days. I need to ace it. For me. I don't want to end up like my grandfather when I'm older. Forgetting everyone. My heart clutches as images flash by of his final year—the long, painful months where he was gone before he was gone.

I've got to keep my mind in as good a shape as I keep my body. I hope I can have a different fate. A different future. And that's what I need to focus on—the future. For my family and for me.

* * *

"Taste test time!" Kade issues the announcement as he runs into The Hand Dipper the next afternoon, rushing to the counter.

I follow him into the shop in Hayes Valley with my mom and dad. Sophie has a twelve-hour shift today.

"He's been talking about this nonstop since this morning," my dad says to me, still utterly charmed by his grandson. "On the way to daycare, he asked us to read him the flavors."

"Gotta love that kind of prep," I say.

"Exactly, and who can blame him? There isn't a better way to spend, well, a day than testing ice cream flavors," Mom says.

Dad goes pensive for a beat when he arrives at the counter. "You know, in my next life, maybe I'll be an ice cream taster," he says, staring at the plethora of flavors.

No, he's gawking. Well, this place is damn good. Wesley recommended it to me, and the dude knows his ice cream.

Mom squeezes Dad's shoulder. "What about in this life, Mike? Let's get started now."

The four of us survey the offerings from the black-berry jam swirl to the pretzel and chips confetti. Kade presses his palms to the glass. "There are soooo many, Uncle Max." He spins to face me, utter concern in his eyes. "Help me pick."

I bend down and read off all the flavors to the kiddo, debating which ones sound the best. He takes his time, then picks out four flavors for us to taste test.

Before my dad can even attempt to swipe his phone, I slide mine over the card reader. It's nice that they don't have to think about whether it's in the budget like they did when we were kids. I like that they no longer have to worry.

And I don't ever want that to change.

Later that night, after my parents and Kade have met Athena and I've said goodbye, my phone flashes with a message from Everly. I sneer at it even while I click it open so fast. It's the time to meet her tomorrow evening. Then a chipper message *can't wait*.

I scoff.

That's doubtful. She probably wishes she were getting a root canal instead of dealing with me. Understandable. I feel the same about her.

I just wish she weren't so distractingly beautiful, and after I get ready for bed and wander past the floor-to-ceiling windows overlooking the city, I wish I weren't wondering where she lived.

11

ONE NEW THING

Everly

This avocado sushi is melting in my mouth. It's so good, I want to groan. No, I want to Food Network moan. But that'd be wildly inappropriate for a business dinner.

Which is clearly what this is with Max, which is why I dressed for work. Trim slacks, a white blouse, and my hair in a high ponytail. I always wear it back at work.

I've learned that in a male-dominated field, it's extra important to have boundaries. I've set plenty for myself—dressing only in a professional way, looking the same day in and day out with my hair and makeup, and acting above board.

Most of all—having no crushes on players.

At least, no crushes on players that I'd admit out loud to anyone but my friends.

"This is amazing," I say after I finish the piece of sushi. That's a much safer assessment than going all orgasmic eye-closing.

"Yeah, it sure seemed like you liked it," Max says dryly.

What's that supposed to mean? Except, fuck a duck. I think I might know. "Well, it's good," I say defensively.

His smile is ludicrously cocky. "I could tell you were enjoying yourself."

Shoot. Was I food moaning even when I tried not to? That's a bad habit of mine, and I blame Marie. Heat creeps across my cheeks, and for a few seconds, I stall, hunting for a plausible excuse, then offering up the first one that comes to mind. "I haven't had sushi in a while. So I was excited."

And that was weak. But I add a big smile to try to sell it. Like, maybe he'll think I've just been smiling because of my love for this food. That's all. Just a sweet, innocent smile.

With his chopsticks in that big right hand—how much of my ass could he cover with that hand? *No. Don't think that*—he reaches for a yellowtail roll, takes his time swirling it in a soy sauce and wasabi mix, then leans closer, dropping his voice to a bedroom whisper. "I think they could even tell you liked it in the restaurant next door."

My jaw drops. I *was* food moaning. And he caught me red-handed. I don't know how to backpedal on this one, but...maybe it'll help us work together. I can admit something awkward about myself, then we can get to the reason for this dinner—the battle plan I have with me on my goes-with-me-everywhere tablet. "I'm sorry," I say, then shake my head. "It's this thing my best friend and I used to do. We had contests every time we went out to eat. We pretended we were Food Network chefs. She wanted to be one—a chef. She was an amazing cook."

And holy shit. I just went full word-vomit confession.

His smug smile evaporates. He sets down the soy-sauce-and-wasabi-drenched roll before he even brings it to his mouth. "*Was?*" he croaks out.

A one-word question that asks everything.

But it's hard for me to say everything that happened the day I lost her, and a part of myself too. So I say the simplest thing. "She died three years ago. In a car accident."

"I'm so sorry," he says, and for a few blurry-eyed seconds, I think he's going to squeeze my hand, and for a few more seconds, I want him to.

Maybe he senses it. As my vision swims and I blink back unwelcome tears, his hand settles on my wrist. Warm, comforting, reassuring. "You must have been close to her," he says gently, squeezing my wrist.

I nod, unable to speak and feeling foolish for the intensity of my reaction. It's been three years. I should be able to say she died without crying. But sometimes I just can't. I was the driver, after all. Even if we were hit by another car, I was still the driver. I'm also the survivor.

Instinctively, I reach for my shoulder, feeling the silk strap of the lacy lavender bra I'm wearing today, then the hypertrophic scar there under my shirt, the harshest reminder of what happened. It's hard not to touch it when I think of her, or that evening, or the terrible broken days that followed as I tried to heal. A choice she never had.

But I have to stay rooted in this moment.

Quickly, I take inventory of the surroundings. How does the table look? Like bamboo. What's on the walls? They have Japanese art, stylized prints of blue waves and orange line drawings of fish. Where is the door? To the left, past the hostess stand. Crowds stream down the corridor of this complex in the heart of Japantown, a mall of sorts full of sushi, ramen, and shabu-shabu places along with gourmet grocery stores and tchotchke shops. I'm here, not caught in the pull of the past.

I blink away the sting as best I can and meet Max's gaze. "She was like a sister. I'm an only child and we were best friends since we were kids. We met in kindergarten, and we rented an apartment together here in the city. Before..." I take a deep breath and scan the room again. The art. The table. The door.

"I get it—why it'd hit you hard," he says, his hand still on my wrist. "I haven't lost a sibling, but I imagine it must be like having your heart ripped out every time."

"Yes," I say, then swallow past the knot of emotions clogging my throat.

His blue eyes are usually piercing, icy even. But now they're softer, gentler. Filled with heartfelt sympathy. He gives one more squeeze then lets go. My skin feels lonely without his touch.

"Tell me more about this Food Network moan," he says. It's asked genuinely, without his usual teasing or taunting—it's like he really wants to know.

I should move on. Talk to him about my three-step plan for the makeover. But I'm a car, stuck in first gear. Or maybe I don't want to shift just yet. "She made me watch a ton of cooking shows, so it became this thing we did. Perfecting the orgasmic food moan."

His eyebrows shoot up, saying *tell me more.*

I can picture Marie perfectly—her short dark hair, cropped in a pixie cut. Skull earrings crawling up her lobes, right alongside butterflies. "I am a rebel and an animal that won't hurt you," she'd said of her favorite jewelry one night when she lounged on the couch in the two-bedroom apartment we shared. Best friends for life.

That had been the plan, at least. But later, I learned that skulls and butterflies had more in common than I'd thought—they could both mean a new life, and the life beyond.

I shake off the memory, focusing on the story instead. "Every time she made a new dish—and she was always making new dishes and always saying *just try it*—if it was good, we'd do the food moan."

I laugh, and wow that feels surprisingly good, the shift from tears to laughter in a few minutes. "Which is weird, I guess." I sigh, then shrug. "It was our thing."

He nods, his eyes serious. "Let's get a new thing."

"What?" I ask, like I didn't hear him right when of course I did. But I didn't expect him to say *that*.

"Try a new thing," he says. "They have a good menu."

Call me skeptical, but one kind moment does not change the prickly dynamic between us. I'm not his buddy. He's not mine. We are strictly professional. I don't want to let him into the food moan world. "So I can food moan?" I ask, my guard all the way up again.

He rolls his eyes, then sears me with them. Now they're piercing again. Gone is the softness. In its place is the cool, unknowableness of Max Lambert. No wonder he's so good at playing the grump. He doesn't act out the role—he lives it. His expression is impenetrable and unflinching for a long beat. But then he shifts again. "Sunshine, I've already heard the sound you make when you like something," he says, his voice deep, raspy, a little smoky—and far too sexy. We're talking about food, but he's looking at me like he knows what I'd sound like if he touched me after dark. If he brushed those fingers along my jaw, down my throat, over my collarbone. "I meant... let's try some new sushi," he adds.

Right. Yes. Of course. I grab the menu from the holder, and scan it again. But it's hard to focus with the heat still flaring through me. I even catch the faint scent of his Midnight Flame cologne, and it's making my mind a little fuzzy as I look at the offerings, barely able to read them.

Focus, girl.

"Have you had octopus?" he asks.

The question grounds me. "Actually, I don't eat fish. Or meat," I say.

He peers quickly at the food I ordered. Avocado rolls and cucumber rolls.

With a quick nod, he jumps to the next page, then frowns. "Well, shit." He looks up, meeting my eyes again. "They only have avocado, cucumber, and asparagus rolls. Also, tamago. You eat eggs?"

"I do."

Then, with a quickness I didn't see coming, he's flagging down our server who's here in seconds. "Question for you, my man. Can the chef put all four of these together? In a specialty roll? If you can, that'd be awesome." Max flashes a rare smile the server's way.

"I think so. I'll ask the chef."

"Thanks. I'd appreciate it immensely."

When the server leaves, I give Max a knowing stare. Maybe topped with a bit of an *I was right* smile.

"What's that for?"

I let my gaze sail toward the server then back to him, like Max has been busted. "You can be charming."

He pffts.

"Don't pfft me," I say.

He pffts again.

"You were charming," I say, pointing at his big, broad

chest. "Like when the Beast didn't interfere with Belle reading at dinner."

He scratches his jaw, all casual. "I don't think we're watching the same movies. Pretty sure he bellowed at her to join him for dinner or else."

"And then he was charming. *Eventually*," I say.

"Fine," he relents. "I was charming with the server. Does that mean I've passed and you'll graduate me?"

I laugh. "Not on your life, Lambert."

"You sure? You seemed pretty impressed I asked nicely for something. Why don't you put in a good word with team management, and we'll call this good?" He pushes back slightly in his chair.

"Nice try but sit your hockey butt down."

With a sigh, he stays put. I'd expect nothing less from a competitive elite athlete, though, than to try to finagle a quicker way through this situation. It's like when he stretches his body in all new directions to prevent a goal, doing the splits, it seems, in front of the net. Hmm. In what other inventive ways can he move his body? Or, really, mine, for that matter? I'm flexible too, thanks to pole. What would it be like to be flexible with him? It's easy to picture in some ways, but hard too. It's been a while since I've been with someone. Or really, it's been a while since I took all my clothes off with someone. The last person was Gunnar—a guy I dated about a year and a half after the accident. An architect, he'd seemed thoughtful and smart on our first date, asking interesting questions and never hogging the conversation. Several dates and a few clothed make-out sessions later, I finally felt comfortable enough to tell him about my body. "I'm not afraid of a few scars," he'd said with a wry smile. But still, once my shirt came off, he couldn't stop staring at them. He never said a word about them, but his eyes said enough.

Pity.

His actions said more. He ghosted me literally an hour later.

Briefly, I think of Lucas, and the second date we're planning. I don't think he'd ghost me for the same reasons, since he knows all about the injuries, the surgeries, the marks on my body. I haven't had sexy thoughts about Lucas recently, but then again, I haven't seen him in a few months. Max is in my face every damn day.

I'm saved from my own wandering thoughts about both men when the server returns with a brand new combination of all things vegetarian. Max points to it with his chopsticks. "Vegetarians first," he says.

I go for it, grabbing a roll, swiping it through the soy sauce and wasabi dish, then bringing it to my lips. I take a bite, and it's...not bad. It doesn't make me want to moan, but it is pretty tasty. When I finish the bite, Max looks at me expectantly.

"It's unusual. And kind of fun. Is that weird for sushi to be fun?" I ask.

"No idea," he says, but he sounds amused. He snags a piece, dips, and chews. Judging from the expression on his face, he's not about to become an aficionado of this invented-on-the-fly roll, but he nods a few times. "It's kind of like a vegetarian party in my mouth."

And I crack up, laughing for longer than I'd expected. When I finally catch my breath, he looks pleased.

But he wipes the look off his face quickly. "All right. You tried a new thing. I guess I gotta try one now too." He nods to the tablet by my side, and it's no longer resignation in his eyes, but he's wearing his game face. Like he's ready to hit the ice. "What have you got for me, drill instructor?"

I flip it open and we get to work at last. There's no need to mince words with Max. "We have one goal—we need to make you sellable again."

His jaw ticks, but he nods, even though I know it can't be easy to hear that he's unlikeable. "No matter how good you are in the crease, no matter how much you love the sport, you have to be marketable these days," I say. "I have some ideas for how to do that. A three-step plan, if you will. We'll need to do a series of community outreach events, charitable appearances, and other fun things."

He snorts. "We might have different definitions of fun."

We probably do, so I soldier on. "And at the risk of being patently obvious, before we embark on the *Max Makeover Tour*," I say, flashing a big, dazzling smile that doesn't land for my audience of one, but so it goes, "you'll need to be on social media again."

I brace myself for a bestial bellow. Instead, he drops his forehead in his big palm, and he's the one groaning now. No orgasmic moans at all. Just one of pure dread. When he lifts his face, his eyes look tired. "Really?"

He doesn't sound bitter. He sounds...dead. My heart squeezes for him. "PTSD from Lyra?" I ask gently.

A long sigh falls from his pretty lips. "Yeah, and everything that came after. The fallout." He's quiet for a beat, then he adds, with rare vulnerability, "It's been kind of nice living my life offline the last year and a half. An unexpected side effect."

I can see that. I have to imagine it was a relief to live a more unscrutinized life. I've researched past posts. Seen what she said about him when they were together. She was fawning, and sweet, and he was doting—a perfect athlete-and-pop-star couple.

Until it wasn't. And a few months after the nasty public split, she released a song about how hurt she was, and the world blamed him rather than her new guy. The upshot? Max is like the grumpy mountain man who retreats to a cabin in the woods to live off the grid and make furniture.

"It does sound nice," I say. But his media disappearance isn't realistic for him at this critical moment in his career. Not with the team's expectations or with the potential of *The Ice Men* documentary. "But even so, before we head down this path of public appearances and photo opps, I think it would be good if we start up *your* social again. Or really, a new one for you." He shut down the old one and killed it.

His face turns stony. "There's no other way?"

I stay strong as I shake my head. "There's not, Max. This is how the world works now."

He rolls his eyes. "I'm not fucking five."

And there's the grump again. The sweetness didn't last long at all. Which means I have to be all the sweeter by reaching for common ground. "Look, I wish we didn't live our lives in a fishbowl. But we do. I promise, though, it doesn't have to be painful."

"More like soul-sucking," he mutters.

"I've got some ideas that can make it more enjoyable."

"Like take-a-puck-to-the-eye enjoyable? That level of pleasure? Because that's what this whole battle plan sounds like."

And he hasn't even heard most of it. But I stay cheery. "It'll be more like vegetarian-sushi enjoyable. We can share more about you on your feed without letting anyone in too deep," I begin. I know how to do this. If he could stop acting like he has the man flu, I could explain it. "I've been working in the sports business for eight years. I have a plan. And here it—"

"Why not just post on the team's social media? Why do I have to have one?"

He's like a lion crying over a teeny splinter in his paw. There's nothing to do but remove the shard so I try gently, saying, "Of course I'll post more of you on the team's social media too. But that's not enough for what the GM wants from you. And what your agency wants. Which is also what *you* want. We need to rebuild *your* social so you have some fan engagement. That's important to your agency, and that's step one. For step two, we'll embark on some meaningful community outreach. Events and such, where you'll need to pose for photos, and"—I pause, take a breath and gird myself for him to breathe a plume of fire —"talk to the press."

He drags a hand down his face, sighing the world's most aggrieved sigh.

What? Did you think you'd pull this off by staying silent? But you catch more flies with honey, so I add, "But I'll be there. I'll be with you at all the events and press opps. I'll make sure you're not blindsided."

"If only that were a guarantee."

Fine. There are no guarantees in life. Still, I add, "I'll do my best, and I'm very good at my job."

He offers me a wry smile. "I know. You're relentless."

It's a small admission, but I'm glad he acknowledges my tenacity. "I am." Then I play my ace. I didn't show him this card yet because I knew he'd push back. I needed him to pull his protest act first before I offered him *this*. "And

I'll run your social for you. You won't have to touch it or do a thing. I'll take care of it all."

His hardened expression softens at the edges. "Really? You can run it?" His voice is wary but a touch hopeful. Damn, this man has trust issues a mile wide and ten miles deep. I've got to remember that. It'll help me deal with working with him. Since it seems—knock on wood—I'm finally getting through to the beast.

"Absolutely. You won't have to touch it. I can take care of it all. Think of me like your...social media bodyguard." I flash him a smile, bright, cheery, and smart. One that says I've got this under control.

His lips curve up in a slight grin. Yes! I'm getting through to him. "Okay," he mutters.

It's hardly a ringing endorsement, but it's not a no, and that's all that matters. "What's step three?"

I shrug happily. "The easiest one of all. You do *The Ice Men* doc."

"Easy for you to say," he grumbles. "I'll be under a microscope."

It *is* easy for me to say, because if I do steps one and two right, my work is done. I can land the promotion I'm dying to get, and get my life back without having to deal daily with a stupidly hot, annoyingly broody, phenomenally grunty man who loves to bicker with me. "But you'll be a pro at it by then. Because of the work we'll do first. I already got you a new handle and everything. The Real Max Lambert," I say.

He seems to give that some thought before he says, "You're taking this seriously."

"Of course I am. It's my job. I love my job. I work very hard at it and I give it my all every day. And I'm in line for a promotion," I say, laying my cards on the table. Since he doesn't trust easily, or at all, it's better if he knows my deal. I don't want him to be surprised later.

With a decisive nod, he says, "Let's get you a promotion then, Everly."

It's a welcome change from him angling to get out of this project.

As he snags another roll, I continue. "Great. Here's how I think we should start. It won't take too long to restart your social before we move onto the community outreach step. I'm guessing a week or so if all we need to do is build out your social with some fresh content. Nothing too taxing. Just pics of your favorite things."

"Like rainy days with my favorite mug? Like soft blankets and the smell of lilacs in the morning?" He flutters his lashes in complete mockery.

But I fight fire with fire this time. "Sure. We can take a picture of you gazing out your bay window and watching the city roll by while you drink chamomile tea. Then we'll snap a shot of you shopping for pumpkins at the farmers' market. And maybe you can even sniff a candle when you get home. How does that sound?"

Oh, did that come out sarcastic? My bad.

"Let's start Monday. I have a candle-making class, in fact," he counters, not one to be outdone.

"Fantastic. I'll be there taking pics."

"And the farmers' market is the next day. Let me just make sure I have my favorite wicker basket to bring."

"The one with the red gingham cloth in it?"

"How did you know? I got it the other day at the craft fair. Then I wrote about it in my journal of good things. Fucking love that gingham cloth."

"It's so you, right? Upbeat and cheery?" I set my chin in my hand, playing it up.

He smiles, showing zero teeth, then says, "So very me."

We're not done yet though. We need to get a date on the schedule for the first pic. "Candle-making it is, then? That's how you want to start with your favorite things?"

"It's either that or the circus," he tosses back.

And oh. *Oh my.* He has no idea what he just did, does he? I jump on the chance he just gave me. "I pick candle-making," I say.

He narrows his brow, tilts his head, studies me. Naturally, being the naysayer he is, he replies, "Nah. Let's do the circus."

I fight off a smile—the one that says *I set you up, Max Lambert.*

I knew he'd pick the opposite of my choice. And I can't wait to snap a shot of Mister Difficult ringside. "The big top it is," I say.

His smile is smug, but he doesn't know who he's dealing with.

12

THE FIRST MOVE

Max

That little stunt ought to buy me some time to get used to this invasion of privacy. Where's she going to find a circus after all? It's not like they're popping up all over the place. The era of circuses is over. So score one for this guy.

"Are there even circuses anymore?" I ask Asher on Monday afternoon as I'm driving to the rink for our game against Chicago tonight. I gave him the download on the three-step-stab-my-eyes-out-with-toothpicks-battle plan. "Besides Cirque du Soleil." Oh, shit. I groan as I flick my turn signal. "Fuck me. What if she takes me to Cirque du Soleil in Vegas this week?"

We're heading there next for a stretch of away games, first in Vegas, then Denver.

He shoots me a look from the passenger seat. "And that'd be a problem for some reason? What's wrong with Cirque du Soleil? That shit is cool. Also, what's your deal?"

"What do you mean?" I ask him as we near the players' lot.

"You want to do this, right? This whole reputation rehab."

"I wouldn't call it *want*," I say dryly.

He makes a rolling gesture with his hands as I pull up to the gate. "Right, right. You don't want to. You have to. Whatever. Point is you're doing it. Why don't you just lean into it and get it done?"

Is it not obvious? "Because I hate social media? Because I hate false things? Because it all sucks?" I point out as I steer the car into the lot.

"But you're doing it because of the potential benefits for your career, your future, your family," he says, and I snag a spot and cut the engine.

We get out. "Right. I am. What are you getting at?"

"So just do it instead of giving her a hard time about it all," he suggests, like it's no big deal to smile and wave and shake hands, because to him it's easy. He's a natural at this stuff. Asher has the Midas touch.

"Not everyone is you, dickhead. We're not all naturally nice," I say.

He rolls his eyes. "Not the point, *dickhead*. The point is you know you need to do this. You seemed resolute the other morning. Why not just tackle it like it's warm-up drills and get it done? Instead, you're setting up circus dates to toy with Everly. Like it's a game. An escape room or something, but you're not really solving the clues. You're dicking around and being difficult."

"I wouldn't call it a date."

"Walks like a date, talks like a date..."

"But it's not a date," I add.

"Keep telling yourself that. All I'm saying is you're making this harder than it has to be."

But he wasn't there when Everly was sassing me at the sushi restaurant on Friday night, tossing out options for my favorite things. The woman has made a game of our one-upmanship. We bicker professionally. There's probably a leaderboard somewhere of our barbs and arrows. "I couldn't just give in. You don't get it. She expects me to be—"

"An asshole?"

I tap my finger to my nose. "Bingo."

"Ah. I get it," he says, nodding in understanding. "Everything makes perfect sense now. You're prolonging spending time with her."

My smile drops like a fly in the summer swelter. "What the fuck?"

"You kind of are. You're going to the circus with her..." He pauses for effect, then cups his mouth. "For a social media post."

Dammit. I feel a little triggered. "Because I have to," I point out defensively.

"And you're finding every way possible to huff and puff and drag your feet."

"Look, you might like everything, but not all of us are wired to wake up on the right side of the bed with the coffee cup already half-filled. Just because I know I *have* to do something doesn't mean I *have* to like it. I change cat litter but I don't love it," I say as we near the door to the players' entrance.

"I would think going to the circus with Everly is better than changing cat litter," he says dryly.

I arch a skeptical brow his way. "Have you ever met a clown?"

"Wait. Do you have that same issue as Dallas Bright?" he asks, mentioning the forward on the Toronto Terror. "Dude is legit afraid of clowns."

"Reasonable. John Wayne Gacy was known as the clown killer. I get where Bright is coming from."

"You afraid of clowns too? Tell the truth," Asher says.

I scoff. "No. I just don't want to watch jugglers. Or contortionists. Or clowns. Or people pretending to be happy."

Asher nods, long and understanding. "Right. I get it now. It's happiness you hate. This makes so much sense. I bet you hate picnics and sunrises too."

I shudder at the thought of dawn. "I'm not a morning person."

"Called it," he says.

We go inside where he spends the rest of the way to the locker room listing things he suspects I hate—stargazing, parks, movie nights with popcorn. Actually, that last one sounds surprisingly good.

"Wait. Was that a flicker of a smile?"

"Fuck you. No."

"Dude, I like popcorn too," Asher stage-whispers.

But as I move through my pre-game ritual—a light jog on the treadmill as I listen to one of my hard-rock playlists—my mind wanders back to his observation—the ridiculous idea that I'm trying to prolong spending time with Everly. *Please.* This makeover is already torture. No way would I try to drag it out. And no way will I pretend I like it. She knows the truth. She'd expect nothing less from me than who I've been.

But who you are is unapproachable, a voice whispers darkly in me.

My own voice from inside my fucking skull. Annoying voice.

It follows me as I text with my parents while I jog. *Still thinking about those bagels from last week. A good son would send them every day*, Dad teases. Mom replies with *A great son would send my favorite Italian food for dinner.*

I write back with one word: *Done.*

Then Mom says she was just kidding and tells me to kick butt tonight.

I always do, I reply then I finish my workout, put on my pads, and lace up. But the voice chases me as I hit the ice for warm-ups, stretching my hammies, hips, and inner thighs, then shuffling back and forth in the crease before my teammates take easy shots on goal.

I don't smile as they shoot at me. Why would I? No one wants an approachable goalie. You don't stop goals by being approachable. You stop them with grit, glower, determination, and absolute unapproachability.

That's really what the team pays me for, and I intend to deliver that tonight. I dial up the unapproachability way past ten once the puck drops.

No one wants a nice guy guarding the net when we're down a man in the second period when one of our defenseman, Hugo Bergstrand, winds up in the box for holding.

This is when Chicago will be hungriest. The second the power play begins, the Chicago center attacks the net, but I block the puck cleanly with my leg pad. It bounces sharply to their winger, who skates around the back of the net, and I track him like a hawk.

Just try me, fucker.

When he comes around again, he takes a shot, but it doesn't stand a chance. I lunge for it, pushing off the posts while scanning the action in the zone. There's Ryker Samuels nearby, but down by center ice is Bryant.

Open. Ready. A long shot.

Fuck it. I go for it, slapping the puck and making a long pass to him. There's barely a chance, but like the brilliant motherfucker he is, Bryant grabs it and tears down the ice, hell-bent on the visitors' net, where he lifts his stick and holy shit.

He sends it rushing past their goalie. The lamp lights.

"Yes! Fucking yes," I shout.

Asher flies by. "Nice assist!"

We go on to win the game, proving my point. Don't need to be nice to get the job done. In the tunnel, I'm ripping off my helmet right as the beautiful blonde who I swear I am not trying to spend extra time with strides toward me.

"Did you know the average goalie scores zero to three assists in a season? A season, Lambert," she says, sounding pleased with her research.

"That so?"

"It's so rare when a goalie gets one, it's the kind of thing that would be worth giving a quote to the press about." Her voice pitches up with hope. Damn, she's sexy when she's hopeful. Which means she's sexy all the time. She tilts her head, the sleek ponytail bobbing to the side. "You could even, say, gee, exactly what I just said to them. Just use my words. Easy-peasy."

She's sing-song, selling this talk-to-the-press idea to me.

Like I'd bend that easily that soon. Besides, Everly wouldn't want me to. Everly expects the volley. She'd think I was an imposter if I didn't give her a ferocious game of ping-pong. No way am I backing down so soon.

I flash her a smile as my teammates walk down the hall around us. "But wouldn't *you* rather put a pic of me and my man Bryant on my social and say just that?" I drape an arm around my friend who nabbed the goal itself.

She huffs, then mutters a "fine" as she lifts her phone.

Ha. I won that round, wiggling out of talking to the press even when I really should. It's a once-in-a-blue-moon hockey event after all. But instead I pose with Bryant for a pic.

As I walk off, I feel a little cocky. Okay, a lot, so I say to her, "Score one for the goalie."

"In what, Max?" she asks sweetly, innocently.

I spin around, trying not to get distracted by her pretty pink lips and those big, brown eyes that hold thousands of stories. Right now, they're etched with a curiosity she can't hide.

"In the game with the publicist," I say.

"Oh, we're playing a game now?"

"Sunshine, we've always been playing and you know it," I toss back.

Wesley points his thumb toward the locker room. "I'm heading off. You two maybe should get a room."

Best to ignore that comment as he trudges down the hall. I turn my focus back to Everly.

"I thought we were playing a game, so that's why I made this move." She swipes a polished silver nail along the phone, then spins the device around, showing me— *The Real Max Lambert.*

The feed she set up. The fresh pic of Bryant and me is the only thing on it. I furrow my brow. "Right. That was the point," I say, like it's obvious.

She smiles, far too Mona Lisa-style for my taste.

"Score's tied, grump. I've got a pic of you on social, and I didn't even have to take you anywhere to get one of your favorite things. Also, it's a *real* favorite thing," she says with the most confident, winning smile I've seen—one that sends heat roaring through my body. It's annoying, my attraction to her. So annoying I don't even have a comeback.

But she does. She waves, then says, "By the way, see you at the circus in Vegas. We're catching an early flight before the team."

Damn her. She's good. No, she's better than good. "Is it Cirque du Soleil?" I ask. I haven't seen it, but if Asher likes it, maybe I can stomach going.

She sears me with a look. "In your dreams."

But my dreams last night involved her spreading her legs on a trapeze so she might be right.

13

SWEET TORTURE

Max

"Welcome to the Most Spectacular Little Circus in Vegas."
A short white dude sporting a twirly mustache and a top
hat waves grandly to the big top he stands under.

Or, really, the little top.

Everly found a tiny shoestring circus on the outskirts
of Vegas to take me to. She's an evil genius. She is
Einstein-ian in her makeover planning, since I'm sitting
on the cramped metal bleachers with my knees in my
eyes.

This woman lives to torture me.

"I'm your ringmaster—Victor Valenti. Prepare to be
dazzled by feats of wonder and magic, where reality blurs
with illusion and dreams come to life before your very
eyes," the ringmaster booms, his voice echoing
throughout the tiny tent. The air is thick with the scent of
popcorn and cotton candy in the early afternoon.

The crowd of maybe one hundred erupts into cheers.

Everly sits beside me, a mischievous glint dancing in her eyes. She knew exactly what she was doing when she suggested we visit this circus. But as much as I want to be annoyed by her cunning ways, I'm too damn impressed. There's no room for a six-foot-four guy here, and this was a brilliant way to make me suffer. She's so beautifully mean, and since she expects nothing less than ire from me, I mutter, "These seats are smaller than coach."

She arches a brow, whispering, "And you would know how?"

That's fair. "True. I haven't flown coach in years."

"So you're not really suffering much then, are you?"

I harumph. She's got me on that too. Still, I counter with, "Define suffering."

As the ringmaster waxes on about the death-defying acts we'll soon witness, she levels me with a stare that's as sexy as it is withering. "This," she says, gesturing to her face. "This is suffering right now."

I smirk. "Good."

"I had a feeling you'd like it."

"Just like you enjoy my pain," I toss back.

She pats my thigh. "It gets better. I promise."

I glance down at her hand on the denim on my leg. Well, *that* is better, truth be told. My body sizzles under her touch, even though it's irritating, this reaction to her. But it's especially irritating when she takes her hand away and I miss it.

How can one person wind me up and annoyingly turn me on at the same time? That's the real feat of wonder and mystery—that the woman next to me in the snug blue button-up blouse with short sleeves that show off toned arms is vexing me every single second.

With a swish of her trademark ponytail, Everly turns

her gaze back to the man in the center of the stage as he says, "And now, the Amazing Valentis."

The lights dim, casting a hush over the crowd. We're wedged in next to the rest of the audience. A spotlight illuminates the center ring all the way to the top of the tent, where a trapeze drops down. A woman, clad in sparkling purple sequins and white feathers that catch the light, has one knee hooked over the bar. The rest of her hangs gracefully upside down. She rocks gently, then quickly as another trapeze drops down. A man hangs from the bar, swinging toward her, and soon he reaches her.

She grabs his hands and he catches her so she's sailing under him.

Everly gasps. Gone is the sassy woman who needles me better than an acupuncturist. In its place is a woman awed by each death-defying move of a pair of trapeze artists. They execute them perfectly, then land on a mat, sticking their arms straight up in the air.

Everly claps loudly, looking like she wants to jump to her feet to give them a standing ovation.

The ringmaster introduces the next act—a juggler who tosses flaming batons high into the air. As he throws higher and higher, I lean closer to my companion, my shoulder bumping hers. "So you're a closet circus fan. I get it now, Rosewood."

She squares her shoulders, defiantly. "No. It's just impressive."

"Right. Sure," I say, doubtful. "That's all it is."

She rolls her eyes at me. "You can't handle the fact that I have a hidden appreciation for the extraordinary."

"Next thing you know, you'll be running away to join the circus."

"Don't tempt me. I might just leave you and the Max makeover behind."

I chuckle, shaking my head. "You wouldn't. You like spending time with me too much."

She scoffs. "Keep telling yourself that."

"Don't have to. It's just a fact."

With a beleaguered sigh, she looks away from the juggler, her brown eyes locking with mine. "Fine. I'll take the bait. Why is it a fact?"

"Because you, sunshine, love torture."

"Is this torture, Max? Is this really sweet torture?" she asks, leaning closer.

Her perfume swirls around me, seductive, alluring. A promise of sultry nights, and long, slow kisses that should never end. And I have the answer. Yes, this is torture. I'm entirely distracted by her scent. And I can't resist stealing a hit. I shift toward her, catching another hit of it as I whisper in a gravelly voice, "The sweetest."

She swallows, then blinks, like she's been knocked off-kilter. "Good," she says, but she sounds a little wobbly.

Like how I feel as my pulse kicks faster just from being near this woman. This attraction is getting to be a serious workplace hazard.

I've got to get a handle on this lust. I tear my gaze from her, forcing my focus on the juggler as he flips the fiery batons higher and higher still.

Everly stares hard at the ring too, like she's also reset-ting her focus. Interesting.

At some point, though, she relaxes, watching the juggler again with avid eyes, then delighted ones. Everly's enrapt. It's kind of endearing, her joy in the show. That's so not what I expected from this tough, fiery, fierce goddess of PR. But then again, Everly finds the bright side in everything—even circuses. I tip my chin toward her, catching her eye as I ask, "Do you have a thing for jugglers?"

"Do you have a thing for talking during a show?"

"Yes," I say, because she smells too fucking good. I can't focus on anything but her. With barely any space on these bleachers, I'm entirely too close to her on this too-small bench with too-little room, while I'm stuck inhaling her scent that's driving me wild. I blame the perfume for what comes out of my mouth next. "Admit it—you've been secretly dying to take me out."

She turns to me, shooting me a *you didn't just say that* stare. But it's not like she's mad. More like she's curious as hell. "What does that mean?"

"That maybe this was part of your plan all along," I say, as nonchalant as I can be. "A date at the circus."

She rolls her eyes. "Max, we're here for a picture for your social feed. Step one, remember?"

"And yet I don't see you taking one," I say, busting her on a technicality, since I can't stop giving her a hard time.

Her eyes widen, like she's just realized that she'd forgotten our raison d'être. "I know that. I have a plan," she says, defensively.

"Sure you do," I tease.

"I do," she insists quietly, but she's already busy snagging her phone from her purse in a rush, like she wants to prove a point. She lifts it and snaps a quick shot of me. Then, the juggler. But she seems...shaky.

I smirk. Yup. She was having fun, despite herself. She was having such a good time she forgot her mission. Because I, Max Lambert, might be an unapproachable jerk but I'm also a damn good time. I inch closer once more, this time setting a hand on her shoulder. Her breath hitches, but she tries to hide it with a quick inhale.

"I won't tell a soul you're loving this," I say, low and smoky in her ear.

She rolls her lips together, like she's holding in words she wants to fling at me, words dipped in her brand of sexy sarcasm. Words meant to dress me down, that I can't seem to resist eliciting from her.

"It'll be our secret," I press on, even lower, even raspier.

She's stoic, her gaze focused on the act on stage doing...I don't even know what. I don't even care. I can't stop teasing her. "It'll be just between us," I add.

Briefly, she closes her eyes. My attention snags on her bare forearms. Oh. *Oh.* Goosebumps are rising on her pale skin, a tell-tale sign she's aroused. My head swims with this new knowledge. My mind short-circuits. Is Everly Rosewood turned on from the things I whispered in her ear at the circus? I raise my face slowly, getting a glimpse of her neck, her throat, the exposed skin at the top of her dark blue blouse.

It's flushed.

She opens her eyes, and I sit back, too pleased, too fucking satisfied. I cross my arms, enjoying...*everything.*

Acrobats soar through the air and the fire-breather commands the attention of the audience. A man in black leather throws knives at a woman dressed in a tight, sleek catsuit. As the show reaches the end, the juggler returns, this time swallowing swords.

Which makes me cringe. My throat hurts from looking at him. "How the fuck does he do that?" I whisper. No low, seductive words this time. Just shock.

"No gag reflex," Everly says, deadpan.

Great. Just great. My mind is off and running. "For real?"

She's quiet for a beat, those pretty lips curving in the slightest smile as she murmurs, "I hear it helps with... swallowing."

My chest burns, flames licking my blood. She went there. She fucking went there, and now I'm a volcano as I picture Everly Rosewood's beautiful mouth doing unholy things to my dick.

I stare at her lush lips longer than I should till her eyes widen, and she pats her own chin subtly, a sign of something.

"What?" I ask, my voice rough.

In a whisper, she says, "Your mouth. It's hanging open."

Busted. But I'm not even sure I mind.

When the circus ends, we make our way down the bleachers and across the sawdust on the ground. As we exit the tent, Everly nods in the opposite direction of the street where the Lyft dropped us off. "I arranged for you to meet the ringmaster."

My eyebrows shoot up. "You did?"

"Of course. This was a PR thing. It's for your social," she says.

Right. Of course. I'd let the moment get away from me. I'd let my thoughts wander too far. She guides me through the fairground to a tiny trailer where the ringmaster waits for us, his mustache curling with a bit of sweat. Hard work, running a show.

"Hello, Mr. Valenti. I'm Everly Rosewood," she says, sticking out a hand. "We emailed."

"Of course," Victor says, shaking hands, as jovial as he

was onstage. He turns to me. "You must be Max Lambert. The hockey guy, right?"

"That's me," I say.

"Everly says you're pretty good on the ice. I'm more of a theater man myself but if you ever do tricks on skates, let me know."

And there's a first time for everything. I was just invited to join the circus. "Thanks. I will. Great show," I say, working on being nicer, more approachable, more outgoing, so I add, "Do you all, um, train and study in the circus arts?"

Is that even what it's called? I have no idea, but it sounds plausible.

"We do. I come from a long line of circus artists. Seventh generation myself," he says, puffing out his chest with well-earned pride, and as we chat more about his family, Everly snaps some pics of us. I guess she was prepared after all.

"And what about you, Max? Does your family do hockey?" he asks.

"Actually, my parents are teachers," I say.

That seems to catch his interest. "What do they teach?"

"Dad is a drama teacher and Mom teaches dance. That's how they met—they had to share space at a little theater in Seattle where he was directing a play, and she was putting on a recital. Been together ever since. And they teach together, too, at a performing arts school in the Bay Area."

"It's lovely that they work together."

"Yeah, it really is. More than thirty years married and still going strong. Honestly, I'm just glad they don't mind watching me play hockey now and then," I say, then shrug, almost apologetically, "even though it's not a play or musical."

"I'm sure they don't mind it one bit," he says, like a proud dad too. "I always like seeing what my kids love. Fortunately, I get to see them juggle every day."

"They're the jugglers?" I ask, a little amazed in spite of myself.

"They are," he says, proudly.

"No shit. That's awesome," I say.

"I think so too," he says.

We wrap up a few minutes later and once we're in the Lyft, Everly lifts her chin and says, "I was right."

"About what?"

"Circuses are your favorite thing."

I scoff. "They're not. I'm not a circus guy."

The smirk doesn't disappear from her face. "But you're wrong."

"I think I know what my favorite things are, sunshine."

She turns to face me with that trump-card smile. "Do you?"

"I sure do, and they're not circuses."

"But you like your family. And you liked talking to Mr. Valenti about *his* family. So, really, it was no hardship going to the circus. In fact, you enjoyed chatting with him about your parents. So that's another real favorite thing."

Holy. Fuck.

Forget evil genius. She is next level. I can't even be annoyed. I'm too impressed with how she plays the game.

"Has anyone told you that you're Machiavellian?" I ask as the car heads toward the team hotel. I'll need to get ready soon for the game. I skipped my game-day nap. I

like them, but I slept on the early flight this morning so
I'll be fine.

"As a matter of fact, yes. *You*. You just did."

"Well, you are."

She's smiling. "I know."

As the car swings onto the Strip, my phone buzzes,
and I check it. It's a text from my mom.

> Guess where I found your kitten?

I groan, bracing myself for Athena's antics.

> Top of the fridge? Bottom of the laundry
> basket? Inside the dryer?

I hope it's not the latter. But I bet it is. She's the
sneakiest.

> Your closet. Top shelf. Sleeping on a tie.

There's a pic attached of the tiny furball curled up on
some sapphire blue neckwear. Fuck, that's cute.

Everly shoots me a curious look, like she wants to
know what's on my phone. "All good?"

But if I let on that I foster kittens, I'll never hear the
end of it from her. "Yep," I say, shutting the text.

She returns to her phone, typing away. Smiling too.
That looks like how a woman smiles when she sets up a
date. A fire rages in my chest, out of control in seconds.

"Got a date?" I ask. It comes out strangled.

"Maybe," she says, a little flintily.

The flames burn higher. Brighter. Hotter. In seconds,
there's a wildfire in me, eating the forest alive. "Is he your
type?"

"I guess I'll find out. We're going to grab lunch on Sunday," she says.

"Lunch," I scoff. "That's weak."

"Why is lunch weak?"

"Because it's lunch. Who takes a woman out for lunch?"

"A nice guy," she says.

I grind my teeth, then stare out the window, my jaw ticking the rest of the way back as I think about her lunch this weekend.

* * *

As I'm heading to the Vegas arena a couple hours later, a text from her lands on my phone. It's a link to my social feed.

She dropped some pics from the circus. The shot of me watching, a pic of the sword swallowing, then the final snap of the ringmaster and me.

The caption reads: *If hockey doesn't work out, I might run off to join the circus.*

I shake my head. She's brilliant. So fucking brilliant. And I bet this fuckface she's having lunch with won't appreciate her clever ways.

She needs a guy who does. A guy who does more than take her to lunch. A friend takes you to lunch. A date doesn't take you to lunch on a Sunday.

Wait. This Sunday. I know something that's happening this Sunday right around noon. I send her a text.

Max: Had a great idea for my next favorite thing. There's a fun bike ride in the city this weekend. Starts at noon on Sunday. You can get another pic.

Who's the evil genius now?

14

ALL THE NAKED GLORY

Everly

On a red mountain bike, a man sits tall and proud, his furry chest on full display, a pair of bright green bike shorts painted on his thighs as he pedals in the city. He rides next to a woman on an electric bike, who's dressed in only a pink bikini, which is painted on her breasts and pelvis.

A pack of men with Superman logos on their chests and tight red thongs painted on their penises cycle along Hayes Street in the Naked Painted Bike Ride.

I can't believe this is where Max took me today, but I'm begrudgingly admitting to myself that he's good. He's damn good at this game. But I will never let on to him. "So this is one of your favorite things?"

"Big time," he says, resting his muscular arms on the parade barricade on the sidewalk as we join the other onlookers here on Sunday afternoon, now that we're back in town. After a quick stretch of away games—the Sea

Dogs won in Vegas *and* in Denver—we're back home in time for what's become a San Francisco tradition each fall. "Come here every year. It's a great cause, don't you think?"

"Sure is," I say, meaning it. This bike ride—where cyclists wear nothing under their painted on costumes—raises money for more bike lanes in the city. It's one of the city's green initiatives funded in part by the city's best-known billionaire, the football team owner Wilder Blaine, who's also a noted green philanthropist. "I didn't realize you were such a supporter though."

"Definitely. I donate to it every year, and I walk the walk," Max says, laying an easy target for me.

I fire away. "Why aren't you out there riding then?"

If he's going to sabotage my date to take me to a naked bike outing for our makeover project, I might as well wind him up.

But he's not a ferocious competitor for nothing. He scratches his jaw carelessly. "My body painter was busy this year. Such a shame. I was going to go as a Sea Dog. That would have been great for the team's image, right? Me, naked, with only a painted dog tail covering my dick?"

This man. I'm thinking of his cock now, and that is not fair. He shifts his gaze to me, his eyes sparkling with trouble. So I give it right back to him. "Absolutely. A naked hockey star raising funds as he *flies free* with his wiener," I say.

"Next year. That work for you? The whole 'try new things' mantra and all."

"Why wait? You don't need a body painter. You can just go au natural," I challenge. "I'll go grab someone's bike for you. Feel free to strip down."

He sweeps out a hand toward the bike parade. "Let's do it. I'm all for trying new things."

I walk toward the edge of the barricade, calling his bluff, when he darts out a hand, and tugs me back, right next to him.

"I'm joking," he says, his hand still covering my arm. His chest, close to mine. We're inches away, and for a few silent seconds under the midday sun, I swear he's going to kiss me. He's staring at my mouth. He can't seem to look anyplace else. And I don't want him to.

But then he shakes it off, reorienting perhaps, as he says, "Next year for sure."

"Definitely," I say, with a feathery breath. "I'm putting it in my calendar now."

A group of riders dressed as woodland creatures pedal past us, colorful leaves adorning their bodies. My gaze lingers next on a particularly eccentric rider sporting nothing but a rainbow cape billowing in the wind. But what's also billowing in the wind? The guy's balls.

I appreciate the fundraising and all, but how do they do it? A woman with flapping breasts, painted like peaches, pedals by. "How the hell does she sit like that?"

"No idea," Max says, like it hurts him to watch.

Same here. I wince a little, thinking of my lady parts. I would not want my free-range vagina perched on a bike seat anywhere. Let alone in public. But more so, I wouldn't want to show...my scars to the world. I reach for my shoulder, briefly touching the one that won't fade.

Max must notice, since he lifts a brow my way in question. Perhaps concern too. "You okay?"

"Of course."

He tilts his head, his sharp eyes that see everything on

the ice cataloging me now. "Did you...hurt your shoulder at some point?"

The man is a hawk. He misses nothing. It's literally his job, but still I'm thrown off. "Why do you ask?"

"You touch it sometimes," he says gently. "Like maybe you injured it. That's happened to me. I've had a couple hits in the past—elbow, knee. And it's like I'm always checking to see if it's still injured."

I don't want to talk about the accident, the injuries, or the surgeries here in public. Not when I run the risk of emotions surging up my throat, and memories pulling me under. But I don't like to lie either. "Car accident," I admit, then try to make light of it with a quick, "It's fine though. I'm fine."

His eyes flood with concern and immediate understanding. "The same one?"

I close my eyes for a second. I don't want to lose myself in time. Don't want to feel that uncomfortable surge of anxiety as images from that night flash before me. I know how to handle them if they do. But I don't want to handle them right now, while I'm working. I don't want to explain everything about me either. The last time I explained that to a guy he shut me out as soon as he could.

"Yes, but I'm okay. Thank you for asking," I say, trying to be kind, because I know it's easier for most people to never talk about hard things. I have to give Max credit. At least he doesn't shy away.

"If you ever want to talk about it..." he adds. The offer is tender, and I'm tempted to take him up on it. But there's a time and place—and now is not the time nor place.

"Thanks. Maybe," I say, upbeat, but noncommittal. I nod toward a pack of cyclists, quickly changing the subject. "So since you're such a regular, what's your favorite view? Front or back?"

Maybe sensing I need an out, he jumps on the changeup. "The 360-degree view, Everly."

"Like that one right there," I say, subtly gesturing to an older man riding by, probably a grandfather's age. He has a soft belly and saggy skin, and he's balls naked, smiling and riding.

Max shifts on his feet, looking uncomfortable. I do so love torturing him, but maybe I should let him off easy. I nod toward a bar up the street. The sign on the window of Sticks and Stones reads: **Have a clothed drink after your naked ride!**

"Want to get a drink?" I ask.

With that cocky grin I know too well, he shrugs. "If you can't handle the view anymore..."

I lift my phone and snap a pic of him as a pack of zombie riders in their birthday suits cruise past in the background. "That's it. You've figured me out."

"I get it. It's a lot of naked. I understand it's too much for you."

Nope. He's not winning now. I hold my ground, staring at the cyclists, musing. "I can't keep from thinking though...what the bike seats are like right this very second."

He frowns, cringing. "Dude. You won. I'm tapping out."

I pump a fist. "Victory is mine."

"You're too good at this game of chicken, woman."

"Chicken? We're playing chicken? I had no idea."

"What a surprise, isn't it," he says dryly as we walk to the bar. He opens the door for me, and we go inside.

The sound of clinking glasses and lively chatter fills

the air, providing a stark contrast to the catcalls and hollers outside at the parade. As we settle into a cozy booth, the dim lighting casts shadows across Max's face, highlighting the chiseled line of his jaw, covered in that scrumptious beard. What would it feel like to touch that beard? To run my fingers along the scruff on his handsome face? To feel him rub it against my...

I blink off the entirely unprofessional thoughts as Max spreads his strong arms across the back of the booth.

Which doesn't entirely clean up my mind at all. The move shows off the muscles in his chest, stretching that gray T-shirt he wears. He's so stupidly hot he makes me ache. I'm tingly all over.

"So, Everly," he begins. "How are you going to dress me down in a social media post today?"

I'd like to undress him.

But I ignore that inappropriate thought too. "Thoroughly, Max," I tease, tracing patterns on the wooden table with my finger. "With a rousing appreciation of all the flesh we witnessed."

He groans, clearly aggrieved. "Right, of course. I can't forget who I'm dealing with."

"Never forget I'm fearless."

"You could never let me," he says, but there's no taunting or teasing. It's like he's talking about something else entirely. But there's no time to figure out what since a server arrives to ask for our order.

I opt for an iced tea, and he picks a beer but then he tips his forehead to me. "You hungry?"

"Sure," I say, then choose a spinach salad while he picks a chicken sandwich. When the server leaves, I say, "Lunch on a Sunday. Isn't that weak, as you said?"

"Nope. Because it's not a date."

No kidding. "You have a lot of opinions on my dates," I say. But I probably shouldn't linger on the way he turned down Joe for me back in Seattle, then announced he wanted a pic taken at the same time that I happened to have a date with Lucas.

Like Max knew I'd prioritize work over a date.

"I have a lot of opinions on a lot of things," he says, evading the question. Maybe he doesn't want to linger on the *why* either.

I glance around, spotting a couple a few tables over on an obvious date. "I bet you have an opinion on whether they should be here. Want to tell them it's a bad idea for a first date?"

"Nah. Damage is already done," he says, then clears his throat. "So where's your date taking you next? Bingo? Bridge? Mahjong?"

His sweetness never lasts long. "No, Max, we're having a drink next Monday night. At The Spotted Zebra. Does that meet your approval? Or do you need me to reschedule it yet again?"

He scowls but then grumbles. "That's better."

"Glad to have your approval."

"I wouldn't call it approval," he says.

"What would you call it?"

But he doesn't answer. Instead, he pins me with a serious stare, his eyes searching my face, his jaw ticking. "Who is this guy?"

Like he needs to know I'm seeing my former therapist for a second date. "Just a guy."

"A nice guy?" It's asked like that's a terrible thing.

"Yes," I admit. "Is that so bad?"

"If that's your type."

"Do you think I prefer unapproachable men? Difficult

men? Grumpy men?" I counter before I think the better of it.

A flicker of a knowing grin coasts across his lips, but then it disappears. "No idea." He holds my gaze, a new form of chicken, a new type of challenge. My heart rate stutters. My skin heats. His eyes roam over me, then he slides his teeth along his bottom lip before adding, "It's hard to say, sunshine."

I swallow roughly, trying to get my bearings. When he looks at me like that, I feel as if I should cancel my date with Lucas entirely.

But it's not like I'm going to date Max. That simply can't happen so I lift my phone, segueing to work mode. "I should post some pics," I say.

"Have at it," he says, looking particularly delectable right now with the lighting and the snug T-shirt and the don't-have-a-care-in-the-world attitude.

"Can I take a pic of you here?"

It takes him a beat to decide, then he says, "Sure."

I snap a shot, and he looks too good for my own good. All broody and intense, but somehow...approachable too. The goalie out of the office. But who is this man for real? Is he the jerk who taunts me, or is he the man who gently offers to talk anytime?

I don't know.

And I want to.

As I prep the post, the server returns with my iced tea. I down some quickly, then show Max the images from today before I upload them. I covered any naked parts of riders with stickers of hockey pucks and added the shot of him here. The caption reads: *Today a friend brought me to this event.*

He lifts a brow in curiosity. "Are we friends now?"

"Don't believe everything you read on the Internet," I say.

"Thanks for the warning."

"Anytime," I say, then hit post. But I can't keep wondering who he really is. Even though I vowed not to do this—I do it anyway. I let down my guard. "Look, I've got to hand it to you. From the circus to the naked parade, you've done a great job keeping your real self off social, and from me." Then I take a chance. "But I'd love to know what you're really like."

Max is quiet for a beat, his brow furrowed, the cogs turning. He takes a deep breath. "You free Thursday afternoon? We don't have a game that night. I can show you."

He didn't pick my night with Lucas, so I say yes in a heartbeat.

15

RAINCHECK

Everly

As I'm chatting with our new communications assistant at the arena before the game Tuesday night, a gruff voice calls out to me in the press box. "Got the injury report, Rosewood?"

I turn away from Jenna Nguyen toward Gus Mitchell, the grizzled sports reporter who's been covering hockey for longer than I've been alive—something he likes to remind me of nearly every time I see him. His face is weathered and his voice sounds like gravel.

He's tough, but fair though, which is all I can ask for. "Don't I always, Gus?" I say, then brandish my tablet and make a show of swiping my finger across the screen. "In your email."

He narrows his shrewd eyes, shaking his head as he grumbles, "Why can't I just have it on a piece of paper like the old days?"

"Because it's not the old days, Gus," I say with a smile.

"Why chop a tree down when I can send it to you in the ether?"

"I hate the ether," he grouses, but he picks up his reading glasses from the string around his neck and shoves them on his face, hunching over his laptop. "Been covering this longer than you've been alive," he mutters, as if on cue.

I smile at Jenna. "It's his love language."

She smiles awkwardly. "Really?"

"I promise. He's more bark than bite."

"I can hear you, Rosewood," Gus chides.

"I know, Mitchell. It wasn't a secret. I'm training a new department assistant on all the media team."

I expect a surly comeback, but instead he snaps his gaze to me. "Volkov is out? He's got an ankle sprain again?"

Jenna gulps, fidgeting with the silver bracelets on her wrists. She knows our center Alexei Volkov has an ankle sprain for the second time in a year. He should be back in a couple games.

"Just a minor lower body injury," I say with a smile, giving nothing away.

"So it's his ankle again?" Gus pushes.

I stare him down. "Gus, did I say it was his ankle? I did not. You have the report. He's out with a lower body injury. And it's minor. Anything else?"

He huffs. "Yeah, can you make sure I get one of those bags of salted chips with the media meal?"

"Salty for salty," I say, then turn to Jenna. "Can you handle Mister Salty?"

"I can," she says eagerly.

He rolls his eyes. "Make them extra salty."

"As if we'd do anything else," I say, then after checking

in with a few other reporters, we leave.

In the hallway, Jenna brings her hand to her chest, like her heart is beating too fast. "I thought he was going to grill us, and then you went all badass boss babe."

I laugh, making light of the compliment that I secretly love. "Thank you. And even if the press grills you on an injury, you don't have to tell them the details."

"Really?"

"Absolutely. While we're required to disclose injuries to the league and the public, we don't have to specify the exact type so we usually share upper or lower body injury. Player privacy is an issue, but we also don't want to reveal weaknesses to other teams. Reporters will try to push, but there's a way around everything."

"Like you did. Can I just imitate you if that ever happens to me?" she asks with a hopeful smile.

"Of course. And if you aren't sure what to say you can always answer any question with a generic *I'll get back to you*. It covers everything."

"Good to know," she says as we walk down the hall, then turn the corner as Zaire—my boss—walks toward us, head high, cutting a powerful image as she strides down the hall. "How's everything going?"

"Great. We were just checking in with the press box before the game," I say, stopping when we reach her.

Zaire turns to Jenna. "And you're learning the ropes?"

She nods eagerly. "Everly is teaching me how to handle questions from the press."

"Excellent," Zaire says with a wry grin, then turns to me. "That's what we like here at the Sea Dogs. We pride ourselves on a mentorship-style workplace. And the biggest tip is working with reporters isn't that different from working with hockey players. It's all about managing the big egos."

"It sure is," I say.

"Speaking of," Zaire says, returning her focus to me. "Great work so far on the social media foundation. I reviewed the updates you sent over earlier. Step one looks great. Now that you're ready for step two, let's all have dinner with Max's agent and myself. We can make sure we're all set for step two."

"I'm there," I say without a second thought.

"Monday night?"

She names the time and I'll still be able to fit in drinks with Lucas beforehand. At least I know Zaire isn't trying to, well, cock-block me.

When she leaves, Jenna takes off for her cubicle, and I return to my office. Along the way, I spot the manager of promotions walking toward me. A clean-cut blond guy, Elias played hockey at his Massachusetts boarding school and for one year in college too—something he loves to remind me of. He's the poster boy for East Coast prep school guys who have uncles who are general counsels for the team. He wears an Oxford cloth shirt and khakis, and looks like he's off to play golf every time I see him.

"Hey, Ev. How's everything going in com?" he asks.

"Great," I say. "How's promo treating you?"

"Fan-freaking-tastic. It's the best. Soooo many fun things going on. I'll tell you all about them soon," he says. "Did you see that slapshot the captain made in Vegas? Not an easy one to make, and don't I know it."

"I'm sure you do," I say with a smile.

He gives me finger guns for some reason, then aims them toward the rink. "We're doing the T-shirt cannon tonight. Bam, bam!"

He works with Donna, the emcee who hosts the fan promo events during each intermission for our home games. "Fans love the cannon," I say.

"More than anything," he says.

Well, not more than hockey, but I don't correct him. He turns to leave, then spins back around. "Hey, did you hear about the new director opening?"

I square my shoulders. I have more experience. I have a great track record. He's only got a few years under his belt. Is he gunning for the post with those ridiculous pistol fingers? "Yes," I say, keeping my answer simple since I don't know why he's bringing it up.

"I bet you'd be great at it," he says, then leaves, and I'm left wondering if he means that or if he's angling for it too.

But I have to put him out of my mind, since there are a million other things I need to think about. Like the Max makeover, which is the key to me nabbing the job.

* * *

With less than three minutes to go in the game that night, Max lunges across the net to stop a ruthless shot from Montreal. He stretches so far I don't know how he's not pulling a muscle and winding up on the injury report for the next game. But he pops back up no problem and fresh excitement zips through my body, then an unexpected rush of tingles skate down my spine. I want to cheer. To thrust my arms in the air. That was a key play. But I'm working the press box tonight, and cheering is frowned on in here. I'm frowning on myself, too, because why the hell am I wanting to root for one guy when I work for the team?

Best not to think too hard on that as I leave with two

minutes on the clock, making my way to the ice level. When the game ends shortly with the Sea Dogs sealing the victory, I'm already waiting outside the tunnel, rounding up the crew for the post-game interviews. Max walks toward me, ripping off his helmet and shaking out his hair. It's sweaty at his temples.

"Nice save," I say, still a little tingly from the last play I saw, which turned out to be the final save of the game. "That last one."

"Thanks," he says, then shoots me a suspicious look. "Is that all?"

He's expecting me to bicker with him. To cajole him into talking to the press. But I like to keep him on his toes, so I don't do that tonight.

"That's all. I need to catch up with Asher," I answer, then pick up the pace till I reach the left winger a few feet ahead. "I hear you and Quinn have become sparring partners." Quinn's the equipment manager and a huge baseball fan.

Asher nods. "He's almost as vicious as the Reddit group members."

"That's what you want? Someone to fight you on baseball trivia?"

"Course. I'm a hockey player," he says. "I live to fight."

"As long as you're not fighting online from your burner account anymore."

"I can learn, Everly," he says.

"I appreciate it and you so much," I say, then continue down the hall. I'm pretty sure Max is watching me as I go. And I shouldn't check, but I can't resist. I turn my head, and yep. He's shooting me a final curious look before he heads into the locker room, like he isn't sure what to make of me.

I'm not sure either, especially since I'm looking forward to Thursday more than I should. I have no idea what he has planned, but I want to know him better.

* * *

On Thursday afternoon, Max leads me past dimly lit empty locker rooms and out toward a community ice rink, pointing to the stands. This place is nothing like the Sea Dogs state-of-the-art arena, with its high-backed vegan leather seats in every row. This run-down rink on the outskirts of Oakland has bleachers only. "Front row seats," he says with a wry grin. "Unless you want to help me coach today?"

It's asked with a challenge in his tone. A tease. "I'll watch, thanks."

"You do that," he says as I take a spot in the first row. A smattering of parents and caregivers are here, bundled up in hoodies, hunched over phones or books. Others are simply watching the action on the ice as their six-, seven-, and eight-year-olds lace up.

Max trots down to the bench where he quickly laces up too. He's wearing a warm-up suit, like the coaches usually wear for morning skate with the players since, well, it turns out he coaches young players. I had no idea. Of course I had no idea. But now he's showing me, and I'm a little gobsmacked.

A woman with long, dark hair sits next to him, striking up an easy conversation I can't hear. She wears a similar outfit and is lacing her skates.

I don't want to miss a second, so I lean forward, perched on the uncomfortable, metal seat as Max gets right into it on the ice with about a dozen or so kids.

"Who brought their A game today?" he asks in a not-so-scary voice.

A young boy waves his hockey stick, shouting, "Me!"

A girl about the same age weighs in with, "Me too."

More kids shout their *me too*.

The woman glides onto the ice. "That's what Coach Lambert and I like to hear. And you know the drill."

"Time for warm-ups," Max says, then pushes backward on his skates. It's an effortless move—one I've seen him do thousands of times on the ice. Except now he's not doing it in a professional rink, in front of twenty or thirty thousand fans who pay top dollar. He's doing it for kids. "Skating backward has to be as easy as skating forward."

"But it's so much easier to skate forward," one of the boys says, not quite whining but getting very close.

"Of course it is. That's because your brain wants to go that way," Max says, tapping the side of his head, talking to them so easily, like he spoke to his nephew the other week. "But the more you do it, the more your brain treats backward the same till you can do it just as well."

"I don't think my brain thinks like that, Coach Lambert," a girl with red curls flying out from under her helmet says.

Coach Lambert. That is too adorable. I'm smiling too big.

"You'll train it to, Hannah," he says. "And your body as well. You ready?"

They spin around, some awkwardly, some smoothly, and work on drills with Max and the woman as they skate backward. He's patient with each kid but also tough. He doesn't sugarcoat how hard the game is. He does talk up the rewards though—teamwork, fun, accomplishment.

"Don't worry. You'll all get the hang of it," he says,

spinning around and quickly shifting into crossovers, then stops. When they're done with the basic skating drills, Max moves them into relay races to warm them up.

He didn't even tell me where he was taking me this afternoon. He just said he'd pick me up at work, to expect a thirty-minute drive, and to wear a hoodie. But Max coaching kids the tricks of his trade in a rundown skating rink? Nope. Never had this on my radar screen. I don't want to take my eyes off the ice as they work on puck-handling drills, maneuvering past cones with their sticks.

Who knew?

I'm shaking my head, a little awed, a lot shocked. He's not the Max he is with me, teasing, goading, pushing. He's a different guy here—direct, encouraging, totally approachable.

I'm clutching my phone in my hands, feeling a little giddy, a little fizzy even. It would go such a long way if people knew he did this. How can he hide this? Why doesn't he tell his agent? Or Thrive? Or the team?

I lift my phone to take a pic of him at work—the approachable side of Max Lambert. The female coach is working with a group of kids on balance drills while Max is showing the kids how to keep the puck close to the stick. I capture this one and several more till a throat clears. Someone behind me shifts around, then clambers down two rows, parking next to me—a woman, dressed in a fleece, her eyes tired, but her smile kind. "Hey, I'm Becca. Just wanted to let you know we're not supposed to take pics."

"Oh," I say, chastened, and setting my phone down. "I didn't know."

"I figured as much. That's why I shared. Which one is yours? Mine is Hannah. The redhead. She wants to skate on a women's pro team someday but she's got a long way to go."

"Don't we all," I say, then return to her question. "And I don't have kids. I work with Max's team."

"Ah," she says, understanding dawning. "Got it. It's great that he does this when he's in town. Even with Coach Gupta here at all the practices." She nods toward the woman on the ice. She must be the regular coach. "But there's no way we could afford this without him."

Color me intrigued. "He pays for all this?"

"Covers the whole thing. The ice time, the gear, the training—everything. Coach Gupta's time too."

"Wow," I say.

She tilts her head. "You didn't know that?"

There's no point playing it cool. "I didn't."

"You learn something new every day," she says, seeming amused. But then her gaze is wary. "Is something changing here? Is that why they sent you?"

There's real concern in her voice. Like I could take this away. I glance down at my outfit—a Sea Dogs fleece but also charcoal gray slacks, low heels, and a tablet in hand. Briefly I wonder what I represent to her. Corporate America? Rules? The proper public image? Whatever it is, it's concerning to her. Somehow in her eyes, I might be the enemy that could end this lovely thing he does.

I shake my head. "He invited me," I say, opting for the easiest answer.

Her brow scrunches then slowly, like the sun rising, her lips part. "Oh. *Oh.* You're his—?" She's waiting for me to fill in the dots.

Vociferously, I shake my head. "No. God no. We just work together. That's all. It's actually frowned upon, dating a player. It can go all kinds of wrong. Management wouldn't like it. It's a rule. Well, an unwritten rule, but those are just as powerful. Since reputation matters," I say, and am I actually in PR? Does a professional sports organization truly pay me to craft and shape images and messages for a living, because I sound like I've never spoken in public before.

"Is that so?"

It's Max's deep, sexy voice. I snap my gaze to the edge of the rink and he's mere feet away from me by the boards, amusement dancing across his eyes while Coach Gupta works with the kids. "So this is forbidden, Everly? You and me hanging out like this?"

Becca snickers.

"Yes," I blurt, then shake my head because that was the wrong answer. He's got me flustered. *Again.* "No. It's not. I mean, they know. Of course they know I'm spending time with you. They gave me this assignment. Because it's work. That's all."

Becca covers her mouth with her hand, chuckling the whole time, then finally lowering it to say to Max, "I think someone has a crush on you." Only she's pointing at me like I don't know she's doing it.

I do not, I want to scream at her, but that'd make it worse.

Instead, Max cuts in, saying, "Don't worry, Becca. She actually hates me."

Then he winks at me. He fucking winks and skates backward, waving and blowing me a kiss.

I'm...mortified.

Becca's laughing.

And I feel out of place entirely.

As the practice continues, Becca excuses herself, presumably for the ladies' room. Once she's gone, a redheaded man with a freckled face appears at my bench. "Hey there. I'm Flynn, Jonah's dad," he says, then nods to one of the kids Max was coaching.

"Nice to meet you, Flynn," I say, and before I can get another word out, there's a spray of ice, then a giant hockey player has appeared at the boards right next to me.

"Flynn," Max says with a smile I don't quite buy. "Want to help me out today?"

Flynn's face lights up. "Yeah. Sure. I've been wanting to."

"I know. This seemed like the perfect time," he says.

Flynn turns to me. "We'll catch up later."

Max chuckles. "We'll be pretty busy," he says, then parks his elbow and waits for Flynn to leave the stands and head around to the ice.

He flashes me one more smile—the kind that says *I won*. This man is like a dog sometimes. Shame I like dogs so much.

* * *

When the kids finish a little later, Flynn is finishing up on the ice, having done nothing but move a few cones around. But Max keeps him busy putting cones away. Becca gathers her things, then says goodbye to me, adding, "I was just teasing. But if you did have a crush on Max, I'd understand."

"I don't," I say quickly. "It's strictly professional."

"Of course."

She sounds like she's placating me, but there's no point arguing with her so I smile weakly as she disappears inside the rink. Coach Gupta is gone too. And Flynn's disappeared as well.

Then, it's just Max and me. He's standing at the boards, resting his elbows on them, smiling smugly my way. "It's so professional, and I definitely don't know about your...*bralettes*." He says it like they're sexy magic. Well, they are. He lifts a curious brow. "Are you wearing one today? Or maybe a lavender bra like you did at sushi?"

Does he have eagle ears as well as eagle eyes? "You remember the bra I was wearing?" I ask, when the real question should be *how does he know which one I was wearing?*

"Fuck yes," he says, unapologetic.

"H-how?"

"Is that a real question?" His eyes are heated as they roam up and down me. "I remember my favorite things."

Like *my* lingerie? Or *all* lingerie? But those aren't questions I can ask. "I meant how did you know what bra I was wearing?" Then I hold up a hand. I shouldn't go fishing for this intel. I shouldn't know if he's wanting me the way I want him. It's better if I don't figure it out. "Forget it. I shouldn't have asked."

"Relax, sunshine. Your shirt sloped down your shoulder for a hot second when we got sushi. I caught a glimpse of the strap—that was all." After a moment, he adds, "Your right shoulder."

He knows the left one is the one I touch sometimes. He doesn't know it has the scar though. But he seems to have sensed I'm cautious about it. "Oh. Okay," I say, unsteady and I'm not sure why, but I feel like I'm walking across a ship's deck in choppy waters.

"It was nice," he adds, but *nice* comes out like *hot*. Or maybe like *I want to fuck you.* Or maybe that's where my brain keeps going lately with him. I do my best to shake off this haze of lust. Trying to get my bearings, I focus on why I'm here and lift my phone. "She said there's a no picture rule. Becca did," I add.

"That's true."

Which means I'm even more confused. I cut to the chase. "Why did you invite me?"

"You didn't like it?" He sounds genuinely hurt.

"I did. I loved it," I say, truthfully. "I just..." I shrug. "I'm thrown off. I thought you were showing me something we could..." But I swallow the word *use*. It feels wrong to say that right now.

"To use?" he supplies, a hint of irritation in his tone.

"I want to help you with this project," I say, pleading somewhat. Sure, he's infuriating, but I truly want to improve his image. "That's the point."

"I want you to," he says, curling his big hands over the boards. "That's why I brought you here."

I raise my hands, helpless. "I'm not getting it."

He drags a hand through that wild, messy hair. "You asked me who I really am. I said I'd show you. So I brought you here," he says, his tone stripped bare. He blows out a breath then glances around, gesturing to the space. "This is who I really am, but I don't want this to be something you use. I want this to be something I keep for myself. I don't do this to fix my image. I do this for those kids," he says, glancing toward the exits, even though the children are long gone. When he returns his gaze to me, his blue eyes hold a new vulnerability. "I know what it's like to be those kids whose parents worry about how to pay for a sport. I don't have those worries anymore. So I do this." He pauses for a few seconds, then adds in a quieter voice, "I know I need to be open and shit. To let people see who I am. And I get it. I dug this hole and all. I have the shitty likability quotient. And I have to fix it, so

I'm trying. But this is the one thing that's mine. That isn't up for negotiation. This is for the kids."

I do understand why he brought me here. He wanted me to know this part of him. The part he's not going to share with the world. My heart feels squishy in a way it hasn't in a long time. I hold up the phone and one by one delete the pics, but stop at the last one. It's a little boy skating backward, looking up at the star goalie as if to say, *Am I doing it right?*

I show it to Max. "Can I keep this for myself?"

"For when I'm a dick and you need a reminder I'm not?"

"Something like that," I say.

"Sure," he says, then nods to the exit, a sign we're done. But instead, he says, "Flynn's a nice guy."

I laugh lightly. "Should I have lunch with him then?"

His smile vacates the premises. His eyes darken. "No."

Well, that's even more clear now. He'll stop dates with guys he dislikes and guys he approves of. Max nods to the ice. "You want to skate?"

I shake my head. "Oh, no. I babysit hockey players. I don't skate."

"C'mon," he goads.

I shake it again. "Nope."

"One new thing to try. Say yes, Everly," he says, and just like that I'm back in time again. Marie's favorite words. The thing she said when she asked me to take a pole class with her on a Post-it note. She was always leaving Post-it notes around the apartment we shared.

Want to go to the movies tonight? Say yes.

Want to grab a glass of wine after work? Say yes.

Want to take a pole dance class? Say yes.

I said yes.

And then a car slammed into us when I was turning left, hitting the passenger side head-on with a horrifying crunch, sending my head snapping back, and the car fishtailing into a truck. The sounds and the sirens and the machines and the hospital come rushing back to me, like it's happening all over again. The noises, the surgeries, the burns, and the news.

The awful, terrifying news.

I look away from Max, focusing on my breathing. Cataloging the surroundings.

The net is made of twine and red metal.

The ice is cold and scraped up from practice.

The metal benches have grooves in them.

The scoreboard. It's a deep red, with *home* and *visitors* painted in bold white writing.

And there's one more thing I can see. Right in front of me—there's Max, with real concern etched in his eyes. But I'm okay. I'm here. I'm alive. I'm not trapped in that car, or feeling my heart rip out of my chest as I say goodbye to the person who was like a sister to me. I kept all her Post-it notes in a little wooden box in my bedroom.

I want to say yes to Max's offer to skate. I said yes to the sushi. I said yes to the naked bike ride. But there are practical matters. "Yes, but I don't have my skates," I say, gesturing to my heels.

His lips quirk up, like he wasn't expecting that answer. "You have skates?" The question's asked with surprise. Maybe wonder.

"Max, I work for a hockey team. Of course I have skates."

"Then...raincheck?"

My chest warms. "Raincheck."

16

A LITTLE LADY BONER

Everly

He drives me back into the city, tossing me a look as we cross over the Bay Bridge and the sparkly blue water below. "I do appreciate what you're doing for me," he says, earnestly. "I know I don't show that much though."

"Much?"

"Fine. At all," he admits, then sighs. "I know I haven't made it easy for you."

"With your game of chicken?"

"Our game," he tosses back as we exit the bridge, heading into the city now.

"Fine. It's our game."

"And you play it too, sunshine."

I hold up my hands in surrender. "I do."

He slows at a light, then looks my way. "What I'm trying to say is I know this is extra work for you...I wanted you to know I'm not just a jerk."

I cup my ear. "What did you just say?"

"I'm not just a jerk," he repeats in a grumble.

"What are you then?"

He's quiet, refusing to speak.

I lean a little closer, stage-whispering, "A nice guy?"

He flashes his gaze to me, his eyes smoldering as he stares me down. "You don't want me to be nice."

My breath catches. My thighs clench. Maybe I don't. But I'm not telling him that. "It was nice of you to let me in though."

The light changes, and he drives, saying nothing for several blocks. As we near my home in Russian Hill, he clears his throat, like he's gearing up for something hard. "Letting people in isn't my strong suit. Especially after... Lyra."

My heart lurches toward him. "Do you still love her?"

He scoffs. "Fuck no."

"Do you miss her?"

"Not one bit," he says, resolute. "But everything we did was so public. It was all out there. Bane knew where I had taken her on dates. He knew what we were up to. When I was visiting her, when I left. She was the one who cheated, but he was the one who used what he knew about me to seize an opportunity. That's why I don't want to put my real self out there."

Fletcher Bane. A forward on the Los Angeles team. The guy he got in that fight with. The guy who threw the first punch that night. The guy who was then seen dating Lyra a few days later.

Bane and Max go way back. They were drafted the same year. They were top prospects in the league together —the best goalie in years, the best forward in years. They were rivals for media attention even though they played different positions.

While I knew about Lyra and Bane's relationship, this is the first time Max has said out loud that his ex-girlfriend cheated on him with his longtime rival. I understand him more now. His retreat from the public eye makes even more sense than it did before, and pisses me off on his behalf too.

"That's terrible," I say, anger rising up in me over what must have happened.

Max doesn't sound angry though. As he pulls up outside my building and cuts the engine, he sounds remarkably fine as he says, "It is but I'm over it. I learned my lesson though."

And I'm pushing him to be public. Yes, I have to. Yes, he needs to be more accessible. But I can see now why he resists so hard. "I understand why you want to keep some things private. Most things, actually," I say, but a thought tugs on my brain. "No one really knows she was unfaithful. Everyone thinks you were a jerk because of that song —'Surprise Me.' You never corrected that notion. Why?"

He shrugs, like *what can you do.* "The song came out three months after she cheated. I wasn't going to get online and say, *hey world, she banged another dude.* There was no winning in that situation."

I nod, my heart heavy. "I get that." I set a hand on his arm. "I've got your back."

He swallows roughly, nodding. "I know you do."

Then his gaze drifts to my hand curled around his biceps, then back up to my face. He looks at my mouth, his breath ghosting across his lips, it seems. When he meets my eyes, something flickers across his.

Want.

Heat.

A wish.

Or maybe I'm the one wishing for things I can't have. "I should go," I say, and as I unlock the door and head inside I keep wondering if I should go on that date with Lucas next week.

Which means I really need girl time. Good thing tomorrow night, I've planned to go to pole class.

* * *

Not going to lie—when I first walked into a pole class a year and a half ago, it was hard. For a lot of reasons. First and foremost, I was supposed to have gone with Marie. We were five blocks away from the studio she'd picked out when that car hit us. It took me eighteen months and some serious therapy to decide to try again.

But I knew I had to give it a go.

That Post-it note from my best friend was branded not just on my brain, but in my heart.

Want to take a pole dance class? Say yes.

We never reached the studio and walked in together. The first time I walked into this studio alone, I had to practice one of my grounding exercises to get through the door. What are five things I see? The door, the name of the studio, the railing along the steps, the chrome poles in the studio, and the other women. What are four things I hear? The faint beat of music from inside, the rumble of the bus down the street, the click of shoes along the sidewalk as people walked by, and the creak of the door as someone exited the studio. I worked my way through three things I felt, two things I smelled, one thing I tasted, and with my heart beating in the next county, I found the guts to make it inside, then walked around a pole.

I didn't fall in love with pole right away. But I kept

going, and by the time I did my first front hook spin, I had one surprising thought—this is fun.

Then a second thought—I wasn't meant to do this alone.

So I invited Josie, knowing deep down that pole was something I was supposed to do with my friends. The women I leaned on, and who leaned on me. Josie didn't take too much convincing. She doesn't come as often as I do—she's here maybe once a week to my three—but she's become a regular.

Soon she'll probably be able to do moves that I can't do.

Correction: *won't* do.

The thing about pole I didn't realize when I walked into Upside Down is that it's not a sport for the body shy. Most of the advanced tricks require a whole lot of skin contact and, of all things, your armpit.

But I've always found workarounds in my life, in my job, and now in pole. There are so many tricks I can do that don't require me to use my sides or my armpit to hold on. So many that don't require me to show my back.

Like the stargazer. God bless this trick. It's all core and legs and strength, and I've got that as I hold onto the pole with my legs and one hand while reaching the other hand behind me toward the wall as I stretch back, eyes toward the ceiling.

"Nice work," the instructor, Kyla, says as she stops next to me. "Loved your jasmine, too, earlier."

She already told me that when I nailed that intermediate trick—it takes the back of the knee contact, hands and core. But I love praise so as I move out of the stargazer pose, I say, "Thanks. I've been working on the jasmine for a while."

"I know, and you did it, Everly," she says, proud, like she usually is for all her students.

Still, I have this foolish worry that she'll ask why I dress like this eighteen months in. Does she wonder why I wear a fitted tee that doesn't move when I move, when the rest of the class wears sports bras?

Like Josie.

Like Maeve, who takes it too with us.

Like Fable, who joins us from time to time.

But I still wear a shirt, because of my scars.

Kyla's also never asked. She lets me be. She lets me take the tricks at my own pace, like she does with all the students, of all body types. But as Kyla moves to spot another student, a woman with blue hair and strong shoulders who's upside down in a butterfly, a pang of longing digs into my chest. I bet I could do that if I let go. I *want* to do that.

Maybe I should just get my own pole for my home. I could do it there. The only issue would be if I needed a spotter.

Best not to think about that for now. There are plenty of laybacks and spins to keep this girl busy for a while.

I hope.

Class ends, and I hustle to my gym bag and pull on sweats, leaving on the workout tee. No heels tonight, so I just pop on sneakers, thank Kyla and head out with my friends.

They know why I dress like this. I've told them about the car accident, and the scars that travel down the left side of my body, covering a large swath of my back, my hip, my upper arm, and my shoulder.

I don't hate them. I just don't want people to see them and stare. To see them and feel sorry for me. I'd rather not have their pity. I had enough of it from my own parents after it happened. "I feel terrible this happened to you. I don't know what I'd do if I lost my best friend, and some of my skin," my mom had said.

Thanks, Mom.

Besides, I work in a world where image matters. I don't want people to construct their own image of me as someone to feel sorry for.

And then, there's simple self-protection. The more people who see them, the more I have to tell the story of *why*. The more I have to go back in time and relive the worst night of my life and feel that pain all over again.

Sometimes—no, most of the time—it's easier to cover them up and move on.

We head out into the October night to a nearby diner, the one we usually go to after class.

"I seriously can't believe you got me addicted to pole," Maeve remarks as she pulls open the door.

"Really? You can't believe it?" Josie asks Maeve. "Pole was made for you."

"Why's that?" I ask.

"Because our dear friend Maeve is not, as you might say, shy," Josie says.

"Facts," I say, then tell the hostess we need a table for four. As we slide in, I'm feeling a little emotional, like I often am after class with them, since I'm so damn grateful to have friends to do this with, so I add, "And I'm glad none of you are shy either. I'm really glad you all said yes to taking this class with me."

"Of course we would," Josie says, heartfelt.

"Are you kidding? Like I'd miss the chance to make a fool of myself physically," Fable says.

"Please. You're doing great. You're making such strides," I say to my redheaded friend.

"If by strides you mean I can walk around a pole in heels without tripping, then yes, sure I have."

"Do not underestimate not tripping," I say.

"Truer words," Maeve adds, then we flip open our menus and order when the server arrives.

Once she's gone, Josie taps the table, her eyes excited. "So, update time. How's the makeover project going with the man who's, ahem, *admittedly handsome*?"

Maeve scoffs, waving a hand. "I want to know how the dick project's going."

I furrow my brow. Does she mean because Max is a dick? Or something else? "Am I doing a dick project?"

She stares at me like I should know. "You were supposed to check out the guy's dick. Your physical therapist."

A laugh bursts from me but it's chased by a kernel of guilt I've been feeling today. I'm not even sure how to deal with it, but I don't have friends to keep things from them. "I'm seeing Lucas in a few days. But is it weird that I feel sort of...uncertain?"

"No, it's a date. If you didn't feel uncertain that'd be weird," Josie says.

But that's not it. I'm not experiencing normal dating nerves. "It's more like..." I pause, take a breath, then confess, "I keep having really inappropriate thoughts about the man who's *admittedly handsome*."

Maeve sets her chin in her hand.

Josie bats her lashes.

Fable gazes at me eagerly. "Well, well, well."

"I know," I whisper-groan. "So should I cancel with Lucas?"

"Is something happening with Max?" Josie asks.

I shake my head. Only in my late-night fantasies. And my daydreams. "Just up here," I say, tapping my temple. "But that's all."

"And is something going to happen?" Fable inquires.

I picture Zaire encouraging me to apply for the promotion. I imagine Clementine telling me it's a bad idea to date a player, because it is. I think about the unwritten rule. There are so many reasons not to get involved with an athlete—top among them, it could detract from my ability to do my job.

Like what would happen if it went south? How would the media perceive me if word got out? Would they still trust me, respect me, talk to me?

There are so many cautionary tales from around pro sports of situations like this, and spoiler alert: The woman rarely comes out unscathed. The guy almost always does.

I see my future—the one I'm lucky to have. The one I want to grasp and hold onto. I want to learn and grow and improve. I'm so fortunate to be alive.

When I woke up in the hospital room after the accident, I made a promise—to live my best life. For me, but also for those who couldn't.

That means *not* throwing away what I've worked for. Not losing sight of what I've built. I need to do things right. I need to say yes to the right things—not the tempting things. Indulging in *anything* with a hockey player on the team I work for would be too risky. Max is already a complicated enough project.

I can't blow this job on a few tingles in my chest. "No," I say, certain, strong.

"Then I say it's a fine idea to go out with someone else

to explore what it might be, even if you have a little bit of a lady boner for someone else," Josie says.

"Sounds like it's not really a *little* lady boner," Maeve says dryly.

I roll my eyes, but she's not wrong. "But nothing is happening with Max. And nothing is going to happen with him."

Fable tilts her head. "This date is exactly what you need then."

And the more I think about that, the more convinced I am she's right.

Later that day when I'm home and my parents call on speakerphone, my mom's first question is if we're still on for our breakfast next weekend (of course). Her second is how's work going (great), and her third question is whether I'm seeing anyone new.

Good thing I'm not on FaceTime. "No. I've been busy," I say.

"Never too busy for love," she chirps.

"Not true, sweetheart," Dad corrects.

My shoulders tighten. Every cell tenses.

"Russ, it is true," Mom says cheerily to him, like I'm not even here, but that's fine. It's totally fine.

"It's true if you pick wisely," Dad says. "Not everyone does that. Isn't that right, Everly?"

What a leading question. What a dig. I swallow the hurt but don't acknowledge the way it cuts. "How's everything at the firm, Dad?" I ask, and turn the conversation around back on him.

I don't want to discuss romance with them. Ever. Or really, much of anything.

* * *

On Monday night, I study my lingerie drawer, considering my options for tonight. Lucas won't see them, but that's not the point. The lingerie is for me. I pick up a few lacy bras and hold them in front of my body in the scalloped mirror in my bedroom. A sheer tulle demi bra, pale yellow with purple lace edging. It's unconventional. A dark blue bustier. That one's elegant. Then, a pale aqua demi bra that's so see-through the color barely matters. It's covered with embroidered roses and it's called a balconette. I don't know why it has that name, but I don't care.

It makes me feel pretty and powerful, so I slip on the set, then grab a black silk blouse and a dark gray skirt. Perfect for my business dinner later, and it'll work for the date too. I catch a Lyft to The Spotted Zebra, my chest flipping with nerves.

Date nerves this time.

It's normal to be nervous before a date. Of course it is. We only have an hour, and I want to make the most of it. Then I'll need to head over to the dinner with Max, his agent, and my boss. It'll be good to have a start and an end. Good for both Lucas and me.

When I reach the trendy bar in Hayes Valley, I clear my thoughts, focusing only on the here and now as I swing the door open and quickly find Lucas.

He smiles, a bright, warm greeting. He's at a table in the corner, and he pops up, runs a hand through his sandy brown hair, then offers that hand in greeting when I reach him. "Actually, wait. Can we hug instead of shake?"

I smile. "I think we know each other well enough to hug."

He gives me a quick one, patting me on the back. It's nice, this hug. I'm not feeling sparks, but who feels sparks from a hug?

I sit, setting my purse next to me on the zebra-print booth by the window that looks out on the street. "I have to do a work thing later," I say, explaining the big work bag.

"Totally get it," he says. "I have a thing too."

Does he though? What would he have at night? But then I tell myself not to be suspicious. To be present. To be engaged.

He asks if I want a drink, and I opt for an iced tea since I don't want to show up tipsy to a work dinner. After he orders, he shoots me a grin. "How's everything going? What have you been up to?"

We chat for several minutes, catching up on life, then trading book and movie recs, but when I'm about to ask him if he's seen the newest episode of *The Dating Games*— a show we were both addicted to when I worked with him —the words die on my tongue.

Since my gaze catches on a man crossing the street.

It's Max, and he's headed this way.

17

JUST A LITTLE SABOTAGE

Max

Almost there.

The destination is in my crosshairs.

My sister shoots me a suspicious look as we cross the street. "Where are we going?"

"Just to grab a drink. That's all," I say as casually as I can, given my secret mission.

She hums doubtfully. "You never call and ask me to grab a drink on a random weeknight."

"Can't a brother take his little sister out after work? It was a long day, right?"

"I'm a nurse. It's always a long day," she says.

"Then it's a good thing I called," I say. "Even better that Kade's on a playdate."

Better still because it means Sophie's here in the city hanging out for another hour, which ties in perfectly with my pre-dinner-meeting plans. Better yet because I've got a wingwoman. "In fact, I'd call it kismet."

She snort-laughs. "Kismet, Max? It's kismet, you asking me to go to The Spotted Zebra instead of, say, McCoy's?"

That's the bar near the urgent care where she works. I shoot her a don't-be-silly look. "You don't want to run into colleagues, do you?"

She points to the pink neon sign for The Spotted Zebra, twenty or thirty feet away now. "This is a trendy bar. A date bar. They have fancy craft cocktails. It's not a hang-out-with-your-sister bar. You're up to something, Max Lambert. Mark my words. I will find out," she says.

She's right. She probably will figure it out. But I don't care. Right now I care about one thing—checking out Everly's date. No way is he the right guy for her.

Like when I'm on the ice, I've got blinders on. I'm single-minded in my mission.

Stop. That. Date.

When I reach the door of The Spotted Zebra, I yank it open, then scan the establishment. There they are, at a table by the window. My jaw ticks. I clamp my molars down. He looks sooo fucking nice, and I hate him on principle.

I march over to the hostess. "We'll grab a seat at the bar, please," I say. *Naturally, I'll stop by her table first, but I don't need to reveal the details to the hostess.*

"Of course," she says, but as we're heading over there, I look toward Everly's table the whole time, waiting, just waiting for her to catch my eye.

Doesn't take long—all of two seconds till she's looking my way.

Like she wants to kick me in the balls. Her annoyance only stokes the flame inside me.

A hand curls around my forearm. "Max." My sister's tone is low and dripping with accusation. "She's why you came here."

I turn to her, grinning like a sly fox. "You think so?"

She shakes her head. "What are you doing?"

"Just saying hi," I say, then I beeline for the table, flashing my best PR smile, my sister trailing behind me. Bonus? I can prove to Everly that I can be a nice guy for the press. I can put on an act. She'll be pleased.

I channel Asher, or Miles, as I say, "Hey, Everly. How the heck are you?"

Her lips part, but she says nothing, just closes them into a tight, angry smile. But she's also the queen of putting on a good face, since in seconds she slides on her happy mask. "Great. How are you, Max?"

"Fantastic," I say, selling it to the jury. "What a surprise to see you here. My sister and I were just grabbing a drink."

I can feel my sister roll her eyes rather than see it. I turn to my nemesis. "Max Lambert. With the Sea Dogs. Nice to meet you," I say, then stick out a hand toward the guy with the woman who I think about far too much.

He stands and shakes. "Good to meet you, Max. Lucas Evans...with Golden Gate Health Center and Services."

I flinch, but only for a second. The dude's in health care. I didn't see that coming. Also, he's not easily intimidated. But that doesn't mean she should date him. That doesn't mean a thing. I shove those thoughts aside and check out the table. He's got a beer, and she has...an Arnold Palmer?

"Your drink looks good. What have you got there, Ev?"

She squares her shoulders. "It's called an iced tea. It

has…tea and ice in it," she deadpans, with faux pleasantry. She's more pissed than I'd thought.

But I'm not easily deterred. "I'll have to try one then," I say, then glance around. "This is such a nice place. I've never been here before."

"How did you hear about it then?" she asks, the clever genius trying to nail me.

I shrug, then scratch my beard. "Googled places nearby."

"How convenient," she says, sarcastic. Then she turns to my sister, her tone genuine as she says, "It's good to see you, Sophie."

"You too," my sister says.

I turn to the golden guy who's dating Everly. Maybe he's a doctor. Instantly, I loathe him more. That means she likes brainy guys, rather than guys who work with their bodies. "So, you're in health care?"

He furrows his brow, perhaps taken aback. Maybe it's a pushy question, but whatever. The dude quickly shifts to a smile though, answering easily, "Yes, I'm a physical therapist and help patients recover from injury or surgery."

Fuuuuck. Is he the guy who helped her with…her car accident? I bet he is. And it's official. No need to ask Reddit. *I am the asshole.* I swallow, then hitch my thumb behind me. "I'll let you—"

"Did you want to join us?" Lucas asks, tilting his head. "Sounds like you two know each other well."

Everly was right. He *is* a nice guy. But the fact that he said that—*want to join us*—means he's also not right for her. Whether I'm the asshole or not, I jump on the chance faster than I'd slap a puck away from the net. "Yes," I say before Everly can say no.

We join Everly on her date. Date-crashing achieved.

Across the table, the blonde beauty with the big brown eyes stares at me like she wants to kill me. Well, she already hates me, so what else is new? But I know this—I did the right thing joining her.

"Why don't I call the server over? So you two can order?" Lucas offers.

"Great idea," I say.

Lucas flags the woman down, and I order a pale ale while Sophie opts for a soda. When the server leaves, Sophie smiles apologetically and says to the table, "I have to pick up my son in a little bit. He has a playdate."

"How is Kade doing?" Everly asks, focusing all her energy on my sister.

"He's great. They're making homemade playdough so I suspect that means *I'll* be making homemade playdough with him this weekend," she says.

"I would count on that for sure," Lucas says, chiming in, then turning to me. "So, how's your team doing so far this season? I have to admit I don't follow hockey that closely. I'm more of a football fan myself."

"I love football," Everly coos. "It's so much more strategic than hockey, don't you think, Lucas?"

He blinks, maybe surprised that a publicist for a hockey team would say such a thing. I'm not confounded though. That comment was a dig at me, and I fucking love that because it says I'm under her skin. Good, because she's burrowed so deep under mine.

"Football has definitely got some great plays to it," Lucas says, diplomatic.

"But hockey's more of a thrill," I say, locking eyes with Everly. "The adrenaline rush. The faster pace. The break-neck speed."

"Speed isn't everything," Everly retorts, those brown eyes saying she is going to lay into me later.

Bring it on, sunshine.

"Truer words," Sophie says, cutting in and playing the peacemaker. "But I do like both. *Equally.*"

I ignore my sister. I've got a game to win with the woman who drives me wild. I keep my gaze locked entirely on Everly. "I read an article that said the average football play lasts four seconds. But the average amount of continuous play in hockey is forty seconds. Which means...hockey lasts longer," I say, full of innuendo.

"But on the other hand," Everly counters, "football players can't be drafted till they're three years removed from high school. Which means they're more...*grown up* than hockey players," she says with a sweet smile as she delivers a beautiful dig.

"In hockey the refs never give you the puck after the other team scores, like they do in football. On the ice, you have to fight for it," I say, and this guy? He'd never fight for her. I know that for a fact.

"In hockey, you don't need much skill. All you do is wave a stick," Everly counters.

I see her bid and I raise the ante one more time. "And finally, the hockey season lasts twenty-six weeks, not including playoffs. Football is eighteen weeks. Ergo, hockey players have more stamina." Crossing my arms, I rest my case.

"You both make great points," Sophie says as the server returns with the drinks.

Once we thank her, I take a sip of my beer.

Lucas shoots Everly a serious look, then me, before he blows out a breath. "I have to ask," he says, pausing to lick his lips, then to laugh, almost apologetically. "Did you two date?"

I nearly spit-take my beer.

Everly coughs. "No. Never."

"Tell me how you really feel," I counter.

"Because I'm getting a vibe," Lucas adds.

"Funny, Lucas. I get that vibe too," Sophie says pointedly.

"We definitely did not date," Everly says, then finishes her tea, takes a breath, and peppers Sophie and Lucas with questions for the next thirty minutes till the date mercifully ends.

I push back first, slap down a hundred to pay the bill for the table, then say goodbye, heading to the street with my sister. Once we're outside, she pokes my chest. "We are going to talk about what you did."

"Yes, Mom," I say, but I don't make a move to leave yet to drop her off at Kade's friend's home. I watch the door, waiting for Everly. They leave a few seconds later, waving goodbye awkwardly, then Lucas walks down the street the other way.

As Sophie waits for me, I trot over to Everly, gesturing to my car down the block. "Want a ride to dinner?"

She breathes fire. "Are you kidding me? I do not want a ride. I'm calling a Lyft."

"I have my car. Let me drive you."

"I'd rather walk barefoot," she seethes as she taps open the app.

"Everly," I say. "We're going to the same restaurant."

"Don't *Everly* me," she hisses as she orders her ride, then stares me down. "Why did you do that?"

"Because he's wrong for you," I say with no remorse. "And I knew it the second he invited me to join you."

"I guess I'll never know now though if he is," she snaps, and seconds later, a red Honda pulls up. She gets inside and slams the door.

On the one hand, she doesn't just hate me. She loathes me till the end of time. On the other hand, she's not having a second date with him.

I'll chalk that up as a win.

18

THE MAX EFFECT

Everly

I'm so ticked off, I'm experiencing the Max Effect. Side effects of prolonged exposure to bossy, overbearing men who think they know what's good for you might include a rage spiral.

Except I can't afford to rage spiral. I need to calm down before dinner with my boss and Max's agent. I have to act like I don't want to throat-punch the star athlete.

On the ride over, I close my eyes and try to let go of my irritation as best I can. By the time I'm a block away, I feel somewhat human, but my brain keeps playing Max's words on a loop: *Because he's wrong for you.*

I hate that he's right.

I hate that I didn't feel the chemistry with Lucas *before* Max barreled into the bar and sabotaged my evening. I already knew there wasn't going to be a third date before he showed up, but I hate, too, that I was secretly excited when Max arrived.

What is wrong with me? I can hear my father's voice slithering in my ear with an answer. *Well, you've always had bad taste in men, honey.*

I try to drown out the comment he made when my last romance went south a few months in. My dad's right though. I don't pick well. I have the track record of failed romance to show for it. I'm nearly thirty, and I've never had a non-toxic relationship.

But at least I'm good at my job, so I vow to focus on that as I arrive at Kitchen Mosaic, an upscale fusion restaurant in the Financial District. It's the kind of place where the city's high rollers take clients to seal deals. After I thank the driver, I hop out of the car and go inside, taking a deep, centering breath before I tell the host I'm joining the Emerson party of four.

Except it's a party of seven, she informs me.

I roll with the change. When I arrive at the table, Max's agent is here, and he's brought two people from the agency. He makes quick intros to a woman named Rosario and a man named John. Zaire's here too. I wasn't expecting Clementine to come but the general manager's at the table as well. I really need to stay calm.

"Good to see you both," I say as I sit.

"I had the night free, so I decided to join," Clementine says cooly.

Translation: this meeting was too important to miss.

And my job is too important to lose my head over because of a guy. "Glad everyone is here, except for the man of honor," I say, and maybe I couldn't resist taking a dig at Max for being late. But he deserves it.

A few minutes later, the troublemaking goalie breezes in, looking stylish and sexy in tailored charcoal pants that hug his strong legs and a royal blue shirt that does unfair things to his strong chest and thick arms. He's wearing team colors. Smart move.

At the bar he was wearing jeans and a polo. He cleaned up even more for dinner with all the stakeholders, and I'm annoyingly impressed. He's striding to the table like he owns the place, all cool confidence and with barely a smile—just his trademark intensity, wild hair, and icy eyes. That's the way he walks through the corridor in the arena before a game, wearing his game-day suit, looking like sex and strength.

My pulse beats faster. My body is such a traitor.

When he reaches us, he says, "Thanks for waiting. I had to drop my sister at her son's friend's house."

I refrain from rolling my eyes. Of course he's angling for I-help-with-my-cute-nephew empathy points.

"That's always lovely to hear," Clementine says.

"Good to see you, my man," Garrett puts in, standing and clapping his client's back.

Max sits, snagging the empty seat across from me. The seven of us make small talk about the restaurant, the weather, and the menu until it's time to order.

I refuse to look at Max. I can't. I can't afford the brand of trouble he brings to my heart and body. Once the server has left Garrett clears his throat, then looks my way. "Everly, before you arrived, we were all chatting. The social looks great. You've done a fantastic job in just a few weeks building it out."

"Yes. It even looks like you're having fun, Max," Zaire remarks with a pleased grin. In addition to the circus, bike ride, and post-game shots, I instructed him to take a picture of the football field when he went to a Renegades game on the weekend, as well as the view of the Golden Gate Bridge from his home. He sent me both and

I posted them too. They don't show his face, but that's fine.

Rosario sits straighter, shifting toward her client. "And we've run some tests and already your likability quotient is ticking up a notch or two."

"Great," Max says dryly. "Gotta keep that thermometer at the bank rising higher."

John smiles. "This is a promising start."

"It is. We adore *The Real Max Lambert*," Clementine says to Max. "You've done a great job."

He's done a great job? Are you kidding me? I did all that. But as a publicist, my role is to stay in the background, to let others shine, so I do my part to praise the star too. "Max has really been helpful at being open and available. He's made it easy."

Lies, tell me sweet little lies.

But rather than finding a way to subtly zing me, the man getting the makeover offers me a thoughtful smile, then turns to the others. "Actually, Everly's the one who's done a great job. I have to give her all the credit," he says earnestly. "She's a delight to work with. She's come up with every single idea. She arranges the events. She plans the photos. She writes the posts. Any increase in the LQ is entirely her doing."

What???

Am I in a time warp? Did he just compliment me in front of the GM *and* my boss? I stare at him like an alien has taken over his body. "Thank you," I say, thrown off but delighted all the same.

Zaire smiles proudly. "Everly is terrific at what she does. I'm so glad you're working well together."

"She's the one who makes it easy," Max says, then sighs, a little apologetically. "I know I've made a lot of this hard for all of you, but putting Everly on this project is what's bringing it all together. She deserves all the credit." He rubs his palms together. "So what's next?"

Holy shit.

I want to hate him, but I want to kiss him too. What is wrong with me?

We spend the next hour of the dinner talking about the community outreach that I'll be overseeing for him for the next month—the meat of the makeover. I've already planned the first event with a local animal rescue I love working with, and it's coming up in another week, after a stretch of away games. I'm calling it Dogs on Ice because I couldn't resist that name. I tell Max the details of the event —we're hosting the rescue's dogs up for adoption—and even though it'll be fun, it'll also be harder, busier, and more challenging for him than usual since it's so, obviously, public.

"You'll have to talk to the press," I say, reminding him.

Max nods in acceptance. "I'm ready."

What universe am I living in where Max is being agreeable? I don't even know.

As the meal nears its end, I push back and excuse myself for the ladies' room. After I freshen up, I touch up my lipstick in the mirror, then head back into the narrow hallway, stopping short when I spot Max. Hard to miss him. He's leaning against the brick wall across from the ladies' room.

Waiting for me. Looking like every sexy mistake I want to make.

"Everly," he says, like this is important, whatever he's about to say. "I'm sorry you're pissed at me, but I'm not sorry I crashed your date."

I groan. Here he goes again, being infuriating. "Why do you do this?"

"Do what?"

I flap my hand toward the end of the hallway, indicating the table around the corner where we just met with everyone who matters to our jobs. "Do something nice like what you said at the table, then return to saying this stuff? This *I know what's good for you* crap."

"Because it's true. You and Lucas weren't even into each other."

"That's not really for you to decide," I say.

He steps closer, his gaze narrowed. "He invited my sister and me to join your date."

"He was being nice! Ever heard of it?"

Max crowds me, his heated eyes holding mine, his body so dangerously close I catch a hint of the bold and spicy Midnight Flame. Chili pepper and cedar and wild nights. I didn't smell that at The Spotted Zebra. Did he splash it on while driving over? Did he do it for me? Change for me to look even more tempting? I don't understand him. I don't understand myself either and why my body reacts to him. The way he looks at me is unfairly alluring.

I'm aching.

And he's shaking his head, like he can't believe I said Lucas was nice. Max lifts a hand, reaches for the collar of my black blouse, and runs a finger gently along the silk, barely touching my skin but lighting me up all at the same time. "For the record, if I took you out, I'd never invite anyone to join my date with you."

I'm thrown off by that statement, the intensity of it, the passion of it. I don't have a comeback, but he doesn't seem to need one since he keeps going. "Besides, drinks is a cop-out. He should take you to dinner. He should drive you home. He should walk you to your door. He should make sure you get inside safely. But before he does that, he should devastate you with a kiss like he can't fucking breathe if he doesn't kiss you."

Forget aching. I'm outrageously aroused. My breath catches. But I say nothing still as he lets go of my shirt, finishing with, "I would never share you."

I'm so off-kilter, because Max is so close to me, the hallway is so narrow, my boss is in the other room, and yet I'm not walking away from the very bad idea of him. "What if I like nice guys?" I counter.

He pins me with his gaze. "You don't."

"You don't know what I like."

He smirks. "I think I do though."

A dish rattles from somewhere in the restaurant, breaking the heated moment. I swirl around and return to the table, putting on a fake front for the rest of the meal.

Fake because it hides this unbridled desire ricocheting through me as those words echo in my mind.

I would never share you.

When the meal ends, I say goodbye to everyone, then head outside to call a Lyft, grateful to put some distance between me and the object of this inappropriate lust.

But my phone is fading fast. The battery's at one percent right as the car options populate. "C'mon," I mutter as I try to grab one before the screen of death appears.

I'm too late. But seconds later, the scent of midnight wraps around me. "I'll drive you home," Max says, striding up next to me on the street, having just left Kitchen Mosaic.

I wince, not wanting to take him up on it. Not trusting myself to. But having no choice.

I turn around and give in. "Fine."

He sets his hand on the small of my back as he walks me to his car, like a man who'd never share me.

19

A PIECE OF ME

Max

The car is quiet for several blocks as I zip along Columbus Avenue, catching all the green lights. Normally, I'd be all over this kind of traffic luck. But tonight I'd like to hit every single red.

Something to buy some time. Slow us down. Figure out what to do next.

The silence hangs heavily in the car. I should say something to Everly. But I already apologized. Plus, I don't want to talk about that guy again. I'm not sure I *should* talk. I've said enough, and I should remember what a bad idea we are.

I need her too much to act on these desires. Need her to help fix the mess I made of my public life. I try to focus on the drive, the surroundings—anything but the way my pulse spikes just being near her.

It's nearly ten. The city is still busy as we cruise toward North Beach, closer and closer to Everly's home, passing smatterings of people walking along the sidewalk, dipping in and out of restaurants, bars and bookstores, chatting with each other.

We're still not talking. I steal a glance at her, but that's a rookie mistake. Now I'm thinking about how her legs look in that skirt. How the moonlight streams across her pale skin as she stares straight ahead out the window, quiet too. I'm picturing how she'd look in her home, dragging me inside, grabbing my shirt and telling me to shut her up with a kiss.

I nearly groan at the thought. Gripping the wheel tighter, I force out a safe question. "Want me to play some music?"

We've got all of a mile left, but I can't stand the company of my own thoughts right now.

"Sure," she says.

Without thinking, I stab the play button on the console to blast the car with the new playlist Wesley shared with me—*Rock Tunes That Put You In A Winning Mood* will do me some good right now.

"Economic forces played a role in the progress of navigation, and in this lesson we'll explore—"

Fuck.

I hit end faster than I bat a puck out of the crease. I don't want Everly to hear what I was listening to on the drive over to the restaurant earlier. It's too personal.

She turns to me for the first time since she got in the car, tilting her head. "What's that?" It's asked with amusement.

"Just a class," I mutter as the light ahead turns red. Great. My wish is finally granted when I don't want it anymore. I don't want her to know this about me.

"The class you've been taking?" she prompts. "You mentioned it in the weight room."

Shit. I did. "Yeah. That's the one." Maybe the less I say, the more she'll get the message.

Her mouth softens. "What's it on? I was curious."

"It's on navigational tools," I say.

And she's not getting the message at all. She's too interested in this detail about me since she asks, "Are you into cartography or something?"

I snap my gaze to her, my jaw ticking. "Are you going to use this somehow? In this image makeover?"

"No," she says, almost offended. I expected her to sound annoyed, but she sounds...disappointed actually. "I was curious. About you, Max. I didn't ask for any other reason."

Shit. I swallow uncomfortably. But the whole topic *is* uncomfortable. "Sorry. I thought..."

I don't finish since she knows what I thought—that I didn't trust her with this information.

"Yeah. I know what you thought," she says sadly, then turns her head subtly toward the window. Like she's giving me space as she gazes into the inky night sky.

Do I want space? I don't know. I don't know what I want. No, that's not true. I know what I want—her. But I know, too, it's a bad idea to do a damn thing about that wish.

At least I can give her the truth though. I blow out a breath as I grip the wheel and I glance at the woman beside me, her face aglow with the lights of the city after dark.

"It's an online class offered by a local university. I listen to it. Been taking this one since the start of the season. It's selfish really. Why I take it," I say.

"Why do you take it then?"

I picture my grandfather, the last few years of his life, but especially the last few months. How he wasn't himself any more. He was a man without history, without a family, without memories. He was a shell of who he'd been. "My grandfather had dementia. It led to his death a year ago," I say, and the light changes mercifully. Good. It's easier to share this awful story when I don't have to look at her. "I spent time with him whenever I could get to Seattle. Sometimes I took him to his appointments. One time, he was in pretty bad shape when I took him to his neurologist. And when he was with the nurse doing labs, I got a chance to be alone with the doctor. And I jumped on it," I say, and I'm not entirely proud of this moment, but at the time, I was roiled with fear. I'd seen the future, and it was awful. I felt like I *had* to make it about me. "I selfishly asked if there was anything I could do to prevent dementia."

"That's not selfish," she says, her voice strong and passionate. "That's smart."

"I don't know. It was kind of a dick move. It was *his* appointment. Not mine."

"But that's proactive. That's wise to ask a doctor. It's wise to think about it *now*," she says, and maybe she's right. But what's done is done.

"Anyway, he told me there are no guarantees. There's no cure. But if he could offer me any advice for brain health it's that the three keys are 'exercise, socialize, and memorize,'" I say as I cruise along the street, climbing a slight hill. "Of course, that's just hopeful advice, he'd said. There's no medical proof that anything can prevent memory loss, but those things could possibly help. I figured I've already got the exercise part aced, so it can't hurt to keep working on my brain," I admit, telling her something I don't really reveal to anyone.

"I'm sorry about the loss. And what he went through. And you," she says with sympathy. "That must have been so hard for everyone."

Apparently now that I've started sharing I can't stop. A valve has loosened in me, so I add, "And maybe this makes me a selfish dick too, but what happened to him? It's my greatest fear," I admit. Maybe even more so than trusting someone else. The only person I know for certain I can trust is me. But what if I lose myself someday? The thought makes me shudder. "I hope I can have a different fate. A different future. So that's why I try to do those things."

"Socialize?" she asks with a quirk in her lips, playfully busting me. "*You* like to socialize?"

"With friends," I say sternly. "Don't get any ideas about me being a social butterfly."

She holds up her hands. "I would never. The memorize part though. Does that mean you do the class, memorize the info, and then take tests?"

"Yep," I say with a laugh. "I take a quiz every week. Like I'm in school again."

She's quiet for a beat, perhaps absorbing that as I near Filbert Street. "Max," she says softly.

"Yes?"

She sets a hand on my biceps. That simple touch from her is almost too much for me to handle as I drive. I do my best to focus on the road as she says, "I do know that some things are personal. I don't want to use everything. I don't want to use most things. I wish you'd see that."

I wish I could too. "I'll try."

"Thank you."

We're a few blocks from her home. She lets go of my arm, sighs, then says, "Lucas was my physical therapist. I was in the hospital for a while from the car accident. It was pretty bad. I had some surgeries. Some injuries. I needed rehab. He was one of the people who helped me a lot."

There are so many questions I want to ask her. So much more I want to know. But mostly I take what she's said for the gift that it is—a piece of her after I gave her a piece of me.

"I'm really glad he helped," I say, meaning it as I pull up on her block, sliding into a spot right outside her town-home. I turn off the engine, then shoot her a cocky smile. "But I'm glad, too, you don't like him. Fucking knew he wasn't your type."

She swats my arm, but she's smiling. "Can you ever just let a nice moment be?"

I scoff. "You know the answer to that, sunshine. And it's no."

"It sure is."

"Like you'd want it any other way."

She rolls her eyes. And *this*? This banter, this needling, this energy? It's a million times safer than sharing these intimate pieces of ourselves with each other.

I nod toward her townhome. "I'll walk you up," I say, then get out of the car. As I stride around the front of the vehicle, I remind myself to behave. I'll escort her to the stoop, then say goodbye. Watch her as she goes up the steps, unlocks the front entryway, then disappears safely inside.

That's the plan as I open her car door.

She steps out, and her brown eyes hold mine. But hers are full of curiosity. "Are you doing this on purpose?"

"Doing what?"

She tips her forehead toward the nearby steps. "Walking me home when I'm ten feet away. Showing me what you think a man should do on a date."

"I am," I say, owning it.

"Why?" Her tone is a touch desperate, like she has to know what's really going on with me, and she pushes for it, asking, "Because you want to keep proving that Lucas is wrong for me? Max, you already won that battle. Why are you doing this?"

That's a great question actually. A fair fucking question too. I could say it's the right thing to do. I could say I'd do this even if I wasn't borderline obsessed with her. I could say that even if she were a friend I'd walk her up the steps. That's all true. It's what a man should do. But instead, I step closer, because the gravitational pull of Everly is too strong for me to resist. "Like I said, because that's what I'd do if *I* were out with you."

"But we're not. And you made your point earlier," she says, lifting her chin, like she's trying to stay strong even as her tone wobbles. Like she's hurt. By my point? By Lucas? I'm not sure at all. "Lucas isn't into me the way you think he should be."

But I am. And it's a big problem. "Don't want to talk about him anymore," I mutter. "Just let me walk you to the door."

"Fine," she says, her palms raised in surrender.

I set my hand on her back again. A slight shiver seems to run through her when I touch her. I try not to let that go to my head. Or my dick.

But as we go, I spread my fingers wider across the silk of her shirt. Press a little harder. Rub a little more. Curl my thumb around her waist. Register every hitch of her breath.

By the time we're at the top of the steps, my hand feels too right on her back to let go. "I'm not sure I *have* made my point, Everly."

She turns to me, facing me, so I have to drop my hand from her back. Her gaze is wary but intrigued, her eyes flickering with questions. "What's your point exactly?"

"Like I said earlier, if this was a date I'd walk you to the door."

"But it's not. You keep telling me it's not." It's like she's trying to catch me on a technicality, or maybe to push me into admitting something. She doesn't make a move to go inside. Her gaze is locked on mine, and the air is charged between us. It crackles with anticipation.

"You're right. It's not," I say, weighing how far I'll go. What it'll cost me.

She rolls her lips together, then breathes out, like she's centering herself. "And you did it anyway."

"True," I say. Like I could do anything else with her. I couldn't have stopped myself from showing up at The Spotted Zebra tonight if I'd tried. I couldn't have resisted driving her home. I couldn't have refrained from walking her up her steps. Now we're standing in the warm October air, the Golden Gate Bridge in the distance, the ocean hugging us. And I'm not walking away—not with her closer than she's ever been. I look at her lush mouth one more time, then her gorgeous eyes. "And if this were a date I'd kiss you at the door."

She's quiet, but her lips curve up. "That's not what you said at the restaurant."

Wait. I'm confused now. "That *is* what I said," I point out.

She crosses her arms, shaking her head, but she's smiling and it's flirty. Inviting. "No, Max. You said you'd devastate me with a kiss."

And that's it. That's enough. Just fuck it. Fuck everything. "I guess I'd better start."

She grabs the collar of my shirt in a challenge. "What are you waiting for?"

20

I HAVE EVERY IDEA

Everly

Max cups the side of my face—but he doesn't kiss me. He slides his thumb along my jawline, but doesn't dip his mouth to mine. He steps closer, but still makes no move to capture a kiss.

I'm trapped in the tease of him. I back up against the railing, needing something to steady myself. He moves with me, still staring greedily at my mouth. Then my eyes. "You have no idea," he mutters.

Those four words rocket through my bloodstream, like a supernova. I'm lit up, sparkling everywhere, and he hasn't even put me out of my sweet misery.

"No idea what?" I ask, my voice feathery with need, with desire.

"How much I want you."

I shiver from the confession. "How much?"

He doesn't tell me. He shows me. He runs the pad of his

thumb along my jaw, like he's memorizing me. Finally, he drops his face closer, but not close enough. I'm caught in the anticipation. His warm breath is like silk over my skin. The vein in his neck pulses. Heat radiates off his strong body.

I close my eyes. It's so much—his words, his touch, his need. I'm too shivery. Too aroused. I don't even know what to hold onto. I've lost every shred of resistance, so I can't hold onto that. But when I open my eyes, those blue irises of his are like flames. And I don't want to hold onto a thing.

I want to let go.

He slides his thumb down to my chin, tilting up my face, like he's finding the perfect position.

I've thought about kissing Max countless times, but I never pictured *this*. I never imagined he'd take his sweet time. I never expected him to slow burn a kiss.

But he's killing me as he travels his thumb up to my mouth then runs it along my bottom lip. My breath catches and I whimper. Everything in me aches. "Just kiss me," I murmur, a quiet demand.

He smiles like a cocky asshole. "Don't worry. I know you want it."

I roll my eyes. "Why do you have to ruin this by talk—"

Then I'm gasping, shuddering when he cuts me off, his lips meeting mine at last. It's the barest of kisses. He hardly touches me. Just dusts those full lips over mine.

But it's enough for my knees to weaken. I curl my fingers around the collar of his shirt. My other hand seeks hold of him too, so I set my palm on his strong chest, drawing a sharp breath as I touch his firm muscles for the first time.

He's so solid. So sturdy. And I need this strength so much.

Max holds my face in the most tender way as he gives me the softest kiss. His beard whisks across my skin. I can taste the hint of his raspberry-flavored lip balm.

I feel like I'm floating.

Like I'm melting too. I'm a liquid woman as Max Lambert delivers on his promise—*he should devastate you with a kiss like he can't fucking breathe if he doesn't kiss you.*

Max does just that. He devastates me with a kiss I never saw coming.

Because I imagined he'd kiss rough and hard. A little pushy. A lot of tongue. This kiss though? It's soft and slow and mesmerizing.

It's the opposite of my expectations yet it's exceeding all of them.

He's letting me feel every second of this moment. He's getting to know my mouth. It's intoxicating as he takes his time, deepening the kiss. I feel like I'm falling into this kiss, like he's seducing me with a brush of his lips, a gentle stroke of his tongue, a confident hand holding my face.

It's magic, wonderful and terrifying all at once, because one kiss and I'm addicted. I don't want him to stop. I want him to take me apart.

I grip his collar more tightly, jerk him closer, and then I feel him.

All of him.

He presses his big frame against me, and the outline of his erection is like a whole new world—hard, insistent, hungry. His kisses build in intensity even as he lets go of my face and he explores my body. He slides one hand down to the neckline of my shirt, then over the soft fabric toward my belly, making me tremble. When he curls the other hand around my hip, the sound I let out is dangerously loud.

A warning bell.

I break the kiss, tip my forehead to the door. An invitation. We don't need words. The second I open the entryway door, he's saying yes by following me. I walk up the steps to the second floor, him behind me every step of the way, our desire pulsing in the air of my building.

I reach my place, unlock it, then drop my bag and phone on the table in a rush. I switch on one light in the living room, but I dim it. I don't plan on taking off my shirt, but it's easier if I don't have to explain anything tonight. Sometimes, I don't want to explain anything. It'll be easier if this is mostly dark in case he accidentally sees my scars, or the ones on my left hip.

"I didn't think you'd kiss like that," I admit.

He shuts the door and moves me against the wall right next to it, staring down at me with those cool eyes. "You've thought about kissing me?"

An ungodly amount of times. No point pretending anything else now. "I have."

"How did I kiss you? When you got off to me?"

A laugh bursts from me. "I didn't say I got off to you."

He shoots me a closed-mouth smile. "You didn't have to say it."

I roll my eyes. "Why do you even talk?"

He smiles wider as he cages me against the wall, then kisses a path up my neck, traveling to my ear. "Want to know why I kiss you like this?"

My breath comes surprisingly fast. "Yes," I say, desperate. I'm dying for his answer.

"Because you need to be savored, Everly. Because I

would never rush things with you. Because you are not a quickie."

His words thrum through my whole body, making me tingle everywhere as I meet his gaze. "What am I?"

He pulls back and locks his gaze with mine, his eyes filled with what looks like raw honesty. "You're a bad idea, and I still fucking want you so much."

Reality slams into me. We should stop. We really should. But Max is leaning against the wall, resting on his forearm, looking down at me like I'm impossible to walk away from.

Say yes.

"This can't happen again," I say as much for him as for me.

"I know."

"This is one time only."

"It sure is."

I'm done talking so I reach for his waist and jerk him against me. I take the lead, and I'm not patient like he is. I'm hungry. No—starving is more like it. I kiss him like a greedy girl. I grow hotter with each press of our lips, each graze of his hands. A pulse beats everywhere in me, most insistently between my thighs.

I can't wait much longer for whatever is coming next. Ideally, *me.*

When he coasts his big palm down my thigh, I grab his hand and cover it with mine. We break the kiss, and his ice blue eyes turn to fire as I guide his hand under my skirt, then up my right thigh.

His mouth falls open on a groan. "You're so fucking soft."

I nibble on the corner of my lips, then feeling bold, I say, "And wet."

His groan is carnal as he glides his fingers across the damp panel of my lacy panties. "Soaked is more like it," he says.

I smile and nod. Just for tonight, I'm done fighting this desire. The morning will be a different story but tomorrow will take care of itself. Right now, I desperately want him to take care of me. I want his fingers deep inside me. I want him to get me off. "You should make it up to me," I say, a little demanding.

His eyebrows shoot up. "Make what up?"

"The way you ruined my date."

"But I'm not sorry," he says, refusing to back down on this count.

"I don't need you to apologize," I tell him. "I want something else. Something better than an apology."

"Tell me," he says, his gaze never breaking mine.

I take my time. Let the moment stretch, then say, "You talked a big game about how a date should go. Why don't you show me?"

Like he's hit all the jackpots in Vegas, he says, "This is how a date should end." He seals his mouth onto mine and kisses me hard. Ruthlessly. A bossy man once more, owning my mouth with his merciless kiss as his fingers slide over the scrap of lace between my legs. His mouth is ferocious, devouring me as he tugs at the fabric, then pulls it aside.

The second he touches me, my body shouts with joy. I've needed this so much. Wanted this from him. I break the kiss, my head falling back against the wall. "Oh god," I gasp.

His eyes are dark, and the muscles in his neck tense. "You're so fucking soft and wet," he says, praising me as he strokes my pussy. "You're fucking perfect."

The compliments light me up, making my skin tingle.

He pushes up my skirt. For a second, I worry. But he's too hungry to notice my hip and, of course, the light's too low to see anything. I'm not in the mood for explanations.

Max doesn't seem to be in the mood for anything except for chasing my pleasure. He grabs my thigh and hitches it up against his hip. Like that, he fingers me, with one leg wrapped around his hip. Pushing me against the wall, pinning me, and touching me.

He slows the kiss as he slides one finger inside me. My breath hitches, then turns into a raspy moan as he fills me with one finger, curling it just so. My stomach tightens.

"More," I whisper, holding onto his shoulders as he touches me.

"Anything you want."

He adds another finger, and I'm fuller, but not full enough. "More," I urge.

He complies, fucking me with three fingers while teasing my clit with his thumb. Bright lights spark behind my eyelids. Electricity crackles over my skin. Pressure builds in me, the urgent need to come as he hunts down my release with his talented fingers, fucking me and crooking them just so till I'm at the tipping point, my world breaking into bliss as he sends me over the edge.

Before I can even catch my breath he eases out his fingers, lowers my leg to the floor, then drops to his knees. He bunches up my skirt all the way to my waist. I hold my breath, but the scars on my hip are the most faded, and he'd really have to be looking to see them. Right now, he's *doing*. He tugs down my panties and slides them over one shoe, not even bothering to take them off all the way. They sit at one ankle.

"Need to taste you. Can't fucking wait," he mutters.

The need in his voice makes my legs shake. Makes me hotter, wetter.

"Please do it. Please."

"I've been needing to eat you for so long," he rasps as he flicks his tongue against my clit, groaning savagely from the first taste.

He's on a mission and before I've stopped moaning from my first orgasm, he seals his mouth to me, then French kisses the fuck out of my pussy. I curl my hands around his skull, my fingers roping through his thick, wild mane of hair, my nails scraping him.

He growls as he eats me, his tongue stroking me deeply, passionately. Rocking into his face, I fuck his mouth, his beard, his lips with a wild abandon I haven't felt in ages.

Or really, ever.

He grabs my ass, gripping my flesh tightly, tugging me impossibly closer, then thrusting his tongue deep inside me.

I scream from the sharp, hot spikes of pleasure. From the filthy delight of his tongue inside me. The grumpy goalie is tongue-fucking me against the wall as I grab his head tighter, pull him closer, and shamelessly chase a second orgasm on his face.

It comes out of nowhere. Slamming into me. Shattering me with a white-hot blur. I cry out, panting and murmuring for a good long time. I can't see straight or even walk but the next thing I know, Max is scooping me up and carrying me through my living room, down the hall, and finding my bedroom. Gently, he sets me on my bed, takes off my shoes and presses a tender kiss to my forehead before he whispers, "That's how you end a first date."

Then, he leaves.

I'm too sex-drunk to even think about what just happened. It's not until twenty minutes later, when I've cleaned up and changed into sleep shorts and a cami, that I start the hunt for my wet panties.

But I can't find them near the door. Or anywhere. Because...Max must have taken them.

21

THE CAT JUDGE

Max

Ten out of ten do not recommend driving with a boner.

Don't ask me how I get home. Pretty sure I drive, but my mind is not on the road. At last, I peel into the parking lot of my building, turn off the engine, and march into the elevators. Swiping my card key for the penthouse, I'm damn grateful no one is in the lift.

I breathe out hard, trying to think about anything but the desire that's got me in a chokehold. An interminable forty-five-second elevator ride later, I'm on the top floor, stalking down the hall, and unlocking the door to my home.

I'm too amped up to make it to my bedroom. The second the door clangs shut, I'm undoing the buckle of my belt and crossing the living room to the couch. I sink into the suede cushion as I unzip my pants and take out my demanding dick.

I can't think.

I can't focus.

I don't even turn on a goddamn light.

I can't do a thing but replay those twenty minutes up against the wall in Everly's home. I grip my cock, stroking it with purpose. There are no lazy tugs here. No test strokes to see if I'm in the mood. I am nothing but in the mood right now.

As I curl a fist around my cock, I jam my other hand into my pocket and take out my prize.

My reward. But these I want to see, so I bark out, "Hey, Alexa, turn on the living room light."

The helpful hub complies, flicking on the overhead.

Yes. Fuck yes. They're light aqua with a delicate rose embroidery thingy all over the sheer fabric, and barely anything covering the ass. Just a fantastic thong that goes to the victor. My pulse pounds as I bring the still-wet panel to my nose. "Fuuuuuck," I rumble, inhaling the scent of her desire.

I jerk faster, my dick throbbing ruthlessly in my hand as I close my eyes and let the flavors of her fill my mind. She smells fucking incredible—like lace and longing. Like all my dirty dreams. Like *her*, turned on by *me*.

I shuttle my fist faster, from base to tip, squeezing out a drop of pre-come at the head, using that liquid to ease the path.

My jaw ticks with all this pent-up tension as I fuck my fist and inhale Everly's panties. I can't stop sniffing them. Don't want to stop inhaling her arousal as I take care of this insistent erection that's been begging for attention for the last hour.

My thighs tighten. My head spins with lust. My bones shake. I stroke faster and faster still as a filthy, beautiful loop plays in my head.

Her fantastic fucking lips. The sweetness of her mouth, the flowery perfume on her collarbone, the way she melted into my kiss. The soft, tempting taste of her lips as I held her in my arms.

The way she fucked my hand as much as I fucked her.

I bring the damp panel of her panties even closer to my nostrils, catching another intoxicating whiff of her.

Heat roars low in my stomach. This is so fucking necessary. I can't last another minute without this release. I'm too wound up with want. And I can't stand how much I want her.

One more inhale. *"Fuck it."*

Letting go of my dick for a second, I switch the fabric to my right hand, turning them inside out. Then I grip my dick with the cotton panel.

They're still a little wet from her, and the idea of getting off with her arousal fries my brain. It short-circuits my entire body. It sends me spinning. I fuck my fist harder with the sheer lace and cotton, jerking and stroking till my thoughts blank out and my vision blurs.

I'm grunting as sparks burst before my eyes. Then punching my hips and spilling all over my hand and her expensive panties.

It's so wrong.

I can't even catch my breath for a long time.

After, my eyes float open finally, and I reconnect to the earth. I swing my gaze down to my hand. I've ruined the lace. But I smirk at the mess.

Worth it. Fucking worth it.

Then, I blink. "The fuck?"

Athena's perched on the coffee table across from me, staring sharply with unblinking green eyes.

"Don't judge me," I mutter.

She turns the other way, lifting a haughty, furry chin.

"You saw nothing," I tell her.

She twitches her tail more. Judging me. Fucking judging me.

But then again, I'm sitting on my couch with my pants down, my dick out, holding a pair of the world's sexiest panties covered in my come.

I'd judge me too.

Fifteen minutes later, I've showered and cleaned up. After I hang up the fluffy bath towel next to the rainfall shower, I pad across the soft carpet in my bedroom suite and enter the walk-in closet. I grab a pair of black boxer briefs from a drawer and pull them on, then head to bed. I sink down on the soft gray duvet on the king-size bed.

I yawn, relaxed at last. But even though we have a game tomorrow, it's not bedtime yet.

Settling onto the pillows, I grab my phone, the lights of the city flickering from beyond the floor-to-ceiling windows.

Time for some detective work. There's no brand name on the tag. Just a size. No way am I going to ask Everly what brand that was. Instead, I google *aqua sheer panties covered in roses* and visit seven different lingerie shops online before I find one that looks right.

"Bingo," I say. Then I place an order for rush delivery tomorrow afternoon.

I close the browser and hop over to my text messages, opening the thread with Everly. I start to tap out a message, letting her know to be on the lookout for a package.

But then, screw it. I'd rather surprise her.

I set my phone down, blow out a very satisfied sigh, and park my hands behind my head. I'm sated.

Well, for now.

There's a soft sound, and I turn to the right. A quiet furball slinks across the bed, and curls up next to my neck. In seconds, she's purring and I'm forgiven.

* * *

In the morning, I'm pouring a cup of coffee in the kitchen while texting with my dad about bagels. He's started sending me daily pics of them, and I don't know why but I fucking love pics of bagels from my parents. *Looks delish*, I respond to today's so-called Bagel of the Day, when a new text blinks up at me from my phone. A damning text.

> Everly: You took my panties.

I down some coffee, letting it wake me up before I dictate a reply.

> Max: Is there a question in there?

> Everly: I can't believe you took my panties.

> Max: That's still not a question.

> Everly: Why did you take my panties?

Well, that answer is easy, so I give it to her.

. . .

Max: Because I wanted them.

* * *

"What is that?" Asher asks as he slides into the passenger seat of my car on the way to morning skate.

"What is what?"

He tips his chin toward me, peering at...my face. "Is that...a *smile* you're wearing?"

I scoff. "Fuck no."

"Dude. I think you're smiling," he says as he buckles in.

"Watch it, Callahan," I warn him as I pull into the light traffic on California Street.

"Did you find a lucky penny this morning? Wait. I bet you found a whole twenty in the dryer and now you're gonna take us out to lunch?" He presses his hands together in mock prayer.

"You're a cheap date. When was the last time you got lunch for one person for less than twenty bucks, let alone a crew?"

"So it was a hundo. Excellent. I suggest we get tacos. You, me, Bryant, and Falcon," he says, then flashes me a grin.

I point at him before I turn at the light, like I've caught him in the act. "That on your pie hole? That's a smile. Me? I don't smile."

"Right." He lowers his voice to a faux whisper. "Your makeover is working. Admit it. This is Max 2.0. *Watch as he helps little old ladies cross the street. Witness as he sings*

'Happy Birthday' at the old folks' home. Grab a seat in the front row as he knits blankets for puppies at the shelter."

I growl again, then stab the button on the console. Thankfully, this time a new tune plays from Wesley's "take-no-prisoners pre-game warm-up" playlist—an Arctic Monkeys tune. I crank the volume to full blast. "Do I Wanna Know" shuts up Asher for the rest of the short drive to the arena. I pull into the players' lot next to Wesley, who's getting out of his vehicle at the same time as we are.

Asher calls out to him, "Dude, Lambert is happy. You know what that means?"

I groan, shaking my head. Asher is a relentless shit-stirrer. He's also unfairly emotionally astute, so I've got to be on my guard. For Everly's sake, especially.

Wesley looks from me to Asher, as if he's assessing us. "The aliens took him yesterday, so we need a new goalie for the game?"

"Exactly," Asher says, then claps my shoulder. "Or dude got laid last night."

I won't give him the satisfaction of a response. "Did you see the Cougars picked up Martinez after all? Dude wasn't a free agent for long," I say, dangling baseball trade talk to distract him, like he's Athena and I'm waving a fake bird toy in front of him. Maybe he won't put two and two together about my good mood. Don't need the scrutiny right now.

Asher shoots me a smug smile. "So I was right," he says, and dammit. He *is* smarter than a cat.

"Pretty sure you said you thought they'd lock him up," I say, trying again since my poker face is tight.

Asher cocks his brow at me. "Nice try, Lambert."

We head inside and down the corridor. Miles is a few

paces ahead of us, so that's as good a distraction as any. "Hey, Falcon," I call out to the center.

He turns around, tips his chin toward us. "What's up?"

"Question for you."

"Sure."

I scratch my jaw. "Do you know anyone who babysits?"

Miles furrows his brow. "Um, no. Is it for your nephew?"

I scoff, then point my thumb toward Asher, then Wesley. "No, it's for these clowns."

Miles waggles a brow, smiling, getting it now. "Speaking of clowns, I hear you're going to join the circus when you're done with hockey. Let me know where you wind up because I will heckle the fuck out of that."

I groan, dragging a hand down my face. "Why are you guys looking at my social media?"

"Everyone needs a good laugh now and then," Wesley says as we head into the locker room.

Hugo's here, tugging on his jersey. Christian, the captain, is lacing up his skates.

When Miles reaches his stall, he looks back at me, tilting his head. "Looks like you had fun at the naked ride. But why didn't you *do* the ride?" He asks it innocently, like he's been educating himself at the Wesley and Asher School of Giving Me Hell. "Were you afraid of scaring everyone with your attire?"

I look to the ceiling in frustration, tossing up my hands. "Why are you all my teammates?"

"You're just that lucky, man," Hugo calls out.

"And don't you forget it," Christian chimes in.

"As if I could," I say, then I grab my shoulder pads from the stall.

As I'm heading to practice ten minutes later with

Asher, my gaze drifts up to the management levels. I picture Everly in her office.

A dirty grin returns to my face.

As we reach the gate at the ice, Asher points to me with a *busted* grin on his face. "Yup. It's working. You've been made over into...a new man, and I know why," he says, his gaze drifting pointedly to the management levels before he takes off and flies down the ice away from me.

I try my best to flip him the bird, but it's fuck-all hard with gloves on.

Still, I really need to get my game face on, especially since nothing can happen with Everly again.

It really, really can't, no matter how much I'm thinking about her and the delivery coming her way today.

22

A THIEF AND A PIRATE

Everly

"He's a panty thief!" Josie issues that declaration with a slap of the table at the diner.

I'm at lunch with my friends after the hottest night of my life. I've told them nearly everything. I only feel slightly bad for divulging all the details of our one-time-only tryst, but they've been sworn to vault-levels of secrecy. And honestly, I couldn't *not* tell them.

"I never expected that. They were just...*gone* when I looked all over for them," I say, a little thrilled all over again as I recall the discovery of his theft. "Like stolen treasure or something."

Maeve arches a brow. "It kind of makes him...a sex pirate."

I laugh. "Evidently."

"Max *is* sort of swashbuckling," Fable says thoughtfully, then asks, "and did he admit to taking them?"

"Yes," I say, still incredulous over Max's matter-of-fact reaction via text this morning. "He was unapologetic."

Maeve stabs a forkful of salad but doesn't bring it to her mouth. "The man wants what he wants. That's impressive."

"Is it though? I mean, what did he do with them?" I ask, then take a bite of my lunch.

But as I'm chewing on the portobello mushroom sandwich, three pairs of eyes from around the table stare wide-eyed at me.

"Is that a real question?" Josie asks.

I set down the sandwich. "What do you mean?"

Maeve snorts, then arches a knowing brow. "I think we all know what he did with them." She finally takes that bite.

A flush crawls up my chest and along my neck, setting my face on fire. "Seriously?"

Josie cracks up. "Sweetie, of course he did."

"I..." I begin, but I'm speechless. And turned on all over again. "I guess I didn't think it through. Really? *Really*?" But of course that's what he did. "I didn't play out the whole 'what happened next' bit in my head."

"Because the act of theft is hot in and of itself," Maeve supplies with a cat-like grin. "You were fixated on the simple fact that he took them."

I wince but nod guiltily. "I was. Since that was just hot," I say quietly, leaning closer to them as I whisper, "No one's ever done that before. But the fact that he did kind of got me going this morning."

Fable's naughty grin spreads. "So what you're saying is you were too turned on from him taking them to even think about what he did *with* them?"

"Girl, what he did *to me* is all I could think about last night when I got into bed. Then this morning before I left for work. And at work while I was supposed to be finalizing the press notes for tonight's game," I say, then lift my iced tea. I need a drink. I'm hot all over. After I take a thirsty sip, I put down the glass with some finality. "But it can't happen again."

"Why?" Maeve asks curiously.

"We work together. It's considered a bad idea to get involved with a player."

"Really?" Josie asks, seeming sad on my behalf.

"It's an unwritten rule. Mostly because of all the ways it could go wrong," I say, laying out the facts. "I'm not his direct report, and he's of course not mine. But that doesn't matter necessarily. If you get involved with a player, it could change the way the other players see you, how the media sees you, and of course how management does. Every move you make could look like favoritism or bias. Someone could think you're promoting the guy you're involved with over other players. And that could hurt the team dynamics. And it could look like I'm trying to use that connection to move up. I don't want to take that chance, especially when I'm competing for a promotion."

"That makes sense," Fable says, nodding thoughtfully. "I know Blaine Enterprises has all sorts of guidelines in its HR handbook about office romances and relationships with co-workers. It's good to be careful." That's the company she works for that owns the city's winningest and most popular football team.

"Exactly," I say, trying to stay as clear-headed as I can about the Max situation—since last night can't happen again. "If a fling goes south, the team doesn't want to find themselves in the position of punishing a player. They spend millions on their players. And it's understandable

—the players *are* the product. But no one wants to handle a broken heart at the office." I pause. "Or worse."

Maeve sighs, then drags a French fry through her ketchup. "I wonder what it'd be like to have an office romance. They always sound so hot."

She's an artist so she's never worked in an office.

"Maybe you could have a studio romance. With a moody sculptor or a tortured painter or something. And then you'd get paint all over your—" I gesture to her chest.

"Yes! I want to find a man who'd like to paint my tits red."

We crack up, but when the laughter fades, Josie clears her throat, turning to me. "But I get where you're coming from, Ev. Your job matters to you. You've worked hard for it. I personally don't think sleeping with a player undermines that, but I understand why you'd worry."

"Thank you," I say with a sigh of resignation. Renewed acceptance, too, that last night was a one and done. "It's hard enough as a woman in sports. I remember reading this memoir by a female sports reporter about all the harassment she had to endure and the sexism. That's the other thing—there's this overhang for a lot of women working in sports. Getting involved with a player kind of goes against years of sisterhood trying to make it an even playing field."

"Sisterhood matters," Fable says, then tilts her head. "But so do your feelings. Do you care about him?"

I think about Max and the things we've spoken about. About his grandfather, about his past heartbreak with Lyra, about his sister. He's been surprisingly open with me, and it warms my heart when he is. Those moments when he shares feel special in ways I didn't expect. But even though I shared about our night together, I won't share the personal details about Max—those are for me and me alone.

I keep my answer simple and truthful. "I care about him. But there's no room for anything more. Our work together has barely begun. There's so much we still have to do," I say. This afternoon I need to focus on the Dogs on Ice event I have planned for next week—part of step two, the community outreach phase we've been building toward. This will be the payoff. Or so I hope.

"Onward and upward then," Josie says, lifting her glass. "But let's toast to knowing a panty thief. Well, besides my dog."

I freeze. "Wait. Pancake is a panty thief?"

She shrugs a yes. "Apparently, it's not that uncommon. Guess he's a horndog."

We all clink, and then drink to that.

When lunch ends, I return to the arena with a renewed focus now that I've gotten that confession out of my system. After I grab my afternoon London fog latte from a shop nearby, I head to my office and sit down at my computer, toggling the mouse. As the machine wakes up, there's a soft knock on my door.

I spin around. It's Jenna. She's standing in the open doorway, holding a pretty dove gray envelope. "This just came for you. It's a personal delivery."

I furrow my brow, thinking on what it could be. Then I brighten. "It must be that new team T-shirt I ordered," I say, then reach for the envelope and rip it open.

I reach my hand inside, fishing around in the soft tissue paper, and yank the shirt out.

Only it's not a shirt, and my face flames hot.

23

MY UNDOING

Everly

I'm praying sweet, angel-faced Jenna who comes to me for publicity advice did not see my new thong.

Please, universe. If you could grant me one wish right now, it'd be that. I'd be super grateful.

I stuff the lace to the bottom of the envelope, then farther, like, say, to the center of earth, and ideally all the way to Siberia on the other side.

I'm not in the spin business for nothing though. I flash an *oh what a silly mix-up* grin, and say to her, "I got the size wrong."

I roll my eyes, like *can you believe it?*

But would my face be as red as a fire engine over the wrong size? Maybe Jenna won't notice I'm imitating a candy apple.

The worker bee tilts her head to the side and says helpfully, "Want me to handle the return? I don't mind at all. I do it for my girlfriend," she says. "She orders way too many shirts to try on all the time, and I'm always the one sending them back."

It's a relief that she didn't see the new lingerie our star goalie sent me. "Nah. I need to return some…" I glance around quickly, but my desk is mostly empty except for a succulent that I've never fed. "Some plant food too. I can do it all."

"I don't mind. I totally have a green thumb."

Jenna is the nicest person in the sports world, and I don't deserve her. "You don't need to spend company time dealing with my mistake. But thanks, Jenna. You're the best."

"Okay, well let me know what I can help you with."

I wrack my brain for a project to keep her busy. "Actually, I need some research done on the upcoming event with Little Friends next week."

Quickly I give her a few tasks for Dogs on Ice, and when she trots off, I shut the door, something I rarely do unless I'm sitting in on an interview, but I need a moment alone with this *treat*.

I return to my chair, take a breath, and then set my hand on my chest. My heart is beating so fast. No one has ever sent me lingerie. I haven't had a relationship long enough to enter the *meaningful gift* stage. My fingers are so eager to touch this pretty thing. To see if there's a note. I dip my hand back into the envelope and pull out the panties, getting a good look at them at last.

A smile coasts across my face. A smile of amazement.

He got me the exact same pair. A perfect replacement. Delivered in less than twenty-four hours. But there's not only a replacement here. There's one more item waiting patiently at the bottom of the envelope. I dip my hand back in, the tissue paper softly crinkling as I pull out another gift.

My breath catches.

It's another pair of panties, and these are royal blue lace. Specifically, Sea Dogs blue. With white lace edging and white embroidered rosettes along the waistband.

He bought me a pair of panties in team colors. I squirm a little in my chair, my chest tingling, my belly flipping. I reach for the small card in the envelope, flip it open, and press my lips together to swallow my gasp.

It's not signed, but it doesn't need to be. There are only five words—*Wear the blue ones tonight.*

I clutch the card in my fingers, not wanting to let it go as the puzzle pieces slide fully into place. Max must have ordered both of these last night, and I try to picture him in his home. I think he lives off Union Street in a tall building, overlooking the city. Was he in bed, scrolling through sites, picking out underthings for me? Including a pair to wear to tonight's home game?

A noise escapes my throat. A soft murmur. Thank god the door is closed since I'm turned on as the late-night reel plays in my head for the thousandth time. I close my eyes, relaxing against the back of the chair, picturing the things he did to me all over again.

Seeing, too, what he might do to me in *these*.

Such a dangerous thought.

Something I can't entertain except in my mind. But here, in the afternoon with my eyes closed, I entertain the hell out of the fantasy. Breathing in deeply, then out, savoring the naughty moments unfurling before my closed eyes.

"Yoo-hoo."

I sit bolt upright. It's Elias in promotions, and he's

rapping on the door. Fear of getting caught fondling a lingerie gift roars down my spine. Hastily I shout "come in" right as he helps himself, swinging the door open. I stuff both pairs of panties back in the envelope like they're contraband and he's border control.

Fresh-faced Elias is smiling because of course he's smiling. Everything goes his way all the time. His gaze drifts to the bag. "Ooh, a fun little gift?"

How the hell does he know it's a gift? Does he even know what it is? "Yes. I mean, it's a shirt. The wrong size. It happens." I wave a hand like this is all no big deal. Then grab my latte and gulp some–that makes my casual routine more believable. At least, that's what I tell myself.

"I hear ya," he says with a solidarity nod. "Like, how hard is it to get a size right?"

"Seriously," I say, trying to mask my breathiness, trying to hide the furious beating of my pulse, and hoping I'm not red-faced anymore. "So, what can I do for you?"

"Just wanted to talk about..." He pauses, *wait for it* style, then booms shockingly on key, "Who let the dogs out?"

It takes me a beat to catch up. "Right. The dog rescue event next week."

"It's going to be great. We used to do those sorts of promos when I played in college," he says in a reminiscing tone, and it only took less than one minute for him to remind me he played college hockey. What I really want to say is *did you do those events?* Because I really don't think adoption events are done for college hockey. But there's no point in calling him on it. I wait for him to keep going and he does, asking, "And you talked to my contacts at Little Friends, right?"

Um, he's not the only one who has contacts at the

city's rescue. I know people there too, and I contacted them. But I don't want to be an asshole, so I say, "Yes, I spoke to Little Friends, and everything's all set for the dog adoption event. Thanks for checking in."

"Sweet. Just want to make sure everything's good to go. And I paved the path for Donna to be there."

Hold on. I don't need the emcee. It's not an in-game fan experience event. It's community outreach. An adoption event we're hosting. "I'm actually going to have some of the players do that. Since, well, they're the draw."

His face falls. "Shoot. Donna loves that stuff especially. Big dog person."

I take a moment to think things over. "I'm sure we can make room for everyone," I say diplomatically, solving the problem with a the-more-the-merrier approach.

"Cool. I'd feel like a jerk if I told her not to come," he says, then turns to the door.

Leave, Elias, leave. I need to ogle my pretties some more.

But instead, he swings his gaze back to me again. "Hey, I wanted to give you a heads-up. I'm applying for the director job too. But I'm totally not going to get it. You have way more experience—*on the desk*," he says, a subtle dig that I don't have on-ice experience. "But I figured *hey, how am I going to get experience applying for a promotion if I don't apply for one?*"

Great. The general counsel's nephew is applying for the job I want. That doesn't hurt my chances at all.

"That's fantastic," I say, and it nearly sounds like I mean it.

He raps his knuckles on the wall for luck. "May the best..." He stops himself from saying man, shifting to, "human win."

"Absolutely," I say.

But before he leaves, his eyes drift to the package on my desk. "Enjoy your gift."

Oh fuck off, Elias.

He leaves. Finally. I grab the package from my desk, do my damnedest to fold it in half, then quarters, and stuff it into my purse. It's not easy. It takes up all the space and makes my purse bulge.

But I'm pissed and annoyed. I've worked so hard for this chance. I show up day in and day out. I travel with the team to a good chunk of their away games. I work late hours. I handle tough questions from the press. And I present the team and the players in the best possible light. Why is he even applying? He manages the in-game fan experience, not publicity.

Then again, Zaire told me she wanted healthy competition for the post. It'd be ridiculous to think I'd be handed it on a silver platter or that I'd be the only internal candidate wanting the gig. There are surely external candidates too. From other teams, other cities. So many of them. All I can do is work harder, try harder, and do more.

I can fight for it. And I'm prepared to do that when a text from Max lights up my phone.

Ignore it.

You don't need a distraction.

But the pull is too strong, so I slide open the preview.

> Max: I see you got a delivery.

My neck turns hot. I want to just rappel down the cave of

texting him. Enjoy some flirty banter, but instead, I shove my phone out of reach before I'm tempted to answer.

For the next few hours, I dive into work to take my mind off Elias. In the late afternoon, there's another knock on my open door.

Is my office a train depot today?

I spin around. Goosebumps rise on my arms. I'm hot everywhere as Max rests his forearm against the doorway. He's wearing a Sea Dogs workout shirt and basketball shorts. His blue eyes lock with mine and his voice is deep and raspy as he says, "Hey."

One word, and I melt a little. "Oh, hi," I say, feeling far too fluttery for my own good.

"Do you have a second to talk about...that thing next week?"

He sounds so believable that no one could know he's here for any other reason.

But I know. I know because of the way he rakes his eyes over me, like he's undressing me, like he's checking to see what I'm wearing underneath my clothes. "Sure," I say, feeling a little hypnotized under his stare. "Don't you have a game?"

"In a couple hours. Gonna work out first," he says, and that's his pre-game ritual. He steps inside and locks the door. "Are you coming tonight?"

I almost always show up at games. I'm about to say yes but wait. Is there a double meaning to his question? I shouldn't ask. I really shouldn't. But I tilt my head coyly as the flirty words take shape on my lips, "To the game? Or did you mean something else?"

His nostrils flare. His eyes darken. "I know the answer to that."

I roll my eyes. "You're so cocky."

He strides closer to my desk, resting his firm ass against it, then bending closer to me. Midnight Flame drifts past my nose. My eyes float closed for a second.

When I open them, he's smirking. "You sniffed it when you opened my suitcase. My cologne."

He says it like he's busting me. And he is.

"What?" I furrow my brow like I have no idea what he means.

His smile deepens. "Rosewood, you're even hotter when you act like you don't know what I'm talking about," he says. "But I know you like it. And I know you opened the bottle." In a stage whisper, he adds, "The cap was a little loose."

Damn him, and damn me. I clench my jaw then breathe out hard. "Why are you so infuriating?"

He ignores the dig. "Want to know how I can tell you like it?"

"No," I say crisply.

"I'll tell you anyway."

"Max," I say, shaking my head. "Did you get the memo? You are extra infuriating."

But we're having two different conversations evidently, and he's not taking the foot off the gas on his. "Because you have the most expressive eyes I've ever seen. Those big brown eyes are a window to all your thoughts. I like to look at your eyes and read what's going on with you," he says, and my throat tightens. His words are terrifying. I don't want to be an open book. I don't want to wear my emotions on my face. He leans closer, the nearness making my skin thrum. He reaches for my hair, cinched back in a ponytail. As he runs his fingers along the ends of it, he adds, "And I could tell from the look in them when you'd get close to me. When you'd smell me. I could tell." I want to jerk him close and smack him until he adds in a tender, sensual voice, "Your eyes are my undoing."

I can't breathe. I can't move. I'm trapped in this swirl of heat and emotion as he does that thing he does—swings from aggravating me to adoring me. I swallow past the desert in my throat, trying to find some kind of words, but all I can manage is a bare question.

"You want me to wear them to the game tonight?" I ask it even though I'm one hundred percent clear on what he wrote on the card. But I want his answer. The truth in it.

He gives it with a long, slow nod and a certain, "I really do."

He steps away, heads toward the door, and exits, leaving me hot and bothered all over again.

"Lambert is extra sharp tonight," Gus remarks as he stuffs a vinegar chip in his mouth, then shoves his readers back on.

"He sure is," I say, hiding how proud I am of his goal tending as the third period begins and the men take to the ice below our spot in the press box that night.

"Wonder what that's all about," Gus grumbles. Trying to get a read on his intentions, I steal a glance at the grizzled vet, who's pecking away on his PC. He's the only reporter who doesn't use a Mac. He's so old school it's cute. Except he's always so suspicious of everyone's motives—players especially. That's not too cute.

Erin's here, too, from our broadcast partner, and she laughs from the water cooler as she refills her bottle during a commercial break. "Can't a guy just have a good game, Gus?"

"No," Gus barks. "There's something to it."

Claudia, the sports blogger next to him, chimes in with a nod of her curly-haired head. "We have to find the story behind everything."

"Bet there's a good reason he's only allowed one goal tonight," Jamie shouts. He's a young, hungry podcaster.

"Because he's a good player," Erin adds.

"Nope," Jamie says, not buying her logic.

Briefly, I understand why Max doesn't want to talk to the press. They *are* pushy, and they're all hunting for an angle.

But then I remember I was one of them once upon a time, leaving no stone unturned as I searched for a fresh way to write about a sport I love. They're simply trying to do their jobs. Heck, aren't we all? And every day it gets harder with all the competition.

Like Elias.

And I plan to stay several steps ahead of him.

Erin sweeps past the guys, heading to the door. "Look, I don't care what the reason is. When Lambert is a brick wall in the net, it's exciting and our ratings go up. On that fun fact, I'm back to the booth."

I wave to her. "See you later."

"We'd still love a comment from him sometime," she says, hopeful. "When he has games like this it'd be great to have him say something."

Don't I know it. This is what I've hoped for from him—even a bland *my team is great* comment would help rehab his rep and keep his face out there for fans and possible sponsors. Plus, I'd love to see him chat with Erin. She's more balanced than the other reporters.

"I'm working on it," I say.

Every head in the room snaps toward me. They all know Max's no-talk rep.

The podcaster arches a doubtful bushy brow. "I swear if he ever talks to the press he better say something really good."

"Like...*we win because I eat raw eggs before a game*," Claudia suggests in her gravelly voice.

"Or *it's thanks to my lucky dirty socks*," Gus barks.

Or *because he sends panties to women whose eyes are his undoing.*

I fight off a private smile as the game picks back up. Wesley and Asher rotate on for their shift, flying down the ice, then behind the Calgary net.

Max is stationed in front of the crease at the other end, ready to defend his turf.

That's Max. A defender. Like he was when I went out with Lucas. The man is wildly protective, both at work and...with me. Warmth unfurls in my chest, but I try not to get lost in the feelings.

Instead, I focus on the action down below.

Miles jostles for the puck with the Calgary defenders, trying to strip it from them. When he finally does, he skates with it for a second or two before he's swarmed and needs to flip it to Asher, who aims it for the net, but their goalie smacks it down. Wesley snags the rebound just past the post and comes around the back of the net, flicking it to Miles again, who slips it through the goalie's legs.

The lamp lights. And the crowd roars.

A minute later, when the puck drops, Calgary jumps on it, fighting to score since they're down by one. But every single time they try to slip it past Max, he deflects it.

Easily. Like it's just another day.

"It's like they're flies bugging him. No. They're gnats,

and he swats them all away," Gus remarks, clearly impressed as he types. He pauses and points at Claudia. "You're right. It's gotta be the eggs. Bet on it."

"I'm betting on dirty socks," Jamie weighs in.

Tonight? My money's on the royal blue lace between my thighs.

And before anyone can read that in my eyes, I check the time. "Maybe someday he'll tell us," I say, then I head to the door. The media will follow shortly, but for now I should meet the players.

Once I'm at the tunnel, the game is locked up with another Sea Dogs win, and I prepare to make my case with Max to tell the press his secret.

When he emerges from the tunnel, he's ripping off his helmet, his wild hair damp with sweat. *Do not be distracted by how ruggedly sexy he looks after a game.* I put on my professional smile. "Max, there's a bet in the press room that you're so good in the net because you either eat raw eggs before each game or wear dirty socks. Want to dispel the rumors?"

He won't want to. But this is our routine. Our back and forth. I'm forcing his hand to come up with a clever retort.

"Maybe I have a special bedtime ritual the night before each game," he drawls out suggestively. "Something to make sure I get a real good night's sleep."

Yep. It's our thing. And it feels dangerously like foreplay. I'm this close to shuddering in front of the whole team from his allusion to last night and what he did when he was home alone. But I can't take that chance, so I try to reset him to business. "Look, I'm pretty sure some of them are convinced you sold your soul to the devil. So there's that possibility too."

"A Faustian bargain. Yeah, that seems likely," he says dryly.

"Do you want to tell them that yourself? Because I know the GM would love it if you did," I say, a subtle reminder of our makeover project. Which is where I should focus, especially with the new Elias threat.

"So they're betting on whether I sold my soul to the devil?" Max asks thoughtfully.

"So you want to discuss it? Perfect. I'll tell them you'll be there shortly."

I brace myself for his retort, since of course he won't talk. But then, in a strangely serious voice, he says, "I'll be there in ten. At the media room."

It's said evenly, with zero snark. A simple promise, and I'm taken aback. Does he mean it? No idea. Max heads to the locker room and for ten long minutes I hope, and I pace, and I pray.

I'm in the media room adjusting the mic for Miles when Max Lambert strides in first, wearing a T-shirt and shorts. It's like a spotting in the wild of a rare Malayan tiger.

I hold my breath. The last time he interacted with the press he told them to fuck right off.

Please, Max, don't do that again.

Reporters whisper. Media members whip out phones. Podcasters stand up, at the ready with mics. I've got my phone lifted too. No idea if I'll use this on our social, but right now I want evidence.

Questions and comments fly with abandon.

"They say you're a difficult guy to coach."

"I hear you don't get along with your teammates."

"Why have you refused to talk to the press for more than a year?"

"Did you know BuzzFeed ranked your fight with Bane as one of the ten best hockey fights ever?"

"Max, what was going through your head that night at your sister's house when you told the photographers to F off?"

My stomach roils. Maybe I should have kept him away from the press. Maybe this isn't worth it after all. I seriously consider running over to him in my heels, putting my hands on his chest and mustering all my strength to push him right out of the media room.

Instead, as I stand inside the doorway, recording the impromptu press conference, I turn to the press in the room. "Please focus on tonight's game or he'll have to leave," I tell them and my tone is decidedly icy.

But it's like Max didn't even hear their questions—or really, like he doesn't care. He leans into the mic and takes the fuck over. "Hear you all wanted to know why I had a good game tonight."

Which is not at all what they said.

Gus sticks up a hand. "Yes, and why have you been so elusive for the last year and a half? What's going on with you for real?"

My blood is pumping too fast. I wanted him to talk to the press so badly that I hadn't considered that it could backfire for all of us—him, me, the team. I have to fix this. "He's not here to discuss anything but tonight's game," I say crisply to Gus and by extension, everyone else.

Then Erin sticks out her mic. "What motivated you in tonight's game, Max? Take us through your performance and what drove you."

It's a softball question, but at least she understood that I simply won't let him answer hardball ones.

"Let me tell you something about tonight," Max says,

staying on message—*his* message. "I've got a great group of teammates. They've got my back and I've got theirs. Thanks for asking."

I breathe the biggest sigh in the world. It's the most throwaway of answers in the history of sports. A harmless cliché reply straight from the school of media training. But that's all I could ask for—a cliché is so much better than the alternative.

He's not telling a reporter to fuck off. He's not yelling at a photographer to get the hell off his sister's property. He's giving the simplest of comments. Nothing earth-shattering. Nothing damning.

But it's an olive branch.

He turns to go, but before he takes a step away from the mic, he whirls back, leans in, and adds, "Oh and I did a lot of visualization exercises before the game. That helps me picture how I want things to go."

I roll my lips together to silence the gasp in my throat. If only I could cool the heat flaring in every damn cell in my body. I'm on fire, lit up in my bones and under my skin. I keep my eyes focused on the floor so no one can read them. So no one can tell Max was thinking of me in my new pair of Sea Dogs blue panties.

He leaves without looking at me, but we both know he wants to. That's the problem. That's the big, huge problem right now.

But I've got a press scrum to wrap up, so I focus solely on my job, which I need to do well to try to win the promotion—the one Elias is angling for. A little later, when I'm finished for the night, I make my way down the corridor toward the parking lot, passing the equipment room.

Up ahead, I spot several players. Wesley and Asher are

in their suits, Miles too. The team is heading out of town tonight for an away stretch of games. Zaire will fly with them this time while I hold down the fort. The team bus will take them to the jet in a bit.

Max will be gone for a few days, and that has to be good for me. Like eating kale is good for me. Like taking vitamins is good for me.

But when I pass the locker room, a voice calls out, "I think you left something in here."

I wheel around. Max is dressed for travel in a dark blue suit and a starched white shirt, looking too sexy for my own good. He's got one hand pushing open the door to the equipment room, his forehead tipped in an invitation.

24

A KISS FOR THE ROAD

Max

By my estimates I have twenty minutes before I have to be on the team bus that'll take us to the airport. Every second counts. It's only fair that I let Everly know why I showed up in the media room tonight. The equipment room seems as good a place to inform her as any. "Come with me," I tell her, as I step into the room full of sticks, pads, and skates.

"You have to leave any second," she says, concern in her brow as she stands in the doorway.

"But not yet. Now come inside."

"So bossy," she says, as I reach for her hand. She places it in mine and I tug her inside.

I close the door. I can't wait a second longer to know. "Did you wear the underwear?"

She jerks her gaze behind her, as if she can check for eavesdroppers, stragglers, anyone in the hallway beyond.

But I'm not stupid, and I wouldn't hurt her by talking

this way in front of her co-workers or mine. The hallway's empty now, plus the door is shut. "I'm paid a lot of money for these eyes. I already checked to see if anyone was around before I pulled you in here," I try to reassure her, then return to the pressing matter—the one I can't get out of my head. "Did you wear them?"

She lifts her chin, a little saucy as she asks, "What do you think?"

She's still not answering me, and it's driving me wild. I try one more tactic—*assuming.* "You wore them."

She moves to the wall, leaning against it, right next to a long row of cubbies holding gear. Dropping her purse to the floor, she bobs a shoulder, giving me a *you'll never know* smile. "I guess you'll just have to wonder the whole time you're out of town," she says coquettishly, and I deserve all her taunts.

But as much as I could chase the high score on our banter leaderboard all night, I legit need to talk to her. I let go of the games we play, asking seriously, "Do you have a sec? It's important."

Her expression shifts instantly, her sass vanishing. She straightens. "Sure."

She's been trying so hard for so long. I need to make some effort too, so I meet her gaze with a serious one of my own. I drag a hand through my hair, taking a breath. "Listen, I know I kind of surprised you back in the media room."

"It wasn't a bad surprise," she says, then winces. "But I'm really sorry that everyone started going after you so quickly. I tried to stop them the second they did."

I hold up a hand, exonerating her from the barrage of questions I tuned out. "They barely even registered. I had a one-track mind in there."

She smiles. "I noticed. That was incredibly impressive, how you shut them all down."

"All that time not talking makes me kind of immune to their questions. I said what I wanted to say tonight. And I noticed you recording it. You're going to put it on my *The Real Max Lambert*, right?"

"I'd like to. We do have to keep feeding that beast."

"Then toss it into the maw."

"Thank you." With genuine excitement in her eyes, she adds, "I love the clip of you saying you've got a great group of teammates. You have their back and they have yours. I know it might seem too practiced and too much of a PR answer, but that's okay. That's exactly what I've been wanting. Just something from you to put you out there, for fans to start seeing you. And I definitely need content for that."

"I'm glad it'll work," I say, pleased I could make her life easier for once.

Her gaze is etched with curiosity as she asks, "What made you do that tonight? Talk to them?"

I do want to tell her the real reason. She deserves to know. But I'm still a little hung up on something. A lot hung up. And the cocky jerk in me has the wheel right now. "So, are you going to tell me? Did you say yes to the underwear?"

She rolls her pretty eyes. "You're still asking me that?"

I fucking love that she never lets me off easily. "I'm not going to stop asking. Tell me, Everly."

"I thought last night was a one-and-done thing," she says, but she inches closer to me.

"I'm not *doing* anything. Just asking," I insist.

"Right. Sure." She arches a playful brow.

"I just want to know," I say, leaning in so we're inches apart, letting her catch a hint of my cologne.

The moment it hits her is clear. It's in the quiet gasp she tries to hide but fails to. A tiny murmur seems to escape those lush lips. Still, she tries to up the ante in our game, saying, "Guess."

Now we're getting somewhere. But because we are, I need to be careful. I dart away from her and close the distance to the door a few feet away, locking it then returning to her. My eyes roam up and down her body. "You have them on, don't you?"

She tilts her head, her blonde ponytail swishing against her shoulder. "Since you did something big for me, I'll answer you—yes. I do."

A rumble works its way up my chest and past my lips. "And I just wanted to thank you for wearing them then," I say.

She laughs. "That's why you talked to the press? Me wearing the lingerie you sent me inspired you to talk to the media? I guess if I'd known all along it was that easy..."

"You wouldn't have promised me a limo once upon a time?"

She shakes her head playfully. "Not now that I know your weakness."

But I correct her. "Your eyes," I say, looking into those deep brown pools. "Like I told you earlier. Your eyes are my weakness. Your eyes are my undoing."

Her breath hitches, but she lifts a doubtful brow since she's not won over easily. "Are my eyes your weakness or is it the royal blue panties?"

Jesus. *She* is my weakness. I can't hide the truth

anymore. "It's not just the panties. Did I love it? Fuck yes. But that's not why I talked tonight."

"Why then?"

"Because of you. How hard you work," I say, my tone one hundred percent serious. *This* is why I waited for her tonight. "I needed you to know that. The real reason I pulled you into the equipment room is to tell you what hit me tonight right outside the tunnel. When you told me the press made bets on me. You—*you, Everly*—have to put up with that shit all the time from them. And you have to put up with me. All of a sudden, I understood what you've been dealing with from their side—not just mine. But in the press box too. You're tough and strong, and you have been putting up with so much. It only seemed fair that I do this for you."

Her lips part in a slow, sweet smile. "Max," she says softly, like she's genuinely touched. "Thank you. That really means a lot to me."

Ah, fuck. My heart lurches toward her. She cares so much. More than I expected. "You really want this to work, don't you? This makeover?"

"I do," she whispers, her voice cracking. "Maybe this sounds silly, but I made a promise when Marie...died," she says, taking a breath, steeling herself perhaps as she sets a hand on the edge of the shelf full of helmets next to her, "to try to live my best life. To work hard, to do good, to appreciate everything I have—my friends, my job, my... body." Something about that last word seems to knock her off-kilter. And it's like she needs a moment. But she pushes on. "To reach for the moon. To be an example. And I want to be excellent at everything I do."

"You are," I say, so damn impressed by her. "You're powerful and strong."

"You're strong too. It took a lot of guts to talk to the press tonight."

I wave a dismissive hand. "Nah. Just some drugs."

"What? You'd better not be on drugs."

I wiggle a brow. "I think I've been a little high all day long." I pause, locking eyes with her. "On you."

"Stop it," she whispers, but it's playful and seems to say *go on*.

Here in the equipment room, surrounded by helmets, sticks, pucks, pads, and all kinds of gear, I reach for her hair, stroking the ends of the ponytail. "I have not been able to stop thinking about what it was like to kiss you."

"Max, you really shouldn't do this. I really shouldn't do this," she says, but she reaches for my shirt collar, her nimble fingers playing with it.

"I know," I admit. Neither one of us stops touching the other.

"Things are intense here at work. I found out today Elias is competing for the promotion now, and it's tougher," she says with a sigh.

A dose of protectiveness rockets through me. "The guy who looks like he's twelve? The one who's always asking us to sign hockey sticks to give away during the intermissions? It's not just me that he asks—he asks all the guys all the time."

She laughs lightly. "That's him. He used to play in college too. Which he likes reminding me of."

"Fuck him. He doesn't deserve the job. You do."

"It doesn't even matter. He used to play. He's got connections. His uncle's the general counsel, and I don't want to be the..." She doesn't finish the thought but it's clear what she means—she doesn't want to be the woman who's getting silky gifts from one of the players.

I think about her dilemma for a minute, but I don't have any useful answers. There's nothing I can do right now anyway. I've got my own problems. "I wish it weren't like this either," I say heavily.

I wish, too, I didn't need her so much right now in my professional life. But there's a message on my phone from my agent telling me he's proud of me for saying something to the media tonight. There's an image of the bagel of the day. There's a memory of the injury in my rookie season that could have been so much worse.

But there's something else I need to say tonight to her too. Something important. I let go of her hair, and she drops her hand from my collar. "You've been trying to do your job for over a year, and I've been an asshole."

She tilts her head, her smile kinder than I deserve, considering how I've railroaded her. "But that's not who you are. You're not a jerk. You're kind of soft underneath."

I growl. "Pro tip: do not ever call a man soft."

She rolls her eyes, then sets a hand on my chest like she's feeling my heart beating under her palm. Hell, I can feel it speed up as she spreads her fingers across the fabric of my shirt, then says, "I've seen you with your nephew. You're soft when it matters. And thank you in advance for trusting me."

I didn't trust her for a long while. But things have changed now that I've gotten to know her. I've seen her heart, her passion, and her hope for the future. "I do trust you, Everly. I didn't when we started this, but I do now."

Her smile deepens, touches someplace inside me that's rarely touched. "I'm glad," she says.

I should say goodnight to her. I should leave this room. I should get on that bus. But a glance at my watch tells me there are twelve more minutes before we have to leave.

My gaze swings down to her pants, then back up to her face. "I really want to see how you look in them," I say in a needy rasp.

She's quiet for several seconds before she whispers, "Do you want me to send you a picture later?"

More than I want my next breath. "Yes," I say in a rough demand. But I know that won't be enough to satisfy me. I tip my chin toward her. "Give me a sneak peek now."

She doesn't need any convincing. As she stands against the wall in her trim slacks, heels, and blouse, her right hand slides down to the waistband and she's unbuttoning then unzipping and...I groan.

How does she get sexier by the day? I didn't know that feat was possible, but Everly Rosewood pulls it off. Here, surrounded by gear, with a fluorescent light flickering overhead, Everly unzips her slacks, spreads the waistband open, and shows me the beautiful blue lace.

It's just a tease, but in a second my chest is a furnace. My dick is a telephone pole. "It's almost better than if you were in my jersey," I rasp out.

She drags her teeth across the corner of her mouth then murmurs, "Bet this is better."

In slow motion, she slides her hand inside her panties, and I think I might combust. I am nothing but one frayed, red-hot nerve as her hand disappears then emerges. She lifts it, steps close to me, presses her index finger to my mouth, and brushes my lower lip with the taste of her wetness. As I lick my lips, I shoot out a hand, grip the back of her neck, and drag her close. Then I growl. "Give me one fucking kiss for the road, and then I swear I'll forget you."

She seals her sweet mouth to mine, giving me a hot, deep, wet kiss that pretty much ensures I'm never going to forget her.

When she lets go, she zips her slacks and tucks in her blouse, but makes no move to leave. Her eyes gleam with something naughty. Something risqué. Don't know what. But I want to. "We're not even, Max."

I furrow my brow. She must mean about the press somehow. "We don't have to be even about me talking to the media," I say.

She shakes her head. "That's not what I mean. I know we said it was a one-and-done last night but the thing is..." Her expression turns flirty. "We didn't really finish."

"Sunshine, you finished twice. All over my fingers and all over my face."

She blushes and it's a beautiful shade, but then she shakes her head. "But you didn't."

Before I even have time to process her words, Everly grabs my shoulders, spins me around, and pushes me against the wall. She gives me the naughtiest look as she drops down to her knees, asking, "Why don't I give you another kiss for the road?"

My voice is sandpaper as I groan, "Fuck yes."

She runs the tip of her tongue along her teeth as she unbuttons my slacks. I help her along, unzipping them. Her quick hands tug on the waistband of my black boxer briefs, pulling them down, freeing my aching cock.

The second she takes me out, those brown eyes of hers light up with a wicked sort of delight. "Looks even prettier than I imagined."

I blink, shock and desire radiating through me. "You imagined *my dick?*"

She's the pleased one now, nodding as she stares at my hard length. "The way you taste too."

It's a miracle I don't come right now. This is going to take me all of ninety seconds. I run a hand down her glossy ponytail. "Show me. Show me how fucking beautiful you look sucking my cock."

She doesn't need any instruction from me because she's already parting her pretty lips. She stares up at me as she flicks her tongue across the head. I grunt at the beautifully filthy sight of this woman on her knees.

Sliding her hands up my thighs, she opens wider, her mouth warm and wet, inviting me in. The clock is ticking, but she doesn't rush. She gives me exactly what she promised.

A kiss on my dick.

And it lights up every cell in my body. She caresses the crown of my cock with her lush lips, then lavishes attention with her tongue.

My eyes roll back in my head. It's fucking incredible, and she's barely touched me. I force myself to keep my eyes open because there is nothing better than this view. She lets my cock fall from her mouth only so she can brush her lips down my shaft—one side, then the other.

With her left hand, she grips my thigh tighter. With her right, she reaches for my balls, cupping them.

"Fuck, baby," I groan, unbidden.

She follows that kiss with a long, lingering stroke of her tongue, from base to tip and back again.

"What are you doing to me?" I murmur.

She smiles as she licks my dick adoringly, then whispers, "Just a goodbye kiss."

And I want it. Dear god, do I fucking want it. I want

everything she's giving me. I don't want to stop her either just because the clock is ticking. Hell, I'll miss the flight for this blow job. I've never had one like this before.

Where she's lavishing open-mouthed caresses on my dick that make me feel like a king.

A king who really wants to come though.

But she must read my mind because she gives my balls a quick squeeze, then inhales my dick.

"Oh fuck," I rasp out as my cock slides past her beautiful lips and hits all the way to the back of her throat.

She lets go of my thigh and reaches for my watch, tapping it. Doesn't need to tell me twice to speed it up. "Can I fuck your mouth?" I ask urgently.

Her eyes glint as she nods. She sets to work sucking in deep and hard while I do my part, thrusting into the paradise of her wet, warm mouth.

"You're a fucking goddess," I say as pleasure rockets through me.

I can barely stand how good it feels. My thighs shake. My muscles tense. I tug on her hair. "Always wanted to do that," I murmur.

For a brief second, she drops me. "Do it again."

"Yeah?"

She gives me a filthy smile. "Say yes and all. So I'm saying yes to you fucking my throat and pulling my hair."

And I'm saying yes to the hottest words ever spoken on Earth. I gather her silky hair in my fist and give it a jerk as I thrust.

She coughs.

I pull out. "Want me to stop?"

She scoffs, then gives me the sexiest look ever. "No. I want you to fuck my mouth like I have no gag reflex."

Lust rattles down my spine. "You're perfect," I say, shoving my dick back in her mouth and tugging on her hair.

As I fuck her throat, the open neckline of her blouse slides over, exposing some of her collarbone and the lacy strap of a pale peach bra, as well as what looks like the edge of a red, raised scar.

I can barely see the scar, and can barely register the mark either since my brain's short-circuiting. I grunt out a *coming* warning. As my legs shake, I fight off an outrageously loud moan of pleasure as I come down her throat. She looks up at me, shaking her head with my dick still between her lips, her eyes saying *be quiet* as she swallows my release.

"Sunshine, your mouth is heaven," I say in a rumble when she lets me fall from her lips.

She runs a hand across her mouth and rises. Adjusts her blouse. Leans in to press a kiss to my lips. "Now we're even."

But she's wrong. I'm not sated. I'm not sure I could ever be satisfied that I've had enough of Everly. I want her more every fucking hour. I wrap a hand around her head, pressing a kiss to her lips then letting go, running my hand along her collarbone where the scar is peeking out, touching her gently there. Trying to tell her something.

But as I near the fabric covering that hint of a scar, she tenses, then lifts her hand once more to adjust her top, lightly brushing mine away.

Not sure what that means. But we don't have time now to talk. Still, I can't stand the thought she'd worry. I meet her gaze, more serious than I was earlier when I told her why I'd talked to the press. "You're beautiful everywhere.

Know that," I say, cupping her cheek, imploring her to understand.

She closes her eyes like something hurts her.

My heart aches for her. I kiss her forehead. "I mean it," I whisper.

When she opens her eyes a few seconds later, she's blinked off the emotions. "Thank you." Then she frowns, her eyes sad. "We really shouldn't do this," she says, repeating—essentially—what she said earlier.

"I know," I say, heavily.

But she puts her hand on my face, her thumb stroking my beard, her eyes swimming with vulnerability—the same kind I've been feeling for her. I cover her hand with mine. "I'll try to resist you. But I make no promises."

She laughs softly. "I'll try too." Then she clears away the emotion. "Have a good trip."

She grabs her purse from the floor, runs a hand over her ponytail, and heads to the door. But before she unlocks the door, she looks back at me, fire in her eyes again, flirtation on her mouth. "You were right. I did sniff your Midnight Flame that night in my hotel room."

She leaves, the door closing with a *thunk*, her parting words like a post-orgasm jolt of pleasure. I glance at my watch. There are seven minutes before the team bus leaves. I can't quite figure out if I reassured her at the end, but there's just enough time for me to do something else for her.

Quickly, I tuck in my shirt and zip my pants. Running a hand through my hair, I try to straighten up so it's not obvious I just got the blow job of a lifetime, then I yank open the door. But the second I step into the hallway, I'm greeted by the smiling face of Elias.

Fuck me.

"Hey, Max! Great game tonight. You were on fire," he says, but his gaze drifts down the corridor, and my brain races with worry. Is Everly walking away? Did he spot her leaving before me? Is it obvious we were in here together? But when I steal a glance down the hall she's nowhere to be seen.

That's good.

"Thanks, man," I say. But I don't make up an excuse about what I was looking for in the equipment room. The more you say, the more obvious it is that you're covering up something.

Elias's brow knits. "Working late?"

"Or hardly working," I joke, keeping it casual. I nod to the end of the corridor, a subtle sign I should go.

But maybe he doesn't do subtle since he doesn't let up. "Anything you need in the equipment room?"

The dude doesn't sound suspicious, but the fact that he's asking the question tells me he is.

Think fast.

This fucker wants Everly's job. I'll do whatever it takes to protect her from him. "Actually, I need a Sharpie. I was going to sign a hockey stick for you to give away during the next home game. If you want to, that is?"

Here's hoping a distraction play works.

His gray eyes pop. A smile forms on his face, big and wide. "I've got a Sharpie on me."

"Great. Then I can do it now."

I head back into the equipment room, grab a stick, and return to the hall, signing it for the guy I hate, then thrusting it at him. "Here you go."

"I seriously appreciate this so much," he says, beaming, and I guess the play worked.

"Happy to help," I say, then nod to the exit. "Got to catch the bus."

"Have a great road trip."

"We will." I take off, but make a speedy pit stop in the locker room before I go. If I'm fast, I'll have just enough time.

25

THE REAL CLICHÉ

Everly

I'm still amped up a half hour later, even after I've edited then posted the video of Max's comment on the team's social media. I'll put it on his feed in the morning. With that done, I slide into bed in a cami and sleep shorts. I open the nightstand drawer, reaching for my favorite toy, then stop. I should take a picture now for him. Since, well, these panties are coming off in three, two, one...

But my phone buzzes before I set up the shot. A text from Max lights the screen.

> Max: There's a package coming to you in ten minutes. Local courier. Can you meet the driver at the door?

I have no idea what it could be but I'm sure I want it.

> Everly: Yes.

I grab a hoodie and tug it on, then wait for a notification that the driver's arrived. When it lands, I race downstairs and open the front door. A man in a ball cap hands me a gift bag that's stapled closed and says, "Here you go."

Anticipation curls through my veins as I rush back upstairs to my home. The second I'm inside, I rip open the staples, and...I know. My nose twitches, and I jam my hand in the bag faster than a kid dipping her paw into a cookie jar. When I pull out the delivery, I swallow roughly.

It's his shirt. The one he wore tonight after the game. The white dress shirt, and it smells like his cologne. I bring it to my nose. I close my eyes, feeling weak in the best of ways. Feeling woozy as I savor the scent of him. What is he even wearing right now on the team plane? No idea, but I guess he has multiple dress shirts in his stall and grabbed another one so he could send this to me— and send it quickly. But then again, services like Uber Connect are ridiculously fast.

When I open my eyes, I feel like I'm melting. I'm not sure I can walk. My phone buzzes again. Tingles spread down my spine as I open the next message.

> Max: Wear it to bed. Send me that picture. Because you're so incredibly beautiful, I can't stop thinking about you. Guess I'm bad at resisting. But you know that.

With the shirt clasped to my chest, I walk to my bedroom in some kind of trance. I set the shirt down on the bed, pull off the hoodie and cami, then strip off my sleep shorts. Briefly, I glance at the wooden box on the lower shelf of the nightstand—the one with the Post-it notes.

All those *say yes*es.

"That's the problem. I keep saying yes," I whisper to my silent home.

But Max makes me feel pretty and powerful. And that's catnip, so I say yes one more time.

Tomorrow I'll do better. Tomorrow I'll be done with this dangerous tryst. For one more night, I'll say yes—this time to wearing his clothes that smell like him. I slide my arms into his shirt, turning my neck to the collar. The shirt hits me at the thighs, and I love how big it is. I'm wrapped up in him, in his scent, in the memory.

Briefly, I contemplate buttoning the shirt before I snap a pic.

But instead, I sit on the edge of the bed, arranging it so it covers up all the places I don't want him to see—my upper arm, then the scar on my left shoulder. The one he possibly caught a small glimpse of. I'm not sure how I'd handle it if he saw more. The memory of Gunnar's shock still stings.

But Max and I are one-and-done. So getting naked with him won't happen.

Making sure my face isn't in the shot, I snap a pic from the neck down. Send it to him. Inhale him one more time.

Then I vow to resist him for real.

* * *

As the sun streams through my bedroom window early the next morning, the light feels too bright on me. Like it's highlighting all my flaws as I get ready for work.

I try to ignore the squirmy feeling in my gut as I pick out a red bustier with embroidered cherries on it, put it on, then slip on black slacks next.

Before I grab the black blouse that's hanging on the door, I look in the mirror in the corner of my room. Each day since I began this routine—I started it after Gunnar ghosted me—I try to like the view more.

"I am pretty and powerful," I tell my reflection.

But the words ring hollow. It's not the pretty part of my mantra that's the problem. It's the powerful part, since that's the lie the morning light is exposing. Lately, I'm powerless to these feelings for Max.

I've been giving in at night when I shouldn't. Taking risks when I ought to be cautious. Listening to the lies I tell myself—that it's no big deal to say yes to these wild feelings.

It *is* a big deal though.

I've worked too hard in my field. But last night I was foolishly risky. Locked doors or not, that was world-class levels of dumb. I can't be the kind of woman who blows superstar athletes in equipment rooms.

Max's words to the press might have been a cliché, but they were a safe cliché. I'm the real cliché. I stare angrily back at my reflection, my jaw set hard, my nostrils flaring.

"You're not powerful when you do that stupid shit," I hiss at the woman in the mirror.

I think of Erin, a woman I admire, and the question she asked last night.

How steady and strong she was in the media room. She wanted one thing—Max on camera. She *knew* she wouldn't get salacious answers from him with me there, so she didn't ask an aggressive question.

And what did I do to show I'm good at my job? I gave a pro athlete a blow job. What the hell would the reporters I work with think of me if they'd seen me on my knees with his dick down my throat?

I jerk my blouse off the hanger, stuff my arms into it, and button it up. I leave in a cloud of loathing.

At the office, I am all business. I repost the clip on *The Real Max Lambert*.

When that's done, I do my morning rounds online, checking sports news sites and feeds. As promised, Erin ran with his comments in a wrap-up report on The Sports Network last night. I hit play on my laptop.

"And in a rare appearance off the ice, the Sea Dogs goalie had this to say about tonight's game," she says, then leads into the quote from Max. When the video returns to her, she looks to her co-host and says with a wry grin, "It's not as if he cracked open the playbook. But maybe he didn't need to."

"His numbers this season have been speaking for themselves," her co-host, Rowan, says.

Erin wags a finger at him. "Hey, don't jinx me, Rowan. I want him to keep talking to The Sports Network," she says, then cuts to a report on the Supernovas, and how Fletcher Bane has been playing recently.

Irrational irritation ratchets up in me as they talk

about what a great season Bane is having on the LA team. Next, they cut to a clip of him in the locker room last night after a win. "We capitalized on the power plays. We've been skating well and matching our opponents. And we just played hard all around." Then he flashes a charming grin worthy of all the toothpaste commercials in the land. "What can I say? You have to jump on the opportunities life affords you."

I want to reach through the computer and smack him. And smack Lyra for hurting Max. And then smack myself for feeling all of these feelings.

I drop my head on my desk, sighing listlessly. I shouldn't care about Max's ex-girlfriend. Or his rival. I shouldn't care about how they hurt him. Maybe I should even be grateful she cheated on him. If she'd been faithful, I probably wouldn't have had that screaming set of orgasms the other night.

I groan. What is wrong with me? I can't actually be glad that he's single so he could...please me?

Besides, nothing more is going to come of that brief two-night tryst with Max. I lift my face from my desk, smooth out my hair, and return to my job. Reading and watching everything that was said last night. Jamie, one of the podcasters, has stitched the barrage of questions from the press together, then his commentary comes next with, "And now, winning cliché of the month, is Max Lambert for this chestnut."

Before I can watch more, my phone trills with Zaire's ringtone.

I answer it right away, and she says, "Good job last night with Lambert."

"Thank you."

"You coaxed more than a one-word grunt out of him.

You got a real comment," she says, laying on praise I don't deserve. "What magic did you work?"

"I guess it was the right time," I say, like it was nothing, when in fact it was my magic panties.

"Keep up the good work. You are a makeover queen," Zaire says, then moves on to other topics.

But the thing is—she's right. I am damn good at my job. I do know how to handle the press. I want the promotion badly. I want to live my boldest, brightest life. I want to be the best that I can.

A tryst in the equipment room simply can't happen again. Too much is at stake. The job, the potential promotion, and especially the reputation rehab. It's too important to too many people.

Which means it's time to call for backup.

When I get off the call, I text my friends and request an emergency meeting this weekend. *I need a girls' night this weekend. Fair warning—I need a major strategy session. Bring wine.*

Seconds later, Josie responds first with: *On it!*

And it's a relief to speak the complete and utter truth.

26

A DAMN GOOD MOOD

Max

I'm still in a damn fine mood a few hours before game time. Maybe because I spent a good long time in my hotel room in Dallas on Tuesday and Wednesday night with the pic Everly sent of her looking like sin in my shirt.

Spent extra time with that snap last night, and this morning, too, here in Nashville.

With the endorphins still fueling me, I'm damn near strutting down the hallway with Asher at the Nashville arena, all cold concrete and an intimidating atmosphere that only fuels my desire to beat the other team tonight.

"Hey, Miles," I call out since he's up ahead several feet, and I can't resist giving my teammates hell. It's part of my good mood.

Miles turns back to me with a chin nod. "What's up?"

"You're avoiding me, and I know why."

Miles isn't a gamer for nothing, since he adopts a blank face as he asks, "What would I be avoiding you for?"

Like he doesn't know. "My three-of-a-kind last night on the plane. I beat you in poker. Bryant and Callahan paid up. You did not. You owe me one hundred bucks too. Don't try to get out of it again."

Miles glares at me as he stops, lifts his phone from a pocket, and makes a show of Venmo-ing me the money. "Someday I'm going to figure out what your trick is with poker," he says, defeated, like he was last night too.

Shame.

Asher snorts. "Good luck with that. Lambert's unbeatable."

I want to bask in the praise and the truth of it. But I can't let either of them think that or they'll never play poker with me on the plane again. "Not true." I scratch my beard, as casual as can be. "I lost the other week. Don't you remember?"

That's a bald-faced lie, but I try to sell it with a lazy shrug.

Asher lifts a doubtful brow, studying me for several seconds. "You're bluffing."

Miles's jaw drops. "Holy shit. He is. That's your tell, Lambert."

"You scratch your beard when you're full of it," Asher adds.

Well, fuck me. I only meant to throw them off the scent, not reveal my hand. So I double down, scoffing as we stride closer to the visitors' locker room. "Don't have a tell."

"Everyone does," Miles says.

I wave a hand to move on. Maybe my good mood has softened me up. "Fine, I'll go easy on you next time."

Miles stares dead-eyed at me. "You will do no such thing. Ever."

"That's what I like to hear," I say, patting him on the back. "Now, let's go make Nashville cry."

As Miles turns into the locker room, Asher hangs back, stopping outside the door. "How's everything going?"

"Good. Why?"

"I saw your comments from the other night got some pickup with the sports press."

"You did?" I guess I shouldn't be surprised Asher noticed—he's observant.

But then he surprises me when he says, "Maeve was texting me and telling me. She said she was trying to scroll through calming, time-lapse videos of people painting murals—they're her favorite, and it's fucking adorable—but then hockey infected her feed."

There's a whole lot going on in that intel drop. I'm not sure where to start, so I say, "That's awfully specific."

"She's a painter," he says, a little proudly. "Anyway, just checking in to see how you're doing."

I'm a lucky guy that some of my friends are so emotionally astute. "I'm actually okay," I say honestly, opening up some more to him. He makes it easy enough, like he did at the smoothie shop the other week, like he does in my car, too, when I drive him to the rink. "It wasn't as awful as I'd thought it'd be."

"Proud of you," he says.

"I just put blinders on, you know?"

"That's what you gotta do," he says. "I'm glad you're finally realizing you don't need to make things harder on yourself. You don't need to fight it. You'll see it becomes painless after a while—talking to the press."

But I'm not buying that yet. "Let's not get too far ahead of ourselves."

"I'm not worried. You've got this," he says.

I wave him along. "All right. If I spend too much time with you and your happy attitude, I might not be a dick during the game."

He scoffs. "You'll always be a dick," he says, then nods toward the locker room. But my phone rings and when I grab it from my pocket, it's my agent's name lighting up the screen. A dart of tension stabs me in the chest. I waggle my cell at Asher. "I'll catch up with you inside. I need to talk to Garrett."

"Good luck, man. Let me know how it goes," he says.

"Will do."

I hit answer then turn around, pacing away from the locker room to a quieter corner of the corridor. "What's up?" I ask with more trepidation than I'd like to feel with my agent. But that's how things have been since this whole makeover project started with veiled threats from my very unhappy team.

"Guess who's not getting fined?" Garrett asks.

Pretty sure I know what he means, but I can't resist teasing him either. "Is it you? Did you get a parking ticket again? I know you like to park that ridiculous Lambo wherever you want. The one I make possible for you."

Garrett groans, all over the top. "You say that like it's a problem that your success and my hard work funded my sweet ride."

"Fine, you deserve your sports car. And ten more. Anyway, what's going on?"

He's clearly in a good mood, and I'm damn curious.

"I heard from Clementine and Zaire this morning," he begins, businesslike. "They're both going to be at the dog adoption event next week, and they were very happy you talked to the press earlier this week. Zaire even said the producers at *The Ice Men* noticed it, and they're glad to see it too. No idea what inspired you but keep that shit up."

I picture Everly. Her effort. Her commitment. Fact is I wanted to do something for her. She's done a hell of a lot for me.

"What can I say? I guess it was just the right time," I reply instead.

"Now, was it so hard to say something nice the other night?"

I roll my eyes but I'm glad Garrett is happy. "You think we can get some sponsorships now?" I ask, shifting gears though I immediately want to take it back because I sound a little desperate. But the fact is, I'd like to start moving forward on this front again. Make some progress with my financial plans. Put away enough to take care of Sophie and Kade for life. Help my parents out even more with a big retirement plan for them too.

"We're not there yet," he says. "I'm not fighting off phone calls to sign you up as a spokesperson. We're gonna need a whole lot more of this if you want that to happen."

I sigh, wishing it were easier. "Can't fault a guy for trying."

"But we'll get there. You keep that up and I know it will."

"Here's hoping," I say. "I'll see you at the event."

Then I go into the locker room. As I'm getting ready for the game, my phone buzzes with a text. Briefly I hope it's Everly. That she's sending me another pic. Saying hi. Wanting to know how I'm doing.

But am I wanting to hear from her too much when I'm supposed to be resisting her? For both our sakes, I do the right thing—I refrain from checking my messages.

* * *

When the game is over and we've won, I head to the team jet that'll take us to Detroit. As I'm boarding, I hop over to my texts at last.

But I stop dead in my tracks at my row. It's not from her. It's from someone who hasn't texted me in a year and a half, since the night I came home early to a hell of a surprise.

Lyra: Hi, Max! Can we talk?

27

THE PLAYER AND THE PUBLICIST

Everly

Before I can have my girls' night in, I have to brave the fire swamp and endure Saturday morning with my parents.

I steel myself for my monthly breakfast with them. I meet them across the Golden Gate Bridge in Sausalito where they live, and go to Gigi's Café—the same place we always go for our regular check-ins. Mom is dressed impeccably in navy slacks and a white blouse, with a fresh blowout of her blonde hair. Dad's in khaki pants and a polo, looking like he's about to work on a Saturday. Which he probably is, since the law business is a round-the-clock one, as he likes to tell me.

And only the strongest survive.

I say hello, then we make small talk as we settle into our regular table and peruse the menu. It's pointless— Dad orders the same thing every time. Two poached eggs, no butter. Toast dry. Mom orders the fruit bowl and claims it fills her up.

I opt for French toast because Marie used to say *life's too short to pass up a good French toast*. She was right—life is too short.

"And how's everything going at work?" my mom asks after the server leaves, then prattles on before I can answer. "I'm so glad you have a good job. Let me tell you— all my friends' kids are struggling these days, living at home. Barely doing their own laundry. But look at you. You've got it all figured out. It's like the accident didn't even slow you down."

Yes, Mom. I almost died and I didn't miss a beat. That's exactly what happened.

"Well, she's not a director yet," my dad points out since nothing is good enough for him. Nothing ever has been.

My gut churns. "I'm applying for a promotion though."

"And she'll get it, Russ," my mom says, patting his hand.

"Nothing's in the bag till it's in the bag," he says, since he's always right.

"That's why I'm devoting every bit of energy toward it," I point out, doing my best to hold my own.

"Good. Everyone your age is obsessed with work-life balance," he says. "But that's bullshit. You have to work hard. End of story."

It's always been the end of the story with him.

"Now, Russ," Mom says, chiding him. "You don't have to work all the time these days." But she stage-whispers to me, "But when your father works, I have plenty of time for my book club. And my yoga. And my volunteer work."

She's the one who has the work-life balance figured out, but maybe it's simply that she's balanced being married to a workaholic hard-ass by savoring every second when he's at the office. Heck, his eighty-hour weeks are probably why they're still married.

Dad downs some coffee, then turns to me, expression still gruff. "And how's everything in the romance department, honey?" That's his pet name for me. The one he uses when he downshifts to what he must think is his *softer side*. "If you let us set you up with a good guy, maybe you'd finally meet a good guy."

It's said upbeat, like he's oh so helpful, rather than delivering a dig.

"But then I wouldn't have time for work," I say, slinging his words right back at him since two can play at his game.

"Good point," he says, cracking a rare smile.

Yes, this is when I make him the happiest—when I prove I'm devoted to the desk.

Josie knocks on my door Sunday evening with the world's loudest bang. I swing it open to find her brandishing a grocery bag. "I've got boxed wine, lime chili-pepper tortilla chips, and instructions to take you to Maeve's favorite bowling alley instead of here," she says with a *please say yes to the change of plans* grin.

I groan, gesturing to my leggings and a hoodie. "I have to go out? A girls' night in is supposed to be, you know, inside. I was going to wallow before we strategize."

"I can see if the bowling alley allows wallowing and bowling?" Josie asks playfully.

I sigh, then acquiesce. "Let me change into jeans. But what should we do about the boxed wine and chips?"

"Dude, they're portable."

LAUREN BLAKELY

"Another reason why I love wine."

Twenty minutes later, we're at Spare Time Alley in the Mission, not far from Fable's place.

Maeve and Fable have already claimed a lane. Maeve is wearing a 60s-style outfit—a pink button-down bowling shirt and capri pants. Her golden-brown hair is curled at the ends, a retro do, while Fable's wearing a letterman jacket. Briefly, I imagine Marie walking in here with me. She'd wear a black leather jacket and matching pants, declare it her bowling garb, then promptly forget the game because she'd want to hear all the details of everyone's week first. She'd fit in perfectly. I know that. It's a lovely picture, the five of us, and one of the first ones that doesn't choke me up.

But I can't live in my head.

"Hello! Did anyone think to tell me there was a dress code?" I glance disapprovingly at my very casual clothes.

Fable plucks at the coat. "I just grabbed this from work." It's a Renegades jacket.

"Did the team owner give it to you?" Maeve asks her, arching a playful brow.

Fable rolls her eyes. "No." It's said like it has ten syllables.

I laugh. Maeve has never let go of the idea that the team owner has a crush on Fable. Not even now that Fable's started seeing a new guy—a stockbroker named Brady who's friendly and fun, Fable has said.

"Someday, you'll admit the truth," Maeve tells her, then looks to me. "And there's no dress code. The style is be yourself. And you look cute in a lavender hoodie. You hardly ever wear colors besides blue, black, or gray. But you should. They suit you."

"Thanks. It's my job to blend in though, so I try not to stand out at work."

"This isn't work," Maeve says, then cracks open the box wine.

"Thank fuck," I say.

Maeve peers at me with studious eyes. "I bet you can bowl. I want you on my team."

"Why do you think I can play well?" I ask.

"Because you do pole like a badass babe *and* you spend all day doing strategy things at work. That's why."

But I don't do pole like a badass babe. I do it like I'm grocery shopping with coupons, and I've found a cheaper way to make chickpea salad. I find substitutions. I don't go all in. I do it like I'm holding back because...I have to hold back.

"I don't feel very strategic these days," I admit, since I'm more than ready for the wallow hour. "Either in pole or life."

Maeve sets down the box wine. Fable shrugs off the jacket and pats the seat next to her. I take it.

Josie sits next to me, wrapping an arm around me. "What do you mean?"

I lower my face for a second, considering whether I'm going to say this or not. But they have to know. They go to class with me, and really, it's easier to talk about pole than to deal with the wild mess of my feelings for Max. I look up and face them. "I just...sometimes really want to do... these other tricks. Ayesha's a dream move. So is Iron X. I'd love to be strong enough someday. But also, I'd just like to do a real outside leg hang. Without holding on, you know? Or...anything. And I should try, but I don't, which is so dumb."

"It's not dumb," Josie says, emphatically. "It's where you're at right now."

"The fact that you go to pole class at all after what happened is a big fucking deal," Maeve says, squeezing my thigh. "The PTSD has to be real."

I sigh. "Sometimes it is," I say. "But is that really an excuse?"

"That sounds like someone else talking," Fable says, then gives me a gentle but firm stare. "And as someone who's got a dad who takes up too much space in the room too, I bet that's where it's coming from. But don't beat yourself up because you're not ready to try a new thing," Fable adds, and way to read me.

"She's right," Josie seconds.

"But it's just such a...vain reason," I say.

Maeve shakes her head. "It's not vain. It's how you feel. You went through something huge, and you don't have to recover at any particular pace. Do it at your own speed. And if I could do a stargazer *at all* I'd be seriously impressed with myself. Don't knock what you choose to do. Maybe the strategy you've taken with pole is exactly the strategy you need."

I mull on that for several seconds. She might be onto something. Perhaps I have been strategic in the way I need when I go to the studio. But I need to be strategic about Max now. I need to *stop* feeling. I need to move forward. "I need a strategy for how to deal with all these wild feelings," I say, squaring my shoulders, looking for help.

"For the sex pirate?" Fable asks.

"Yep. Because I need to resist him. I mean it this time," I say, then because I'm trying to be more strategic, I peer around, checking my surroundings. You never know who might be here. Satisfied that it's not crowded in the alley tonight, I turn back to my friends and lower my voice as I update them on everything from Elias to the equipment room to Max's shirt, while Maeve pours the wine.

"Damn, he is down bad for you," Fable says, with a low whistle.

"I don't know. I'm pretty sure he hates me." But that doesn't ring true anymore at all.

Josie shakes her head. "I think hate turned to not hate pretty quickly."

My chest tingles, but that's the dangerous feeling I'm trying to avoid. "Same for me. That's the issue," I say with a helpless shrug, then asking the big question. "How do I handle seeing him again? Every time I see him I—"

"Take off your panties?" Josie offers.

I laugh, but I'm laughing *at me* because she's so right. "Yes, get me panties that lock, please."

With a thoughtful gaze, Maeve taps her chin. "I saw a pair just like that at Risqué Business. They have a padlock. And you have to open the padlock with your tongue," she says, and she's totally serious.

"That's a whole new form of tongue exercise," Fable remarks.

"Yes, and if a man can open a padlock with his tongue, I'm not sure I want to resist him," I point out.

"That's sort of the point of the panties," Maeve stage-whispers.

"Gee, thanks. I didn't realize," I say dryly.

"But the point is, you need the equivalent. What if we're your padlocks?" Maeve suggests.

I arch a brow. "Um. Explain."

"We can be your accountability buddies. If you're tempted, just text us instead," she offers.

"And you'll be my...no-sex-with-Max sponsors?"

Maeve smiles. "Exactly."

Josie's eyes light up from behind her glasses. "If you want us to be, yes. Just reach out and say *I'm tempted to rub myself against him like a cat. Come toss water on me.*"

"That sounds fun," I say, but the truth is it's a good idea—this impromptu support group. So good that Josie takes out her phone and makes a production of changing the name of our group message thread to The Padlockers.

I breathe deeply, feeling like I can do this. I can actually resist the irresistible Max Lambert. "He's behind me now," I say. "I'm going to focus on the makeover. The first event is later this week. And I need to make sure his *public appearance* goes off without a hitch."

"You're going to do a great job. Because, see my earlier point—you are a badass babe. Who can throw strikes," Maeve says.

And I do throw a strike when it's my first turn at the lane.

Because I'm here, trying to live my best life, and it turns out I'm pretty damn good at bowling. When the night ends, I've drunk some boxed wine, eaten some spicy chips, and found a little bit of my power again.

I've found it with my friends, and that's what matters —not this brief tryst with a sexy hockey player I used to hate.

Someone I definitely don't hate now.

* * *

Everything is ready for Wednesday. We have an afternoon game that day against our crosstown rivals, the Golden State Foxes. When it ends, the Zamboni will clean the ice and then we'll lead right into a dog adoption event with

Little Friends. The players will be in their jerseys. They can play with the dogs on ice, and then we can hopefully send all the pups to new homes that day. The rescue will bring the dogs over before the third period and they'll hang out in a media room till the game ends and then it's showtime.

It's going to be great, even with Elias popping by my office every day this week to check on details. To remind me that Donna is sooo excited. That he is sooo excited that I got in touch with his contact at Little Friends.

"I even wrote a press release," he says on Wednesday morning when he catches up with me in the hall.

I turn to him, taken aback. That's my area, and he's encroaching. "I did that," I say, trying not to let on I want to kick him in the knees.

He flashes me a smile that probably charms others. "Maybe just combine them? I have some fun facts in there. I know you love fun facts. Since you pitched The Sports Network to put them on the broadcast," he says, which he knows from our departmental meetings when we all update Zaire on what we've been working on. "And they did. Go you." Then he swivels his tablet around and shows it to me.

I read it, my jaw ticking. I'm annoyed that I like his fun facts about dog adoption. Annoyed I didn't think of it too. I have to do better. But then I remind myself, it's natural that the competition would be fierce. I'm going after a coveted post. The Sea Dogs don't want to hire light-weights. Elias, for all his annoyances, isn't a lightweight.

And if I want to be the director, I need to get along with everyone. Hopefully, even guys who might—gasp—work for me. I look up, returning his tablet to him. "This is great, Elias," I say with a professional smile. "If you email it to me, I'll layer them into mine as you suggested. I appreciate your collaborative spirit."

He beams. "Thanks, Ev."

The nickname from him grates on me, but I don't let it show. "You're welcome."

I'm about to head down the hall when he adds, "And speaking of collaboration—I've got that hockey stick signed from Max. Is there a time when you want me to give it away?"

I rack my brain, trying to figure out what he's referring to, but I draw a blank. "What giveaway? What stick?"

He gives me a curious look. "You know," he says, taking his time. "The one Max was getting when you were in the equipment room with him last week."

What the hell does he know about the equipment room? A damning flush crawls up my neck, threatening to reveal my secrets. I swallow roughly. *Don't let on, don't let on, don't you dare let on.* "Oh. Okay," I say, buying some time, trying to figure out what he knows—or thinks he knows.

"Where Max signed the hockey stick for me," he prompts, rolling his eyes like he can't believe I forgot.

But I did because I wasn't there to remember it. I'm guessing, though, that Elias must have run into Max after I left, and Max finessed the situation with an excuse about signing a stick. Smart move on his part, playing into Elias's love of giveaways. Now it's my turn to finesse an explanation as to why I was there. "Yes, I was chatting with him there before the Dallas flight so reporters wouldn't overhear me giving him tips on how to handle the media," I say, spinning my ass off like I've never spun it before.

Elias's eyes light up, twinkling even. "Damn. That's smart. Seriously smart."

It is? I mean, yes it is. "Thanks. That's your pro tip for the day," I say playfully.

He taps his temple. "I'll have to remember that."

I'm about to leave having gotten away with murder, when I remember—he asked when to give it away. I can't leave without answering. "Oh, and why don't you decide when to give the stick away? You're so good at the fan stuff, and you really know best."

It's actually the truth, even though it sounds like I'm sucking up to him. So I add, as earnestly as I can, "I mean it."

"Thanks, Ev. I'll find the perfect time."

I grin and bear the nickname, then head on down the hall, whipping out my phone to text Max. I should let him know that Mister Hockey Stick might be onto us.

But I stop when I open his contact info.

Our last exchange was the photo the night he left town. I *have* resisted him. He's resisted me. And he's going to hit the ice in a couple hours when the puck drops. I don't need to text him about Elias before the game starts since there's nothing to really worry about anyway.

Instead, I text The Padlockers.

> Everly: It's been more than a week since I even texted him. I want a prize for my resistance.

> Maeve: I'll send you a new vibe tonight as a reward! That is impressive!

> Josie: Gold stars for you, strategy queen.

> Fable: Is anyone else wondering if we can all get that reward? Just me?

> Everly: Yes, Maeve, make it a group reward.

> Maeve: Bankrupt me, why don't you?

> Josie: But it's for a good cause.

> Maeve: You don't need one, Josie! You have a hot man obsessed with your pleasure at your beck and call.

> Josie: That doesn't mean we don't enjoy vibes!

> Fable: I'd like to say TMI, but I'm mostly just jealous.

> Maeve: Me too.

> Everly: Me three thousand.

I smile, then put my phone away as I march down the hall, doing a double take when I pass the coach's office.

"Leighton!" I say when I spot the back of the pretty brunette sitting across from her father.

She must not hear me though, because she doesn't turn till her dad tips his chin in my direction, as if he's letting her know I'm here.

When she looks my way, her eyes brighten. "Hey, Everly! How are you? Good to see you again."

I step inside and give her a hug. I met Leighton a few years ago when she was still in college and interned at The Sports Network as a photographer. "Did you graduate last year?"

"I did. I'm doing some freelancing now," she says.

"She's so talented," her father says proudly, and gone is his usual tough guy coolness. He's all dad now, praising his daughter.

"I should have hired you for today. To take pics of the dog adoption event," I say. "I didn't realize you were back in town. I'll just have to hire you the next time I need a photographer. I'm guessing you won't have a problem with that, Coach?" I ask playfully, turning to her dad.

He adopts a faux stern expression. "Let's see. A job for my amazing, talented daughter? I'd have no problem with it."

"Can you come to the event today?" I ask her.

"I'm not sure. I actually have another freelance job with the Renegades."

"That's awesome. Seriously excited for you. Let's catch up soon. Want to grab a bite to eat with my friends and me? One of my girlfriends works for the Renegades."

"I'd love that," she says, then I say goodbye to her and her dad.

I spend the next few hours before game time hustling my butt off. I haven't even seen Max since he's returned, but that's okay.

We are just player and publicist—that is all.

With everything set for the event, and all sorts of media coming for photos, I head to the press box as a high school choir sings the national anthem. I arrive right before the one o'clock puck drop. The game begins, and two minutes into it, everyone's eyes are drawn to the Jumbotron.

Lyra Raine's face is on it, and she's here at center ice, sitting in the stands.

28

SNEAK ATTACK

Everly

It's my job to know how to handle surprises, but I am simply stumped. She's not here to sing the national anthem. I don't know what to make of this surprise appearance—nor do the members of the press. Gus peers at the Jumbotron with his brow pinched, then looks down at his screen, like the answer will materialize there.

Claudia's jaw drops, and in a raspy, former two-pack-a-day, awed voice, she says, "No way."

Jamie, the young podcaster, points at the huge screen above the ice, and blurts out, "Holy shit. Is that her?"

Her.

That's all he says.

Her.

She's so famous, she doesn't even need to be called by her name, Lyra Raine, or as she's more often known, *America's sweetheart*. She's famous enough that she's just... *her*. Bloggers, reporters, and talk radio hosts scramble.

There's a shuffling of equipment, phones, cameras. And then it's complete and utter chaos as reporters text their editors, lift their phones, and tap out social media posts, stat.

Jamie hoots then rubs his palms together. "And today, Jamie will be playing the role of an entertainment reporter."

Gus turns to me, always the news hound, tilting his head. "Did you know she was going to be here?"

My skin is as cold as my confidence is shot. "No."

Jamie is studying the Jumbotron where Lyra's chatting and smiling with a familiar-looking female friend—an actress perhaps. "Holy shit," Jamie says. "She's not with Fletcher. She's just with a friend." To no one at all but the computer screen, he adds, "I bet they're back together. Why else would she be here? A year and a half later? She shows up at his game on the day of a charity event? They've got to be a couple again."

Gus scoffs. "She's probably just trying to get his attention."

Claudia snorts as she types. "I bet she already has it. She used to do this when they were together. Just show up as a surprise for him. He loved it. And when he'd lose, she'd console him in the corridor right after."

My stomach pitches. My throat tightens. My hands feel clammy. Is she here for him? Are they back together? Is that why we didn't talk when he was on the road? It's completely possible that she could be here to see him again. Why else would she show up at a Sea Dogs game in early November on a Wednesday afternoon? There's no reason for her to be here other than to see Max and to get him back.

I wrap my arm around my waist like I need to protect

myself from all these possibilities as I stand here in the corner of the press room, the most surprised of all of them, with nothing to say because I don't have a clue what's going on.

I don't know the answer to any of the questions, but I do know how I compare to America's sweetheart and that's...disappointingly.

* * *

The worst part? He lets in a goal in the first five minutes when the Golden State Foxes send a puck flying through his legs. From three floors away, all the way up in the press box, I swear I can see him curse from behind his goalie mask.

I can't.

Of course I can't, but I can tell that's how he feels. He's surprised she's here—so surprised he's off his game. But is it a good surprise or a bad surprise? Those questions gnaw at me through the first period as the Foxes score again on the type of easy shot that Max almost always blocks. When the first period ends, no one leaves the press room because a Sports Network reporter is down there in the stands, sticking a mic in the pop star's face, and the Jumbotron is carrying the broadcast. "What a surprise to see you here. I would've thought you would be singing the national anthem," he says to her.

The pop star smiles, so self-deprecatingly, the kind of smile the world loves, then says, "That would be so great. What an honor that would be."

"Maybe you can come back for it?"

There's another dazzling smile from the pop star. "Maybe I can."

It's a promise she dangles that makes it sound like she has her sights set on a reunion. Or, that this *is* one.

The reporter asks another question. "Are you rooting for the Sea Dogs or the Foxes?"

Lyra's green-eyed gaze drifts to the net, empty now, of course, and my gut churns as she answers sweetly, "I'm rooting for the Sea Dogs."

Then the reporter cuts away and returns to the broadcasters.

Heads whip in the press room. Jamie and Claudia huddle as they toss ideas at each other.

"She's totally here for him," Claudia says.

"They're already back together," Jamie suggests.

"Do you think they're going to hard-launch their second chance at the end of this game?"

I grab hold of the wall. I won't let this get to me. That can't be happening. He's not going to post a picture with Lyra on his social media at the end of this game.

Then I tell myself to get a grip.

Whatever he does is fine. I'm not with him. I'm only the publicity manager for the team. I'm not his. I'm just the girl he sent a shirt and underwear to, but that doesn't mean a thing.

When the media peppers me with more questions, I smile and say, "I don't have any information." And finally, when the game ends with a terrible six goals scored on Max Lambert, I'm already at the tunnel, waiting for the team, knowing only one thing—I'm not asking him to talk to anyone right now.

It's not just because he won't. It's not simply to protect him. This time, it's to protect myself. I don't ask him because I don't want to talk to him right now. I'm too terrified of the emotions he'll find in my eyes.

Since Lyra's waiting in the corridor with her body-guards and her entourage. Waiting to console him, like she used to do after a loss.

I can't. I just can't.

I grab some of the guys and bring them to the media room. When that task is done, I hustle back and forth between Penny, who runs Little Friends, Elias, who's handling Donna, and the cheery, rosy-cheeked emcee herself who's saying hi to all the dogs like she's a dog whis-perer, then the Zamboni driver.

Finally, Max emerges from the locker room. I try to school my expression. To clear away any emotions. I'd thought, or maybe I'd hoped, that he'd look like he wanted to tear something apart.

But he seems shell-shocked. Maybe even empty. That doesn't give me any more answers. I have to remind myself it's not my place to find answers about his personal life. It's my place to rehab his public image. We don't have a romance. We have a business deal.

When he trudges over to me, I don't give him a chance to say a word.

I go first, fastening on my most PR of all PR smiles. "Let's get you out there playing with dogs."

"Everly," he says, a little imploring. The sound tugs on something in my heart. Something terrifying. Something tender that hurts to the touch. Like a bruise. Something you want to keep touching but probably shouldn't.

I cut in. "We really need to get you out there. This is going to be such a great event," I say, and I do deserve a promotion for spinning that lie right now.

29

ALL THE HOUNDS

Max

What the *fuck?* Seriously.

What the hell is my ex doing here? And why didn't I stop it? This is all my fault. I should've replied to her text. With one quick stab of my finger, I deleted it the other day, figuring I'd ignore her. Figuring that would make her go away. But maybe if I'd replied to it, she wouldn't have sabotaged this event.

I've got to tell Everly I had no idea Lyra was coming. Don't want her to think I had anything to do with this sideshow my ex has engineered out of nowhere. I can't even imagine what Everly must think. But I can't tell her *now*.

I clamp my molars together, grinding them in annoyance as I skate onto the ice with my teammates. We're in jerseys, jeans and skates—promo wear.

The ice is packed—Donna the emcee, a photographer Everly hired, a ton of local lifestyle media, and a

Chihuahua mix, a Beagle mix, a terrier of some sort, a lab-husky mutt, and a dog that looks like a Corgi met a Great Dane, and I really am not sure who was the mom and who was the dad in that situation, but if the dad was the Corgi I'd be real impressed.

As they promised they'd be here, the GM is sitting in the stands, just behind the bench, and she's next to Zaire. Garrett's sitting with them, too, and I feel like the bad kid at school, with Dad and the principal watching over me to make sure I behave.

Which is even harder because, oh right, there's one more person. Lyra's standing casually by the boards, the queen of surprises, like she's a part of this. Because of course, that's what somebody like her can do. Somebody world-famous can drop in and become a part of things where she doesn't even belong.

As her bodyguards flank her, she coos and smiles at all the dogs. The press snap pictures of her kissing the mutts like she's a politician with babies. She's dressed in her trademark ripped jeans, with a T-shirt that slopes down her shoulder, showing off her tattoos and her silver star, sun, and moon necklaces, her wavy red hair falling down past her shoulders.

Elias latches onto her, grinning like this is the highlight of his life. "Would you want to adopt one and take it home?"

The question is dripping with hope. Obsequiousness too. Bet he's crossing his fingers that this will be his breakout moment. That he'll get some comment from her and use it somewhere to level up in his promotion battle. I hate that guy more than I did before.

Lyra brings her hand to her chest, a practiced move that I've seen from her a dozen times before, but it still convinces everyone she legitimately means what she says. "I'd love one of these sweeties if I wasn't on the road so much."

Everly stands like a sentry a few feet away, patiently waiting to take over the event again since hockey players are nothing compared to a pop star. We're chopped liver, and the media wants the porterhouse of Lyra until the redhead who was supposedly brokenhearted when our romance ended—or so the public thinks—seems to notice the commotion, saying, "Oh my gosh, I did not mean to steal the focus. Let me get out of your way."

With a wave, she takes off, leaving the ice with her entourage, her havoc wreaked.

My heart rushes to Everly, and I want to skate over, grab her, and explain that if I'd only answered Lyra I could have stopped this circus. But Everly's on the move already. She scurries over to bubbly-faced, rosy-cheeked Donna, whispers something to her, then steps away.

With a nod, Donna strides in front of the photographers, her trademark mic in hand. "It's always great to have a surprise guest. And dogs love surprise guests because they love everyone. We've got some amazing mutts here that are looking for homes. And some of our guys are going to show them off to you."

Damn. That was some impressive ringmastering from Everly.

Donna introduces the first pup, a dog named Prancer who comes running like a springy pony toward Asher, who hugs the little guy. Photographers snap pictures. Then it's Asher's turn to introduce the next one. Miles goes next, then Wesley, until it's my turn to introduce Simon the Corgi-Great Dane.

"And this guy loves long baths in the sun," I say to the crowd, but I sound...gruff. Distant.

Like how you always sound.

Maybe no one cares. Maybe they're all used to that from me. But I'm so thrown off that I'm barely even sure how to fucking talk anymore.

There aren't the usual sports reporters here. These are lifestyle reporters. TV anchors. Influencers. It's a whole new ball game, and when I pose with a cute little Chihuahua named Lulu, I feel like I'm someplace else.

All I want to do is talk to Everly and tell her I'm sorry I didn't reply to Lyra's text because this event going sideways is all my fault.

When the photographers lower their cameras, one of them thrusts out a phone toward me. "Is it true that the two of you are back together? Did Lyra come here for you?"

Are you kidding me? That will never happen. I steal a glance at Everly, and hurt flashes in her eyes.

Shit.

She thinks that's why Lyra's here too. But does she think I want that?

Briefly, the words Everly fed me flash through my head—*I love animals, and I just want to help them all find a home.* And I do hope they all get adopted today. But the words that come out of my mouth are, "Do you want to talk about the charity and the dogs, or do you want to gossip?"

In no time, Asher arrives next to me in a spray of ice from his blades. He pats my shoulder. "They are kind of gossip *hounds*, aren't they?" he adds a wink. "But they're here for the dogs too. Maybe we can find a new team mascot."

He always knows what to say, and I'm so fucking grateful. I should follow his lead. "That's a great idea," I say, with as much pep as I can muster.

"Let's do it," Asher adds.

"They're all adorable," I add and maybe, just maybe I haven't dug myself a bigger press grave than the one I was already in.

A few seconds later, Everly steps into the fray holding Donna's mic, standing next to the emcee. "That's a great idea, Asher," Everly says. "We can actually help Donna find a new Sea Dog. She just said she wants to take a pup home today."

With a coolness and a savvy that never ceases to amaze me, Everly guides the reporters over to the pups and they spend the next hour helping pick a new rescue dog for Donna.

Somehow Everly saves the event. When it's over and I finally head off the ice, Asher asks where I'm going. "Need to find Everly," I grunt out then leave. Garrett tries to flag me down, but I give him a quick wave and shake of the head. Don't have time for him. Don't have time for anyone but the woman who has to think the worst.

What else would she think?

Lyra is spinning some narrative, and the media is eating it up, thinking we're back together. But what does Everly think?

I search for her in the arena, marching down the hall to her office even, but I can't find her anywhere. She doesn't answer when I call her. Or when I text. But as I'm stalking down the hall to the players' lot on the way to my car, Asher catches up to me. "Lambert, Everly's the one who told me to say that," he tells me.

My brow knits. "The gossip hound thing?"

"Yeah. She saved the whole damn thing," he says, clearly impressed with our publicist, then blunt as fuck with me as he adds, "Maybe you should...talk to her."

"I should. I will," I say, owning it. "Thanks, man."

I really fucked this whole day up by doing...nothing. Which means it's time to do something.

30

UPSIDE DOWN DAY

Everly

"When you've had a rough day at work...hang upside down."

That's what Kyla says to me when class ends that night. After I hightailed it out of the arena, I went straight to a pole class solo. I didn't want to talk to my friends about what happened today. But that's because I didn't want to talk to anyone. I just wanted to move.

"Is it that obvious?" I ask.

"A little," she says with a smile. "But then again, I can kind of recognize the feeling. It was a rough day at the day job too." She glances around the studio as most of the students shuffle out. I'm grabbing my water bottle as she asks, a little nervously, "Hey, any chance you can stick around to shoot some videos?"

"Of course," I say immediately, since I've done that in the past for her as part of her efforts to promote the classes she teaches here.

"Thank you," she says, flashing a grateful smile. "Marketing is nonstop these days. The Upside Down owner told me the landlord is upping the rent, so she's marketing it even harder. Translation: I'm marketing it even harder."

"I'm at your service then," I say, happy to help. I like having something to do. I like being useful.

"Give me five minutes to straighten up so I don't have to kick myself if I find a stray towel in a video," she says as the last student waves goodbye. "You can climb or play on your phone or whatever."

"Thanks," I say, and I have zero interest in getting on my phone. I turned it off when I left work. I don't really want to turn it back on. There's a part of me that likes being unreachable right now.

No—there's a part of me that *needs* it.

I spend so much of my life plugged in. Maybe too much.

As Kyla tidies the room, I return to the pole, wanting to keep moving. I already burned off my frustration in class. I'm not upset anymore. My job is handling problems, and I did it today. I'm proud of how I handled a complicated situation. I'm proud of how I took an event that was spiraling out of control and yanked it back into the orbit the team wanted.

So I savor one more moment on this chrome pole that has meant more to me than I ever expected. Or maybe I should have expected this connection. This pole has given me so much. It's been a reconnection with friends. But also with Marie. We were supposed to do this together, and that was why it was so hard for me to start this class. But I know—*I really know*—she'd be proud of me. She'd have cheered me on when I walked through the studio door more than a year ago. She'd have been telling me I could do it each time I came back. She always believed in me, more than anyone. Certainly more than my own parents. I was the same way with her, encouraging her to go to culinary school, to pursue her dreams to be a chef, to explore the world.

Grabbing the pole with my right hand—my stronger side—I do a one-armed spin. It's a simple move—one of the first I learned. I fly right past the mirror, checking my form. Objectively, it's good. But I can see the flaws. I'm not sure anyone else could. Because the flaws aren't in the execution. They're in my head. In my choices to *only* do certain tricks.

But is that a flaw? I remember Maeve's words from the other day—*do it at your own pace.*

Maybe my workaround isn't truly a cheat. Maybe it's the life hack I've needed. But what if I didn't need one?

That question echoes in my head as I shift to another trick, one I've been doing for a while—an outside leg hang. I do it at my own pace. Grabbing it with both hands, I kick up my legs into the air while dropping my head toward the floor. I hook my left leg around the pole, my ponytail spilling toward the mat while I hold on tight.

"Nice work!" Kyla shouts from the cubbies.

"Feels pretty good," I say on a sharp breath, not breaking the hold. It feels great actually. It's everything I needed tonight.

A reset.

Even though I keep wondering.

What if...?

"Do you want a pic?" she asks, waggling her phone as she walks toward me.

It's not the first time that she's asked. I normally

decline. When a kernel of tension forms in my gut, I know I'll do it now too. Maybe I'm not ready for my what-ifs.

I flip over and stand upright again, shaking my head. "I don't have social media," I say.

She gives me a look—a friendly one, but a look none-theless that says she knows that's an excuse. "I hate to break it to you but you can take a picture just to take a picture." She pauses, her soft blue eyes thoughtful. "You've made a lot of progress in a year and a half. You can take a picture just for you. It doesn't have to be for the world."

Like I wear lovely lingerie—so I can take back my power, even if it's just for me.

I glance at her racy red sports bra, then down at my beige fitted tee that covers so much skin—skin I need to show to do the moves I crave. We've never discussed why I wear short-sleeve shirts to class. Kyla's never asked, nor has she butted in to suggest I wear a sports bra like she does. She accepts her students for who they are, where they are, and however they feel comfortable in their skin.

But I came here tonight for a reset, not to document it, so I shove those nagging little wishes far away. I stayed to help, not to make this moment about me. "Let me get your videos."

She pauses, but then acquiesces. "Sure," she says, handing me her phone.

She grabs the pole and whips through several advanced tricks like a dance ninja, moving from a Superman to the Titanic, a shoulder mount to a brass monkey, till she executes an Ayesha—an upside-down V where she's holding on with only her hands. It's so good I don't dare breathe as I shoot the video. I don't want to be the one to mess up this moment. When she flips off the pole, I clap loudly. "You look like a goddess."

She catches her breath, then says in a warm, encouraging voice, "So do you, Everly."

I peer around the studio for good measure. It's just us. No other students, and none are coming.

It's been a year and a half of me wearing T-shirts.

A year and a half of holding back.

A year and a half of longing to let go.

Maybe it's time to stop hiding.

Pole isn't just for my friends and me. It's also for only me.

After today, and how I handled the event, maybe I am ready. Or maybe I'm not but I think I'm doing it anyway. Courage isn't always something you're ready for. Sometimes you have to choose it. I hand her the phone. "Will you take a picture...for me?"

Her smile is proud. "I will."

Then I do something incredibly hard. I take off my shirt, leaving on only my sports bra with my short shorts. I roll my lips together, bracing myself.

But Kyla doesn't cringe at all the scars on display, the zigzags down my back, the jagged cuts on my arm, the raised one across my shoulder. She looks at me...the same. Before and after, scars and all. I walk to the pole, feeling horribly vulnerable that the parts I like least are visible at last.

But then...fuck it. I grab the pole and kick up into my outside leg hang, dropping my head toward the floor. I'm still holding on like I've done every single time, in every single class. My life hack. My workaround.

Except...*what if?*

I let go, and press the outside of my now bare arms against the pole—skin to metal for the first time ever.

She snaps a shot and cheers. "You nailed it," she says, even brighter than before.

I stay upside down for a beat, savoring the way my arms tingle, how I feel the slightest bit lightheaded but in a good way. Mostly, how I'm strong and powerful.

When I step off the pole my throat is tight. Quickly, I pull the shirt back on. "I don't know if I'll do that in class," I say quietly.

She gives a one-shoulder shrug and a smile. "We're all ready for things at different times in our life. Wear what you want. Try what you want. Just keep coming."

"I will," I say, then I leave, feeling like I've reset my mind in the most necessary way—through my body. Pole dancing has always done that for me since I started it. It's a reclaiming of my body. Of myself. Of being alive.

I head home, hop into the shower, and wash off the chaos of the day and the hard work of the class. When I'm done, I tug on sweats and a tank top, then head to the kitchen as the door buzzer sounds from my phone. Worry races through me. It's evening. I'm not expecting a delivery. And I certainly don't answer the door to strangers.

Like it's a gun I need for protection, I grab my phone from my sweatpants pocket.

Oh.

The camera app tells me it's not a stranger with a delivery. It's Max with a delivery. An annoying burst of excitement rushes through me, along with nerves too. No idea why he's here. I wish I weren't excited at all to see him. I wish I felt nothing.

But I don't. I feel too much for a man I can't have. That's the problem.

I grab a hoodie and zip it up halfway since I might be ready for my teacher to see my scars but I'm not ready for Max to see all of me.

I buzz him into the building, and it feels like it takes an eternity and no time at all for him to bound up the stairs. When I open the door he's holding two paper cups, like he's weighing them as his eyes lock with mine. "I didn't just get an extra London fog that day in Seattle by chance. I got it for you."

31

THE BOYFRIEND TREATMENT

Everly

My heart bounces from the admission. But does it really change anything? I don't know. That's the problem with Max—I've never had answers. Maybe because I haven't ever known the questions.

Or the score.

I try to tamp down my emotions as I hold open the door for him. He's a guy coming to apologize, and that's that. "It's a London fog latte," he explains as he hands me a cup.

It's just a caffeinated beverage. I take it, trying not to clasp it as if it's some incredible gift while I berate myself for wishing it were one. I shouldn't want his gifts so much, or the boyfriend treatment behind them. I shouldn't want them to mean something...big.

Like he's mine.

He swallows roughly, then nods to the cup in my hand.

"I didn't know if you liked decaf at night. So I got you both. That's the caffeinated one."

I clutch it tighter. "I live for caffeine."

"Me too," he says, but his voice sounds raw. "Everly, I didn't know she was coming." It's said like a confession—one that's vital for me to know.

"It's okay. I'm not upset." That's mostly true. Pole got me through my topsy-turvy, terrifying feelings—I have too many of those when it comes to this man. But I don't have a right to be upset. He's not mine, and he can't be mine.

Max steps closer, pushing the door closed behind him. The last time we were alone in my house I wound up against the wall, in his arms, falling apart. I can't let that happen again tonight.

"I feel like shit because she texted me a few days ago," he adds.

I freeze. "She did?" I'm so confused now. I don't know what to think.

"She said hi and asked if we could talk. I ignored it," he says, like that was the worst thing he could have done when I probably would've done the same if I were him. "That was a mistake. I have no idea why she showed up today. No clue what she's up to. But I probably could've stopped her if I'd picked up the phone and talked to her." He drags his free hand through his wildly messy hair that he's likely been making messier all night. "Like I could have stopped all those goals tonight. I fucked that shit up too."

"It's one game. The season is long. You put it behind you like you always do," I say, reassuring him because he's surprisingly hard on himself tonight after a loss. He's not usually like this.

"Yeah, maybe," he says, but his eyes betray his frustration.

Then I remember what the press said—that she consoled him after losses. Maybe they know more about him than I do. Maybe this is how he normally behaves when they don't win. Maybe I know him less than I'd thought I did.

I feel so unmoored. I take a drink of the beverage rather than speaking. I'm not sure what I'm ready to say to him.

When I lower the cup, he says, "I brought you something else too." He dips a hand into the back pocket of his jeans and takes out an envelope.

I wasn't expecting anything at all. I gesture to the purple couch and we sit down, setting the cups on the French blue wooden coffee table across from me. He hands me the white envelope, and it's from You Look Gorgeous Today. "That's my salon," I say.

I look at the card as if it's an oddity, then at the man who's not scowling at me, or smirking. Those are his usual expressions. But right now, his face is open, hopeful.

Curious, I slide a finger under the flap, then take out the card and flip it open. "A lifetime supply of blowouts for Everly Rosewood," I read out loud, my mouth falling open in shock before I say, "You covered all of my blowouts for the rest of my life?"

Max smiles, that familiar cocky variety that hits me right in the heart and in the panties. "You once said if you had a dollar for every time I turned down a media request, you'd have enough for a lifetime supply of blowouts from your stylist, Aubrey. So I googled stylists named Aubrey in the city and went to her salon tonight." His smile burns off. "I wanted to give you something you wanted. Something you'd never do for yourself. Something that mattered. Because I know the event didn't go perfectly and even if she wasn't there, I wasn't..." He stops to collect his thoughts. "I'm not some affable guy. Like Asher. Someone the press loves. Or even Wesley who has this easy way about him. That's not me. I don't know if it will ever be me. I don't know if I'm going to be able to pull this off. I really don't like all the attention."

He's not complaining. He's simply laying himself bare.

Something in me softens. I want to wrap my arms around him and tell him he should just be himself and that none of this image stuff matters. But we live in a world of reputation and perception. We work in that world. We don't have the luxury of shying away from the public. "It can be hard and uncomfortable," I say gently, wanting him to know I understand where he's coming from. "But for what it's worth, you're doing a great job. I don't think anyone expected you to transform overnight or to become somebody who loves that stuff. I know I didn't expect that."

He sinks into the couch, blowing out a breath like that eases his mind somewhat but perhaps not completely, since he adds, "But you are good at it. You're good at all of this. And I want you to know how much it means to me. If it wasn't for you, I probably would've gone full beast in *Beauty and the Beast* today. And I mean the bellowing beast," he says with a wry grin, and it's like he's waiting for me to laugh, but with that comment I'm even more confused by this gift. Is it a professional gift or a personal one? I turn the card over a few times, wondering if it's a thank you for my hard work, or if it's...more?

There's no room in your professional life for more. "You

didn't have to do this," I say of the gift, since that's the easiest reply to give.

He sits up straighter. "I wanted to. I wanted you to have something you like," he says, then goes quiet, perhaps waiting for me to look at him again in the silence. And I do because I'm too drawn to him. When our gazes connect, he says, "The only thing on my mind during the event was you. All I could think about was you. I was so fucking worried you'd think I was back together with Lyra."

You. All I could think about was you.

Those words wrap around me, like an embrace from a lover. Like a whispered confession. Like everything I secretly wanted to hear. My chest swells with emotion. I close my eyes because it's all too much tonight. All these feelings I never wanted to have for him are bubbling up, overwhelming me. I hardly know what to do with them— whether to give them voice or keep them safe, locked up inside me.

Another question I don't have the answer to.

His strong hand cups my chin, his touch tender. My eyes fly open, and he's looking at me with so much longing in his blue eyes. "The whole time I was there, the only thing that mattered was what you thought. I know what everyone else was saying. They were acting like I'd gotten back together with her. They were trying to create this story that she was there to support me. But all I cared about was what *you* thought. You, Everly. Just you."

My heart pounds mercilessly against my rib cage, fighting to get into his arms. It's such a lovely, gorgeous admission and such a dangerous one too. And I hate that I love it so much. But he's cracking open his heart. I can try to open some of mine. "I honestly wasn't sure what to think. And I didn't want everything we'd worked for to fall apart. I felt so much pressure. I feel all this pressure every day at work—pressure I put on myself. Pressure they put on me. It's good pressure, mostly. But it's still pressure, and I really needed the event to go well. Then, out of nowhere she appeared, and everything went off the rails. The press lost their mind, and she became the story—not everything we were trying to build. And even though I felt so unsteady, I had to ignore all these feelings inside me and...right the ship somehow. I had to find a way to put everything back in order. It's silly but I felt like I was the only one who could do it. I wouldn't let it fall apart," I say, taking a small step closer as I speak the truth on all those fronts. As I let him in.

"And you did it. You're a fucking goddess. But you have to know why I'm so bad at pretending in front of the media. I couldn't think about the event, not even the dogs, not the script you gave me. All I could think about was you. And whatever it is that you're doing to me...that I just can't stop," he says, and this feels so unreal. Like it's happening to someone else in another world, in another story. Someone who has a different job that isn't hemmed in by so many unwritten rules.

"Max," I say, my voice breaking because I'm too scared to say anything more. Like if I open my mouth, I'll tell him that I could fall for him and never look back.

He reaches for my hands, takes both of them in his. "I was worried about you during the game too. What you were thinking about when I was playing, and it messed with my head."

That was why he had a bad game. I fight off a smile because I shouldn't enjoy this. But I do. "I wasn't sure what to think when I saw her," I admit, since we're not holding back anymore. And since we're laying ourselves bare, I add, "But I was hoping she wasn't there for you."

A small smile tips his lips—one of relief maybe. Like he can relax now that I've shared some of myself too.

"Know this," he says emphatically. "I think about you far too much. I think about you all the time. I've been thinking about you for so fucking long and denying it. For the last year, I've been thinking about you and thinking I didn't like you." The words seem to pour out with no sign of stopping, though I make a mental note that I've been on his mind since several months after his painful breakup. That surprises me, but also kind of thrills me. "But I don't think that was the case at all." He pauses, breathes out hard. "It's the opposite."

My breath catches, and I feel like I'm going to cry. My throat is tight, and my eyes are shining, and my heart is beating too fast. This is a new kind of courage, but I'm pretty sure I'm ready for this. "It's the same for me," I admit.

When he smiles, there's nothing cocky in it. It's utter relief.

"Good. That's so damn good," he says, resting his forehead briefly against mine. I feel caught in this heady world with him, where it's only us, and he's breathing against me in the night.

My fingers trace his bottom lip, and I take another chance. "You hardly smile...but you do with me."

"I guess you've figured me out," he says quietly. Then he pulls back. "I came over here, too, to tell you what happened that night a year and a half ago. A week or so after the fight, when everyone showed up at my sister's house. I want you to know everything."

My heart clenches at the way he's letting me in so

deeply, so freely. I want to hear all his stories. I want to know him better. I want to understand him even when I shouldn't, even when it's risky.

But right now, I don't want to talk.

"Tell me later," I say.

I grab the back of his neck and pull him against me, then I slide down on the couch, dragging this big hockey player with me, the full weight of his big frame on me.

This delicious feeling of being surrounded by him spreads through my body. By his strength, by his scent, by his passion. That feeling takes over everything, including my scarred and broken heart.

I don't text my friends. I don't want to stop. I want to unlock all these feelings for him.

I look up into his heated eyes, then say something risky and true. "Show me how much you think about me."

32

THREE TIMES

Max

She kisses me hard enough to hurt. She's all tongue and teeth and need, kissing and biting and devouring. My pulse surges, and my brain is spinning out just from the hunger of her kiss. The desire in it. The urgency.

Everly's frenzied tonight, and it's mind-bending to get to know this side of her. It's such a fucking privilege to know *any* side of her. But especially the intimate one.

The one I suspect she rarely shows a soul.

I'm such a lucky fucker, and I'm going to do everything I can to deserve this luck. Every damn thing.

It feels too good to be with her. Too right.

As she explores my mouth greedily, she pushes at my gray Henley, tugging at the hem with eager hands ready to strip me.

What the lady wants...

I wrench my mouth from hers. Her lips are bruised,

and it's a beautiful look. I pluck at the fabric of my shirt, then ask dryly, "I think you might want this off?"

"Yes. Now," she says in a ravenous demand that sends electricity sparking down my spine.

I tug it off. Her eyes flutter closed for a second like the view is too much. Masculine pride surges through me from her reaction.

When she opens her eyes, I reach for her hands and guide her palms to my pecs.

With a shudder she spreads her fingers over my chest, then slides them down my stomach, tracing the ladder of my abs, traveling to the waistband of my jeans. Teasing at the button. My breath halts, and now I'm the one shuddering from her touch.

Everly's eyes go big and wide, gleaming with heat as she rubs the heel of her hand over the ridge of my hard cock. "Ohhh, I see you do think about me," she says wickedly.

"Take it out to be sure," I toss back.

"Patience," she teases, then strokes me more through the denim, her smile vanishing and unabashed lust returning to the sensual curves of her mouth. An unbridled sort of lust I've been craving to see in them for so long, it turns out.

"Fucking love the way you look at me," I rasp out.

She drags her teeth across the corner of her lips. "You sure do," she says, calling me on it.

I grab her hand from my cock so I don't get too aroused too soon, then slide both of her hands back up my stomach to my chest. "I'm obsessed with it."

She flicks a finger against one of my nipples and I groan, unbidden. I close my eyes and lean into the thrill of her exploration of me. The way she seems to want to take the lead. How she's memorizing me with her palms.

She slides them down my shoulders. Over my biceps. Down my forearms. When she wriggles out from under me, I open my eyes again to find she's risen and is sitting up. She reaches for my face again and hauls me close to her mouth. "Kiss me again, Max," she whispers in a desperate command. "Kiss me like I'm all you could think about."

"Easy. Because you are," I say, then I rope my hand through those glossy strands of hair. Right before I drop my lips to hers, I whisper against them, "This is the first time you've had your hair down. You always have a pony-tail, and it drives me fucking insane."

"Because you want to tug on it," she teases.

"No. Because I want to be the one to undo it. Because I want to be the one to undo you."

Her eyes are thoroughly unguarded as she runs her hand along my beard, whispering, "You do."

That confession clearly costs her something. I want to take her honesty and hold it safe, and I try to show her that in how I kiss her. I give her a kiss that is all for her, pouring every bit of my ferocious heart and filthy mind into it. Trying to put all my longing into the way I touch her. Showing her with my lips and my mouth how she has absolutely consumed me.

We kiss till we can't breathe. We kiss like the world is burning. We kiss like it's everything we need. When I pull away, she's panting hard, her eyes glossy with desire. But, something like apprehension flickers in those soulful irises, too, as she asks, "Do you have a condom?"

"Yes. But are you okay?" I ask because I'm more

concerned about that flash of worry than I am about my dick. "You look..."

"It's been a while," she says with some vulnerability.

"Same for me. I haven't been with anyone for a year and a half."

The corner of her lips curve into a grin, then she's sassy again as she says, "Are you worried you won't last, Lambert?"

My eyes narrow, and I stare harshly at her. "For that I'm going to give you three orgasms before I get one."

Her eyes sparkle. "Threaten me again, Max."

"And I thought I was the troublemaker," I say.

"You are."

"Pretty sure you're trouble too, sunshine," I say, then shift gears as I tug on the waistband of her sweatpants. "Can I take these off?"

She turns her face to the overhead light. It's bright, and I flash back to the night we were here. How she dimmed the overheads when we walked in. Wait—is that what the apprehension was really about? Before she says anything else, I ask gently, "Do you want me to turn the lights down?"

She draws a shuddery breath as she sits straighter. "It's not so much that it's been a while," she says softly. "It's that I...have some scars. Kind of all over. And they're not like hockey player sexy scars." Her voice breaks off. My heart squeezes for her as her hand moves to her left hip and she rubs it, while meeting my eyes. "There're some here."

"Do you not want me to see them?"

She doesn't answer. Instead, she pushes down her sweatpants, and holy shit. She's wearing an even sexier pair of panties than last time. How is this possible?

They're sheer lavender, and they barely cover her sweet pussy. When her sweatpants hit the floor, she cups my face, grabs it, then pushes me down to the floor too.

The woman knows what she wants.

She doesn't want to talk about scars anymore. She wants me to use my mouth for other things. So I listen to her. I settle between her thighs, staring wantonly at the tiny scrap of lace. "Sexy on. Even sexier off," I say, then I yank them off in a heartbeat so I can bring them to my nose.

Her breath catches. "Is that what you did with them when you stole the pair?"

I draw another inhale of her sexy, aroused scent on the damp fabric, then meet her gaze. "What do you think?"

"You fucked yourself with them," she says, a grin coasting across her face.

"You bet I fucking did, sunshine," I say, then I drop the pair to the floor so I can touch her thoroughly, properly, reverently. I slide my hands along her thighs, then hike them over my shoulders, yank her to my face, and kiss her slick, hot pussy.

One taste and I'm groaning. One kiss and my cock is aching harder than it has before.

My hands slide up her thighs as I eat my woman.

She's hot and wet, her juices covering my beard as I devour her. Her moans grow louder. They go to my dick. They go to my head. They go to my goddamn heart. She grips my face and pulls me close, crying out as I feast on the taste of her. Soon, she's letting go of all her inhibitions, rocking harder against me, and riding my mouth like a queen. When she digs her nails into my skull, she screams my name.

My mind short-circuits. Pleasure rockets through me

in a neon burst. I'm so fucking turned on from her coming fast and hard. When I look up, she's more beautiful than she ever has been. "That's one," I say.

She smiles woozily as I run my hand along her hip where she placed hers earlier—where her scars are. I move my face closer, bend down to her thigh, and press a kiss to her hip where two thick jagged scars crawl along her flesh here. I travel over one with my lips, tenderly kissing its path, then the other.

When I come up for air, I look her in the eyes. It's like she's holding her breath. Waiting, hoping.

My brave woman. "There is nothing about you that isn't beautiful," I say honestly.

Something serene passes in her eyes as she says a quiet, "thank you."

I rise, grab a condom from my wallet, then brandish it. "I got this for you."

"Another gift?" she teases.

"A selfish one. Bought it tonight. What can I say? I was hopeful."

"So presumptuous," she says.

I give her a cocky grin. "And I was right."

She rolls her eyes, but then says, soft again, "You were."

I push down my jeans and my boxer briefs, freeing my eager dick. Then I sit on the couch and I pick her up so she's straddling me. She's naked from the waist down, but she leaves her tank on and her hoodie. It's zipped up half-way. I don't try to take it off. I tuck my fingers under her chin. "We can take everything at your pace," I say, then I run my fingers along the edge of the scar I saw last week so she knows what I mean. "You know that?"

"I do, and I will." It feels like a promise. Like she's

saying she'll get there—she wants to, and the look in her eyes makes my chest swell with emotion. Then, my cock swells more when she turns her gaze to the foil packet in my hand. "Why don't you put that on so I can ride this big dick of yours?"

"Your filthy, beautiful mouth," I praise as I open the condom, roll it down my length, then smack her ass. "Get the fuck on me. Let me show you how much I want you."

She sinks down on my dick and inhales sharply.

I shudder. Then I unleash a long string of curses. "Fuck, fuck, fuuuuuck."

She lets her head fall back, her long hair spilling down her spine.

I grip her ass and move her up and down my cock. "Look at me while we fuck," I tell her, my voice stern. "Look at my face. Know how much I want you. You. All of you. Every part of you."

She rolls her lips, then nods before she murmurs, "Look at me."

"That's right," I say with a dirty smile, proud of her. She keeps her gaze on me the whole time as the slap of flesh grows louder. As our bodies come closer. As I grip her ass harder. Then, as I fuck up into her, I take a chance, dipping my face to her left shoulder and pressing a reverent kiss there on the sliver of exposed skin.

She gasps.

My fingers tease at the fabric. "Can I?"

She winces, but nods a yes. I push the hoodie over to the top of her arm, revealing her flesh as I thrust into her. "Gorgeous," I say on a raspy groan. "So fucking gorgeous."

Her breath catches.

I kiss her there like I adore her, because I do.

I fuck her and tell her with my body that I crave her, all of her.

And she rides me, faster, harder, more furious, sending the pleasure in me kicking up. Her voraciousness is a filthy thrill.

"That's right, sunshine. Use me. Use my dick," I urge her.

She's trembling and moaning as I drop a hand between her thighs, rubbing my thumb against her clit till she's shaking in my arms and falling apart on me.

"Max," she calls out, my name a filthy prayer as she comes.

Pleasure blasts through me in a hot burst that makes me want to come so fucking hard in her. To meet her there on the other side. But I made her a promise so I say, "Two down. One to go."

"Get it," she says, giving me a command.

"I fucking will," I promise.

I ease out of her briefly, then lay her flat on her back on the couch. I settle between those perfect thighs, my hands spreading up the sides of them.

"Put my dick back in you. I want to watch as you slide my cock into this perfect wet pussy," I say as I reach for her hand.

Covering it with mine.

Bringing it to my throbbing dick.

Her lips part as she grips the base and guides me back to the pink paradise between her thighs. I stare until my cock disappears inside her once more.

Where it belongs.

Her head falls back against the couch cushion, her eyes closing while her arms reach for me.

The gesture—the need in it—hooks into my heart.

I lower myself onto her, my body covering hers, then I find a pace and fuck her good and insistently until she's moaning and begging me to make her come again.

Another thrust. Another drive into her. Another electric, white-hot connection, then she's crying out once more.

I can't even crow. I can't even boast with a *there we go* because I'm too far gone. Words lose meaning as I stop fighting the pleasure. I give in to it, lust jolting through my body as I come hard, blurring out the real world.

I don't want to return to it. The world is so much better like this, close to her.

33

A BRAND-NEW GAME

Everly

The Beast storms into the kitchen, losing his mind as Lumiere and Cogsworth make dinner for Belle.

I point to the TV screen my computer is casting to as the fuming beast blows his top. "See? That's you. It's totally you," I say, as we lounge on the couch an hour later.

Max scoffs, then grabs a kernel of popcorn from the bag, tosses it in the air, and catches it on his tongue. "Can the Beast do that?"

"I bet he can. That seems like a Beast trick."

Max rolls his eyes.

I poke his side. "C'mon. You even said you were going to bellow. I'm not wrong here, Lambert."

As the Beast fumes in the film, Max grabs another handful from the bag. "What does it say about you that you like a beast?"

I arch a brow. "Did I say I like the Beast?"

"I'm pretty sure your three orgasms said you liked what the Beast did to you. Do you want me to give you another one just to be sure?"

I stare him down. "Are you threatening me with orgasms again? Because I could get into this brand-new game."

Setting the bag on the table, he tugs me closer on the couch, then pulls my pink fleece blanket up to our waists. He's in his boxer briefs and I'm wearing my hoodie and a pair of sleep shorts. The night is coasting close to midnight. I'm not sure what happens when the clock strikes twelve.

But I don't see any signs that Max is leaving since we're already in the middle of the flick, and he's only getting comfier. When the Beast returns to his lair and demands the mirror show him the girl, Max takes another handful of popcorn, his gaze transfixed on the screen.

"You're a popcorn junkie," I say, more delighted than I should be about this detail. I don't know why it excites me to know this about him. But it does.

"Because it's fucking delicious." He actually ordered a couple bags from Ding and Dine when he saw that I didn't have any. "I can't watch movies without popcorn." Then he tilts his head, seeming thoughtful for a second. "I'm going to have to tell Asher that he was wrong when he said I hate everything."

I'm too intrigued to leave that alone. "I'll bite. What does that mean?"

As the movie plays on, he meets my gaze. "A few weeks ago when I was telling him about the circus you were dragging me to, he was giving me a hard time because he said I hate everything, and I maybe let on that I didn't hate movie nights with popcorn."

I take a beat, savoring this fact—this little true detail about Max Lambert. "So you're doing a real favorite thing with me? *Again?*"

He tugs me closer on the couch, grazes those full lips along the side of my neck, traveling up to my ear. "Sunshine, I'm doing all sorts of real favorite things with you."

He presses another kiss to my forehead and my whole body crackles and sparks. Electricity surges in me, chased by something warm and comforting.

The feeling is only intensified when he whispers, "Ask me to stay the night."

My stomach swoops. "Is that one of your real favorite things?" Maybe I'm fishing for compliments, but I don't care.

"I'm confident it will be."

"Will you stay the night?"

"Yes," he says, then he cuddles with me until we finish the tale as old as time. When it's over, he says, "The Beast definitely had it bad for Belle."

That's what my friends said about Max and me. Maybe that's true. But it's too early for me to linger on that especially when I still have so many questions about him.

As the credits finish rolling, I return to the reason he came over earlier. "So tell me your story, Max. The one you wanted to share when you came over."

He runs a hand through his messy hair, blowing out a breath, then sits up. "You know that fight at the end of the other season?"

It was front-page sports news. "Of course. Goalies don't usually fight."

"I came home one night to them in bed," he says, wasting no time with the details. "Looking back, there were signs—but I didn't see them at the time. Instead, I'd been looking at rings."

My chest tightens with hurt and rage. *For him.* There's no jealousy, which surprises me—just fury that she hurt a man who cared so deeply. "That's awful. I didn't realize it was at that point."

"I didn't buy one," he says, and his tone is surprisingly free of emotion, unlike mine. He doesn't even sound that bitter even when he says, "Fun fact: *that* made it super easy to get over her."

I can't help it. I smile at his deadpan tone.

"You like hearing that. That I got over her," he says, an observation.

"Well, yeah."

He moves closer to me, whisking his beard across my cheek, making me shiver. "I am so your type."

I fight off the spark of lust to roll my eyes since he deserves a big old eye roll. "Only you would taunt me about liking you."

He wiggles his eyebrows. "Yep."

But then his mirth burns to ashes. He's dead serious again. "Obviously we broke up. Even though she didn't want to. She tried to convince me it was a mistake and it wouldn't happen again, and that it was a one-time-only thing. But it wasn't. I knew it wasn't," he says, then he blows out a heavy breath. "But I was still pissed then. Hurt then. And hurt people hurt people. Since I had better stats than Bane and had beaten LA in the Cup a few years before, I said something to the both of them like 'You fucking deserve a guy who comes in second.' It wasn't my finest moment but in my defense he was fucking my girl-friend at the time," Max says it without remorse and I'm glad.

"They both deserved that."

"I think so too." He pauses, then continues. "A few weeks after I caught them, I'm playing LA. He's chirping at me the whole time. He's taunting me. He's trying to score on me constantly—like he needs to prove something. But he's not getting the puck in. I block every shot. Only every time I do, he gets more and more agitated and then he gets right in my face in front of the net and says, 'Your ex tastes like mine.'"

My jaw comes unhinged. That's villainously awful. "He said *that?*"

Max just nods heavily, breathing out hard. "And I put down the stick and pulled off my gloves, and I was ready to throw the first punch even though I know I'm not supposed to. But I was fucking ready, and then he laid one on me. Right in the jaw."

It was a brutal fight. I saw it. And I know the rest. It's one of the sport's most famous fights. "The benches cleared because you don't hit goalies. That's another unwritten rule," I say. "Bane looked pretty bad after the game. But that's probably not any consolation."

Max looks at me, an apology in his eyes. "It wasn't my finest moment." My heart squeezes for him. I reach for his hand, holding it. He grips me tighter, like I'm his lifeline. "And I had no idea it was going to get so much worse."

34

THE UGLY TRUTH

Max

It was inevitable that I'd tell her the ugly story. At first, I figured I'd tell her so she could do her job better. So she could help me with my image. Now I wonder if my intention was always for other reasons.

Because I want her to know me—even the ugly parts.

I go down the cave of the past to places I don't want to go. But she's worth it.

"And Lyra was at the game. After we were tossed out for the fight, she was there in the corridor, checking on him. The press saw her take care of Bane," I say, his name tasting like acid on my tongue.

Everly sighs sympathetically. "And that's when it began. It became a full-on feeding frenzy."

In retrospect, how could it not? "Yep. They thought I was fighting him because I was jealous. They all thought I was pissed that she didn't pick me. Nobody knew what had really happened, and the gossip rags became obsessed. They kept pressing me all the time, and I wouldn't give an inch. They wanted to know if I was really over her." I huff out a breath. "But it's honestly amazing how quickly you can get over somebody when they fuck someone else in front of you."

Everly's smile is understanding as she says, "I imagine so."

"But they kept pressing me and pushing me and they wanted to know what happened. Why it ended. I never said she screwed my rival. I never said she cheated on me. What would be the point? It would make me look like a whiny child. I didn't need that."

"I understand. It sucks but I do understand."

I thread my fingers more tightly through hers. "A week or so after the fight, the press was going at it. Trying to get to the bottom of the story. One night after a game, I left to go to Sophie's house to get away from it all. I just needed a break. She was living in an apartment building then, and as soon as I got there, they were all waiting outside. So many paps. Everywhere, like flies at a picnic. This is America's sweetheart, after all. All my protective instincts kicked in. Sure, they weren't trespassing technically. They couldn't actually be tossed off the lawn, but I wanted to throw them the hell out." The memory rears up, along with it the residual anger over the invasion of my sister's personal space.

Everly waits patiently for me to keep going.

"Sophie comes down to let me in and she's holding Kade, and the photogs all start pestering her and rushing over to her. Kade was crying. More like bawling."

I clench my teeth at the memory of my little nephew, and how scared he was in his mother's arms. With no remorse for my actions, I shrug. "And I snapped, Everly. I snapped and shouted, 'Get the fuck away from my family. Get the fuck off her property, you vultures. Leave my sister alone.'"

She presses her lips together, perhaps reining in her emotions, her reactions. But holding my hand and not letting me go. It feels like a metaphor or maybe I just want her hand in mine to feel like one.

"And it was all caught on camera. Every shitty word I said. The next day the reports were everywhere that I was so mad about Bane and Lyra that I made my nephew cry. I became the monster who scared his own nephew. That's how they spun it." I scrub a hand across the back of my neck, latent irritation rising up in me, but also…acceptance. Maybe the acceptance I didn't have then. My gaze drifts to our fingers, twined together, then back to her warm, accepting eyes. "And there was nothing I could do or say. Because all the neighbors had cameras and had captured me swearing at the press. All the press caught was me telling them to *get the fuck off her property,* and they had Kade bawling as I did it," I say, my jaw ticking, hurt coursing through me over my little nephew's reaction. "No one caught me going inside and hugging the kid and comforting him. Didn't show my sister giving me a hug. It just showed me looking like—"

It's ironic we were watching that movie after all.

"A beast," she says softly, with no irony this time, even though she squeezes my hand harder.

"And then a month or so later, Lyra goes on and she releases that song, and I'm the angry asshole ex who broke her heart. That was it. I shut down. I went from being somebody who had a fun comment now and then for the media to someone who was rude and standoffish. Her song made it seem like I'd hurt her, like I'd left her, and she'd sought solace in Bane's arms. She has always spun everything to be good for her."

Something seems to flicker in Everly's pretty eyes—like she's adding up details. I'm not sure what to make of that look. I'm not sure what to expect next either. But I know what I didn't expect—Everly to climb into my lap, wrap her arms around me, and give me a big hug.

"I get it," she says softly. "All of it."

I band my arms around her too, holding her close. Neither one of us lets go.

She holds me tight like I matter to her, like she needed tonight as much as I did. Everly isn't an open book. She doesn't let you in right away. You have to earn trust with her, and I want to earn everything with her.

When she lets go, I cup her cheek. "I want your stories someday, too, sunshine."

She smiles tenderly with real affection in those eyes that are my undoing. "I had a crush on you when I was a reporter. Before all of this."

This is news to me. "You did?"

"You were charming and funny, and you always talked to me, and you were just so..." She nibbles on the corner of her lip. "So hot." Then she adds, "Still are."

My heart thunders, then kicks in my chest when she comes in for a long, slow kiss that feels like more than a kiss. It feels like she's telling me something. I don't know what, but maybe it's that she's learning to trust me too.

Or maybe that's just what I want it to mean. I don't really know, but I want to find out.

When I let her go, the story's done. It's been told. But there's one part I just don't get. "What I don't understand is why she was there today though. I really don't get it. Just to come in and wreak havoc?"

Everly's eyes twinkle darkly. "I think I know," she says in a bit of a whisper.

"Enlighten me."

"The other morning when I was doing my online media rounds, I realized that shortly after you started posting on social media again, Lyra and Bane started liking your posts. After a few more posts, I think they realized this was real. You weren't quiet anymore. And that scared her. So she reached out to you. She's clearly all about image, and I think she's afraid you're going to say what really happened," Everly posits.

"Okay, that makes sense, but why show up today?"

"It's a distraction ploy. They're afraid she's not going to be America's sweetheart anymore so they're trying to change the narrative. She came without him, but I don't think they're actually broken up since they're still liking each other's posts. But they're letting the media believe she wants you back. They're creating this idea that she's trying to get back together with the man she really loves because they're afraid you're going to tell everyone what happened. She's trying to take over the story again. To drown out *your* voice with her louder one."

I sneer, but then I also shake my head in amazement, not at Lyra, but at Everly. At her beautiful brain. "Fuck, you're hot."

"Why is that hot?"

"Because you're smart. I love the way your mind works." I take a beat, mulling over her thought process. "You really think that's what they're doing?"

"I do. She's trying to *stop* you. But in this case—she wants to stop you from potentially saying something bad about her."

"I was never going to," I huff. "How the fuck would

that help me? Especially now, when I'm trying to fix my rep? It doesn't help me to talk shit about an ex. Garrett has even said as much—that brands don't look fondly on people who badmouth their exes."

Everly's smile is soft as she says, "He's right. But she's scared. She's worried you'll ruin her reputation, so she's trying to control the story. To remind the media that she's beloved. It's like she's trying to build a wall around herself. So even if you revealed what happened, no one would believe you because how could they? She's this popular singer who shows up at a dog adoption event and kisses puppies."

That's...insidious. I breathe out hard, but after a few seconds, I make a choice. To let the frustration go. To stop talking about her. To focus on this beautiful present and the woman in my arms. "I've had enough of Lyra. Enough of Bane. I don't want to talk about them anymore. They don't matter to me," I say, running a hand over her hair. "But you do." And to show her she's the only one on my mind, I say, "Do you know what my favorite part of your beautiful brain is?"

"Which part?"

I tap her temple lightly. "The part that said yes to me, and now I want you to say yes to something else."

She inches closer. "You do know you make it impossible to say no."

"That's my goal. So go on a secret date with me."

Her flirtiness vanishes. "Max, that's so risky. I'm trying for this promotion, and so is Elias and..." She stops, tilts her head, like she just remembered something. "Speaking of, did he see us in the equipment room?"

"I'm not sure. But I ran into him right after," I say, then

I tell her about the encounter. "You don't think he suspects something?"

Everly closes her eyes, blows out a breath. When she opens them, she says, "He made a comment about it, and he also came into my office the day you sent the panties. Right after I opened them."

"Shit. Did he see them?"

She shakes her head, but she winces. "No. But maybe he's suspicious...and he really wants the promotion. He pretends he doesn't, but he does. And he's so connected, and he plays into the whole *I'm a former athlete* thing. Like he thinks that makes him a better candidate."

My chest caves. I hate that she has to face these challenges. I pull her closer. "I'm sorry, sweetheart. I don't want to do anything to hurt you. Especially at work."

"We just have to be careful around him. Around everyone," she says, then frowns. "You know the team has this unwritten rule that employees can't date players."

Right. She said that at the rink with the kids when Becca teased her about having a crush on me. I wasn't sure she'd meant it. My heart sinks to the ocean floor. "You mentioned that before. That's real?"

She explains the reasoning, and I hate how she has to deal with this sexist rule.

"This *thing* can't be anything more," she says, but her tone sounds heartbroken, and *that*—that emotion—tells me something important. "Especially in the middle of us working so closely together on this makeover. We have the next event in a week or so. And then another one."

Right. Step two—a series of community outreach events. And I don't want to cause any problems for her at the next one like I did today. The next one needs to go perfectly, and I'll do my part.

"I know," I say. But I also plan to hold on to that emotion I heard in her voice. I plan to hold on to it and figure it the fuck out. Because I don't know how to change that rule but I also don't know how to change these feelings for her that grow stronger by the day. "That's why I said go on a *secret* date with me."

"Max," she says, but it hardly sounds like a protest.

"You know you want to."

She doesn't fight it. She melts into my arms. "Of course I do," she says, vulnerable and open and a little sad.

I'm not letting her go.

"Then say yes," I say, wiggling my brows.

She narrows her eyes, swatting my chest playfully. "Are you going to ruin it like you did all my other dates?"

"Did I really ruin them?"

"Yes. You did. You turned down Joe. You didn't even let Flynn get a word in so he could ask me out. And you sabotaged my date with Lucas."

"Sounds like I was helpful."

"Is that so?" she asks, but she's smiling.

"It was in your best interest," I say, unrepentant.

"And what is my best interest?"

I meet her gaze unflinchingly. "Me."

"So you're my type?" she asks.

"Fuck yes," I say, then I sweep kisses up the side of her neck, then down her throat and to the top of her breasts, making her tremble everywhere. "So say yes."

When I meet her eyes, they've already given me the answer before her lips do as she says, "Yes."

35

THE FAKE OUT

Max

On Friday morning I'm in my kitchen, making coffee and plotting my secret date with Everly for Sunday...with my dad.

"I think I'll take her to Theo and Soren's restaurant," I say to him on FaceTime, mentioning some of his married friends who run a restaurant an hour or so away. That's key because I need to make sure we avoid the arena area and, frankly, the city too, where most of the people who work for the team live. Sure, there's always a risk I could be recognized anywhere, but I won't touch her in public. I don't want her to deal with an in-person encounter with a co-worker though, so getting away from here will help. "Think you can get me a res?"

Dad chuckles from a couch in the teachers' lounge at his school. "I'm pretty sure you could get your own, but I'll be happy to do it for you."

"No one answers the phone anymore these days."

He clears his throat. "You know you can get reservations online, Max?"

"Really?" I deadpan.

"Technology is an amazing thing."

"So much sass from such an old man," I tease.

"And you wonder where you got it from," he says.

I shake my head. "Nope, I don't. I know it came from you."

"I'll send them a text to get you a good table," he says, understanding *why* I asked him for help rather than making one online. I want the best for Everly. Dad pauses, then asks seriously, "So, the woman must be special?"

Easiest answer ever. "She is," I say, but I don't tell him anything more. I'm in the *convince her* stage anyway.

Those two words seem to be enough for him though. A small smile coasts across his weathered face. "I hope it stays that way."

I hope it *becomes* that way too, for her.

I say thanks and hang up as Athena saunters into the kitchen, looking ready for some playtime. I pick up her favorite toy from the floor—a ball of tinfoil. Of all the toys in the universe, why do cats dig this one the most? No idea, but that's the mystery of felines. After I hurl the tinfoil into the living room, my gaze strays to a bag on the tiled floor full of my gear. Gloves, shoulder pads, and helmet...Not the ones I wear in Sea Dogs games, but the ones I use when I coach the kids.

A couple sticks too.

Sticks...

That reminds me of Everly's warning about Elias. We'll have to be extra careful at work. But maybe there's a very specific way to do that.

Jerseys.

When Athena rushes under the kitchen table batting her shiny prize, I head over to her, extract the tinfoil from her tiny but mighty paws, then scratch her chin. "You know who's brilliant?"

Ignoring me, she stares murderously at the silvery ball in my hand, like she's licensed to kill. Well, she *is* a cat.

"Me, Athena. Me," I say, but she has no interest in my self-praise. She's poised to vanquish tinfoil.

Like I'm going to toss the ball across the kitchen, I lift my hand and fake her out, sending the crushed ball hurtling down the hall and the other way. In a blur of gray fur and the cutest white paws ever she skids out, then spins around to chase after it. My coffee's brewed, so I pour a cup, head to my room, and grab a couple jerseys from a drawer. I keep extra here since you never know when you might need one.

But now I need two. If Lyra can pull off a distraction ploy, so can I. I text my friends and tell them I need their help. They say yes when I ask them to bring extra jerseys to practice.

Back in the kitchen, I grab a Sharpie and sign both of mine, adding a paw print at the end of my name for fun. Then I toss them into a big canvas bag, snagging a second bag since this will be a double decoy.

But right as I'm about to leave, I get another idea about jerseys. I grin wickedly because this new idea is indeed proof that I'm brilliant. I've got a few extra minutes so I flop down on the couch with my tablet and do a little online recon. I'm fast and I know what I want so when I find a store that can do it, I place the order right away, even though it won't arrive for a couple weeks.

And because I can learn, I send this gift to her house instead of to work.

* * *

A couple hours later, I'm in the locker room collecting signed jerseys from Miles, Wesley, Hugo, and Asher—two from each of my friends. "You're a good man," I tell Hugo as he drops his into the bag.

"No problem. You got a couple relatives who are hockey fans? That's what I got my aunt Cindy for Christmas. She lost her mind. Actually, I should have you guys sign some pucks for her next."

"Happy to do it," I say, and while I don't want to give them the details on *why* I need two sets of signed gear, I don't want to lie to my friends either. But I have to protect Everly as much as I possibly can. I've got to do everything I can for her—including subtly trying to win Elias over. Make him think I'm on the same team as him. "These are actually for Elias. As a thank you. And Everly."

Miles laughs. "He's going to be your best friend. Nothing that kid likes better than giving away swag during the intermissions."

"Seriously," I say, then frown, which is easy for me to do since I have a master's degree in glowering, but it helps sell the reason. "And that event earlier in the week was kind of a mess, thanks to my ex. I'm just trying to thank everybody who helped out."

"Aww, you're not such a dickhead after all," Wesley says.

"And if anyone talks shit about you, I'll say *this* right here is proof that you're not a hater," Miles adds.

As Asher puts on his watch, he looks up and asks, ever so innocently, "Where's my football tickets, then, for helping? If memory serves, I did kind of save your ass too so I should be included in the gifting. We all should, in fact."

Wesley seconds that with a vigorous nod. "We don't have a game on Sunday. I hear the VIP suite at the Renegades is real nice."

I owe them big time, so I easily say, "Consider it done." Doesn't matter that I won't be there with them.

As I head to the management level a few minutes later, Asher catches up to me before I reach the stairwell. It's just the two of us. "So, things are going well?"

I furrow my brow. It's such a broad question, and I'm not sure which target he's trying to hit. "Yeah. Why do you ask?"

He nods toward the stairwell. "With..."

I scratch my beard. "With the makeover?"

He points at me, like he's caught me in the act. "Fucking knew you had a tell!"

I roll my eyes. But there's no real point denying it. He put two and two together last week when we hit the ice before practice. I push open the door to the stairwell, and he follows me in. "One, I scratch my beard at other times too."

"Be that as it fucking may, you also do it when you're bluffing."

"And two, don't say a fucking word to anyone."

He gives me a look like *c'mon, man.* "You don't have to say that. I know."

"I do have to say that. I have to protect her however I can," I whisper.

He claps my shoulder. "I get it. And if you need anything, I've got your back. Know that."

I smile. "I do. Appreciate it, man."

"And I appreciate those tix."

"Asshole," I mutter playfully.

"Dickhead," he says in the same tone then returns the

way he came, and I head up the stairs. As I go, I lob in a call to Garrett. He's got clients in every sport. "Any chance you can get me four tickets in a VIP suite to the Renegades for Sunday? I need them for a friend. Put them under the name Asher Callahan, please."

"Happy to do it," he says, with no questions asked. "And I spoke with Zaire this morning and after everything that went down, we still got some good press from the other day. And everything is on track for *The Ice Men.*"

That's a relief on all fronts. "Great. I hope my likeability quotient is going up," I say, mostly meaning it. I do hope it's on the rise. I want this makeover to work. For me, for my family, and for my plans. For my team. I want to stay with the Sea Dogs more than ever since Everly's here.

But mostly now, I want this makeover to work for her. So she can have all the good things. So she can gain the promotion she deserves. If I'm the path to it, I want to ease the way for her.

"And you've got the next community outreach event on Thursday," he says, reminding me.

"I'll be there."

"With a smile on," he adds importantly.

"With a motherfucking smile," I say.

But the smile will likely be for her since she's at the front of my mind.

After I hang up, I stop by her office and hand her a bag of jerseys. She looks up from her desk, quirking a brow as she cautiously asks, "A gift?"

"For Little Friends," I clarify, and yes, it's a legit gift, but I also gave them to her in case word got out that I was giving some jerseys to Elias. Don't want Elias to try to claim to management that he's *tight* with the athletes more than she is. They both get the same thank-you gift.

"From my friends and me. For putting up with all the shenanigans the other day. I figure they can auction them off on their website if they want and raise some more money."

Her smile is bright and genuine. "That is very thoughtful."

"I can be a nice guy," I say.

And since I heard her loud and clear the other night, I don't stick around and flirt. I leave, even though it's hard as hell and I already miss her. As I'm heading down the hall, I send her a text.

> Max: You have no idea how hard it was not to kiss you.

> Everly: Actually, I do. I felt the same with you.

My pulse speeds up, and I want to frame her last note. The admission from her. Dear god, the fucking admission.

But instead, I school my expression as I stop by Elias's cubicle. He gulps when he looks up from his computer. "Hey, man, how's it going?" he asks, sitting up straighter.

"Just wanted to thank you for your help earlier in the week with Dogs on Ice. It was kind of crazy but I appreciate everything you did," I say evenly, like I don't have a single ulterior motive.

He waves a dismissive hand. "No worries, man. That must have been rough. My ex-girlfriend keeps trying to get back together with me too."

Oh, wow. He's really going there, playing the bro-bonding card. But that just makes this visit easier.

"What can you do, right?" I ask, sympathetically, like we're just two dudes with the same problems.

"It's tough," he says.

"Anyway, I wanted to thank everyone who helped out. So I got some of my buddies to sign jerseys. Figured you can give them away at an upcoming game," I say, then hand him the bag.

When he peers inside, his eyes pop. "This is amazing. Thank you so much."

I clap him on the shoulder. "I figured, you know, athlete to athlete, that you'd appreciate it."

If I'd thought his eyes sparkled before, it's nothing compared to how they look now. And that, ladies and gentlemen, is what you call a fake-out.

He thinks I'm his friend now.

36

MY ESCAPE

Everly

When the buzzer rings on Sunday, my chest is flipping. My heart feels far too fluttery for my own good.

It's just a date.

That's all it is.

It can't go anywhere.

But as I tell him through my camera app that I'll be right down, I sound like I've been counting down the hours to see him—and I have.

I grab a sweater, then stop at the door, pausing before I reach for the knob. A memory flashes by of my last date—not with Lucas, but the one with Gunnar. The one where he ghosted me after he saw my body. I shudder from the hurt and shame I felt in every cell.

But I try to stay in the present, using my tools. I catalog my surroundings. I'm in my home, the door is red, my shirt is lavender—Maeve was right about the color—and my hair is...down.

Not only down, but blown-out and smelling faintly of gardenias.

Gunnar is the past. Max is the present. I peer into the mirror by the door, checking my reflection one more time. I'm wearing jeans, short black boots, and a stylish T-shirt with the neckline cut so it slopes down my shoulder—my left one, showing everything. That's on purpose. I swear I can hear Marie's voice, saying, "Damn, you look good."

I do look good. I feel good. And still, my stomach churns with nerves.

You can show him who you are.

With a resolute nod at my reflection, I leave, heading down the steps and out the door to the stoop. At the curb Max is leaning against his car, looking like a tall drink of a man, wearing jeans that hug his muscular thighs and a Henley that shows off all his rippling muscles. Aviator shades cover his eyes, but he whips them off the second he sees me.

A quiet *wow* forms on his lips, and that settles the last remnants of my nerves. I walk over to him, but I'm careful not to touch him in public. "Hey."

That one syllable sounds like it contains the multitude of my messy feelings for him. Feelings that get messier by the hour.

"Your hair," he says, sounding mesmerized, like he can't even finish the sentence. He simply stares, transfixed.

I touch the soft strands. "I got a blowout this morning." Then, feeling daring, I add, "Someone who has a thing for me got me a lifetime supply."

I'm not usually that forward in assessing a man's feelings, but Max has made that easy too.

And I'm rewarded when he nods approvingly. "A very big thing."

That fluttery feeling returns in full force, getting stronger. He opens the door and I slide into the passenger seat and buckle in. When he gets into the driver's seat, he turns to me, filthy appreciation in his eyes. A rumble seems to coast past his lips. "It's impossible not to touch you."

This man makes me feel so wanted. "But you have to behave."

"I don't want to," he says.

"Do it anyway," I say in a sensual tone.

But because he's Max, he slides his hand down my thigh, stealing a caress, then leaning in just a little bit as he inhales me. "Mmm," he murmurs.

I tremble.

Then he lets go and says with so much honesty in his voice, "I love this shirt."

He couldn't have said a more perfect thing. My throat tightens as I say, "Thank you."

He starts the car and cruises out of Russian Hill, past the Marina. As we're crossing the Golden Gate Bridge, my shoulders feel lighter. My mind, a little more free. The city fades away and with it, my worries about being with someone I'm not supposed to be with vanish into the distance.

Or really, I choose to leave them behind.

He drives farther, past Petaluma and toward Lucky Falls, a small town in Wine Country where it's always sunny and sixty-five degrees. Once we're there, he cruises through the town square, then past it, toward the outskirts, where he pulls over outside a red farmhouse on a hill. But before he gets out, he runs a hand along my exposed shoulder. "I love that you wore this," he says, his tone straightforward, no teasing in it.

"It's for you," I say, because he deserves to know how he makes me feel—wanted, accepted, desired with no reservations. "I wore it for you."

He holds my gaze for a long beat, his eyes darkening as he says, "I want to keep earning that."

I swallow roughly, unsure what to say next, but loving that he's noticed I'm wearing less and showing more than I have in the longest time. And that he likes it. "I bet you will," I finally say.

He scans outside of the car then, satisfied the coast is clear, he reaches for my hand and presses my palm to his mouth, giving me a soft kiss. "And now I get to show you what a date should be."

I arch a challenging brow, returning to our playful ways. "But I thought you said lunches were weak," I say, turning his words around on him.

His jaw drops. "Holy shit. I did say that."

"What do you have to say for yourself now, Lambert?"

But his cocky smile returns as he runs a hand through my hair. "Don't worry. I'm going to have you all to myself," he says, then he lowers his voice, and repeats in a more sultry tone. "And then I'm going to have you all to myself."

Arousal floods me from the double meaning, and I both want the lunch to last forever and to end.

With a deep breath like he has to gird himself to not touch me, he gets out of the car and comes around to my side, opening the door. "I love this place. I can't wait to show it to you."

There he goes again, making it harder for me not to fall.

* * *

I don't want to ever leave. The menu is full of fresh salads and inventive risotto dishes, gourmet sandwiches and yummy pastas. But the view. Oh, the view.

"I've never been at a place more...serene," I say, drinking in the surroundings. Since it's, as promised, sixty-five degrees, we're sitting outside under a huge oak tree that canopies our table. String lights hang from the branches. A few feet away is a stone path that travels up a small hill, bursting with golden and maroon fall colors, and hardy aster flowers. There are only a few other patrons, and their tables are at least ten feet away from us.

It's a secret hideaway and that's not the glass of wine I've had talking. It's the quiet, warm afternoon away from the madness of our daily lives. "This place is like an escape. Where we don't have to think about the promotion or the image makeover."

"Good. That's what I wanted for you," he says, then adds, "My parents' friends—Soren and Theo—run this restaurant and have for a couple decades. I asked my dad to text them for a res today."

I lift a brow, pleased with this bit of intel—the level of planning he went to. "Nice of them to fit you in." Even though I want to say *I kind of love you asked for your dad's help for this date.*

He laughs softly. "Yeah, I'm glad they had a table. It's changed over the years but I love the feel of it."

I look around at the quiet charm of this place. "Me too. It's like I can...let go." I relax into my chair with a sigh. "I guess I needed this."

"I had a feeling," he says, then leans closer, almost, *almost* like he wants to take my hand. He doesn't, though, and I half wish I hadn't told him the other night that we had to be cautious, because right now I want to feel what it's like when he takes my hand at the table. But instead, he relies on words and says, "This place...it reminds me of a time before the cameras and media. When hockey was just my escape." He tilts his head, then asks with real curiosity, like he's been wanting to know this for ages, "What's your escape, Everly?"

For a second, maybe several, I sit with that question. I know the answer. I want to give him the answer.

Even though there's that worry in the back of my mind —what if he doesn't receive what I have to give? What if he doesn't want what I have to share?

But he's opened up about his family, his grandfather, his sister. I need to give him more of me.

No. I want to. "This might sound...strange," I begin.

"Try me," he says.

"I escape into the studio."

He tilts his head, clearly intrigued, but also surprised. Before he can say another word, I add, "It's called Upside Down—the studio I go to. It's a pole class."

"Pole?"

It's like his brain is reassembling what a lot of people think of pole—isn't that what strippers do? And sure, it is.

"It isn't just for strip clubs. It's for fitness and for fun. And also for escape. I was there earlier on the night you came over. It's..." I stop and compose myself, but it's easier to say this than I'd expected. Maybe because I've needed to for a while. "It's where I was going the night Marie died. The night I almost died."

JUST IN TIME

Everly

Max's face is ashen. "I knew the accident was serious. But I didn't know it was that bad," he says, then shakes his head like he's mad at himself. "I should have realized."

"Of course you wouldn't know because I didn't really say how bad it was," I say gently, since I'm the one who held back.

He reaches for my hand this time. "What happened?" It's said like he's imploring me to tell him, but he doesn't need to because now that I've started I'm not going to stop.

"You know how I told you she used to have this thing about saying yes?"

"I do."

As a gentle fall breeze rustles the leaves in the nearby trees, I begin. "She loved to try new things and admittedly, I did too, so that was something we did together, but she took the lead. She'd leave Post-it notes in the apartment about different things she wanted to try. Pole dancing was one of them. I don't know why. Maybe somebody came to her restaurant who was a dancer, but she got it in her head that we had to do it. She looked it up and found the studio through their online videos and signed us up for a class." I pause for a moment. Max waits patiently for me to share more so I keep going. "So we were all set and I was running a few minutes late, which never happens, but it happened then. And I drove us."

I stop to take a breath since this is when it gets harder. When the memories threaten to slam into me at a terrifying speed. "We were almost there. I was making a left turn. Nothing out of the ordinary. But out of nowhere, a car slammed into her side."

My heart seizes as the images flash fast, hard, relentlessly. Hitting me in the chest, in the mind—everywhere. But I have the tools to stay grounded in the present. In the smell of the fall flowers, in the feel of the wood of the table, in the bell-like jingle of the wind chimes, and...in Max's bright eyes. "The next part I don't remember clearly. I only remember snapshots. The airbags releasing at record speed. A horrifying sound of crunching and metal. The car rolled. I felt a...snap. The world turned upside down. I was trapped against the door, I think. The window shattered. There was glass and metal all over my side, and I could feel the heat from the fire somewhere, but all I was doing was trying—"

I stop. Cover my mouth with my free hand. Fight off the onslaught of tears. But I can't smother them. What's the point in even trying? Some stories just come with tears.

I lower my hand, and let them fall as he grips my other hand, like he'll hold on for all time.

I try again. "I was frantically trying to unbuckle her—I

don't even know why. I think she was already gone. But I didn't know that. I had to save her. Then I heard sirens and fire trucks and they were pulling us out...The next thing I remember was waking up from surgery. There were all these machines and noises, and my throat hurt and my mouth was dry. My head was aching. I was thirsty. Then I remembered—*her*. What happened to her? Where was she? Was she okay? The nurse kept saying, *you're okay, honey. They got you out just in time*."

Max rolls his lips together, clearly holding in his own emotions as I wade through the ocean of mine. I can't stop the crying. The tears and me are one. "But there was no *just in time* for her."

I stop because it's too hard to talk past the noose tightening my throat. I need several seconds to breathe, and I take all of them fully. "My mom was there. She's the one who told me that Marie was gone. And I felt like I'd died too, but I was still alive to feel all the hurt."

"I'm so sorry for all of this. I'm so sorry she's gone. I know you loved her," Max says, with so much hurt in his voice too.

I never used that word with him—love—but I never had to. He *knew*. He could tell.

"She was like my family," I say. "I'd known her since I was five. I'm not close to my parents. They're complicated and critical. But Marie was the opposite. She was like my sister. And somehow, incomprehensibly, in the middle of all this, I was alive and in this very broken body."

"You're not broken," he says with so much intensity but also with cracks in his own voice too. His eyes shine.

But I was. Parts of me still feel that way. "I had a lot of surgeries for broken bones and for burns, and I went to rehab for my injuries." I look at him straight on and I might as well be naked as I say, "But I still have scars all over my back and my left side. I didn't hate them at first. I don't even know that I do hate them. But when I tried to date again, the first guy I went out with..."

I stop because I hate how weak this makes me feel. How insecure. How...vain.

Max hisses, "Who made you feel this way? Who made you think you're less than?"

Less than.

That's exactly how I've felt ever since I last took off my clothes for another person. "He was just some guy. We dated for a month. He seemed...decent. Like a nice man. But once he saw—" I gesture to my upper arm, my back, my hip. "He ghosted me."

Max clenches his jaw. His eyes brim with fiery rage. "He's the one who made you feel like you're not good enough. He's the one who hurt you."

"Maybe," I say, then shrug, because I need to take some responsibility too. "But I think I did as well. I didn't want to show anybody my body anymore. I didn't want anyone to see all these imperfect pieces."

"He's wrong," he says, emphatic. "You're beautiful everywhere."

I love that Max says that, but he hasn't seen the worst parts of me. Even so, I'm trying to feel that way on my own too. Trying to trust myself. Trying to trust him. "Thank you. That's why I go to pole. To escape from these *less than* feelings. To find myself again. To say yes again. But it's taking me a real long time," I say, forcing out a laugh—at myself—even though it's not really funny. But I don't want to drown in tears anymore. I try to swim out. "The other night, I finally took my shirt off at pole with my teacher, and I did some tricks in a sports bra and shorts for the first time. I hadn't done that before. I didn't want anyone to see me. I don't really show the scars to anyone. I honestly think my teacher is the only one who's seen them. But I felt safe there."

Max runs his hand along my bare arm. His touch is gentle this time, reassuring. "How did you feel when you did the tricks?"

I don't fight off a smile now. "Pretty damn badass."

He presses his forehead to mine. "You are badass. And beautiful." He pulls back, pinning me with his strong gaze. "And today, out like this...you've never looked sexier."

I run one hand over my shoulder. I'd almost forgotten my skin was on display, but none of the wait-staff have looked at my shoulder with a *poor you* look in their eyes. No one has noticed the scars except this beautiful man sitting across from me, and all he's done is praise them.

"You don't have to show them to me until you're ready, but you need to know this, Everly—I'm not *that* guy."

It's my turn to reassure him. "I know you're not. And it means a lot to me to know that. Truly, it does."

"Good." That one word has more passion than anything I've ever heard. "Like I said, we can take everything at your pace. But I'm not going to freak out. You have to trust me."

I want to trust him. But trust is a blade that could cut me all over again. "I'll try. I promise."

"I promise to always earn it."

My chest tingles and a warm, heady pull tugs low in my belly. His eyes say he does too. For a second, I'm convinced he'll risk a kiss and that I'll say yes and melt into his arms. But the moment is broken when a server comes out and brings us our food. Maybe we needed this levity. This break.

When he's gone, Max says, "Thank you for telling me."

I tug on the neckline of the kind of a shirt I've only had the guts to wear with him. "Thank you for giving me a chance to wear a shirt like this."

His eyes fill with warmth. And a tenderness that says he understands exactly what that means. "You can have all your chances with me."

The thing is, I think I know that.

But I wish that I hadn't found all these chances in a man I'm not supposed to be with. A man I can't figure out how to fit into the rest of my life.

I made a promise three years ago to live my best life. I don't know how to fit all these wild feelings for him into that promise. I don't know how wanting him so deeply aligns with my career. With my need to support myself.

This job pays for my life. I don't have any fallbacks. I can't rely on my family. I can't take the risk especially when I'm lucky to be alive.

But right now, I have to hold on to that luck for exactly what it means—*today*. This moment. I look around, soak up the sun, and tilt my face to the sky. I'm not trapped in a car that's starting to burn. I look at Max once more. "At least there is this beautiful day."

We eat.

When we're done, Max says like it's a dare, "Say yes to dessert."

"That's easy. You know I like cake."

"Then say yes." He's so bossy.

"Yes."

A few minutes later, a coconut cake with mango filling arrives, and we share it. When we're done, the sun dips lower in the sky. Max looks to the nearby gravel lot, then me. "Say yes to coming to my place now."

As if I would say anything else. "Yes."

Then he flashes me an *I've got a secret* smile. "Good. Because there's someone I want you to meet."

I blink. What? Who the hell could that be?

38

A STRIPTEASE

Max

As Athena curls her furry, little body around my hand, trying to kill my fingers and bring them home to me to prove she thinks of me as part of her clan, Everly declares, "You're a cat person."

She says it like it makes all the sense in the world.

"Does that surprise you?" I ask, sinking deeper into the couch in my living room.

She's right next to me, shaking her head. "The cat fits you."

"I'll take that as a compliment," I say.

"Of course you would."

"Of course you meant it that way," I say as I hand wrestle the huntress I live with. "You're a dog person, aren't you?"

"Um, yes. But you," Everly says, and she's too delighted. "You foster kittens and you've been keeping that a secret."

I shrug. "Can you blame me? If I'd told you I fostered kittens, you would've had a field day with it."

"You're right. I would." Her lips twitch with amusement. "Imagine if people knew what you're really like."

"What am I really like?"

She raises a hand. Counts off on her fingers. "A guy who fosters kittens. Who coaches underprivileged kids in hockey. Who asks his dad for help planning a date. Who cannot stop romancing me. You're too sw—"

I cover her mouth with mine before she can say *sweet*. I give her a hard, punishing kiss, letting go of Athena. There's nothing sweet about this kiss at all. It's rough and demanding, full of teeth and fire. I tug on her bottom lip, then let go. "Don't make me give you too many orgasms again."

"Oh, please. Punish me," she says, then fiddles with the bottom of her T-shirt. "You know why I wore the shirt."

"Because it shows off your sexy shoulder?" It's such a gift to compliment her.

"Sort of," she says, then tips her forehead toward the hallway. Don't have to tell me twice. I offer my hand, then pull her up. Once we're standing, she says, "I wore it because...it's easy access."

Oh, hell yes.

I scoop her up, toss her over my shoulder, and carry her to the main bedroom in seconds. I set her down on the plush carpet and she turns, checking out the floor-to-ceiling windows and the view of the city, lit up and sparkling, from Richardson Bay to the Golden Gate Bridge. But nothing compares to the view in front of me—Everly walking over to my king-size bed. She sits on it and pats the mattress, looking my way. "Is this where you fucked my panties?"

Jesus. Her mouth. Her filthy mouth.

I stalk over to her, cup her chin, lift that gorgeous face. "No. I couldn't wait. Fucked them on my couch."

Her smile is filthy. "You dirty, horny man."

"Yes," I say unapologetically.

She teases at the bottom of her shirt. "Bet you fucked your fist, too, the night you found my lingerie in Seattle."

"I fucking did."

She nibbles on the corner of her lips, then asks, "Want to see all of *that bralette*?"

That bralette.

Those words echo in my mind. "You wore that bralette for me?"

"Yes," she says with a too-pleased smile.

"Want to show me, sunshine?"

It's a question, not a demand. I'm not going to pressure her to take anything off. I don't know if she's stripping naked or not. She can take the lead.

"I do," she says, then stretches out on the bed, shimmying up to the pillows. She's still wearing her jeans and the shirt, but in no time she whisks off the jeans and she's down to the shirt, and the panties that match her bralette —they're red lace too.

I run a hand along her calf, savoring the soft feel of her skin. She takes the bottom of the shirt, slowly teases me with it and pulls it up, up, up, revealing her stomach that I want to kiss and lick.

I take her invitation and climb onto the bed right as she's pulling up the top to show me her bralette. Cherry red, with a dainty ruffle along the top.

It hits me—this is the first time I've even had a peek at

her tits and my mouth is watering. My chest is a furnace just from the hint of nipples under that sheer red lace.

"Like it?"

"Fucking love it," I say, mesmerized as I roam my hands up her soft belly, push up the lace and free those tits. "Fuck me, they're perfect." They're tight and the nipples are a dusky rose, and all I want to do is bury my face against that gorgeous flesh. I bend down, and suck on her right nipple, tugging on it, then drawing it between my lips. She gasps. And arches into me.

It's fucking glorious, the way she responds. She grabs my head, determined to keep me right there.

Like I'd go anywhere else.

I move to her other breast, kissing, then flicking my tongue along the nipple.

"Max," she moans, her fingers gripping me impossibly tighter, like they're a vise, and she refuses to let go.

Good. I love that she wants this so much. Wants me this much. I spend several lust-fueled minutes sucking on her tits till she's breathless and arching her hips, begging for me.

She pushes my head away.

I rise up. She sits, then reaches under her shirt, and performs the calisthenics that women can do, tugging her bra out one sleeve, then tossing it to the floor.

My chest floods with filthy gratitude. Is that a thing? I think it is, and I am feeling it in every cell in my body.

It's not lost on me that our intimacy has been a strip-tease. Each time we're together she takes off one more item of clothing. Every night she sheds one more garment. Shares more of herself. She's down to nearly nothing, and this is huge for her. I want to keep earning the chance to please her.

She lies back down and pulls her shirt above her tits so the fabric is on top of her chest. She's on display, and it can't be easy for my woman. More of her scars are visible to me for the first time—the two jagged lines on her hip that I've seen, and now a hint of reddish-pink raised skin all along the side of her body. Those must extend to her back, the ones she's most self-conscious of, the ones I can't see now, and that's okay.

This is her pace. This is what she needs from me. But this is what I can give her—the truth of my heart. "Love the way you look right now," I tell her.

Her smile is instant and it's mine. All mine.

I reach for her and slide my hands up her sides, touching the smooth skin on her right side, the bumpy skin on the left. I hate that guy who hurt her self-esteem, but I fucking love that he showed himself the door so I could kick it open. "In case you're wondering, I'm calling you tomorrow. I'm dirty texting you tomorrow. I'm bringing you a London fog tomorrow," I say.

She breathes out a long, shuddering sigh. "Fuck me tonight."

And my clothes vanish in seconds. Then I run a hand up her leg and across the red lace of her panties. "Let me take these off too."

"You better," she says.

I slide them down her legs, taking my time, enjoying her being exposed to me. She's glistening and the more I see, the harder I get. When her panties are all the way off, I bring them to my nose and inhale her greedily. "Fucking delicious," I say, then, like the filthy man I am, I flick my tongue along the wet panel and taste her arousal.

She gasps, then shoves a hand between her thighs, playing with her clit.

Yes. Fucking yes.

I drop the panties to the floor and kneel between her legs, spreading her thighs. As she watches me, I stroke my dick. "Trust me, Everly," I say, shuttling my fist down my hard length. "I want you even more than I did before."

"Then get a condom, Max Lambert, and fuck me like you mean it."

Yup. I'm even harder than I'd thought possible. Seconds later, I'm covering my dick, then hiking up her legs, pushing her knees toward those gorgeous tits so her pussy's spread for me. "Look how wet you are," I say.

"Do something about it."

I notch the head of my cock against her wetness, then hiss in a sharp breath. I close my eyes. I need a moment. This is so fucking good. All this slickness, all this softness, all this arousal for me. I open my eyes and I sink into her, filling her completely.

Her breath comes in a staggered gasp. Then, I comply with her demand. I fuck her like I mean it. I grab her hips, jerk her down on my cock, then work her on my dick. She's moaning and gasping, her lips parting, and it's so damn good. And it's even better when her hands fly to her tits and she plays with them.

"Mine. Those are fucking mine," I say, possessiveness gripping me.

"Then touch them," she challenges me.

With one hand holding her right hip, I thrust into her again and again, reaching for her breast with the other hand, playing with the nipple.

She shudders with each touch. She gets wetter. Her pussy grips me. I'm so turned on from her desire, but I want her to truly understand the depths of my lust. That nothing stops me from wanting her. That no scars will scare me away. I lean closer and rasp out, "Want to get you naked. Put you on all fours. Fuck you from behind. Touch you everywhere."

I'm taking a chance but that's my nature.

"You do?" She gasps, a little disbelieving, a lot turned on.

"I really fucking do, Everly," I say, making a dirty promise I plan to keep. "You want that?"

She nods quickly, desperately. "Yes. Soon, I promise soon," she says, and lets go of her breast to grab the neckline of her shirt. In one quick move, she tugs it over her head.

My breath halts. I'm floored. "I wasn't expecting that," I whisper.

"Me neither," she says, her eyes wide, her voice nervous as she drops down to the bed. The view is no different for me. I can't see her back. But I *can* see the courage that move took. The guts. She's naked with me.

I lower my chest to hers, feeling her against me as I find our pace again, picking up the rhythm, thrusting deep, the way she likes it. She wraps her arms around my neck, holding me close.

"You have no idea how sexy you are," I tell her, because it's what she needs to hear, and because it's true.

She tosses her head back against the pillow and unleashes the hottest groan ever. "Coming," she cries out, shuddering.

Pleasure charges down my body in a hot, sharp, electric spike. I come hard, then collapse onto her, kissing her face, her neck, her hair.

She bands her arms around me, keeping me close to her for a minute till she whispers, "Give me a sec."

I take my cue, ease out, and head to the bathroom,

giving her privacy. When I return to the bedroom, she's put the shirt back on. After she pops into the en suite, she comes back to bed, and I pull her next to me, then inhale the last traces of gardenias in her hair. Hair that I'm privileged to touch, that I mightn't have been able to touch if those emergency responders hadn't arrived when they did. All I can think is *just in time*.

I don't say that though. I'm not sure that's what she needs to hear. "So, when's our

next secret date?"

"Better be soon."

Perfect answer. "Ah, so you learned saying yes to me is your real favorite thing."

She laughs softly. "You and your ego."

"You like both," I tease as I pepper kisses along her neck.

"Clearly. Since I'm not very good at saying no to you."

"Let's keep it that way," I say, because I don't intend to back down. With her like this, here with me, it's hard to believe we can't date. It feels like we could be so much more.

She might have said this *thing* between us can't be anything more.

But I heard in her voice what she *didn't* say.

And I see the emotions in her big brown eyes when we're together.

I feel the way she melts in my arms when I touch her.

Most of all, I *know* we have to be a thing. She might not know that yet, but that's okay. I'll convince her with my actions that I'm worth saying yes to, one secret date at a time.

* * *

In the morning, she's awake first, dressed in last night's clothes. Groggy, I push up in bed, yawning and bleary-eyed. It's six a.m. and there's a kitten on my pillow.

"I have to work," she says quietly. The skies are still dark. The sun hasn't risen.

"I'll drive you home," I say.

She shakes her head. "I'll call a Lyft."

Athena stretches her front legs against my head and Everly laughs. "I don't think you're fostering this cat. I think you're going to adopt her."

I toss off the covers, swing my legs out of bed, and pull on some clothes. "You're probably right," I admit. "But I'm right too."

"About what?"

"I'm driving you home," I say.

When we're in the car, one thought runs through my head — *It's what a boyfriend would do.*

39

MY GREEN THUMB

Max

Let the record reflect that I am not a gardener. But I'm playing the role of one today, and I'm going to win the Stanley Cup of gardening.

That's my goal—be as excellent on the soil as I am on the ice.

It's Thursday morning and we're helping The Garden Society with its final plantings for the fall season. It's the second community outreach event that Everly had planned as part of step two in her so-called Max Makeover Tour. I breathed a sigh of relief when I arrived this morning and Lyra wasn't floating over the garden in a hot-air balloon, waiting to rappel down and crash the event with a fake-ass smile.

I didn't think she would since Everly told me Lyra had returned to going out on the town with Fletcher, breezing in and out of LA establishments with him. What she does with him means nothing to me, but it was sexy as hell that

Everly's theory on Lyra was right. The return to her so-called "regularly scheduled programming" seems to prove that.

But even if she shows up, I'm not letting a damn thing go wrong today as I plant peas at an abandoned-lot-turned-community-garden at the edge of the Mission District. The Sea Dogs are one of the sponsors of these community gardens, along with the Renegades, so there are hockey players and football players here planting veggies in November for a spring harvest.

Since it's a promo opportunity, a handful of photographers are here too, snapping pics, along with Everly, who's capturing the event on her phone. She's next to a brunette a few years younger than she is, who's got a big Nikon in her hands and is snapping images too.

I'm digging up the soil to plant some pea seedlings when Asher says, from his row of peas, "Dude, you're doing it wrong. They need to be two inches apart—not one."

I glance down at my row, then his, then him. "You know how to plant?"

"What? Do you think I'm just a pretty face?"

Miles coughs from a row over. "That's kind of what I thought."

From his spot on the other side of me, Wesley shoots Asher a deadpan look. "Aren't you, though?"

Asher sets down his garden shovel and lifts his gloved hands our way, like he's going to flip us the bird, since we're classy like that.

Laughing, Miles makes a subtle slicing motion at his throat. "You can't do that right now. There're photographers around," he whispers, nodding to the pack with cameras, but the end of the sentence dies off when his gaze lingers on the brunette next to Everly.

But Asher's eyes widen, then he mutters a curse, like he's pissed with himself for forgetting the media. "This is your fault, Lambert. It's like I've been infected with your grumpy attitude. I almost flipped you assholes off in front of reporters," he says under his breath.

Wesley wiggles a brow. "Maybe this is like one of those movies where someone trades souls with another person. I saw that in a flick the other night on Webflix," he says. Then more earnestly, he asks me, "Come to think of it, how's everything going with the Webflix doc? When does that start?"

"Supposedly they're coming to town pretty soon for some pre-interviews," I say as I plant more seeds, two inches apart this time, like Asher the Gardener told me to. "Sounds like everything's on track from what my agent's told me. And Everly."

I steal a glance at the corner of the gardens where Everly's now chatting with a lifestyle reporter and a couple influencers, I think. Maybe garden influencers? She'd said some were coming along with a few of the usual sports crew, but not the beat reporters. But I don't linger on the press here. I linger on her, in her black slacks and gray blouse, a silky scarf around her neck, her blonde hair high in a ponytail, and damn, my heart thunders. My chest swells with pride, too, for how she's pulled this event off.

She wanted a different type of community outreach than the rescue dogs one—something where we had a chance to help people living right here in this city.

I want the event to go well because I want everything to go well for Everly—every job, every chance, every opportunity. I return my focus to the soil and shoot the breeze with the guys as I pull weeds and plant peas.

A little later, I grab a bag that needs composting and walk across the gardens to drop it in a bin. Everly's standing next to a raised silver planter, chatting with a man who looks familiar. He's wearing jeans, but his shirt is clearly custom-made. Pretty sure that's Wilder Blaine, the owner of the Renegades football team.

Is she networking with him? Oh, hell yeah. That'd be a smart move. When I'm closer, I pick up their conversation as he says to her in a cool, confident tone, "You did a great job with this event. Thank you for putting it all together."

"It was my pleasure. I'm so glad both teams could do it," she says.

He glances around once more, his gaze shrewd, assessing. "I'm a good businessman, so I'm not going to poach you, but I appreciate what you're doing and how you're handling your team."

She beams. "Thank you," she says. "It's a good thing I love what I'm doing."

"Keep up the good work. You'll go far."

That makes me think...what if, what if, what if?

When the event winds down, I grab a minute with her in the corner of the gardens as I'm gathering the little shovels we used. "Would you work for him?" I ask quietly.

"He's not going to make an offer. He has a great relationship with the Sea Dogs team owner, so he meant it when he said he wouldn't poach. But it was nice to hear he admires my work."

"Who wouldn't? You're amazing."

She offers a closed mouth smile before she says, "My, my. Isn't your tune changing, Max Lambert?"

I scoff. "I've always thought you were good at your job."

"You had a funny way of showing it before."

And a good way of showing it now, I want to whisper, and I'm tempted to, especially since Elias isn't here. But reporters are, and this is how rumors start. A whisper here or there. I know what it's like to be the subject of them, and I can't let that happen to Everly.

I have to find the will to tear myself away. "Good job with the event," I say, perfectly businesslike, then I return to my friends without giving her a second glance. But I pull out my phone and tap out a text.

> Max: I deserve a medal for resisting kissing you just then.

> Everly: I want one for not flirting with you.

> Max: And I'll accept mine for not touching you.

> Everly: I'll take another for not getting in your car and leaving with you when this ends.

> Max: Fuck, baby. I want that.

And I do want that. *Badly*. How to get it is the question though. When I'm heading to the gate of the garden to take off, a reporter calls out to me. It's Jamie, a hockey podcaster. "You've been doing a lot of appearances lately," he says, and he sounds incredibly skeptical.

Here we go again. But I smile, waiting for the question

that's coming any second—the one that tries to call my bluff.

"Is this a new Max? A Max who's focused on charity, or is this just an image makeover? Now you see it, now you don't?"

Out of the corner of my eye, I see Everly striding over. This is her turf, and she's not going to let a reporter corner a player. Even though I know the answer to his question, I still wait till she arrives before I answer him. "This is the real me. I just haven't shown it before."

Jamie blinks. Maybe he wasn't expecting that reply. He recovers quickly though, adding, "So will we see more of this you?"

If this me helps me win the woman, then yes.

I don't tell him that. I don't let on, either, that most good stories start with a woman. That most people change when they realize there's someone worth changing for. I don't tell him any of that because we're still a secret. But if I can help her rather than create more problems for her, that has to assist our cause.

"You probably will," I say, meaning it.

He asks a few more questions, and when he wraps up, she thanks him, then says I'm free to go. When I slide into my car, there's a text waiting for me on my phone.

> Everly: I could kiss you for those answers. They were so good! So natural, so real, so simple. The Real Max Lambert indeed!

My chest is warm. A little glowy even. I've made her happy. That's something. No, that's everything.

I don't turn on the car yet. I stare at the message for a good minute, enjoying this feeling till I catch sight of her in the rearview mirror, heading to her car.

But that feeling in my chest shifts. Turns into a pang. An empty ache. I want to be the man to walk her to her car, open the door, and kiss her cheek—the kind of kiss you could give your girlfriend in public.

As she drives away, I mull on what it's going to take to make that happen somehow. How many jerseys do I need to give to Elias to solve this? How many upbeat comments do I offer up to the press? And would all of that even be enough to counterbalance the weight of an unwritten rule that she has to bear?

Is she going to have to take a job someplace else for this to work? Could I ask her to? Could I schmooze Wilder Blaine on her behalf?

Not if you want to keep your nuts.

I shut down those ideas so fast. I can't do either of those things. Or ask her for either of them. That's not fair to her and all she's worked for as she aims to live her best life.

I resign myself to figuring that out later. For now, I need to focus on something that's in my control—winning her heart.

Without that, I've got nothing.

40

ICE KISS

Everly

I'm on my way out the door Friday night when Zaire stops me in the hall. "The documentary filmmakers are going to be stopping by next week for B-roll," she says.

My ears perk all the way up. "Does that mean it's officially happening? Are they going to feature Max in an episode?"

Zaire crosses her fingers. "It's an excellent sign. It's not a done deal yet and B-roll is the kind of thing they can toss if they decide not to feature him. But it's a positive indication that they want to have it in the can. They said, and I quote, 'We're happy with how things are going so far.'"

I smile brightly. That's what we've been working toward. "That is great news."

"And let me tell you something, Clementine is happy, too, so you know what that means?"

"You're happy?" I ask playfully.

364   LAUREN BLAKELY

"I am cautiously happy," she says, then spins on her heels and leaves.

I'm glad she feels that way. I don't want anything to destroy that happiness. I have a father who's disappointed with me most of the time. I have a mother who barely cares. But I have a job that has given me a lot of joy and I don't want to risk that.

That's why this thing with Max has to stay a secret. Truly it does.

Even if I've started entertaining possibilities for the future.

Even if I've started wondering if we could make a go of it.

Even if sometimes I think about smashing unwritten rules to smithereens.

The more time I spend with him, the less I want to be hidden.

This woman has serious shutterbug skills. "These are amazing," I say to Leighton a little later at Elodie's Chocolates because why have business meetings anywhere else?

She already showed me the pictures I hired her to take at the gardening event yesterday. I posted some on the team's social and one on Max's, but now we're reviewing the rest of them for a bigger photo drop over the weekend.

"I love this shot of all the guys huddled together planting," she says, and I peer at it on her tablet. It's such a cute picture of Max, Miles, Asher, and Wesley.

"The hockey players planting the seeds of victory," she says, then laughs—at herself. "That's super cheesy. Do not use that as a caption."

"Don't worry. I won't," I say with a playful smile, then pick the photos I like best and ask her to send them to me. After we've done our work, Maeve, Fable, and Josie sail into the chocolate shop. I smile even as nerves flutter in my chest. But they're butterfly nerves.

"I'm excited for my friends to meet you," I say, and I know they'll like her since I do. Leighton and I have become friendlier over the last week or so. I sort of feel like a friend matchmaker tonight.

I wave the group over then make quick introductions. "This is Leighton McBride. She's a freelance photographer I hope to work with more. She's phenomenally cool so I wanted you phenomenally cool ladies to meet her too."

Josie flashes her trademark welcoming grin. "That's good enough for me. How about us phenomenally cool ladies get chocolate and hang out?"

"I'm game," Leighton says.

The five of us order a chocolate sampler and catch up on our weeks, but mostly my friends want to get to know Leighton.

"What kind of photography are you into?" Josie asks, ever the inquisitive one.

Leighton smiles, and it's both a little bit sneaky and a little hopeful. "I'm trying to figure that out, and I'm dabbling in a bunch of things," she says, then lowers her voice and says almost in a confessional whisper, "But I actually kind of like boudoir photography. I've been assisting at a studio and helping out a bit with that. I've done a couple shoots so far."

Maeve clears her throat as her eyes bug out. "Ma'am. Show us."

"Really?" Leighton asks, but it's clear she wants to share.

Fable nods, then makes grabby hands. "Now. Show us now."

Leighton swipes her finger across her tablet. "Just don't tell my dad. I don't know exactly how to have that conversation with him."

I give her a playful look. "Right. I was totally going to tell the coach," I say, then gasp when she shows us her shots.

They're artful and sultry, pretty and powerful.

"I've been researching why women do boudoir shots, and some do it for their partners, but a lot of times it's because it makes them feel...beautiful in their own skin," Leighton says.

I sit up straight. She can't know how that hits, but it's like she's speaking to my soul.

"I'm in," Maeve says. "I want to do one."

"Surprise, surprise," Fable teases.

"Me too," Josie says. "But I also want to give them to Wes. He'd like them."

Max would too, I want to say.

Then another surprising thought hits me—a few weeks ago, I might have slammed the door entirely on a boudoir shot. I'm not saying yes to one, but it's no longer an immediate no.

That change in me feels like something I can be proud of.

This is a project I took on just for me. An image makeover for how I see myself. One that is further along than I'd suspected.

After we finish our flight of salted caramel chocolates, I say, "I have an announcement."

Josie gapes at me, like she's worried I'm about to tell everyone that I'm involved with Max even though pretty much everyone knows how I feel for him except Leighton.

But instead, I say, "Why don't we go lingerie shopping right now? I happen to be a huge fan of satin and lace, and I can help you pick out the best sets for your shoots?"

They're pushing back their chairs and getting up and out of there in no time. And that's another thing that feels empowering—shopping for pretty things with my friends.

And I make sure to pick out something special for me because I have a feeling I'll be ready for it on a secret date very soon.

* * *

But not in Vancouver, where we go on Sunday for a quick away game. Though Max and I do have a secret date there. That is, if you count Max sneaking down to my hotel room to rip open a bag of popcorn and watch *Pretty Woman*—since we're still in our makeover movie era.

When the credits roll, he says, "I have an idea for our next date. Something you owe me."

I arch a brow. "I owe you now?"

"You offered me a raincheck."

Oh. Right. When he asked me to skate. I actually haven't been on skates in a year. No particular reason. I've just been busy. "You were serious about that?"

He holds my gaze, his blue eyes intense. "I'm serious about everything when it comes to you."

Talk about subtext.

My heart catches then speeds up, beating too fast for my chest. How is this man my former nemesis and now he's romancing me like no man has romanced a woman before?

"Yes," I say, then I tug down his gray sweats and show him how much I appreciate him sneaking down to my room.

* * *

We return with a win and some good media coverage, including a feature on Wesley Bryant. Feeling accomplished, I get ready for my next secret date with Max. It's Wednesday evening, and I slip into the new lingerie I bought for him the other night, looking at myself in the mirror in the white lace before I put on a sweater. It's my morning ritual but I'm doing it before our evening date.

I don't do it because I need to, but because I want to. Maybe, too, because I believe in my mantra now. Completely. "I am pretty and powerful," I say, and I believe it. *I am pretty and powerful.*

But it's not because of how I look in lace.

It's because of what I can do with my body.

I have a body that's strong. That can climb a pole. That hangs onto it while letting go at the same time. I have a body that takes me to work, up stairs, around the city, and out with friends.

I have a body with a wild, beating heart.

And tonight, I can use this body on the ice.

* * *

I walk into the rundown rink on the outskirts of Oakland with Max. It's empty. The quiet is serene. "No one's here," I say, stating the obvious.

"I rented it out for the night," he says. "I get to have you all to myself."

And my heart somehow impossibly beats faster. If he keeps doing this, I'm going to...

Actually, I don't know what I will do. I truly don't, and it's a little terrifying. But then again, so is ice skating so I focus on that.

"This is ridiculous," I shout, feeling like a baby foal as I try to glide down the ice alongside the man who could truly do this in his sleep.

"You've got this," he says, encouraging me as he spins around, so he's now skating backward. In slow-mo. And doing it perfectly. Of course he does it perfectly. It's literally his job.

"Why isn't this like riding a bike?" I ask, my ankles wobbling.

"Hockey is the best sport there is because it's hard. But if you can pole dance, you can skate."

I laugh. "I'm pretty sure pole dancing and hockey have nothing in common."

He shrugs. "They have us in common."

This man.

Another minute or so later, I bend my knees and lean forward like I was taught to do.

"There you go," he says with pride in his voice. "Now push off with one foot, glide on the other."

It's a basic move and I do it. Soon, I'm getting the hang of skating again. I'm pushing off with both feet and gliding with both skates on the ice.

"Beautiful," he says.

Then, I do a snowplow stop out of nowhere. "How about that?" I say, smiling like I've pulled off an Olympic feat.

"I knew you could do it, Ice Queen," he says.

"Is that a new nickname?"

"No. It's how you were with me till I melted you," he says with a playful wink.

"You are so ridiculous," I tease, "but I love it."

"I know you do," he says, then offers me his hand.

We're not about to audition for the Ice Capades, but we don't need to because he takes my hand and skates slowly and easily with me. We go round and round, picking up a little more speed each time. But mostly we're just laughing and having a good time. It's as perfect as a night can be.

After several laps, we stop in the middle of the rink, and I'm breathless but exuberant. He tugs me against him, then runs his knuckles against my cheek. His eyes blaze with need. "I want to kiss you on the ice."

A shudder rushes down my body as I lift my chin, offering him my mouth. "Do it."

But he pauses, his eyes holding mine. "I mean at our arena."

My heart catches. Does he know what he's saying? Of course he does. "Yeah?" I ask because I don't know what else to say.

"I do. I really do," he says, as serious as he was when he asked me on this date.

"I want that too, but I don't know how to get there," I say honestly.

He leans in, presses his forehead to mine. "We'll figure it out together."

Will we though? I don't know how we can do that. So I don't make any promises. But I can give him *this*. "Until then...practice now."

He cups my cheek and kisses me like I matter. Like he means it. Like he wants more than secret dates.

And the more I feel that certainty with him the more I start to think about how much I want to find a way to get there.

But I'm also thinking about something else entirely. Something I'm finally ready for. I break the kiss, then say, "Come to my place now. Say yes."

"You had me at *come*."

We're out of there in seconds.

41

ALL THE IMPERFECT PIECES

Everly

The lights in my room are soft, but not dim.

The music beats, low in the background—a playlist I cued up. I don't even know what's on it. I don't really care. It just covers the jackrabbit pace of my heart. The *thump, thump, thump* that's hard and insistent against my rib cage.

And far too fast, but there's no way to slow it down. We kick off shoes, and in the doorway, I reach for Max's hand and lead him across the hardwood to my bed. I stop a foot away, facing him.

"Hi," I whisper. I don't know why I'm saying that. I'm just nervous.

"Hey," Max says, soft and tender, too, and maybe also a little bit nervous. But I think they're nerves of anticipation. Perhaps of hope.

I didn't tell him what I wanted tonight.

Just in case I back down.

My stomach swoops, dipping like a boat battered in

the North Sea as I fiddle with the top button of my jeans, fumbling once, then undoing it, then the zipper. It sticks and I laugh. "These zippers," I say.

"Let me help," he says, steady and reassuring. With a quick tug, he gets it unstuck. He unzips it the rest of the way. With strong, sure hands, he skims the denim down my thighs to my ankles.

I step out.

His eyes drink me in from my bare legs up to the white sweater I'm wearing, landing on my face. He runs his thumb along my jawline. Then he waits for my next move.

But that's easy still.

"Your turn," I say as I tug on the bottom of his dark blue Henley and whisk it off. A sigh of appreciation escapes my lips—he's so strong. But he's not simply carved and toned from the gym, like an athlete should be. He's rippling with rugged muscles, tough and battle-tested. He looks powerful in his own skin. His body is trained to stop goals but he can also carry you across the room and set you gently on a bed. Wiry chest hair descends from his pecs down to his abs. His biceps boast a few scratches. A couple blue bruises decorate his forearms.

I want to keep exploring all of him. I run my hands down his arms, tracing all the lines and marks on him, the little blue lakes, the scratches, and even the scar on his eyebrow—that unfairly sexy scar.

My hands roam back down to his strong chest, and I cover his pecs then play with his nipples. He groans, quick, unbidden, a gust of breath coasting across his lips that forms my name like a plea. "Everly."

Chills erupt over my skin from the sound of him. I drag my nails down his abs.

He shivers.

I inch closer, dip my face to his chest, and run my nose from his pecs up to his throat, where I kiss his Adam's apple. "Midnight Flame," I say. Then I revise that to, "My midnight flame."

He runs his fingers through my hair. "You're possessive."

"And you like it," I say.

He presses an equally possessive kiss to the top of my head. "No. I love it."

I look up and he lets go of my hair, one hand capturing my waist. I blow out a breath and reach for the hem of my white sweater and tug it off. I'm wearing a tank top along with the white bra and panties. But still I'm standing in front of him with no wall behind me, no couch against my back, no pillows to sink into.

No safety net to hide behind.

I don't think my heart has ever beat this fast. "Why does this feel like the first time with us?"

He swallows, his expression shifting instantly to something vulnerable and earnest too. "Maybe it is."

There's that hope in his voice. A tenderness as well. And something else—something so safe I didn't know I was looking for it until I found it in him.

Another song begins and that's as good a reason as any for me to reach for his jeans. He helps me along, unzipping and pushing them down, and in no time they're off. He's wearing only a pair of snug boxer briefs that don't do a damn thing to hide his obvious—very obvious—arousal.

That thrills me. It thrills me so much. I don't know that I will ever get enough of his want. It's the opposite of my last experience. It's the other side of how I felt with Gunnar. It's the evidence I constantly crave. So I reach for his hard-on, squeezing it, drawing out a sharp gasp from his lips. I run my palm up and down the steely length of him, then look in his eyes. There's lust there of course. But patience too. He's been so patient with me.

My heart beats furiously in my throat as I grab the bottom of the tank top and tug it off. I'm standing only in the white lace set I bought last week—a demi-cup bra and bikini panties with little embroidered flowers on the waistband in pinks and purples. His eyes glimmer with heat and also something like awe. "You are just... extraordinary."

My breath catches but I don't say a word. I'm afraid to talk. I'm afraid I'll just sob. I'm not sad. But I am one exposed nerve. I take his hand and walk backward to the bed, bringing him with me. He's facing me the whole way. I sit on the mattress and look up at him. Like I'm at the edge of a cliff and the water is an inviting crystal blue, I slide a finger invitingly along the strap of my bra then jump off. "Do you want to take this off me?"

He grabs my face and holds me with such intensity that I feel precious as he says, "I do."

It's said urgently, with a wild desperation and, more so, a complete understanding of the question.

Max starts with a kiss on my right shoulder since he's sitting on that side. Then he blazes a trail of kisses up to my neck as his hand slides around to my lower back on my right side—the smooth side.

Then he shifts me so I'm turned toward him. He dips his mouth to my left shoulder, kissing me there, journeying along that raised, red scar. He's kissed me there before, many times. Touched me there every night. Seen that scar and the ones on my upper arm in the past. But we both know where this moment is going—well beyond my shoulder, well past my arm.

With a firm hand on my chin, he raises his face, and with his eyes on me, he says in a steady, confident voice, "I'm going to unhook it."

He's not simply giving me a play-by-play. He's giving me a heads-up that he's going to touch my back for the first time. Everywhere. I swallow and nod, granting permission once more, even though it's already been given.

His big, calloused hands cinch around my stomach, sliding over both sides of my back. They reach the hook and he undoes it, then lets the delicate lace fabric fall free, slowly sliding down my arms. He catches it. Sets it down on the bed.

He's seen my breasts before, of course. But it feels different when he cups them, weighs them, then lets go. It feels different because when I lift my chin and meet his honest gaze, I say, "You can look."

There's a pause as he runs the back of his fingers along my cheek. He drops a tender, adoring kiss to my mouth, then shifts his weight. The mattress sinks. He moves on the bed, kneeling behind me for the first time.

I hold my breath. I've been here before. I've been left alone here before. My heart beats in my throat. Emotions swim up my body. Memories, too, along with images from the night of the accident. But I breathe through them, past them, cataloging the beat of the sultry song in the background, the faint scent of midnight and longing, the softness of the duvet.

And him.

While I want to lower my face, I don't do that either. I

stay strong because I am strong. I know that now. I believe that now.

A second later, Max's big hands cover my shoulders, then glide slowly, tenderly. He's like an archaeologist touching a treasure for the first time. One hand coasts down the smooth skin on my right side, the other along the bumpy, scarred, once-burned skin on the left.

He touches each side of me the same way. His touch is hungry and reverent as his hands travel all over the terrain of my body, the map of the last three years of my life. Then it's no longer just his hands on my back. They're joined by his mouth. Hands and lips and the scratch of his beard as he kisses all the imperfect pieces of me.

"I love them," he says in a gravelly rasp.

I turn back to him, unsure I've heard him right. Because I'm not sure anyone could say that. "What?"

He clasps my cheek, drops a kiss to my lips that he finishes with a desperate sigh, then returns to my back. "I love them so much," he says, his own voice full of emotion, like he's fighting to keep it together. With a shudder, he kisses my back more urgently, all over. "Because they mean you're alive," he says, then he raises his face and bands his strong arms around me, pressing his warm chest to my back, clutching me against him like I'm the treasure he's keeping safe. "You're alive and here with me."

Just in time.

I clasp his hands in front of my chest and hold on tight. But I can't hold back the tears that flood down my cheeks. He is so much more than I'd ever imagined. "I'm here," I say, but it's not a whisper this time.

It's steady and strong, like how I feel with Max Lambert.

"And I love them. I love everything about you, and

most of all, this," he says, his hand sliding up and between my breasts where he spreads his palm across my heart and covers it. Like he's protecting it. Like that's all he wants to do for me. Protect me.

And I believe he does.

I close my eyes because this moment is overwhelming. But I lean back against his shoulder, resting on him. The tears slide down my cheeks, and when they slow I say, "You make me feel everything."

I can feel his smile. Can hear his grateful murmur. He kisses the salt from my face until I turn and capture his mouth.

We kiss, and it's hot and needy and unstoppable.

We're clawing at each other, grabbing at the last bits of clothes. He whisks off my panties, and I tug down his boxer briefs, and we're tumbling together on my bed. A tangle of arms and limbs, skin and flesh, bodies and hearts. He's on top of me, and then I'm on top of him. His hands coast up my back again, fearlessly, then into my hair as he hauls me back down for another passionate kiss.

When he lets go, I'm so amped up, I blurt out, "Put me on all fours."

His fantasy.

His wish.

But mine too.

He closes his eyes for a brief second, but he's smiling. He's smiling so wide, like I've given him a dream come true. What a wild thought. When he opens them, he says, "Are you sure?"

My lips curve up. "I'm serious about everything with you."

He holds my face. "You're my real favorite thing."

Some men just say things, but I know Max means his words. This man adores me, and it's such a thrill to feel the full weight of his affection. "And you're mine," I say.

I move to my hands and knees, shifting into a position I *never* thought I'd want. Or really, I never thought a lover would want to see me like this.

But as I bow my back, I'm hardly thinking about how I look to him. I'm simply feeling. The ache inside me. The trembles racing over my skin. The curl of pleasure intensifying in my stomach.

And the heady anticipation as Max kneels behind me, rubs his hands over my ass, then covers himself. He notches the head of his cock against me, and I gasp, sharp and fast. He pushes in. My skin tingles. He groans. He sinks into me all the way. Then he does as he promised a few nights ago.

I can still hear his words echoing in my mind. *"Want to get you naked. Put you on all fours. Fuck you from behind. Touch you everywhere."*

He fucks me like that. It's hard and passionate and fearless. No one would look at us and say we're making love. But as he fucks me, I know that's what we're doing. He runs his hands up and down my back. He doesn't shy away from my scars. He doesn't hold back his lust. He groans and he grunts. He touches and he explores. Most of all—he *shows*.

He shows me with his actions that he's not leaving.

As we're both getting closer, he pushes on the small of my back and rasps hotly in my ear, "Lower your tits to the mattress."

I shudder from the command.

That wasn't what I expected him to say, yet it's perfect too.

I drop down and with my face turned to the side, pressed into the bed, he covers me. Roping a powerful arm around my chest, he tugs me impossibly closer. Then he fucks me hard and powerfully, and I don't even need a hand between my thighs to help myself along. All these raw emotions, all these wild, risky feelings storm inside me, whipping into bliss till I grab the sheets. I fall apart beneath him, and he pumps hard a few more times, then jerks, stills, and groans my name like I'm all he's ever wanted.

The world spins away, and I let it go.

This is all there is, and I don't want to give him up.

42

A BEAUTIFUL TRIAD

Max

I'm playing a long game, but sometimes the long game involves little things.

Like a regular London fog latte. Like her favorite egg sandwich for breakfast. Like an invitation to watch another movie.

I send the first two to her office a couple days later because I reason those can be easily passed off as something she'd ordered, if need be. Then, after I finish listening to a new class—I aced navigational tools and started one on the Pyramids of Giza—I toggle over to a graphics app I downloaded and make an invitation for movies and popcorn in a few nights' time.

I've got an ulterior motive though. Maybe we can talk then. At the ice rink the other day, she said she wants the same things I do. Maybe we can start to figure out how the hell we're going to get them. We've got one more community outreach event next week, so the timing feels right for a deeper conversation. A roll-up-your-sleeves kind of talk.

As Athena saunters into the kitchen with a sassy meow, I send the invite to Everly, then add one more note.

> Max: You were right.

> Everly: Yes to movies and popcorn of course. Also, what am I right about? Tell me now.

I scoop up the furball and snap a shot of her in my arms. I make sure she's nice and snug against my bare biceps. I'm not above a little arm porn. I send the pic and a note.

> Max: I sent in the adoption paperwork for Athena.

Everly doesn't text back, but a minute later after I've pulled on a sweatshirt so I can head to morning skate, my phone rings. "You kept her! I'm so excited."

So you can spend every night with us?

But Everly is a flower that opens slowly. You can't rush the bloom. So I don't say that. "Me too," I say. "Especially since Athena is excellent at watching movies with us, and she doesn't try to steal the popcorn."

She's become our movie companion at my home.

"She is," Everly says, then takes a beat. "Thank you

again for the breakfast and the latte. You've been spoiling me. This is the third day in a row."

"Good. I like spoiling you."

And I want to do it every damn day. Just let me.

"You really do," she says, and briefly I wonder when my special gift will arrive. The company emailed that the custom order had been delayed, which is annoying, but it should arrive soon.

I hear the sound of a door snicking shut. "What can I do for you?" she asks quietly, even though she must have privacy now in her office. "You do so much for me and I want to do something for you."

"Sunshine, there's no ledger here."

"But you give me all these gifts and do all these things."

"And you give me you. It's more than fair," I say.

"Max, you know what I mean. What can I do for you?"

Tell your boss you want her to bend that rule. Tell her you're falling for me too. Tell her to let you keep your job and date me.

But nothing worth having comes easily, and this is not a convo for the phone. It's too important to have offhand. "My parents are coming to the game this weekend. I want to introduce them to you."

"That's what you want me to do? Let you introduce your parents to me?"

"Yes," I say, emphatically. "I told you my dad knows about you. So my mom does too. And Sophie figured out long ago that I had it bad for you."

"I like her," she says, then her tone shifts. "How will you introduce me? Will you say I'm your secret girlfriend?"

I punch the sky. She's calling herself that. That has to be a good sign. "Works for me," I say.

"Then I want to meet them," she says. "Also, don't forget *The Ice Men* producers are here today shooting B-roll. Garrett's already arrived. I've been keeping an eye on them. Everyone seems to be in a good mood. He's been chatting with them the whole time."

"Look at you. You're like my inside woman, spying for me."

"It's secret girlfriend work," she says, and that excites me more than a saved goal. I say goodbye, then head downstairs to my car. I swing by Asher's place to pick him up.

The second he slides into the car, he says, "What are you going to do about the auction?"

"What auction?" I ask, wondering if that's a new event Everly will want me to do.

"The annual player auction. I'm doing it. Gotta keep up my streak of going for the highest bid. Every year I've gone for higher and since I first entered the auction I haven't missed a game."

"I guess someone has to get the sympathy vote," I needle him as I pull away from the curb.

"When they drop that hammer in a couple months' time, I think you'll see it's lust in the ladies' eyes." Asher corrects me then grabs his chest, as if he's been mortally wounded. "Wait—no. Are you jealous cause you didn't get an invite? I mean, I figured it would be part of your makeover."

"Ah, the bid-on-a-date-with-a-player thing. No, they didn't ask. But I'd say no."

"Because you're taken," he says in a leading voice as I cruise toward the arena.

"I fucking hope so," I say seriously.

"How's everything going with her?" he asks, dropping the teasing.

"She's...incredible. I don't deserve her and somehow she still wants me. She's smart and bighearted, and cares deeply about her friends and the team and her job and the world. She likes to try new things, and she's a great listener. She keeps me on my toes and doesn't stand for any shit. She's fiery and easy to talk to and she also likes to hang out at night and watch a movie, and she's abundantly honest. Like, I *know* I trust her. I *know* she trusts me. She's perfect for me."

He whistles. "Damn. That's quite a speech."

"It's just the truth," I say as we reach the players' lot. But even though it's true doesn't mean it's easy. It's harder than it should be. "Trouble is, I don't know how to make it work since she faces most of the risks."

He sighs thoughtfully. "We're lucky, being athletes. A lot of things are easier for us. We're forgiven for breaking rules. Well, not *in* the game itself," he says wryly.

"Exactly. No one's going to give me a hard time about wanting to be with her. And really, I have very little to lose at this point. She's already done the hard work *for me* of rehabbing my image. She faces all the risk. So what the fuck do I do for her?" I ask as I pull into a spot and cut the engine. "I feel a little helpless."

His expression is pensive, but then he shrugs. "I really don't know...except be there for her, one hundred percent. Be there and mean it every step of the way."

He's right. "Good advice."

We head inside, where Garrett's waiting for me near the locker room, chatting with a woman with sleek black hair. He looks a little like a proud dad. I smile when I reach him since that's probably the documentary producer Everly mentioned. Asher heads into the locker room while I join my agent and the woman.

"I'm Lily," she says to me, extending a hand. "I used to play hockey myself, and I knew I had to have you in an episode."

"Glad to do it. Well, if it all works out," I say, shaking hands.

"I bet it will," she says with a hopeful grin. "We can start with some B-roll of you at practice."

"Have at it," I say.

We chat for a few minutes, then she takes off to set up. Once she's out of earshot, Garrett is practically bouncing again.

I arch a suspicious brow. "What's up with you?"

He slugs my shoulder. "Guess who got you a new sponsor?"

I blink. "What? You did?"

"I sure did. Sooner than expected. You're in, baby. It fucking worked," he says and he's...ecstatic. It's a little infectious. Sure, I *could* make do on my hockey salary. That's no hardship. But hell, some extra to set aside for my family, for me, for a future in case I'm injured and can't play? I wouldn't mind that at all.

"Who is it?"

"Date Night. The dating app. Or, I should say, the premier dating app."

I flash back to our first meeting about this makeover. "But you said you didn't want me fake dating?"

He scoffs. "Not fake dating, man. Real dating." He waves a hand airily. "Or real...making a profile on it."

I furrow my brow, trying to process this news out of

left field. "You want me to just...set up a profile and then what? And *say* I'm using it?"

That sounds like a recipe for disaster but maybe I'm missing some key detail. Well, I probably am.

Garrett's face lights up. "Yes, my man, yes! It's so easy. They're one of the advertisers for *The Ice Men*. They've been a lead ad partner for every episode so far, and they're booked for the episode they're considering you for too. Plus, they sponsor fan engagement promotions during the month of February for the Sea Dogs. It'd be like a beautiful triad—the Sea Dogs, *The Ice Men*, and you." He stops, his expression more contemplative. "Or is that a quartet? Since we do need to include Date Night. Huh." But then he shakes off the philosophical debate even though my mind is still reeling on what this might mean. "Point is it's a win-win-win-win. It'd be a great partnership. And it'd be an excellent way for you to keep your face out there." Shoes click from behind me, growing closer, and he pauses, but only for a second. "Plus, your likeability quotient is so high right now that this could be the thing you need to land other sponsors. They'd see you out there even more with your new good guy rep, and then...bam."

He mimes shooting a basketball. Nothing but net.

"So what do you want me to do for them exactly?" I ask, since something isn't adding up. "Posting a profile on it feels like a lie that'd be easy to sniff out. And we know the press loves to sniff out a lie. I'm amazed no one has sniffed out Lyra's lies yet, but she's the mistress of fables, so there's that."

"Then maybe don't lie," he says, oh so helpfully. He pats me on the biceps. "You could actually go on a couple dates if you want."

The fuck I will. But before I can say a word, he adds, "So you'll think about it. Excellent."

"Garrett," I warn him.

"Just think about it," he adds as the sound of clicking shoes turns even louder, and multiplies. Everly's here, tilting her head in curiosity. But she's not alone. She's flanked by Elias, Jenna, and Zaire.

"Think about what?" Everly asks.

"I hope he's thinking about it," Zaire says in a smooth, confident tone.

Garrett beams and looks to Everly. "Thanks to your kickass makeover work on our guy, my agency got him a sweet new deal with Date Night. Think you can convince him to take it?"

The look in Everly's easy-to-read eyes is crystal clear to me. But can Garrett tell she wants to murder him?

43

CAN I GET A FIST BUMP?

Max

"Dude! That's sweet!" Elias offers me a fist for knocking.

What's the etiquette for turning down a fist bump? I do not want to knock fists about a sponsorship deal for a dating app with the guy who wants my secret girlfriend's promotion. I don't want to bump fists with him about anything.

I hold up a stop sign hand instead. "Nothing's signed yet," I say.

With a pfft, he says, "It'll happen. I'm confident for you." Like that's the issue. Like I'm just being superstitious. "And if you need any tips let me know. I signed up for it a month ago," he says, like he's beyond stoked to have a buddy on the app. "Definitely the best one out there, especially for—"

He cuts himself off, maybe realizing it's best not to discuss how it's the best app for single dudes in front of the boss.

"I'm glad to hear Garrett brought you the info," Zaire says in a professional tone, since she's always a professional.

"Me too. But I don't know about going on dates," I say, since I'm not going to act like that's cool with me.

Zaire offers a placating smile. "Of course you don't have to do that. There's no requirement. We would never expect it of you. That's not fair and certainly not appropriate to ask you to."

I whip my gaze to Garrett, a little annoyed he suggested I go on dates. But my agent reads me like that, jumping in with, "I was saying you could, Max. That's all. No worries if you're not ready."

I appreciate his support now, but it sure sounded earlier like he thought it'd be a good idea if I were.

And I'm sure it would be for a dating app. Doesn't take a genius to figure out a brand could benefit more from a partnership if the athlete actually used the product. So while Date Night might not make using it a condition of a partnership, I bet they'd sure as shit like me to.

"I don't know," I say, since I need to buy some time. No way do I want to make this decision now in front of an audience.

"Think about it," Zaire says in a calm tone. "There's time. I'm just glad to see the work you and Everly did is paying off so soon."

Zaire shoots a pleased look to the woman I adore, but Everly might as well be a mannequin, standing there with a frozen smile. Jenna softly clears her throat, likely for Everly's benefit.

Everly blinks then says woodenly, "It's so great."

"It really is," Jenna seconds, "but only if Max truly

feels it's right for him. Brand deals need to be right for the athlete."

"I think you'll like it," Elias says to me, selling it once again. "And really, there's no reason to turn it down, since you're not seeing anyone, right?"

He says it so earnestly, so hopefully, that he legit sounds like the dude-bro he is, wanting to hang with the big dogs and shoot the shit about girls. But I don't trust him. Hell, I'm not sure I trust anyone right now. I don't know who Jenna's loyal to. I don't even know what my agent truly wants for me.

I feel entirely unmoored.

"I'll think about it," I say, more gruff than I'd intended.

Or maybe exactly as gruff as I'd intended.

"Great. Maybe we can let them know by the end of next week," Zaire says, "after Meals on Wheels?"

Right. We're delivering food to seniors on Tuesday. "Sure."

"I'd love to go to that," Elias says.

What the fuck does that have to do with the fan experience?

"Me too," Jenna says.

And I feel like I'm on the ice and a tough team is taking shots left and right, and I don't know who to block next.

With a happy shrug, Zaire turns to Everly. "It'd be great for them to see how you pulled this off. Does that work for you?"

Everly's eyes flash with confusion or maybe mistrust, but she blinks it off a second later. "Of course." She turns to me, swallows, then says, "And congrats, Max. I should... go sit in...on this Zoom call. Good luck."

She heads off before anyone else. We need to move up the timeline on our convo real fast.

Because this potential deal has the power to trip us up big time. It's a damned-if-you-do-damned-if-you-don't kind of problem.

44

OUT LOUD

Everly

When Max buzzes that he's at my place later that night, I hit the open button on my app so fast. My nerves are frayed thin after this morning.

I swing open the door to my home in record time and he's bounding up the stairs two by two.

I peer around the hallway cautiously, even though my building is small and I never see my neighbors. But there are cameras everywhere. What if someone sees us hanging out? My stomach churns. How long can we get away with this? This morning wasn't even a close call, but I hated myself for standing there and patently lying by omission.

I wiggle my fingers, urging Max inside my home. When I lock the door and shut out the world, I breathe a bigger sigh of relief than I want to feel. "Hey."

"Hey, you. You okay?"

"Yes. No. I don't know," I say. We texted during the day,

but I was busy with meetings and couldn't let myself get distracted by spiraling too far into a relationship funk. I really can't do that. I can't risk being distracted. Well, any more than I already am. "Are you going to take it?"

He doesn't answer right away. Instead, he tilts his head, studies me, then takes my hand and leads me to the couch. "You jealous?"

"Yes!" I say, aggravated.

"Is that why you're asking? Because I hope you know there is no other woman in the entire universe who could interest me. You have ruined me for everyone. So there."

My nerves settle but only somewhat. "I'm still jealous."

"Why?" He sounds amused. Maybe delighted.

I groan, frustrated with the way we're hamstrung. "Because I want to stake my claim on you and I can't," I blurt out. "Do you have any idea how hard it was to stand there this morning and just listen to all those dating suggestions? I wanted to drape an arm around you and say, *he's taken, back the fuck off.*"

His smile is the biggest cat-who-ate-the-canary grin ever. "That is the hottest thing you've ever said, Everly."

Maybe it is, but I can't enjoy it. Because I can't enjoy him the way I want—out loud. I want him to be mine. All mine. So I ask again, "What are you going to do about the deal?"

He sighs heavily, his smile burning off. "This deal is a big problem." He takes a beat. "If I turn it down, it looks like I have something to hide. If I say yes, what if someone figures out we're together? And then I look like a liar."

I recoil at the prospect. "That's bad. It would ruin all the work we've done."

"Exactly. That's not good for my rep. But if I turn it down, then it looks to the team and my agent like I'm not playing along. Then Clementine might think about not renewing me."

My gut churns harder. I don't want him traded away. I want him to stay. But the powers that be want him to take this deal. "But do you want to take it? You didn't answer when I asked earlier," I say evenly. Well, as evenly as I can. The thought of Max being the face of a dating app makes me want to claw things.

He sneers. "I thought I made that clear. In case I didn't —fuck no."

"Are you sure?" I ask, but this time I'm asking because I like this one-track mind side of him.

He grabs my jaw. "Sunshine, you are the only woman I want. Full stop. Me promoting a dating app is like you promoting a butcher."

I can't help but smile, but it doesn't last since I can't figure out how to solve the problem. "So what happens next? I don't want to make more complications for you."

"You're not making them." He drags a hand through his thick hair. "I just wish it were coming to me next month, once everything is done, and the doc is about to shoot. Right now if I turn it down, I look like a jackass to management," he says, frustration in his tone.

I sigh heavily, racking my brain. "Well, is it the worst thing if you just make a profile?" The question tastes bitter on my tongue.

He narrows his eyes and inches away from me like he needs some distance. "You want me to do that?" He sounds offended.

"Max, I don't want you to. I'm just trying to figure this out."

"Is there a reason you want me to?" He's tense everywhere, his muscles tight.

Oh god. This is a man who has major trust issues. "No," I say, meaning it from the bottom of my heart as I rope my hands around his neck. "I'm trying to weigh all the options, but you have to know—I meant what I said earlier. I don't want anyone else to even think they have a chance with you."

He presses his forehead to mine, relaxing again. "Good. Because no one does. You have me, Everly. You fucking have me."

I feel his certainty in my bones. It gives me the courage to even think about doing something risky. I pull back to meet his face. "Max, let's get through the next event, but once we do, I could try to talk to my boss."

His eyes light up like a thousand sparklers on the Fourth of July. "Yeah?"

I nod, even though the prospect is terrifying—like offering my job for the chopping block. "There's not really any other way around this than for me to ask Zaire if I can keep my job, while..."

"Being with me?" he supplies.

I love that he says *being* rather than *dating*. Being feels deeper. A promise. A commitment.

"Yes. But I don't know how to say it to her or when exactly. And I don't want to organize it while I'm still working on this makeover. I just need a little more time to plan out how to do it. Can we figure it out once we finish the project? In a week or so? Does that buy you enough time without giving Date Night an answer?"

His smile isn't disappearing. It's growing. "I can buy all that time for you. You're worth it," he says, then he kisses me like we're together.

Except the clock is also ticking, and it sounds a little more foreboding than it did before.

* * *

In the morning, he takes off early to work out with the guys while I get ready to meet up with my friends for a Saturday morning pole class. Before I leave, my camera app shows there's a delivery for me. Curious, I head downstairs and grab a soft padded envelope.

From Lace and Wishes.

Huh. I'm not familiar with that shop. I don't remember ordering from there. I trot back upstairs, anticipation crackling under my skin. Before the door even closes behind me, I rip it open.

When I take out the soft seashell pink tissue and unwrap the gift, my breath catches. He sent me a pair of panties. Again.

They're royal blue again—team colors. Again.

But this time they're custom-made. With his number stitched on the front.

45

INESCAPABLE THINGS

Everly

I'd thought this trick would be hard. But after I invert to a leg hang and drop my right arm, it feels smooth and easy enough to release my back leg.

"Yes! I knew you would get your butterfly on the first try," Kyla says as she spots my hips.

I swear her faith in me before I had my own has helped me pull this off. I'm smiling stupidly, even with my nose against the pole since I'm fully upside down. Or maybe because of it—I didn't expect to see this view. I like this view.

After a few seconds, I flip back over, releasing from the move I didn't truly expect to nail on the first try. "I didn't think it would be that easy," I say, kind of amazed. "But thank you—for everything."

"You did it all. You've been doing inverts and you're strong," she says and there's that word again—*strong*—one

I'm trying to step into more and more. I feel stronger every day.

"We knew you'd get it too," Maeve says proudly, clapping from a few feet away.

Josie's cheering too, and so is Fable. The whole class is, actually, including the woman with the blue hair who nailed this move a few weeks ago—when I longed to be like her.

I still feel self-conscious walking around the Upside Down studio in only a sports bra and shorts, my scars on full display. I'm still hyper-aware of the ways my body is different. But one look around this place with women of all shapes and sizes—tall, short, pear-shaped, plus-size, rectangular, thin, athletic—and I should have known no one would look at me differently. But some things you just have to experience to believe.

When class ends, we leave and for a brief second, I imagine Max waiting for me after class—well, when I don't go with my friends. I picture us grabbing a bite to eat, doing life together like that.

It's such a lovely image it makes my chest ache. Because I know it'll be hard to get there.

On the street, Maeve declares, "We need to celebrate your butterfly with lunch."

I put Max out of my mind. But that's easier said than done since once we've ordered at our favorite diner, Josie turns to me and says thoughtfully, "Your makeover project is almost over, and it looks like you've pulled it off. The perception of Max is way more positive lately."

"You've been checking?"

She gives me a look like *what did you expect*. "I'm a librarian. I like information. I like understanding things.

So yes, I did a little poking around into how the Max image makeover was going."

"I love you," I say with a laugh.

She preens, then says, "I know."

Fable looks my way. "Maybe that makes *you* the kickass movie heroine who takes down bad images in a single bound."

Maeve shrugs happily. "Whatever you're running for, Everly—you have my vote."

Their support, both of my efforts in pole, but also with work, lifts me up. Makes me think I really can take the next step. And because they are such unapologetic friends, I don't need to call upon Herculean strength to say the next thing. In fact, it's really easy to tell them what I told Max last night, "I think I'm going to try to talk to my boss about that whole unwritten rule."

Maeve's hazel eyes sparkle. "And you're going to smash it," she says excitedly.

"We're here for you," Fable says, and I think that's exactly what I needed to hear.

"Yes, we are," Josie seconds.

"You've got this," Maeve adds. "Because you two have that no-question-about-it love."

I pause, tilting my head. "I didn't use the L-word."

Maeve smiles. "My sweet summer child, you didn't have to."

"Is it just that obvious?"

Josie snort-laughs. "Like an open book."

But Maeve sighs contemplatively, her eyes a little dreamy. "With love, I don't think you handle it. It handles you. It's like a painting you're working on, and you think you're making the art but really the art's making you."

I let that soak in—the idea that there's an inescapability to love. With Max, I feel like there's a riot in my heart, and I can't do a damn thing to stop it. Still, I want to be prepared. "So what happens next in this *inescapable* love story? When I go into the office and talk to my boss?"

Maeve reaches into her bag and takes out her tarot deck. "I could ask Tatiana?"

Fable stares at her, too amused. "You named your deck?"

"Of course I did," she says, then shuffles and proceeds to draw—rather deliberately— the Three of Cups, an image of three maidens holding up three chalices. There are four of us here, but it feels like Tatiana knows something. "Tatiana says we're here for you, babe," Maeve says.

"We are," Josie and Fable echo.

Maybe that's some of the strength I needed too.

* * *

After I shower and get ready for a game night, I slide on the panties Max sent me, admiring the way I look in them. Claimed. Then I take a very sexy selfie.

> Everly: Some pre-game inspo.

> Max: I fucking love them. And I have never been more inspired in my life.

* * *

That evening I'm watching from the press box as Max maneuvers a puck around the trapezoid, flipping it to Miles, who tears off down the ice. For a few seconds, I think Max might get another assist, but New York blocks Miles's shot and one of their forwards gets the rebound.

The New York forward flies down the ice, trying to score on a breakaway. But my sexy beast of a goalie drops to his knees, leg pads spreading out to the sides, saving the goal.

I gasp audibly. "Yes," I say with a quiet fist pump.

Someone gently nudges me.

It's Jenna.

Oh, shit. Maybe I wasn't so quiet. I'm not supposed to show favoritism, even though of course I want us to win.

She smiles my way.

I whisper a quiet *thank you.*

I bite my tongue the rest of the game, but it's getting harder to swallow this four-letter word.

* * *

After the shutout, I'm waiting by the tunnel when Max emerges, sweaty and victorious. "Want me to get you a yacht tonight to talk to the press?"

"Yes, sunshine, a four-hundred-footer," he says.

I freeze. But then I remind myself he's called me *sunshine* in front of people before. At least I think he has? I rack my brain. Yes, he has. I breathe again.

But working with him is starting to feel like watching my own back all the time and that's a tall order. I ask, as professionally as I can, "Can you talk to the media? Shutout and all."

"Yes." His eyes sparkle when he says that one word, and I bet he's thinking of our *say yes* mantra. But that's a problem too. Everything between us means something else. Everything could trip us up.

When he finishes chatting with the press and strides back into the corridor with me, he nods toward a man with a similar jawline to his and a woman with cool blue eyes, who are waiting there along with Max's cutie-pie nephew.

I home in on Kade. "Did you see your uncle save all those goals tonight?"

The kid beams. "I did and he blocked *alllll* of them."

"He's very good at that," I say, then come face-to-face with the parents of the man I've fallen for. I stick out a hand to shake with his mother, then his father. "So great to meet you, Mr. and Mrs. Lambert."

"It's lovely to meet you, Everly," his mom says, and her smile is knowing.

"Max raves about your work," his dad says, his eyes twinkling with a secret.

My throat is tight with emotions from this simple fact—that his parents are playing along. But I wish none of us were. I wish this were real. I wish I were telling them how hard I've fallen for their son. What a good man they've raised. What a wonderful person this grumpy, broody, storm cloud of a goalie turned out to be.

But I can't here so I smile and say, "I'm so glad. Max is great to work with."

And I've never felt like more of a publicist, spinning a story, than right now.

* * *

"What's wrong?" Max asks me later that night at his place.

"Nothing," I say flatly as I play with the kitten, dangling a feather toy I bought Athena.

"Something's wrong," he says, setting a big hand on my thigh.

This man can always read me, so I sigh and let go of the toy. "I loved meeting your parents but I wanted to tell them how amazing you are. I wanted to say *your son is incredible and he takes care of me and adores me and I adore him,* and I couldn't say that. I just couldn't."

His lips quirk up. "You adore me."

I roll my eyes. "As if you didn't know."

"Say it again though. I like the way it sounds on your lips."

"I adore you," I huff.

"Still like it even when you're irritated."

"I just...I want to speed up time," I admit. And I want to tell him how deeply I feel. But I don't want to say I've fallen in love with him while we're *only* together in the dark. I want to tell him outside, under the sun, when I don't have to hide. I'm tired of hiding. I've stopped hiding my scars in pole class. I've stopped hiding them from him. I don't want to hide *us* any longer.

"Me too," he says with a sympathetic smile, then he runs a hand down the buttons of my blouse. "But until then, I know how to pass the time."

I've learned how to not slide back into the past thanks to my grounding exercises. Surely, I can root myself in the present. In his touch, in his scent, in our...inescapability. I hold all that close as we head to the bedroom. I undress to my bra and panties, and while it's obviously not a pole I grab hold of the doorway like I'm doing a trick, strike a sultry vixen-like pose, then toss my hair back.

From the bed, he growls as he sheds the rest of his clothes. "Get over here in my jersey."

"Oh, these?" I ask, hooking my thumb in the waistband of my very sexy panties.

"Yes. Been thinking about them all day."

I undo my bra and drop it to the floor as I walk over to him, teasing at the waistband of the lace as I do. Running my fingers down the thirty-three on the front. "So what exactly were you thinking about?"

"That you had my number against your very pretty pussy. Now why don't you put this gorgeous pussy on my face," he commands. "Because I'm really, really hungry."

I take my sweet time, sliding off the panties, then tossing them to him. Because my man's addicted, he brings them to his nose and inhales before he lets them go. "Now, sit on my face. Since what I've really been thinking about all day is eating you. You're mine, Everly. All mine."

I feel like his. But I'm not yet. Not really. That doesn't stop me from climbing over him and straddling his face. He eats me like I'm his last meal.

I come so hard, I nearly black out. I nearly forget that everything we share is a secret.

Maybe soon it won't be.

And maybe, like the butterfly, it'll be easy.

* * *

This is hell.

A few days later we're back and in an SUV we rented. Max is driving, Zaire is in the passenger seat, and I'm in the back seat with Jenna and Elias. I didn't hire Leighton or another freelance photographer for this job since it's more personal. A cell phone camera seemed the right speed for today.

But Elias evidently made a pitch to Zaire about taking the photos, so he's here like he's Ansel freaking Adams with his iPhone. We've already visited a number of homes, with Max delivering meals for seniors who still live alone but have diminished mobility. Now, we're making the final stop at a senior center. "You know," Elias begins as Max nears the Aquatic Park neighborhood, "I volunteered with Meals on Wheels during college."

Of course he did.

"And it was so eye-opening," he says, bloviating even more. "I felt like I learned so much. Truly, it's been an honor to be a part of this today. Thanks, Zaire. Thanks, Max."

Zaire inclines her head, giving a crisp nod while Max grunts out a thanks.

"Where did you go to college?" Jenna asks, seeming intrigued.

Thank god she's here to handle him. It's too hard being in this space with all these people and all this pretending. It's wearing me down. It's stressing me out. It's driving up my anxiety. I feel claustrophobic.

As Jenna peppers Elias with more questions about his supposed glory days, Zaire asks Max if he's given more thought to Date Night.

I feel queasy as he says blandly, "Every day."

My thoughts start spinning, so I do one of my grounding exercises, focusing on things I can see, hear, and sense, till Zaire says, "Would that work for you, Everly?"

I snap to it. "I'm sorry. I didn't hear you."

"I thought it would be nice to have dinner with Garrett and Clementine again. And you and Max later this week.

Just to go over everything you've done and make sure we're all set with this project."

And to decide on Date Night.

The clock keeps ticking. Louder and louder still. "Of course," I say quickly, then brace myself for Elias to invite himself.

And on the count of three...

"I'd love to come too," he offers.

"That won't be necessary, but thanks for the offer," Zaire says, and I fight off the world's biggest grin.

When we arrive at the senior center, Max gathers the meals from the back while Elias snaps more pictures of him taking out the food. Once inside, Max drops them off in a community room that's bustling with older San Franciscans. I hang back near the entrance, staying out of the way as the once grumpy goalie chats with nearly each person there, saying hi to some women knitting, asking questions of a couple guys doing a jigsaw puzzle, and making small talk with some men playing cards. Max said he wasn't naturally affable, but here he seems most at ease. I bet it comes from how he helped take care of his grandfather. As he moves from table to table, it looks like his cup is full. Like this is more than part of his image makeover. Like this is The Real Max Lambert.

It's a good look, and I'm seriously proud of him.

A man with wispy strands of hair who's hunched over his table calls Max over. The older man tilts his face toward Max and asks him something. Max shakes his head and replies. The man keeps asking questions and Max's expression turns more concerned, more worried. I wish I could make out what they're saying. It looks like Max is trying to reassure the man but doesn't know how.

Soon, a woman who works at the center comes over and intervenes.

With tension in his jaw and sadness in his eyes, Max heads for the exit where I'm standing with Elias. He swallows roughly, uncomfortably too, then mutters as he passes us, "Excuse me."

And Elias has the audacity to snap another picture. But as Max turns into the nearby men's room down the hall, I wheel on Elias, raising a finger. "Don't."

"Don't what?" It's asked so innocently.

"Don't use that picture."

"Why not?"

"He's obviously upset."

"It's a real-life picture. It shows Max has feelings."

Elias has no idea. "No," I say firmly, standing my ground.

He gives me a look like I'm a Pollyanna. "This is the stuff people love, Everly. Seeing the real side of an athlete. I know it because I played sports." Of course he went there. "And I know because I interact with the real people at every game," he adds.

And he went there too.

"And I know that part of the job in PR is to protect our players. This is personal. Please delete it," I say, standing my ground. I don't care what Elias suspects about me. He's not posting a photo of Max visibly affected like that.

Annoyed, Elias stares at me for several seconds then relents. "Fine." He makes a show of deleting it.

"Thank you."

Max comes out of the bathroom, dragging a hand through his hair. It looks like he's been hit with bad news, and I want to run to him and comfort him.

But I can't.

When we get to the car, I tug him back, a few feet away to quickly ask. "What happened? Are you okay?"

"That man was asking about his son. If he was coming to visit. And I tried to talk to him, but then the woman who came over, she said his son had already visited and —" He stops like there are stones in his throat, then he pushes on. "This is how it started with my grandfather. The forgetting."

My throat swells. My eyes sting. "Max, I'm so sorry." He takes a small step toward me before he must think the better of it.

I can tell he wants to hold me as much as I want to be his shoulder to lean on.

Instead, I have to wait till later that night, when he comes over for our movie night that he invited me to. It feels like an endless wait, but as I curl up in his arms, I try to believe that soon we'll have more than stolen moments.

* * *

One more night.

That's what I've been telling myself. That's what Max tells me on Thursday evening as we get ready for dinner together at my place. I feel antsy but in a whole new way. In a Christmas Eve kind of way. Once we make it through dinner, I can devise a proper plan for talking to Zaire. One that's thoughtful. One that shows this relationship with Max is serious. One that shows how much I want the promotion or at the very least to stay in my job. If she doesn't make an exception to the unwritten rule, I don't know what I'll do, but I know I'm strong enough to handle it.

I button my blouse and fluff out my hair in the bathroom mirror. It's down tonight. "Like my blowout?" I say to Max. I used one of the lifetime supplies this evening.

"Love it," he says, then comes up behind me and presses a kiss to my neck. "Have I told you how much I appreciate what you're doing?"

I smile. "Yes. But I'm not doing it tonight. I have an early Zoom meeting at eight tomorrow with the East Coast and you have that interview tomorrow with The Sports Network," I say, reminding him of both our schedules, and of the interview he agreed to do with our broadcast partner. Plus, I don't want him to get too excited. I need to get some rest after this dinner—not come home and brainstorm how to save my job. There will be time in the near future. "Let's focus on this dinner and we can start figuring it all out tomorrow. And come up with a smart plan. I promise."

Tomorrow night Max leaves for a week-long stretch of away games on the East Coast—ones I'm not attending—so I'll have some time to put plans into motion.

"I know, sunshine. I know. But I'm here for you."

I turn around, smooth a hand over his purple shirt, then meet his eyes. "We've got this."

"We do."

He kisses me and then we head to dinner together in his car. It feels like the start of the next phase of us, even though we walk in side by side like colleagues rather than lovers. Still, I can't help but feel that fizzy sense of hope. Soon, very soon, we might not have to pretend. We've made it through this project, and we're almost out on the other side where we can sit down, talk, and figure out all the next steps.

That feels even more possible when we reach the table

and Clementine is holding a glass of champagne. "To the makeover queen," she says to me.

Her praise makes me feel like I'm valuable to them, regardless of who I love. That I'm useful even if I've bent a rule. That they'll understand I'm too important to let go just because I fell for an athlete.

I hope so. I really hope so. "It was a tough job, but someone had to do it," I say playfully, then we sit, and I take my glass and clink with the others.

But when I steal a glance at Max, something like suspicion passes in his eyes. I write it off though. I must just be seeing things.

46

A CON JOB

Max

"Did you enjoy the eggplant salad?" the server asks, and the question sounds like it's coming from the bottom of a well.

Is he even asking me?

I tear my gaze away from the water glass in my hand, condensation sliding down the outside of it. I look to the kind-faced server who's standing by my side, clearing my plate, and yup—he *is* asking me.

I try to reconnect to the present moment. But it's hard because my mind is stuck like a tire spinning in the mud. It's not here at this dinner with the VP of Communications, the general manager, my agent, and my secret girlfriend. It's not at this table in this trendy Moroccan restaurant in Hayes Valley that Zaire loves.

It's back in Everly's house an hour ago. And I can't stop playing her words on an endless loop—*but I'm not doing it tonight.*

"The eggplant salad was great," I say flatly, finally managing to muster a response.

"Wonderful. Would you like any more water?"

I don't want water. I don't want an eggplant salad. I don't want couscous. I want to understand what the hell is going on with my girlfriend, who seems far too fixated on the project rather than *us*. "No thanks," I mumble, then stew some more as he moves down the table.

Fine, her comment about *not doing it tonight* technically makes logical sense, but tomorrow is a game day. Which means I have morning skate, then the fucking game itself, then thirty minutes later we get on the bus to the airport.

Plus, she said she had an early Zoom meeting, and I have The Sports Network thingy when I'd normally nap. When did she think we were going to talk about us? She's not going on our road trip. I can't imagine she'll want to talk about it on the phone when I'm on the East Coast.

Is she...putting this off? My jaw ticks as my mind runs wildly into these woods, all while grabbing the branch of this terrible possibility—what if she's putting *me* off?

"Max, are you excited?"

I look up from the water glass that I'm practically crushing in my hand. My agent's sitting next to me, asking a question. "About what?" I ask.

Garrett gives a smile that feels like a correction, like a *pay attention, buddy* grin. "The documentary episode is a go," he says. "The producers gave the green light. We've been talking about it for the last few minutes."

"That's great," I say flatly, clenching my fist in annoyance under the table, or maybe it's worry. Looks like Everly thinks this documentary news is great too. From across the table, she's smiling brightly even as she shoots me a curious look. "Isn't that fantastic, Max?"

She might as well kick me under the table. But is that coming from the girlfriend side of her? Or the publicist one?

"We are truly so happy," Clementine says from the head of the table, looking regal with her cinched back hair and strong profile. "It all really came together." Her pleased gaze turns to Everly. "All that one-on-one time paid off."

Everly smiles. "I've never had to do so much one-on-one work with a player before, but clearly it's worth it. I was hoping this project would show you what I'm capable of."

What the fuck? I snap my gaze toward her, narrowing my eyes. What the hell does that mean? I try to ask it silently through, I dunno, mind waves.

But Everly furrows her brow my way, like she's asking right back *what's wrong with you?*

I'll gladly tell her. What's wrong is that the woman I love thinks I'm just a project. That's what's wrong.

But I clamp my teeth together instead of talking.

Like a puppet master, Garrett claps my shoulder. "Max isn't the easiest to work with. But he's worth it. So worth it," he says, all smiley and shit.

"Thanks," I say dryly. "Appreciate the vote of confidence."

He squeezes harder. "C'mon, man. You aren't, but you two pulled this off. Well done."

"Yes, you two really pulled off a banger," Clementine says.

Pulled off. Those two words echo ceaselessly in my head. We pulled it off. Like it was a heist? Maybe a con?

And now we're celebrating with the crew. Like we stole the diamonds and we've got them all in our pockets and now we're getting away with it—the remake of Lambert.

The project.

Everly shoots me another one of those cautionary looks. Probably because I'm just a project to her. Probably because she doesn't want me to ruin her project. Probably because she wants to make sure we can indeed pull off this whole thing.

I drag a hand down my beard as I slump back in my chair, like a fool. How did I miss this?

The same way you missed all the signs that Lyra was involved with someone else. Signs that were right in front of you. Signs you barely paid attention to while you were falling for her.

Because I *wanted* to believe in Lyra. I wanted to believe in an *us*.

Garrett jumps in again, taking over the conversation like it needs saving. "And it looks like you're well positioned for the promotion," he says to Everly, then shoots that perfect agent grin of his toward Zaire and Clementine. What the hell is going on? Is he in on it? Was this always about her getting a promotion?

Everly demurs, holding up her hands. "That's not what tonight is about," she says, but it sounds *too humble.* Too much of a deflection.

Zaire lifts a champagne glass Everly's way. "I certainly don't want to offer any promotions over dinner, but I will say we're pleased with your work," she says, mostly diplomatic even as she leaves a big, tasty hint.

Everly dips her face, as if she's trying to hide her smile. Yup, that's what my girlfriend wants. The promotion. My muscles tense. My heart shrivels.

"And now you can finally move on to other things," Garrett puts in. "Other projects. Other opportunities. Like, I don't know, maybe Date Night."

It's said oh so casually, like he clearly knows he shouldn't push, but like he also wants an answer badly.

Zaire offers me a hopeful grin. "I spoke with Webflix today. It looks like it could be a great partnership all around." She pauses. "If it works out with Date Night. And I know that's an *if*."

"No pressure," Clementine adds, and they're all so diplomatic. I should appreciate it. Truly, I should.

But I feel like I've stepped into quicksand in the middle of a murky night, so I shift my gaze to Everly, adopting a perfectly curious look. "Is there anything that would hold me back?"

Her eyes widen, and she swallows roughly. "I think it's entirely your decision," she says.

Ironic. The other night she didn't want me to do it, but now it's my choice.

Because she'll be moving on.

Because what if that's all I ever was to her? Work. Just work. The times we spent together never felt like work to me. I never felt like I was doing anything but falling head first into a big, spectacular, move-mountains kind of love. But the last time I fell for someone, my happy, easy, nice-guy life crashed head first and I was left to pick up the wreckage.

I know Everly isn't cheating. I truly know that, but my nerves are strung tight. My heart hurts. And my hackles are up. I don't know how to trust a damn thing anymore.

Except...*me*.

I'm the only one I can trust, and at some point I have

to trust actions, rather than feelings. Deeds rather than words.

Fact is, Everly's been putting this off time and time again.

She said *let's get through this makeover and we'll figure it out*. She said *let's not do anything tonight*. She said *a partnership with Date Night could ruin all the work we've done*.

What if I leave tomorrow and she gets that promotion, and then I return and she dumps me on my ass?

"So, we really should get things going with Date Night," Clementine adds. "Perhaps tomorrow?"

She looks to me hopefully, and I steal a look at Everly. Her face is unreadable now. Her eyes give nothing away. They're just...hard.

But I'm good at memorizing. And I remember all too clearly something she said last week. *"Max, let's get through the next event, but once we do, I could try to talk to my boss."*

Could. She only said she *could try*. I am such a fool. I push back in the chair. "Excuse me," I say, then I step away from the table, but instead of heading to the restroom, I beeline to the front door, a man on a mission. Once outside, I draw a huge breath.

This is how I feel when an opponent slams into me. When the wind's knocked out. When the world has turned upside down.

A minute later, Garrett's pushing open the door, joining me in the cool late November night. "What's going on?"

"Nothing. Just needed some air."

"You okay?"

"Yes," I say.

"You don't need to make this decision tonight," he says. "Actually, maybe don't make it tonight."

"It's fine. I'm fine."

"You don't look fine."

"I'm fine," I snap.

Garrett holds up his hands in surrender. "Okay."

"Are you trying to help Everly get a promotion?" I ask like it's a crime.

He tilts his head, studying me quizzically. "It'd be nice if she got one. She works hard. She's good at her job. Maybe fix your shit and act the same way," he says, for once not playing the smooth, cool agent role, but instead the kick-a-client-in-the-pants one.

He stares me down, hands on hips. Waiting. He's not leaving me out here alone because he doesn't trust me. And really, maybe I don't deserve trust with the way my brain has turned black and dark. I heave a sigh then say, "Fine. Let's go back inside."

He sets a hand on my shoulder. "Shake this mood, man. It's not good."

"Yeah, I wouldn't want to ruin anyone's project."

Then I shrug him off and go back inside, slapping on a false smile for the rest of the meal.

47

THE GREAT UN-SPIRALING

Max

The second we're in my car, she slams the door, then looks at me with both concern and accusation in her eyes. "What is going on with you?"

Like she doesn't know. I fling the question right back at her. "What's going on with *you?*"

She yanks the seatbelt on, then crosses her arms. "Why would you ask me that question about Date Night? *Is there anything that would hold me back*?" She mimics me, but her voice is laced with hurt.

So is my whole body.

"Because I needed to know." I stab the on button and hit the gas. But as I cruise through traffic, I can't escape the weight of her stare.

"What is going on, Max?" she asks again, pressing me, with genuine concern in her voice.

Fuck, what is wrong with me?

I grit my teeth and try to fight off the hurt. I truly do.

But when we're close to her house, I'm too caught up in this swirl of doubt. It's like chains wrapped around me. "Are you moving on?"

She narrows her brow. Studies me like I make no sense. "What are you talking about?"

"Moving on. You said that at dinner," I bite out.

"Garrett said that," she corrects me, a little incredulous. Actually, *a lot* incredulous.

I take a deep breath. "He said, and I quote, *And now you can finally move on to other things.*"

"Those were his words!"

"You didn't deny them."

"It's not my job to deny something your agent says," she says, her voice rising as I pull up to her home, parking at the curb with an unnecessary squeal of tires.

"He seemed awfully fixated on your promotion. The entire dinner seemed to be about the project," I say, building up a new head of steam.

She holds her hands out wide. "News flash: It *was* about the project. That's literally why Zaire asked us to dinner. We just worked on a project together." She takes a beat and draws a deep breath, then pins me with a sharp stare. "So what are you getting at, Max?"

I shouldn't say it. I really shouldn't. But it's weighing on me. It's gnawing at me. It's eating away at me. Because I know what it's like to be burned and to be burned publicly. Before I can think the better of it, the words tumble out, "Did you just use me for the promotion?"

Her jaw falls open.

I always thought that was just a saying. But now I know it's the truth. Everly Rosewood stares at me slack-jawed, like she can't believe I've said that. Slowly, she lifts her hand, pointing to her chest. "Are you equating me to your ex?"

"No!" I say it so fast because she needs to know that's not what I meant.

"Then what are you saying?" The question is a quiet hiss.

"I'm saying that the whole night was about the project, and it just made me wonder—"

"Wonder what, Max? Make you wonder what? If I'm willing to put my head on the line for you? If I feel everything for you? If I'm willing to take all these chances *for you?*"

Her questions cut me to the core, and I deserve every single nick.

She pushes open her door and awareness crashes into me all at once. The spiral un-spirals and I snap back to reality. I fucked up big time.

I race out of the car to the other side as she's trotting up the steps to her place. "Everly, I'm sorry. I'm so fucking sorry. I spiraled, and it's all my fault. It's hard for me to trust." I reach for her, but I don't feel like I have the right to touch her, so I pull back my hand, trying to use my words and voice instead. "Forgive me. Please."

She inhales—a long, thoughtful beat. "It's hard for me to trust too, but I did it anyway."

Her voice is breaking apart, and I am the worst boyfriend in the world for hurting her like this. I try to take a step closer. "I didn't mean anything by it. My thoughts just spun out. All my fears climbed back up."

"I can tell," she says, but her voice is cool, and she's wearing the armor of self-protection.

"I was making up conspiracy theories in my head at

dinner. I was freaking out. Let me make it up to you. I'm crazy about you. I'm madly in—"

But she holds up a hand again, stopping me from saying the words, maybe because it's not fair to tell someone you love them for the first time in the middle of a fight. "You *were* making up conspiracy theories. Because I would never do those things. I would never use you. I hope you know that."

"I do."

"I was ready to put *everything* on the line for you, and you had the audacity to say *that*."

Was. She *was ready.*

"Are you ending this with me?" I ask, the words like razors in my throat.

She gives me a look that says *how can you think that* but then turns her gaze to the doorway. "Max, I have an early Zoom meeting with an East Coast team. At eight. And I do not have the luxury of earning a hockey player's salary. I am going inside so I can get some rest and not make any more mistakes at my job."

"Can I go upstairs with—"

"I need some space tonight. Please just let me have some space tonight."

My heart caves in, but the woman asked loud and clear for one thing—*some space tonight.*

And I have to be the kind of man who listens. "Okay," I say heavily.

Then she walks up the steps and opens the door, and I watch her go. My heart's been punched.

By my own stupid fist.

48

MY NEW BED

Max

I don't leave right away. I stare at her window on the second floor, debating.

I should go back in, right? Knock on her door and grovel on my knees.

I should buy flowers and chocolate and cake and lattes and bring them all upstairs and say *I fucked up big time.*

But her last words are on replay. *Please just let me have some space tonight.*

I hate doing this. Truly, I do, but I've got to listen to the woman, and she needs to *not* see me.

I don't get out of the car and barrel inside like I did when I crashed her dates. I drop my head on the steering wheel. How can I fix this? How can I convince her I'm worthy of all her chances? But a few minutes later, I'm no closer to an answer than I was before.

I turn on the car and go. No clue where I'm headed. No

way can I sleep. I just drive through Russian Hill, passing...wait.

Is that her pole studio? I hang a U-turn so fast, jerking the car to the curb. It's late and the studio is closed, but I bound up the steps to the door of Upside Down, like I can find a clue there to fix this mess I've made with my own stupid trust issues.

Maybe I could buy her a lifetime supply of pole classes? Would that help her see I'm all in? I google the name of the studio to find the contact info, then send a quick email to the owner as I head back down the steps.

But it's not like I'm going to hear from the owner overnight, so once I'm back in my car, I do the next logical thing. I call my dad. "I need your help. I fucked up big time."

"Come on over, kid," he says.

I leave the city behind.

* * *

Dad grabs a bag from the pantry and tugs it open, offering me some of the Himalayan salt air-popped popcorn. "Your favorite."

I shake my head as I slump down into a chair at the kitchen table. "I don't deserve it."

He gives me a sympathetic smile. "I doubt that, but what's going on?" He pops a handful of kernels into his mouth. He's in plaid pajama pants and a sweatshirt. His hair is sticking up. He was probably asleep, but he got out of bed for me.

I blow out a breath. "I kind of have trust issues," I begin.

"You do."

I drag a hand through my hair. "And I sort of freaked out tonight, and thought maybe Everly didn't really mean the things she'd said about her feelings for me. What would come next in our relationship."

He winces, like he can't believe I did that. Yeah, I can't either. I tell him the awful story of where my mind went at dinner, and then what I said to her after. "What do I do now? How do I convince her I'm not—"

"A dick?"

"Yes, Jesus. I've just spent nearly two months convincing the public I'm not, and in one dinner, the woman I'm in love with thinks I am."

He sighs but then shoots me a serious look. "Does she though? Does she believe that?"

"She probably should," I say.

"But did she say that?" he presses.

"She just said to give her space tonight."

"And are you doing that?"

I gesture to his kitchen. "Yes. I'm here. And I apologized already. As soon as she called me on it, I realized I was wrong, and I apologized right away."

"That's good," he says, but he's hedging.

"It's not enough though?" I ask, my gut churning with worry. But before he can answer, I say, "I'll get her a lifetime supply of London fog lattes every morning. A diamond necklace. Her dance studio membership for the rest of her life?"

Chuckling, he holds up a stop sign hand. "Slow down. You can't buy your way out of this or gift your way out of it or play your way out of it, Max. You have to use words and your heart."

I stare at him. "But I tried."

"Try again," he says then adds thoughtfully, "When you've given her exactly what she asked for. She asked for space. The greatest thing you can do right now is listen to her. Give her that. Then try again. Own your shit."

"Own your shit," I say, repeating those words of wisdom from my dad. "That's what I have to do?"

"Yes. Own your shit because relationships aren't easy. And they can't always be fixed with gifts. You win her heart with the way you care for it, and the way you listen. Have you won her heart?"

I flash back to all our nights together. To our days. To our secret dates. To the way we connect, to how we treat each other, and then to what she did for me a couple days ago. She told me about the picture Elias took at the senior center, and how she made him delete it. She protected me. And I missed the full meaning of that moment. I missed how deeply she cares for me because of my own fears.

My fears that have nothing to do with her.

The wounds she didn't cause.

The past she had nothing to do with.

I need to leave my trust issues behind once and for all. To trust that this love between us is real, and do my part to help my girlfriend do the hard thing. She's the only one who can, but I can do a much, *much* better job supporting her. "I hope I've won her heart, Dad."

He pats my arm. "Give her the time she needs and then be there when the night is over."

He's right. That's what I have to do. Show up, let her know I might make mistakes, but I'll do everything I can to un-make them.

"Love you, Dad," I say, then give him a hug and take off.

I return to the city close to midnight, pull up outside her place, and cut the engine. Then I lower the driver's seat, grab a ball cap from the back, and cover my eyes. I'm not going anywhere. I'll be here when she wakes up. Just like I'll be here for her, whatever she needs.

49

THE PADLOCKERS ASSEMBLE

Everly

I don't go to sleep right away. Correction: I can't fall asleep. After an hour or more of tossing and turning, I grab my phone and ask for help.

I text The Padlockers.

> Everly: Are my no-sex-with-Max sponsors still awake?

Maeve replies first.

> Maeve: I have the heart of a vampire. What's up???

. . .

Fable is next, cutting to the chase.

> Fable: Uh-oh. Are you cutting him off?

Josie is the last to answer the SOS, but she does a minute later with her loyalty on full display.

> Josie: Who do I need to beat up?

I write back, asking if they can FaceTime. A minute later, we're on a video call. Maeve's lounging on her couch, one of her bejeweled liquor-bottle lamps glowing softly in the background. Fable's in her bed, her red hair piled high on her head in a messy bun. Josie's on her couch, with her dog, Pancake.

"Max was possessed by an alien tonight at dinner," I say, then explain what happened.

Maeve cringes.

Josie frowns.

Fable sighs heavily, shaking her head as I tell them the tale while I pace around my home. When I'm done recounting the things we said outside my house, I sigh and ask, "Why men?"

"Exactly," Maeve says.

I blow out a breath and sink into my soft, fluffy purple couch pillows. "I can't believe he thinks I did this for my job," I say, annoyed all over again, hurt all over again. "How can he think that? Why would he think that? I would never do that, and I'm the one who's taking the big risk."

They're all quiet for a beat, but Josie opens her mouth as if to speak then closes it again, and I latch onto her silence since it means she's thinking. "Okay, help me out, Josie? Where did your big brain go?"

"Well," she begins thoughtfully. "I think sometimes men and women—well, humans—are just so scared of real love, real vulnerability, real trust...that it's easier in the moment to regress. That's what happened with Wes and me last year."

I remember that. They hit a rough patch, as all couples do, and had to figure out how to get *in* each other's way rather than *out* of each other's way. "And *maybe* this is when the two of you need to really lay your hearts on the line," Josie adds.

"But I did, and he still asked if I was using him," I say, except once I say that I'm keenly aware I didn't completely put myself out there. I said *I adore you*. I said *I feel everything*. I said I was ready to put everything on the line. I avoided the L-word because it scares me. Because the last time I loved someone so deeply that I felt it in my soul, I lost them. Even though that was platonic love, it was still love.

I haven't told Max I love him because I'm afraid of losing him. Because I'm terrified of what might happen if I love so completely and then lose someone again.

But he tried to tell me he loved me tonight, and I didn't

even let him finish the sentence. I also didn't clarify when he asked if I was ending it with him. I groan. "What if I'm the asshole?" I say, then I tell my friends what I just realized.

Maeve scoffs. "Well, he's the asshole too. The bigger one, honestly."

Fable nods. "Let's not give him a get-out-of-jail-free card just because you didn't let him say he loved you when he was in the middle of apologizing. *As he fucking should*. He did spiral. He did suggest you were using him. Just because you didn't soothe his worries doesn't make what he said okay."

That's true too, but I'm also more confused now than I was before. I furrow my brow. "I'm lost. What do I do? Especially if we're both...assholes. Um, whatever-size assholes. Why are we talking about assholes? Can we stop talking about assholes?"

"Please! Yes, anything else," Josie says, then smiles. "Here's what you do. Apologize. Then kiss and make up. Forgive and move on. And keep on loving him."

Fable smiles and gestures to Josie. "Both things can be true at once. You can both be jerks and you can also forgive."

Tears prick the back of my eyes, and my throat clogs with emotions. But my heart swells, too, with so much love for these women. And I don't have to keep that to myself. "I love you. All of you. So much," I say, and that feels like the start of a brand-new day.

"Love you too," they all say.

Then, I yawn, feeling better, and feeling like forgiveness is possible. And honestly, maybe as easy as a butterfly.

Since he's probably asleep, I send Max a text.

Everly: We're not breaking up. You can't get rid of me that easily. I promise you.

I fall asleep.

50

EARLY MORNING DELIVERY

Max

My joints are stiff. My muscles bark. My neck is filing a lawsuit against me for indecent sleep. But when I finally manage to open my tired eyes and fumble around for my phone on the console, two beautiful notes flash on the screen.

The first is from Everly, and it makes my heart soar. I grip the phone tight almost like I'm hugging it in my hand. I needed *this*. I needed this from her so badly. But I need *her* even more. One quick glance at the time and I get the hell out of my car before the sun comes up. I'm not going to try to buy her love back with gifts, *but* at the same time, I've got a streak going.

And athletes don't mess with streaks.

I google the nearest coffee shop, place an order to go, then jog down the street to Doctor Insomnia's two blocks from here. But along the way, I catch a scent of my morning breath.

That won't do. When I dart into the shop a minute later to scoop up the order, I spy some mints at the counter. I buy a pack and stuff some in my mouth, chewing off the morning breath as I rush back to Everly's place with her daily morning London fog latte. Outside her place, I peer upstairs. The light's on.

Good.

I park myself on the steps of her building as the sun slowly peeks above the pale blue light of the horizon, pulling up a new day with it. Stretching my neck from side to side, I answer the other note on my phone as I wait for her to come downstairs. As I do, I feel...hope.

Because of her.

Because even when I freaked the fuck out, she looked out for me. She sent me this text last night. She didn't want me to wake up and worry that we were over.

I need to earn her trust. Every damn day.

Five minutes later, the door swings open.

"Oh!" She stops in place, startled.

I stand and thrust out the cup. "Hi. It's your morning London fog latte. Personal delivery. And today's order comes with an apology," I say, then I don't waste any time speaking straight from the heart. Owning my shit. "I fucked up last night and made a mistake with the things I said, and I promise I'm going to try to do better if you'll let me."

Her smile is like the sun rising, slowly, beautifully, lighting up the dawn. Her big brown eyes tour my frame as an eyebrow rises. "Why are you wearing the same clothes as last night?"

I glance down at my purple shirt. It's wrinkled and probably stinks. My hair's a bigger mess than usual. "I slept in my car."

She shakes her head like there's water in her ears. "You slept in your car?"

But the sleeping arrangements make perfect sense to me. "I wanted to be here when you woke up. To deliver your drink. And to take you to work. And to say I'm sorry. And most of all to tell you I love you so damn much," I say, and that smile of hers? It grows ten million times bigger. But I have more to say. So much more. "You don't need to say it back. I don't expect an *I love you*. I'm not telling you to get it in return. This is how I feel, and I want you to know that I am all in. I believe in you. I believe in us. I trust that this real favorite thing we have is going to work, and I will do whatever you need from me to make this easy. Just let me know."

She takes the cup, lowers it to the concrete, and loops her arms around my neck. The last remnants of the tension I woke up with miraculously fade away thanks to her touch. I shudder from the feel of her hands on me once again. Her fingers play with the ends of my hair.

"I have a bunch of things to say, but the most important is this—I love you too, Max Lambert," she says, and those words are all I've wanted to hear from her, and I am so damn glad she didn't listen to me and make me wait for them. I need them now, like I need her now.

She kisses me, and her kiss is everything good in the world, but it stops too soon. When she breaks it, she shoots me a curious look, asking, "Why do you taste like a mint farm?"

With a laugh, I nod to my car. "See above. I slept in my car. So I ate a bunch of mints this morning."

"I can't believe you slept in your car," she says, sounding kind of amazed, and maybe even delighted.

I curl my hands around her waist, not caring if her

neighbors or anyone else sees us right now. She lets me hold her too, telling me she doesn't care either. "I slept in my car because I needed to be here when you woke up. I needed to be here to bring you your latte. Because I want you to know I will show up for you every day. Even if I make a mistake, I will keep showing up. I spiraled because of my past and my fears, but they have nothing to do with you, and you're not responsible for them. I am. And I promise I will do better. And I wanted to tell you that. And also I really needed to tell you that I love you." I kiss her forehead. "I love you." I kiss her eyelids. "I love you." I kiss those beautiful lips and taste all her love too.

When we break the kiss, she strokes my beard slowly, like she's memorizing the feel of me. Maybe confirming I'm really here with her. "And I love you, Max. So much," she says softly but with the strength too that I know is bone-deep in her. "But there are other things I need to say."

I give a crisp nod. I didn't expect to spackle over last night with an *I love you* and a latte. We need words too. "I'm listening," I say.

She lets go of my neck then sets her hands on my shoulders, giving herself a little space perhaps to say what needs to be said. "You hurt me last night when you asked if I was using you for a promotion. I hope you know I would never do that."

"I know," I say, ashamed I went there.

"That's not who I am," she says, as if she's imploring me to understand. "I would never use you. Everything I feel for you is so real. And trust me, I tried, I really tried, to fight how I was feeling for you."

A smile tugs at my lips, but I deny it, focusing instead

on her. "I know you did, sunshine. I know this isn't easy for you."

"Yes, I want the promotion, and yes, I want to be with you. And, like my friend Fable said, both things can be true at once."

I nod again, because she makes perfect sense. "She's right."

"And I didn't start planning what to say to my boss yet because it's terrifying," she says, her tone so vulnerable as she lets me deeper into her heart. "I don't have any idea how she's going to respond. I don't know how they'll handle it. I don't know if I'm going to be fired," she says, desperation coloring her tone, and I hate that dismissal is even a possibility for her. "And that's why I needed to wait till we got through the last event and dinner. Not because I was putting off this big thing that needs to be done, but because I didn't want to be overwhelmed with everything that it entails."

"I get it now. I appreciate you explaining it to me."

She takes a beat, as if she's gearing up to say something harder. "Sometimes I do get overwhelmed. Sometimes my mind fixates on the past and what happened three years ago. Sometimes I picture it and remember it so clearly I'm afraid I can't move forward. That I'm going to be stuck in that night all over again," she says, and with a deep breath that seems to steady her, she keeps going. "When that happens, I do these grounding exercises to stay in the moment. I haven't told you about them before because there wasn't really a need. It's just something I do in my head. Something I learned about in therapy after the accident. I catalog my surroundings and it helps me stay in the moment so that I don't get lost in the past."

My heart aches for her, for all she's endured, but it

also thumps louder and harder over the ways she starts over and how she thrives as she moves past that terrible day. "I hate what you went through—all of it, just all of it. Every single part. But I'm so glad you have these..." I pause, thinking of the best words to use. "Tools. Coping mechanisms. And I love learning all of these details about you—even the ones that are hard for you to share. Maybe especially those. So thank you for telling me that."

She gives me a soft smile. "I want you to know me. I want us to know each other. And part of why I'm telling you this is that I can't always plan everything all at once. If I do, I'm going to get overwhelmed with the future too." Her hands grip my shoulders tighter as she continues, "I'm truly trying to live and make the best decisions I can for each day. That's the only reason I didn't make a detailed plan yet. Because I didn't want to spiral either. But I already submitted a calendar request for Monday morning. That way I can plan what to say over the week-end. I can rehearse it with my friends. And go into the meeting from a position of strength."

My heart catapults in my chest. "You already requested the meeting?"

"I did it when I woke up."

"Fuck, I love you," I say, then I laugh lightly. "Also, I think you're better at not spiraling than I am." I reach for her right hand on my shoulder and press a soft kiss to her palm, then I link my fingers through hers. "I love that you told me about what's going on inside your head. I love understanding you better and knowing you better. You've let me in, and I want you to know I'll do everything I can to support you. And also to listen."

"You are a great listener," she says. "But I do need to

point out that you're wrong about one thing that you said."

I furrow my brow. "What's that?"

"You said your fears and your past have nothing to do with me." She pauses for a moment. "But they do matter to me because I care about you. Because I love you. And because I want to be your safe space too just like you've been for me. You don't have to be perfect for me to love you. You don't have to be the perfect man for me to stay with you. Just be you. It's okay if you feel doubts now and then. It's okay if you worry. Just talk to me about them like we're in this together rather than apart, okay?"

I understand now that it wasn't so much how I *felt* last night but how I *handled* those feelings. It was my tone. It was the way my questions came out like accusations. But her willingness to love me with all my flaws just makes me fall even harder. "How do you make me fall more in love with you every single second?"

Her smile is like sunshine. "It's my special skill."

"You're excellent at it. Don't ever stop."

"Same to you."

But then more seriously, I add, "I want to keep earning your love, Everly. Every damn day."

She rolls her eyes. "Shut up. You had me at London fog latte."

I relax again, flashing her a grin. "I won you over that day I bought you one in Seattle, didn't I?"

She plays with the wrinkled collar of my shirt as she says, "I couldn't stand you, but yes, you also won me over...because, guess what? Two things can be true at once."

This is officially the best day ever. I don't even try to act cool. "So I'm really your type. I was right."

She laughs. "Yes. Maybe even especially because you slept in your car to wait for me and deliver a latte." She bends to pick it up and takes a drink, then hands it to me —an offering. I down some; it's not my favorite drink, but I don't care, especially when she says, "You've been so patient with me. And so sweet, and so…" Her voice catches. "Uplifting. The way you tell me I'm beautiful makes me feel…like…like I am living my best life."

That is all I want for her. Well, not true. I want something else too. "Sunshine, live it with me."

"I will." She drops her mouth to mine and kisses me— a tender, London fog kiss as the sun rises on a December morning. It warms not only my heart but my whole entire soul that has come back to life thanks to her.

But even though I could spend all day here, she has a meeting to go to so I break the kiss, hand her the cup, and say, "Let me drive you to work. So we can get you to that meeting on time." Then I add, "And so I get more time with you."

Because there's one more thing I need to tell her.

51

WHEN YOU GOT UNDER

Everly

I open the door and slide in. It feels right to be in his car again. Max must like the sight of me here too, since he hums approvingly then bends down, tugs the seatbelt across me, and gives me one more possessive kiss once I'm buckled in.

He hustles around to the driver's side, and when he shuts the door, I nod to the stoop—the scene of our very public reunion. "I feel like we got away with something."

"Me too," he says, then turns on the car and heads to the Sea Dogs home as I drink my latte. When we arrive, he parks right outside the arena. I still have at least fifteen minutes till my Zoom call. Max must realize that too because he glances at the time on the dashboard then picks up his phone from the console. "I have one more thing for you."

"What is it?"

He swipes across the screen, then shows me an email.

I blink when I see the name. I've never met her but it's the woman who owns the pole studio. "This is from the owner of Upside Down?" I ask, just to be sure I'm reading it right.

His smile is pleased. "Sure is."

The world slows. I read the short note like it's a message from another world then look at this man. Searching his eyes for...confirmation. Because this is too much. "Is this for real?" I ask in a hushed voice, like saying it louder might break something.

"It's not a done deal yet. We haven't signed any paper-work. We just emailed overnight. But I made her an offer to buy the studio, and she said yes."

My heart stutters, then beats in double time.

"I know how important that place is to you," he says, and it's good he's talking since I'm not sure I can. "I emailed the owner late last night, and we exchanged a couple more emails this morning while I was waiting on your steps. Apparently, they're struggling with rent. I wanted you to have something that's just yours. So you always have a safe space to go to."

I bring my hand to my mouth. I don't even know what to think or to say. So I start with the simplest thing. A whisper. "I can't believe you're buying the studio."

He shakes his head, adamant. "Just to be clear—I'm not buying it for me. It's for you. It's a gift. I'm giving it to you. It'll be all yours, free and clear. You can always go."

Tears of love, gratitude, and inimitable joy slide down my cheeks. I throw my arms around his neck. "I love you. I love you. I love you. I love you. I love you."

I can't stop saying it. But I'm pretty sure he loves the chorus of my words.

Max has never looked happier when he pulls back and

says, "I'm not even ashamed about how ravenous I am for those words from you."

I drop one more kiss to his lips. "Thank you," I say, then with some reluctance, I reach for the handle. "I'll see you at the interview."

I get out, feeling overjoyed as I head across the concourse toward the main doors. But as I'm pushing one open, someone calls out, "Good morning, Everly."

The sound of Elias's voice crawls up my spine like a snake.

I turn around, bracing myself.

He's the picture of smug. "Don't worry. You don't need to deny anything. All you have to do is step down from the promotion competition," he says, then waggles his phone, like it's a prize. "And if you do it by the end of business today, I won't post the picture of you getting out of his car right now at..." He stops and makes a show of looking at a watch he doesn't wear, then adds, "Seven fifty-one in the morning. There's no professional reason for him to be driving you to work at this hour." And really, Elias is right. Which is probably why he laughs victoriously. Or really, he cackles. "I can only imagine how it'd look as a woman who's worked *so hard* to succeed in sports if everyone finds out you got ahead because you *got under* a hockey player."

I'm cold everywhere, shaking in my bones from his threats.

And they just keep coming. "But it'll be worse if all the press finds out that's *why* you got a promotion."

52

CHANGE OF PLANS

Everly

This is all my fault. This is exactly how people get caught. I was careless. I was caught up in the euphoria of being in love, and I let down my guard. Yes, Max kissed me outside my home this morning, and that was risky enough, but it's also far away from the office. But to let Max take me to work this early?

That was a rookie mistake.

I can't move. My head feels like it's stuffed with cotton, and my heart is pricked with needles. For a long, terrible minute, I feel like I'm sinking in quicksand. I don't know what to do or where to go. All I can do is watch as Elias sails off into the arena, la-di-da-ing his way inside on a cloud of blackmail and smiles.

I try to shake off this funk. I have a job to do. I can't let him throw me off. I can't go into the Zoom call all shook up because of that little man. I take a deep breath and catalog my surroundings. I'm standing in front of the Sea Dogs arena. The door is made of glass.

Beyond it, the signs for concessions are visible. Buses rumble by a hundred feet behind me. When I grab the door, the cool metal is reassuring in my hand.

There. That's better. I can do this and move forward.

I walk inside, picturing the ice rink that sits below this level, where the team fights to win every goddamn game.

Fight.

That's what I'm going to do. I'm going to fight for my job, sooner than I'd planned. I won't let Elias scare me because I'm good at what I do. That means I have to take a meeting right now because that's part of the job.

I pass Jenna's cubicle on the way to my office, and she gives me a cheery wave. "Everly, I have the research you asked for before the interview Max has with Erin later today."

She's here early too? She's not usually here before nine. Did she see me outside as well? But then I talk back to my worries—*You know who to trust. You can trust her. You can't trust Elias. You've never been able to.* "Thanks, Jenna. I appreciate all you do," I say.

I head into my office, close the door, and log into the call. I shut off everything else as I focus on the Zoom with the team in Boston about some joint press coverage for the upcoming game.

When that's done, I grab my phone, leave my office, and walk down the hall. The corridor is concrete. The walls are covered with framed photos of the Sea Dogs. At the end of the hall is my boss's office.

I catalog one more thing—my pulse.

It's calmer because I'm not waiting any longer. I won't

have the weekend to rehearse. I can't practice with my friends. Sometimes, you just have to jump into the fray.

Without a plan, without a strategy, without anything but guts, I walk into my boss's suite.

Her assistant flashes me a bright smile from his desk outside the door. "What can I do for you?"

"Hi, Trevor. I need to see Zaire today," I say, then add a smile. "Could I please get on her schedule as soon as she's free?"

"She's out of the office this morning at an appointment," he says, and I have no idea what that means—if it's personal, if it's business, or if it's something else entirely. But it's not for me to know. I simply tell him I'll take the next free slot on her schedule.

"That'll be three-thirty," he says. That's a lifetime from now, but I take it. At least it's before Elias has said he'll drop his picture online.

I return to my office and text Max about what happened, telling him I'll share the rest when he's done with morning skate and we head to the interview.

I feel calmer—maybe because I'm not in this alone. Then, I flip open my laptop and get to work on a plan for that meeting.

53

THE REAL MAX LAMBERT

Max

The thing about hockey players is we're known for fast reflexes on the ice.

But sometimes people underestimate us when it comes to how we react out of the rink. Reflexes matter, too, even if you're not wearing a mask or holding a stick. The second Everly tells me what went down this morning, I think fast. My brain whirls with ideas as I drive us over to The Sports Network.

Along the way, she's telling me her plans for her meeting with her boss this afternoon. And damn, they're so brilliant, they're beyond brilliant. They're scorching hot.

But I can't let her do all the work. We're a team of two right now, and I know how to help a teammate out. Sometimes you need to block, sometimes you need to shoot, and sometimes you deflect. But a good hockey player also knows how to do something else—how to set up a shot.

When we reach The Sports Network offices in downtown San Francisco, Everly shifts into work mode. I get that. She doesn't want to miss a step when it comes to her job. Erin is interviewing me for a piece in the pre-game show, so Everly's reminding me of my talking points as we walk down the hallway to the studio.

"And now that your episode on *The Ice Men* has been given the go-ahead, Erin will ask about that. I told her this morning about it, so she'll include a mention in her segment. What I want is for you to say something like— *this documentary is a great chance to show the daily routines of a goalie, what it takes to get into the mindset to defend the net every game.* All of those things are exactly what *The Ice Men* will want you to say."

"Got it," I say, and fact is—Everly's right. Those are great points.

I'm not going to say any of those things though.

When we reach the greenroom for the studio, she looks me up and down, and with a smile, she says, "By the way you clean up nice."

"A shower and fresh clothes help," I say, glancing down at my slacks and royal blue dress shirt.

An assistant calls us into the greenroom and mics me for the interview. When I head onto set, Everly follows, standing backstage, watching in the wings in case anything goes wrong.

I join Erin, sitting across from her in a chair with the bright lights beating down on us. She asks me easy questions about the game tonight, our opponents, and how the season looks. Then she says, "You're going to be featured in *The Ice Men* documentary. Can you give us a little preview of what to expect from that?"

I *could* use Everly's lines right now, but I don't. Instead, I say something else that's true about goalies.

"It's all about the ins and outs of being a goaltender, and the biggest thing we do is watch the game like a hawk. See plays before they even happen. And sometimes when you do, you have to set up the shot. Like this," I say, then I barely pause before I say the next thing. "For a long time I never wanted to share my true self with the press, like you, frankly, or anyone else." Erin's eyes register surprise, but she nods quickly. That's good, but I was barreling on anyway. This guy knows how to crash an event, after all. "I'm not a charming guy. I can be kind of unapproachable, but I think it comes with being a goalie. I don't think people want to have a friendly goalie on the ice. I've been trying to change how I am off the ice though. I've been trying to be a little more accessible. A little friendlier. And there are a couple of reasons why I'm doing that. One is for my family. But mostly, it's because of a woman. And that's why I want to tell you a little bit more about who I am."

Erin's a pro so she rolls with the change. "Tell us about the real Max Lambert then."

Here goes nothing. I don't steal a glance at Everly, since I want to keep my focus on Erin as I share the truth of who I am. "Fun fact: I foster rescue kittens. Actually, I adopted one recently. She's a tiny spitfire. She's the sixth rescue kitten I've fostered in the last year but my first foster fail."

"That's adorable," Erin says.

"She's a hellion, and she has me wrapped around her little paw. Other things about me—my parents are teachers. I like to hang out with them. I like to spend time with my little nephew. My favorite place to eat is at a restaurant that my parents' best friends own. I take online classes to keep my mind sharp, and I can and do destroy all my friends in poker on the team jet. And one of my favorite things to do is to watch movies and eat popcorn and spend time with..." I pause because I was going to say *the love of my life*. But my reflexes are really sharp, so I make a game-day decision and change it up. Might as well tell the whole truth. "My future wife."

Erin's eyes widen to saucers. "You're...engaged?"

"Not yet. But soon. I will be," I say, believing it completely. "There's a woman I'm madly in love with. It's the kind of love that makes you get on TV and tell everyone. The kind that makes you want to do whatever it takes for her. The kind that changes you."

I don't name Everly. I don't drop a hint as to who she is. I don't say she works for the team. But when Everly walks into that meeting with her boss today, I want her boss to know that I'm behind her completely.

And I suppose in an hour when this airs, the world will know too.

54

BREAKING THE RULES

Everly

"You. Went. Off. Script."

In the elevator one minute after I watched them record his interview, Max shrugs, giving me the most easygoing grin I've ever seen. I'm still in a state of complete and utter shock, but it's the kind of shock that makes my bones hum and my heart sing.

"What were you thinking?" I ask as thrills race through me.

"I was thinking of you," he says, like it was the simplest thing in the world that he did.

"Future wife?" I ask, because I still can't believe he said that. I also can't wipe the smile off my face.

"You will be," he says, cupping my cheek. "I know your type. I'm your type."

I'm barely able to process his bold, out-on-a-limb words, but they're going to live rent-free in my head for the rest of my life.

Because...he's probably not wrong.

But there isn't much time to bask in the sheer audacity of his mic drop—not when I have a meeting to get to at the Sea Dogs arena. A meeting that will probably be helped by his statement. The fact that he said all of that has to give my boss some confidence that our romance isn't a one-way street. That will matter. I'd never thought to ask for his backup. But I have it.

Max takes me back there quickly, parking in the players' lot, then walking me to the stairwell, where I say, "Wish me luck."

He shakes his head. "Nope, because you don't need luck. You have facts."

Facts matter. And with the facts in my pocket, I head upstairs to the management level and walk down the hall with a plan.

When I first contemplated telling my boss about my relationship with the goalie, I figured I'd plead for her to let me keep my job.

Not anymore.

I'm not going into Zaire's office to ask to stay.

I'm not going in there to beg for her permission either.

And I'm not going in there to lay my head on the desk and ask whether she's going to drop the guillotine on me or not.

I am powerful, and I'm going in there from a place of power.

I march down the hall in my black pantsuit like an avenging goddess of business, ready to take on whatever comes her way.

But along the way, I spot the back of a preppy blond head. Well, this calls for a quick detour. I stride right toward Elias's cubicle and knock on the half-wall. He looks up with a smug look on his face, like he thinks I'm about to cave to his demands.

I get the first word in. "I don't care what you do with that photo."

"W-w-hat?"

"Post it," I spit out. "I don't care."

"But, but, but—" he sputters, clearly unable to form a single sentence.

I lean closer. "You don't scare me. You're a small man with a small, shriveled heart."

I turn around and walk away from him.

As I'm leaving the cubicles, Jenna pops up from hers, clapping and cheering. "You go!"

I'm so glad I never truly doubted her.

As she cheers me on, she swivels to face Elias. "And you never volunteered for Meals on Wheels. I called the organization in your college town and looked it up. They don't have a record of you."

I grin at Jenna. "You are a tenacious, inquisitive, brilliant human," I say and offer her a palm for high-fiving. She smacks back, and then I resume my march down the hall.

Because I am not walking into my boss's office. I am marching in.

Along the way, I catalog my surroundings. The corridor is blue. The air is cool. The chance is mine.

When I reach her suite, Trevor waves me in. The door is halfway open and I push it the rest of the way.

Oh.

Clementine is here too, sitting on the couch next to Zaire. That throws me for a loop but only for a second. It's even better that the general manager's here. I can say my piece to both of them.

"I saw you on the schedule. Tell me what's on your mind," Zaire says.

"Yes, I'd love to know too. Sit," Clementine says, then gestures to the chair across from the couch.

But I don't want to sit. I shake my head. "I'm going to stand." I don't waste another second. "And I'm not here to try to keep my job. I'm here to tell you why *you* should keep me."

Zaire squints. "What exactly are you talking about, Everly?"

Clementine shoots me a skeptical look. "Yes, I'd so love to know too."

"You have an unwritten rule that says employees shouldn't get involved with the athletes. You told me about it on the first day I started here. It's a rule we're all expected to follow because it could end badly for the employee. Because it could affect how they do their job. Because it could affect how people see them. But I'm here to tell you it's a bad rule. And the fact that I've fallen in love with one of our hockey players hasn't affected a single thing about my ability to do the job. And if you fire me for falling in love with a player, here's what else you'll lose."

Shaking her head, Zaire holds up a hand. "Hold on. You've fallen in love with one of our players?"

"The pre-game show starts in about ten minutes on The Sports Network, and you'll hear Max Lambert talking about it. But I want you to hear from me about what I've done so you can think about the value I bring to this organization."

For a beat, both women look floored. No surprise there. But they're not top executives for nothing. "I'd love to hear," Clementine says in her cool British accent, sweeping out a hand.

"My personal life hasn't hurt my ability to do the job at all. Since I've been here, I've helped develop segments with our broadcast partner that drive up ratings. I've spearheaded a project to pitch features on players across mediums, and we've seen a thirty percent increase in our coverage in the last year because of that. Our social media engagement has already increased since October, and is now up sixty-three percent over the last year, which has led to forty-seven percent more jersey sales. I've also planned events with our key partner organizations throughout the city," I say, rattling off some of my major accomplishments. "I did all this while falling in love with Max and making him likeable again. He went from being a recluse to being a reliable player who regularly talks to the media and presents well." I stop and take a fueling breath since there's one more thing to say. "Also, other pro sports team owners recognize my talent and want to work with me. I'm not saying this to worry you that I'm leaving. I'm telling you that I'm valuable. I contribute every day to this PR team. And I will continue innovating."

Zaire's brow furrows right as she tilts her head, as if she's adding up all the facts. "That is quite a speech, Everly."

But I'm not done. "And since the interview's about to air, I'm going to let you watch it. And I would love if you could let me know if you're going to not just bend that rule for me but to get rid of it entirely for everyone."

I thank them and leave.

55

ABOUT THAT SIDE HUSTLE

Max

I'm in the locker room and in my gear early. I've taped up my stick. My pads are on. My skates are laced. We have an early puck drop tonight, so we'll hit the ice soon for warm-ups.

A couple of my teammates are here, too, getting ready. Wesley's next to me, lacing up.

I could hit the ice now and do some stretches, but my mind isn't on hockey. It's on Everly. I hope her meeting's going well, and I also don't want her to be blindsided. I do something I never do. I google myself—to make sure nothing's gotten out yet. That Elias hasn't tried to preempt Everly by dropping that picture of us online.

Even if she's going to neutralize him with her badass approach, even if she has a brilliant plan, and even if she's one thousand times smarter than that prick, I need to be ready.

I swear, if I see him...

I breathe past the anger then plug my own name into Google. The first result is the brief interview from the shutout the other night. Then something about the documentary from today. Next are photos and social posts and articles from the charitable events Everly shepherded.

Fine.

That's all fine.

There's nothing to worry about, and Erin's piece hasn't aired yet. It will in a couple more minutes. I hunt around a little more when something catches my eye on the second page of results. Something I didn't expect to see at all.

A photo of a jersey. A jersey that has a signature of my name on it, with a paw print beside it.

"Holy shit," I mutter to myself. That's the jersey I signed a few weeks ago.

I click on it and do a little digging on the site. It's a sports auction site and there's a whole new set of memorabilia for sale right along with a photo of five jerseys spread out on a table. Mine, Miles's, Asher's, Wesley's, and Hugo's. It's not the set that Little Friends auctioned off the other week—I know because those were indeed auctioned off.

This is the set that I gave to Elias weeks ago. The name of the seller is CollegeSportsGuy. That little fucker has been selling our signed gear all along.

What a liar. What a thief. What a total piece of shit. And I'm smiling so wide because this right here is better than punching the guy.

Though punching him would be so gratifying. Only I've learned that fights don't do me any favors. Good thing I can use my brain.

I mull this over for a minute until I come up with the perfect play. At least, I hope it is. I don't have much time.

We need to be on the ice any minute. I turn to Wesley. "Do me a solid, will you, Bryant?"

"Sure," he says as he tightens his laces.

"Can you call Elias and tell him you have a stick for him? A signed stick?"

He arches a brow in question. "Okay, but why?"

"I need some bait to get him to come down here. And I'm pretty sure he won't take my call."

His easy shrug says yes. "I'm in." He grabs his phone and dials the main number for the front office, asking for Elias. I fucking love my teammates.

Next I hunt around for Coach. I need him—or someone like him inside the Sea Dogs—to pull off this play. But he's the best place to start since he ought to be easy for me to find right before a game. Only, he's not in the locker room. Or the athletic trainer's room. He *might* be in his office, but first I pop into the video room, since he's often there with his assistants before a game. Yup. The captain of the ship sits in a leather chair with an assistant coach, peering at a tablet, probably reviewing plays.

"Sir, how's it going?" I ask.

Coach raises his face, his expression serious because he's always serious. "Good, Lambert. And you?"

I scratch my beard, then sigh. "Pretty good, but you gotta see what's going on with Bryant and this stick. It's messed up."

He takes a breath, then asks, "And you need me? About a stick? Not Quinn?"

Quinn's the equipment manager, and honestly, that's not a bad idea. But the clock's ticking, so I say, "Both of you would be great."

Coach rolls his eyes. "I'll let him know if I see him." He

tells the assistant coach he'll be right back, then pushes up and follows me.

He's a little irked, but I can handle an irked coach. I've got the crew assembled now. Timing is everything in sports and if I've engineered this play properly, Elias ought to be in the hallway outside the locker room right as we walk up to him.

Like...now.

Wesley's handing a signed stick to my enemy as we turn the corner. I fight off a winning smile as I call out, "Hey, Elias."

The prick turns to me, his beady eyes flickering with worry. But he tries to cover it up with a, "Hey, Max. How you doing?"

Like we're friends.

His gaze shifts nervously to the man in the suit next to me. "Hey, Coach. Good to see you too," Elias says, playing up the buddy-buddy card with him.

"Elias," Coach says, with a crisp nod and a tone that clearly says, *Max, why the hell did you pull me out of my meeting for this?*

I tip my chin toward Elias, playing innocent. "I saw you were selling our stuff online. Sweet, man. You must have a nice side hustle there?"

Elias freezes. Aww, poor baby didn't expect to get caught. "Um..."

That's all he says. *Um.*

"But good for you," I add, then clap him on the shoulder before I turn toward Coach, since I need to deliver this message to someone internal to the organization—someone with power. "Finding workarounds and whatnot. Right, Coach?" I turn back to Elias. "That's the kind of sportsmanlike conduct the Sea Dogs really embraces, and you are an enterprising young man, selling signed gear from players instead of giving it away. And well, the other side hustle you tried to launch this morning." Then I whisper, low and menacing in his ear, for him only, "Do not ever fuck with Everly again or I won't be so nice. That clear?"

Elias gulps and nods.

I back off right as Coach sighs heavily, then peers at me like *I do not have time for this shit.* "This is what you called me out for?"

But I have faith in Coach. He runs a squeaky-clean ship. He doesn't like weasels, and he doesn't like distractions, and he really doesn't like people who fuck with his team.

The man with more power than me grabs his phone from his pocket. "I'll call Clementine and let her handle this."

My mind throws a ticker-tape parade. Yes! Fucking yes! I pulled off the play.

"Good call, sir," I say, like he needs me to approve of his decision. "I should have thought of that. But that's why you're the man."

He waves a dismissive hand. All is forgiven with these *athlete shenanigans.* "Clementine, I need you to deal with something," he says into the phone, and I flash a very, *very* satisfied grin at Elias.

Wesley lifts a finger the weasel's way. "Actually, I'll give this stick to Donna," he says, then takes the bait back.

I hit the ice for warm-ups and a few minutes later, my future wife walks to the gate, like she owns the world.

56

GET A ROOM

Everly

My pulse is thundering. My blood is rushing fast. And I feel on top of the world even though I don't have an answer to my work fate.

But that's okay. I have other answers. Ones that will carry me through. I have friends I love, a man who's my soulmate, and a life well worth living.

On the ice, the Sea Dogs are warming up as I walk through the tunnel, heading straight for the players' bench. Some players are stretching on the ice. Others are taking easy shots on the net.

When I reach the bench, I shout at the goalie. "Hey, handsome! Get over here and kiss me!"

Max flies over, ripping off his helmet and meeting me right by the boards. He drops his gloves, holds my face, and kisses me in front of the early crowd, just like he wanted to do.

It's a soft, slow kiss that melts me. It's a kiss that says *I love you, I need you, I care so much about you*. It's a kiss that says *I'm going home with you every night*.

When he lets go, his teammates are whistling. Wesley shouts, "Get a room."

Asher barks out, "Finally! It's about damn time."

Miles catcalls with, "Will you stop being a dickhead now?"

I laugh, and Max hauls me in for a hug. "So what happened? How did it go?"

I shrug, but I'm strangely happy. Because I didn't back down. Because I stood my ground. Because I took care of myself. "I told them everything about how I'm good at my job, told them to watch the piece, then walked out."

"You walked out?"

"Yes, they can come and get me if they want to keep me. If not, I'll get another job. And until then, I have a pole studio to keep me busy."

He smiles and kisses me one more time. "You do," he says, but then breaks our embrace and nods. "But I think there's someone here for you."

I let go and turn around. Zaire's heading from the tunnel to the players' bench too. When she reaches me, she says, "You got the promotion." She points from Max to me. "And you two better keep this up. I want to know you meant every word of what you said." Then to me, she adds, "And we'll take care of your suggestion—about that rule."

"Great," I say. "Then I accept."

"I'll put the paperwork together." She turns around and walks up through the stands.

I snap my gaze back to Max. "I got it," I whisper, awed I've pulled it off.

"Of course you did. You are badass and beautiful," he

says, then he scoops me up and lifts me over the gate and onto the ice where he dips me and kisses me good and long, making my breath catch and my heart race with happiness.

When he lets go, he looks down at the ice and the lines marking it. "I guess this is the romance line now."

I like the sound of that.

* * *

But I also have work to do and Max has a game to play. I leave and head to the press box. As I near it though, I stop, take a moment, then remove my jacket. I'm wearing a sleeveless blouse. The scars on my upper arm are on display for the world to see.

Let them.

I walk inside, and say, "Any questions?"

* * *

A few days later, two people I adore have new jobs. First is Kyla. I hired her as the full-time manager of Upside Down and the head teacher, giving her a raise too. I don't have time to run the studio, and besides, it's been her dream to run one. It's a gift to make someone's dreams come true, so I feel pretty lucky to do that for someone who's done so much for me.

The other person is Jenna, since there was an immediate opening at the Sea Dogs for the manager of promotions. She got the job, so I take her out for a celebratory lunch.

"You are a rock star," I say after we order.

"Speaking of rock stars..." she begins.

I tilt my head in curiosity. "Yes?"

"My girlfriend is a big Lyra fan, so she dragged me to a concert recently."

My eye twitches. My jaw tightens. "How was it?"

She holds up a hand. "Enlightening. My friend won VIP tickets and we maybe, possibly saw Lyra leaving the show with one of her backup dancers."

My jaw drops. "You did?"

She nods impishly. "And I maybe, possibly got some pics. And I maybe, possibly dropped some hints about her extracurricular affairs to a gossip blog."

"Jenna!"

She bobs a shoulder. "Well, she deserves what's coming to her."

Two days later, what comes the rock star's way is front-page news on the celebrity sites—Lyra Raine is cheating on Fletcher Bane. America's sweetheart isn't so sweet after all.

I sigh happily. I can't think of a better way for the truth to come out than a story that doesn't once mention Max.

57

MY REAL FAVORITE THING

Max

Seven long days. Seven long nights. But they end tonight. I'm tapping my foot against the floor of the team bus, willing it to pull faster into the players' lot.

"In a rush, Lambert?" Miles asks dryly from across the aisle.

"Yeah, just a little bit."

Wesley's right in front of me, and he shoots me a sympathetic look. "Know the feeling, man. These long road trips are hard."

"They sure are," I say.

"I miss Josie way too much. But you're lucky. At least Everly will be on the next one," he says, and there is that. I am lucky since she travels with the team half the time. But the other half is still hell.

I need to see her, stat.

The bus comes to a stop and I bound off with my

duffel. I make it to my car in record time, then head home even faster.

Home…where my two favorite ladies will be waiting for me. I peel into a spot in the parking garage, then rush to the elevator, and punch the button for the penthouse.

Forty-five interminable seconds later, the doors slide open and I walk down the hall then unlock the door.

Everly hasn't moved in with me *yet,* but she will. She is, however, waiting for me when I come home. And…I can't breathe.

She's wearing white lace panties and a white dress shirt of mine.

That's it. Nothing else.

Oh, wait.

She's got a kitten in her arms. "Hey, you," she says as I drop my bag. "We missed you."

I tear my gaze away from her for a hot second, doing a double take when I take a better look at Athena. "Is my cat wearing clothes?"

"Oh, this little thing?" Everly plucks at the blue shirt she's somehow wrestled the cat into. "It was sent in from an animal rescue. She has so many outfits from animal rescues and fans thanks to your interview. Little Friends even made her one with a Sea Dogs number. Six. Since she's your sixth foster," she says of the tiny hockey jersey my cat is wearing.

I reach for the furball and hold her for a second before she squirms in my arms.

Well, she is a cat. I set her down and she runs off somewhere, probably to get the touch of human off her.

"That is fucking adorable but you…are…" I stop and gaze in lusty admiration at the half-naked beauty.

Then I do more than look. I touch. Running a hand up

her stomach, over her breasts, up her neck, and around to her hair, all lush and silky and blown out.

"Beautiful," I say, "and all mine."

"All yours," she says, then she takes my hand, leads me to the bedroom and strips me naked. When I'm down to nothing, she shrugs off the shirt she's wearing, pushes me to the bed, and climbs over me.

"Missed you," she says.

"Missed you so much," I say, then I haul her close and kiss her until she's squirming and panting and begging. I skim off her soaked panties, then put on a condom. "Get on my dick and show me how much you've missed me."

"Oh, I will, Max. Because I missed you so damn much."

She rides me, and shows me, and loves me, and comes hard all over my cock, and it's glorious.

After, she curls up next to me and, with a little bit of nerves but excitement, too, in her voice, says, "I have something else for you."

I scoff. "Name something better than you and Athena waiting for me."

"More me," she says playfully, then reaches for her tablet that she must have left on the nightstand. She nibbles on the corner of her lips before she clicks on the screen.

A link from Leighton McBride.

It opens to a stunning photo of Everly on a sapphire chaise longue, wearing the first set of panties I bought her and nothing else. She's cupping her breasts and sitting with her side to the camera lens. Her hair's tossed back, and her gaze meets the camera.

Straight on, fearless, and brave.

I trace the outline of her body in the picture, amazed

that this woman loves me. "Are there more?" I ask, hungry for all the pictures.

"I did a whole session. I did it for me," she says. "But I wanted to show them to you."

I kiss her cheek. "It's a beautiful gift for you to give yourself, and you deserve it."

Then I settle in with my woman as she shows me the rest of the pictures.

This, right here, is my real favorite thing.

EPILOGUE: SAY YES

Max

Man, these team executives love to have dinners.

But no complaints. I like food.

And I really like this—holding Everly's hand as we walk into a sushi restaurant together several days later. *The Ice Men* producers are joining us here too, and so are Zaire and Clementine, as well as my agent. Everything is a go for the documentary to start shooting next month, and I'm still grateful for the opportunities that it might bring. The chance to put some extra money aside for my family.

But the best part of this dinner is that I don't have to pretend I'm not madly in love with the woman by my side. Garrett asked me to come a few minutes early so we find him at the bar, nursing a glass of what looks like a seltzer and scrolling on his phone. When he looks up, he smiles, sets down his mobile and the glass, and stands to give me a clap on the back. He shakes Everly's hand. "Good to see you again. Both of you," he says, then turns to me. "And don't worry. I did it," he says emphatically. "I turned down Date Night for you."

I laugh. I asked him to do that on the day Everly and I went public.

"I appreciate it," I say earnestly, looking him square in the eyes. "I appreciate all that you do. I know I'm not easy to work with."

He waves a hand dismissively. "The job's not supposed to be easy. We're all good." He shifts to Everly. "And congratulations on the promotion. I was rooting for you."

"Thank you. And I'm always rooting for you," she says, and that's my sunshine woman.

"And before we start dinner, I have some news. Rosario snagged a brand-new deal for you," Garrett says to me.

I tense, briefly wondering if this is going to be another one that won't work out. "Please don't tell me you want me to be the face of a circus or something," I say. "Or a naked bike ride."

Everly taps her chin. "Oh, I didn't tell you? The naked bike ride already requested for you to be their spokesperson next year and of course I said yes."

I shoot her a warning look. "You troublemaker."

"And you love it," she says right back to me. That's my woman. Always keeping me on my toes.

Garrett takes a beat then says, "How about a brand deal with a popcorn maker?"

A laugh bursts from Everly. She turns to me, those big brown eyes playful and bright. "Max, say yes."

My heart thumps harder from those two words.

Our words.

I kiss her on the cheek, both because I can't resist and because I can. Then I look at Garrett. "Yes."

But there's something else I need to say to these two people who put up with me and turned my reputation around. "Thank you."

* * *

Everly

After dinner, we go out on a date that's not at all a secret.

We don't need to peer around corners or peek down blocks. We don't need to leave the city or hide behind tinted windows. And we certainly don't need to worry if we make a mistake like kissing each other in public because we just can't help ourselves.

We wander along the bustling blocks of Hayes Valley on our way to The Resort, a hotel in the heart of this neighborhood since Max got us a room for the night... because.

Just because.

We pass trendy boutiques and record shops with garlands in the windows and Christmas lights sparkling over the doorways, then into the hotel where we'll meet his sister for a quick drink.

In the lobby, we pass artful bouquets of dahlias and an elegant waterfall structure when I catch sight of the familiar silhouette of my redheaded friend. "Fable's here. I didn't realize the team party she's going to was tonight."

"Your friend who works for the Renegades?"

"Yes." And she's walking across the lobby right now with Wilder Blaine, who owns the team and the hotel.

"Are they together?" he asks of the man I chatted with at the city vegetable garden.

I make a seesaw motion with my hand because I

know a lot of the details of what's been going on with Wilder and Fable for the last few weeks since the guy she was dating—Brady—showed his true colors. "Not exactly," I hedge, then tell him what happened at Thanksgiving. Max cringes when he learns what her ex did that day. "But then Wilder—her boss—asked her to be his fake girlfriend for the holiday season."

"So the billionaire needs a fake girlfriend," he says quietly, sounding intrigued.

"But don't tell a soul because it's a secret, and nobody knows it's fake."

Max mimes zipping his lips. "You know I know how to keep a secret."

Fable must catch sight of us since she stops and beelines for me. "Good to see you," she says, then makes quick intros to everyone even though I've already met Wilder.

He looks me in the eye and says, "Good to see you again. And congratulations on the new job. I'm not at all surprised."

"Thank you so much," I say. "And your vote of confidence meant a lot to me. It was part of what drove me to go after the promotion with everything I have."

"That's fantastic. I like it when good things happen to people who deserve them." Then to Max, he says, "And congratulations on...your future wife." Wilder's lips curve in a grin.

Max laughs, dragging a hand down the back of his neck. "I guess you saw that."

"A lot of people saw it," Wilder says with a clever smile. "Like, the whole world. That was quite a gesture. You set the bar awfully high for men everywhere." He steals a glance at Fable, then something like longing passes in his eyes as he adds, "And it should be high."

We say goodbye and they leave. But as they go, he sets a hand on her back. Possessively. Maybe more possessive than a fake boyfriend should be.

I tug Max close. "I can't wait to tell Maeve she was right. She's had this theory that he's had a massive crush on her for a long time."

Max checks one last time then turns to me. "Maeve is definitely right." He makes a move to go to the bar, but then stops. "Speaking of massive crushes, I'm pretty sure Asher has exactly those kinds of feelings for Maeve."

The corner of my lips curves up. "You don't say?"

He gives me a curious look. "What does that mean?"

"It means I've had that feeling for a while too. But I don't know if he'll ever do a thing about it. Since he's her brother's best friend and all."

Max drags a hand through his hair, like all this romance stuff is too complicated. "Sometimes you just have to screw all that stuff and go after what you want."

"True," I say.

He runs a hand down my back, sending shivers through my whole body. "Because it's worth it."

I smile. "Yes, it is," I say, as we head to the bar.

We quickly find Sophie and her date.

Lucas.

After a warm hello, Max clears his throat and says to my former physical therapist, "I need to apologize for my behavior when we first met—"

Lucas waves him off. "No need. That date played out perfectly." Then he kisses Sophie's cheek.

Sophie looks at him with genuine affection and says, "It sure did."

We join the new couple for a drink.

After, we head to our room. When the door closes, shutting out the world, Max picks me up and carries me to the king-size bed. He sets me down and holds my face, his eyes filled with both a love and lust that I hope never ends, especially when he says, "And now I'm going to undress my future wife and kiss her everywhere all night long."

I run a hand along his arm. "Get to it, future husband."

And he does.

* * *

Want another spicy, emotional, laugh out loud, he-falls-first MF hockey romance with a hero you'll be obsessed with? Go grab **The Boyfriend Goal** available to download now and experience Josie and Wes's roommates-to-lovers, teammate's little sister romance FREE in KU!

Turn the page for a sneak peek of My Favorite Holidate, Fable and Wilder's fake dating the billionaire boss romance that's coming to you in Kindle Unlimited this fall. Asher and Maeve's best friends-to-lovers hockey romance is coming to you early next year in The Proposal Play!

For more Max and Everly, click here for an extended epilogue or scan the QR code!

Bonus Scene The Romance Line

EXCERPT - MY FAVORITE HOLIDATE

Wilder

She grabs the wreath from the bag and hangs it on the hook. It's made with burlap and colorful ribbons. She adjusts it so Santa's ass, stuck in a chimney, is sticking out of my door.

But I'm still stuck on the last thing she said. "You made *this*? For the contest?"

She gives me a soft smile. "Yes. Well, it's really for you," she says, a flash of nervousness in her eyes, but hope too. "I wanted your office to look the best. And you've been so generous with your gifts. The least I could do was make you something from scratch."

I stare at the wreath, even more astonished. "This is incredible."

"You think so?" she asks, beaming.

"I do." I roam my eyes up and down the door, then turn my gaze to my designer. The woman who enjoys making homemade items. The woman who went all out for me. The woman I can't stop thinking about. Decorating might not be my thing, but I could decorate all day

with her. "It's not fine," I say, correcting my earlier statement. "It's the finest."

"Thank you." Her smile is its own reward. It's wide and
joyful, and I want to swipe my thumb along her bottom
lip, kiss the corner of her mouth, taste her.

Which brings me to a vital topic in the do's and don'ts.
I've been tiptoeing around the main attraction. Avoiding
it. But I can't any longer. Since this topic is best addressed
behind closed doors, I motion to my office. "Let's finish in
here," I say.

"Perfect. Because I brought lights for your desk."

I stare at her, a little amazed. She goes above and
beyond in her creativity. "You did?"

"Yes. But will it cramp your style if some corporate
bigwig comes into a meeting and sees the flashing lights
on your desk? I don't want to ruin the big bad wolf vibe
you've got going on."

I lift a brow. "Is that how you see me?"

Her lips curve up the slightest bit. "I don't know,
Wilder. Do big bad wolves send mint ice cream?"

Two can play at her game. "Perhaps they send them to
little red riding hood," I say as we head into my office.

"Well then, little red riding hood approves."

"So does the wolf," I say, and I am so fucked. Five
minutes after telling myself to follow some rules for self-
protection, I already know that I won't stop sending her
gifts. I won't stop texting. This has been the most fun I've
had in a while and I'm...addicted—and I'm allowed to be.
Nothing can come of this ruse, of course. How could
anything come of a romance that started as a lie? But I'll
enjoy it while I can.

I shut the door behind us.

She beelines for my desk, fishing around in her bag of

tricks for lights, presumably. In no time, she gets to work on stringing them around my desk. Yes, this is the moment. She's occupied with a task, so I say as coolly as I can, "And what about a kiss?"

She spins around, a string of lights in her hand, question marks in her eyes. "Now?"

What? Now? Before I can even answer—and I'm too stunned to answer—she adds, "Sure. A practice kiss couldn't hurt."

I can't think. I can't breathe. She keeps surprising me left and right, and I barely know what to do. I'm a man who prides himself on control, on strategy, on knowing what cards to play at all times. With her, I'm knocked senseless, especially as she sets the lights down on the desk, then closes the distance to me a few feet away.

I still haven't said a word. I really need to say something. *Anything.* She tips up her chin, offering her pretty lips to me. Questions rattle in my head. Should I do this? Is this crossing a line? Is this wrong?

Finally, I manage to ask, "Are you sure?" It comes out like it scrapes my throat.

A tilt of her head. A curve of her lips. "You don't bite, do you? Like the big bad wolf?"

A bolt of lust shoots down my spine. I try to ignore it, to resist it when all I can think is *the better to eat you with.* "Only if you want me to."

Her eyes flicker with something that looks a lot like lust. "I'll take a rain check on the biting. But it's a yes on the practice," she says, then parts her lips the slightest bit.

I didn't plan this meeting as a dress rehearsal for a kiss. But I also know how to spot an opportunity and how to seize one. I step closer, run a finger along some silky strands of auburn hair, taking my time to sweep them across her face and tuck them behind her ear. Her breath hitches. I let go of those strands of hair, then brush the back of my fingers along her jaw. Her chest rises and falls. Her eyes track me the whole time, watching my face, then my hand. I'm drawing out this moment, stretching it like elastic till my fingers reach her chin, holding her.

Preorder Fable and Wilder's holiday romance coming this fall to Kindle Unlimited in My Favorite Holidate!

BE A LOVELY

Want to be the first to know of sales, new releases, special deals and giveaways? Sign up for my newsletter today!

Want to be part of a fun, feel-good place to talk about books and romance, and get sneak peeks of covers and advance copies of my books? Be a Lovely!

ACKNOWLEDGMENTS

Thank you to KA Linde for the pole insight! You are a goddess and a dog lover and I adore you! You helped the story immensely and your guidance shaped it in beautiful ways. In amazing ways. In ALL THE WAYS! THANK YOU!

Thank you to Jill for her insight into trauma, grounding exercises and PTSD. Thank you to Lo for her guidance too on the details of Everly's injuries, as well as her overall guidance on the whole dang thing! Thank you Kayti and never leave me. Thank you KP for, well, everything.

I am so appreciative of Sharon for checking all the hockey and guiding me through the sport. Thank you to Rae and Kim for helping me fine tune details.

With gratitude to my author friends who I rely on daily — Corinne, Laura, AL, Natasha, Lili, Laurelin, CD, K, Helena, and Nadia, among others.

Thank you to my family for putting up with me and my wild hours and need for sandwiches and cookies.

Most of all, I am so amazingly grateful to you — the readers — for picking this up! I hope you love Max and Everly like I do!

ACKNOWLEDGMENTS

MORE BOOKS BY LAUREN

I've written more than 100 books! **All of these titles below are FREE in Kindle Unlimited!**

The Love and Hockey Series

The Boyfriend Goal

A roommates-to-lovers, teammate's little sister hockey romance!

The Romance Line

An enemies-to-lovers, player the publicist, forbidden romance!

The Proposal Play

A best friends-to-lovers romance!

The Girlfriend Zone

A coach's daughter romance!

My Favorite Holidate

A spinoff from this series! Fake dating the billionaire boss!

The My Hockey Romance Series

Hockey, spice, shenanigans and cute dogs in this series of standalones! Because when you get screwed over, make it a double or even a triple!

Karma is two hockey boyfriends and sometimes three!

Double Pucked

A sexy, outrageous MFM hockey romantic comedy!

Puck Yes

A fake marriage, spicy MFM hockey rom com!

Thoroughly Pucked!

A brother's best friends +runaway bride, spicy MFM hockey rom com!

Well and Truly Pucked

A friends-to-lovers forced proximity why-choose hockey rom com!

The Virgin Society Series

Meet the Virgin Society – great friends who'd do anything for each other. Indulge in these forbidden, emotionally-charged, and wildly sexy age-gap romances!

The RSVP

The Tryst

The Tease

The Dating Games Series

A fun, sexy romantic comedy series about friends in the city and their dating mishaps!

The Virgin Next Door

Two A Day

The Good Guy Challenge

How To Date Series (New and ongoing)

Friends who are like family. Chances to learn how to date again. Standalone romantic comedies full of love, sex and meet-cute shenanigans.

My So-Called Love Life

Plays Well With Others

The Almost Romantic

The Accidental Dating Experiment

A romantic comedy adventure standalone

A Real Good Bad Thing

Boyfriend Material

Four fabulous heroines. Four outrageous proposals. Four chances at love in this sexy rom-com series!

Asking For a Friend

Sex and Other Shiny Objects

One Night Stand-In

Overnight Service

Big Rock Series

My #1 New York Times Bestselling sexy as sin, irreverent, male-POV romantic comedy!

Big Rock

Mister O

Well Hung

Full Package

Joy Ride

Hard Wood

Happy Endings Series

Romance starts with a bang in this series of standalones following a group of friends seeking and avoiding love!

Come Again

Shut Up and Kiss Me

Kismet

My Single-Versary

A group of friends in New York City find love and laughter in this series of sexy standalones!

Satisfaction Guaranteed

Never Have I Ever

Instant Gratification

PS It's Always Been You

The Gift Series

An after dark series of standalones! Explore your fantasies!

The Engagement Gift

The Virgin Gift

The Decadent Gift

The Heartbreakers Series

Three brothers. Three rockers. Three standalone sexy romantic comedies.

Once Upon a Real Good Time

Once Upon a Sure Thing

Once Upon a Wild Fling

Sinful Men

A high-stakes, high-octane, sexy-as-sin romantic suspense series!

My Sinful Nights

My Sinful Desire

My Sinful Longing

My Sinful Love

My Sinful Temptation

From Paris With Love

Swoony, sweeping romances set in Paris!

Wanderlust

Part-Time Lover

One Love Series

A group of friends in New York falls in love one by one in this sexy rom-com series!

The Sexy One

The Hot One

The Knocked Up Plan

Come As You Are

Lucky In Love Series

A small town romance full of heat and blue collar heroes and sexy heroines!

Best Laid Plans

The Feel Good Factor

Nobody Does It Better

Unzipped

No Regrets

An angsty, sexy, emotional, new adult trilogy about one young couple fighting to break free of their pasts!

The Start of Us

The Thrill of It

Every Second With You

The Caught Up in Love Series

A group of friends finds love!

The Pretending Plot

The Dating Proposal

The Second Chance Plan

The Private Rehearsal

Seductive Nights Series

A high heat series full of danger and spice!

Night After Night

After This Night

One More Night

A Wildly Seductive Night

Joy Delivered Duet

A high-heat, wickedly sexy series of standalones that will set your sheets on fire!

Nights With Him

Forbidden Nights

Unbreak My Heart

A standalone second chance emotional roller coaster of a romance

The Muse

A magical realism romance set in Paris

Good Love Series of sexy rom-coms co-written with Lili Valente!

I also write MM romance under the name L. Blakely!

Hopelessly Bromantic Duet (MM)

Roomies to lovers to enemies to fake boyfriends

Hopelessly Bromantic

Here Comes My Man

Men of Summer Series (MM)

Two baseball players on the same team fall in love in a
forbidden romance spanning five epic years

Scoring With Him

Winning With Him

All In With Him

MM Standalone Novels

A Guy Walks Into My Bar

The Bromance Zone

One Time Only

The Best Men (Co-written with Sarina Bowen)

Winner Takes All Series (MM)

A series of emotionally-charged and irresistibly sexy standalone
MM sports romances!

The Boyfriend Comeback

Turn Me On

A Very Filthy Game

Limited Edition Husband

Manhandled

If you want a personalized recommendation, email me at
laurenblakelybooks@gmail.com!

CONTACT

I love hearing from readers! You can find me on TikTok at LaurenBlakelyBooks, Instagram at LaurenBlakelyBooks, Facebook at LaurenBlakelyBooks, or online at Lauren-Blakely.com. You can also email me at laurenblakely books@gmail.com

Made in the USA
Monee, IL
05 March 2025